Deadly Kin

'Quizzing glass and quill, into my sedan chair and away —— the 1700s rock!'

Lucinda Brant is a *New York Times*, *USA Today*, and *Audible* bestselling author of award-winning Georgian historical romances and mysteries. Her books are renowned for wit, drama and a happily ever-after. She has a degree in history and political science from the Australian National University and a post-graduate degree in education from Bond University, where she was awarded the Frank Surman Medal.

Noble Satyr, Lucinda's first novel, was awarded the $10,000 Random House/Woman's Day Romantic Fiction Prize, and she has twice been a finalist for the Romance Writers' of Australia Romantic Book of the Year. All her novels have garnered multiple awards and become worldwide bestsellers.

Lucinda lives in the middle of a koala reserve, in a writing cave that is wall-to-wall books on all aspects of the Eighteenth Century, collected over 40 years—Heaven. She loves to hear from her readers (and she'll write back!).

lucindabrant@gmail.com

A GEORGIAN HISTORICAL MYSTERY

ALEC HALSEY MYSTERIES BOOK FOUR

Lucinda Brant

A Sprigleaf Book
Published by Sprigleaf Pty Ltd

Deadly Kin: A Georgian Historical Mystery
Copyright © 2019 Lucinda Brant
Editing & proofing: Martha Stites
Cover art and photography: Larry Rostant
Design, and formatting: Sprigleaf
Cover model: Dan Cook
All rights reserved

Typeset in Adobe Garamond Pro.

ISBN 978-1-925614-51-0

10 9 8 7 6 5 4 3 2 1 (i) I

for

Aarin

PROLOGUE

FIVETREES KENT, SUMMER 1764

THE BEAST LAY DEAD AT THEIR FEET.

Blood, bright red, seeped from the wound in tiny bubbles where the arrow had pierced the flesh, entered the heart and clipped a lung. When struck, the beast had lifted its heavy head, startled. It then turned and fled, frantic, from the open pasture to the safety of cover deep in the wood.

One last spirited display of life in the fading light of a summer's day.

Two of three youths gave chase, crashing through bracken, dodging branches, slipping and sliding in the sodden leaves and mud, prepared to run until their lungs burst. This beast was theirs, and it wasn't getting away.

A hundred yards into dense forest and they found it collapsed by a lichen-covered tree trunk, gasping its last.

They approached with caution, unconvinced such a mighty animal could be brought down by a single arrow from a crossbow. They feared it could still have some fight left in it yet, and rear up in one last act of defiance. And if it did, and they were too close, it would gore them and they would find themselves wounded and bleeding.

But the beast did not rally.

Emboldened, one of the youths stuck out his muddy foot and gave the inert body a prod with his toe. When there was no reaction, he moved closer and pressed his foot into the wound. Blood oozed and pooled around the arrow and dripped into the leaf litter. His friend snatched up a stick, and holding it at arm's length, poked the beast's flank. And like his friend, when the beast did not react, he moved closer and poked again, and a third time. Each poke more forceful than the last.

They taunted the beast in death to rise again, caution extinguished with its demise. And now that it was dead and stared out at the world without blinking, they were brave and triumphant. Never in all their thirteen summers would they have dreamed of being so close to such an animal. Such beasts were only glimpsed at dawn and at dusk, and even then they were out of the reach of mere mortals. They and the herd were the property and hunted playthings of kings and nobles.

And here they were, village boys without a pair of shoes between them, victorious hunters. They wanted to shout their triumph from the tree tops.

It was a foolish want, and one that would be denied them. They were trespassers—in this wood, on this estate, and at this particular hour such trespass was a hanging offence. Not that anyone who had been caught had ever been hanged. A caution from the gamekeeper was enough to be warned off, for a few weeks at least. But a caution would not do for them this time. This time they had killed, and His Lordship's most prized stag. This time, if they were caught, they would dangle from the end of a rope.

Such a shared thought, as if it were a startling revelation and only now realized, made the youths step away from the beast. They stared at one another, and then without warning, surprised themselves by bursting into laughter. It was the sort of high-pitched nervous laugh that derives from absolute panic. But neither wanted to admit to being frightened or show they cared in any way about the consequences of their actions. And to their relief, neither was required to admit to it.

A third youth, the ringleader, and the one who had shot the fatal arrow, pushed between them and ordered they shut up. Had they forgotten they'd heard voices deep in the wood? It could be their brethren looking to net a couple of hares or a brace of partridges. What if it were Adams the gamekeeper and his assistants, who always made a habit of prowling at sun up and sun down? Did they want to get caught and hanged?

That wiped the smiles from his friends' faces. They obediently shook their heads and shut their mouths, a wary look about, as if these men were behind them.

The ringleader put aside the crossbow and went down on bended knee before the beast. But he did not prod or poke it. Nor was he wary. He gently placed a hand on its flank and caressed the soft fur with his palm, and bowed his head in veneration.

He knew this stag. It was no ordinary beast. It was king of its kind. The elder statesman amongst the harts in His Lordship's herd. Close up, it was larger than estimated, the neck thick and strong, the antlers wide and heavy. With sixteen points, it was a rack worthy of display in the Great Hall, along with the other prize racks from impressive beasts slain by noble ancestors down the centuries. But this one deserved pride of place above His Lordship's enormous hearth. But Lord Halsey, lord and master of this deer park and of the thousands of acres surrounding it, was to be denied the privilege of claiming his own stag. So too his land-owning neighbors.

This kill was no mere trophy for a nobleman to strut before. This kill was not for Marquess Halsey. He, Hugh Turner, was laying claim to this magnificent stag on behalf of the poor and the dispossessed— those poor sods who had been evicted from common land which they had farmed and grazed their cattle for hundreds of years. This beast was for the parish, and every parish in the kingdom, left with nothing and nowhere to turn since the notorious Black Act had robbed them of their livelihood. And while they starved, His Lordship's deer ate what had once fed the poor's pigs, and grew fatter. The local landowners grew fatter, too, and more prosperous, and emboldened, and hunted His Lordship's lands without fear of reprisal. For who would dare prosecute the prosecutors?

Beating these men at their own game was the only answer. Hurt them where it hurt most—their pockets and their paunches. This beast was to be their example. To prove a point. To show His Lordship and his landowning cronies that if they treated those beneath them with disdain and indifference, then just like the stag who proudly strutted about its dominion as if it owned the world, they would discover they, too, were not invulnerable.

Hugh's friends were not sure what he meant by his impassioned speeches about the poor and the dispossessed. And they had no idea about the Black Act. But they were all in for the excitement and the thrill of the kill. And they rubbed their hands in glee at the anticipated fortune this beast's venison would bring them. And then as now, Hugh reminded them of their pledge.

"Not a penny," he hissed, getting to his feet and turning to face them. "We agreed. Remember? Nic? Will?"

The youths looked at one another, and Will said what they were both thinking.

"Aye. We did. But this one's got to be twice the size and so worth twice as much, and with enough meat for every—"

"No. We're not common thieves. This beast is to be a symbol. It can't have died in vain."

"It's not in vain if it feeds a village!" Nic argued.

"And think of the coin we'd get for selling its meat."

Hugh took a menacing step forward. "Sometimes I wonder if you two have listened to a word I've said! And I said no!"

"We do. We have. But the days aren't like they used to be. Since the new lord has come to live amongst us, it's a different world, ain't it?"

"It's not like families starve these days, is it?" stuck in Nic. "There's plenty of work up at the Hall for all of us."

"And Pa reckons with all the improvements His Lordship's makin', they'll be more than enough work until our graves are dug."

"Sally says Her Ladyship takes a keen interest in everythin'!"

"What would your silly sister know?" Hugh spat out. "She's a laundress."

"She hears things," Nic mumbled.

Hugh looked from one to the other, then crossed his arms.

"In one breath you're tellin' me we should cut up the beast to feed a starvin' village, and in the next you're sayin' His Lordship has made us all fat and happy and we got work till we drop dead! Which is it?"

When his friends opened their mouths but looked confused, Hugh shook his head and grinned. He put his arms around their necks and pulled them in. "I'll say one thing we can all agree upon," he whispered conspiratorially. "We don't want to get caught. So let's get what we came for and get out of here before night's upon us."

"The rack?"

"The rack."

"What about the rest of it?"

"Seems a shame to let it waste."

Hugh let go of his friends with a clap to their backs and stood straight.

"Old Bill. He'll know what to do with the rest. Always has. You may even get a portion when he finds out who sent good fortune his way."

It was said that Old Bill had been a poacher all his life until a man-trap cut off his leg, and his livelihood, and forced him indoors. Now he acted as go-between in the distribution of illegal kill. Not that anyone had ever seen Old Bill. But everyone knew where his cottage was to be found in the forest. That decided the youths, and their smiles returned. But just as quickly those smiles disappeared again.

Not far off amongst the trees there were men calling to one another. It couldn't be a rival poaching gang, or His Lordship's game-keeper and his assistants. The former wouldn't make a sound whilst stalking, and the latter wouldn't either if they hoped to catch trespassers on His Lordship's lands. So whoever it was, they must be searching for something or someone.

The boom from a blunderbuss had the youths leaping and jittery. It had the opposite effect on Hugh, who grinned. He tried to calm his friends.

"It's Adams. That's a warning shot. And it's the only one he'll give. We've got to hurry."

"What? He knows it's us?" Nic hissed.

"Not us precisely. But he's lettin' any trespassers know there are hunters—"

"Squire Ferris?"

It was Will who blurted out the name. When Hugh nodded, Nic and Will stared about wildly, as if the man himself was behind them. Sir Tinsley Ferris was the largest landowner after Lord Halsey. And while his lands were a fifth the size of His Lordship's estate, he was the local magistrate. Which meant he held the power of life or death over all those beneath him, which was everyone except His Lordship. Ferris was feared and loathed in equal measure.

Hugh huffed and returned to the fallen stag.

"Don't tell me y'scared of another poacher?" he taunted, fighting back his fear but not his loathing. "That's what Ferris is, ain't he? This is His Lordship's land, and yet Ferris and his friends have been stalking upon it for years. That's stealing in anyone's books, ain't it?" When his friends nodded, he added with a wry grin, "Adams did us a courtesy by discharging his shotgun—"

"—to let us know the Squire was about?" Nic interrupted, awed.

"I reckon so. Dare say that blunderbuss scattered the herd too. Which wouldn't please His Lordship's neighbor, now would it?"

Nic and Will grinned at the thought of the frustrated and angry Sir Tinsley returning home empty-handed.

Hugh went down on his knees in the leaf litter and pulled the bloodied arrow free from the stag. He held it out to Nic.

"Put this in the quiver," he ordered. "And bring me the knife and saw."

Nic took the arrow but remained rooted to the spot.

"You still goin' to take the rack? There ain't time now to do what needs doin'!"

"A'course there is! They're not nearly as close as you think."

"We won't be able to carry it away fast enough," Will added.

Hugh looked over his shoulder. His friends were both white-faced. He resisted the urge to huff again, and said flatly, "Then we'll carry it just over there, behind that stump, and hide it. Cover it in leaf litter and come back for it tomorrow. But first I got to hack the head off, don't I? Oi! What the—Nic! Nic?"

With the words *hack the head off*, Nic flung the arrow down and fled into the wood.

Hugh wanted to shout that he was a sniveling coward, but that would surely give away their position. Instead he quickly searched out the arrow, thrust it into his quiver, and returned with his knife and small saw. Before he knelt again he stared at Will.

"You goin' to be a girl about this and run off too?"

"I reckon you need me to hold the rack steady while you saw."

Hugh relaxed. "Aye. I do." He held up the knife. "Best get to work."

Will tried to be a man about it, but he'd never seen freshly-dead kill of this size skinned, least of all a head sawn in two. Rabbits and chickens, yes, even a sheep, but the crack of bone being split and muscle being hacked was a grisly business, and soon Hugh was elbow deep in blood and sinew, the front of his shirt splattered with the same. The final straw was the exposed brain, and Hugh's fingers moving about inside the animal's head. Will let go of the antlers, staggered, and vomited.

Hugh was so engrossed in the task and completing it as swiftly as possible that he only noticed Will wasn't there when he had to quickly put up a hand to catch at an antler before the lot toppled and the saw slipped. He paused. Will was over by a tree, heaving. There was no time to waste while he threw up his guts. The stag and its rack were almost separated.

Hugh put aside the saw. He needed the knife to slice off the skin more cleanly. Checking his handiwork and holding the rack with one hand, his fingers searched out the knife which he'd dropped in the leaf litter by his knee. When he couldn't put his fingers on it immediately, he took his eyes from the skinned, decapitated head of the stag, and looked around. That's when he caught a glimpse of boot and glove.

He twisted about and looked up. Recognition sparked in his eyes and his mouth dropped into a frown.

"Why—Why are you here?"

The gloved hand clamped under his chin and jerked his head back until his nose pointed skyward, exposing white throat and a prominent Adam's apple.

Hugh's eyes widened, darting this way and that, mind reeling, wondering what game his attacker was playing at. He was held firm against a booted leg, and the gloved hand under his chin kept his teeth together. In his shock he did not think to struggle, and with his mouth shut tight he couldn't protest. And then he knew. In that second, with his head pulled back until he thought his neck would snap, he knew his attacker's intent. He did not see the knife nor did he feel it.

Hugh Turner's final thought was not of his mother, or his father, or of his brother. He thought of Tabitha.

ONE

WRAPPED IN A SILK BANYAN, ALEC STARED OUT AT THE PRE-
dawn darkness as the first rays of summer sun banished the night.
This was the quietest part of his day, the few moments of utter peace
before incessant noise and constant interruption. Whoever said the
country was a haven of tranquility had never renovated a sprawling
Jacobean manor the size of a medieval town.

How many acres did the house cover? Four? Yes, *four* acres of
buildings. And his steward said there were seven, *seven* acres of roof.
And after twenty years of neglect much of it required repairs of some
sort or another. The list was endless: Repointing the ragstone bricks,
re-laying uneven flagstones, stripping and re-plastering and painting
most of the internal walls, fitting new glass to leaky mullioned
windows, replacing rotted timbers in flooring, staircases, and ceilings.
These were just a few of the monumental tasks to be ticked off. And
that was just to make the house habitable. It did not account for the
modernizations he intended to introduce for his family to be
comfortable; most would have to wait until the major repairs were
done.

Half the buildings that constituted the daily living areas were now
covered in scaffolding. The other half had been stripped internally.
And all four acres of buildings and the seven acres of roof would be
crawling with workmen come sun up. Sawing, hammering, nailing,

shoveling, scraping, and shouting; the continual din of fixing, fortifying, and repair would continue until sundown.

How had he lived in London for most of his life and not been aware of the noise? Was it because the city never slept, not even when the sun went down? Whereas here, deep in the country, when the sun disappeared, so did the noise. The night was deathly quiet. Perhaps the noise continued indoors in far-off parts of this collection of buildings, in the servant areas, and where those workmen who were living on site hunkered down for the evening.

And the incessant racket was only going to get louder.

The day before, he had agreed with his steward and the head foreman to take on another twenty men, bringing the total workforce on the house alone to eighty-five. He already employed most of the able-bodied men, women and children within a twenty-mile radius. But more skilled labor was required, and that had to come from further afield. This number did not include the servants who kept the house running, and those personal servants who looked after his family's immediate needs.

As for the fifteen thousand acres that constituted his estate, and the men employed in its upkeep, from the parklands and the deer forest to the tenants who farmed his lands, that was a whole other area of his inheritance that was beyond his expertise, and one he gladly left to his steward, his gamekeeper, and the workmen they had under their jurisdiction. For now, he intended to concentrate on making the house a home.

He gently put up the window sash and leaned on the sill so he could feel the cool air on his cheeks.

The dawn was so restful. The undulating parkland that stretched to the wood glistened and twinkled with dew. The awakening sun filtering through tree branches diffused in a low-lying mist that had settled in pockets. Deer had come out to graze and roamed across the park. In groups of three and four, timid red deer does, with their calves under hoof, nibbled on the tender, newly-emerging leaves, while speckled fallow deer fawns and yearlings playfully pranced about each other. His gamekeeper told him that the harts—older stags—rarely showed themselves, and then only at dusk and at dawn, keeping to the edges of the forest, ready to flee to the safety of the canopy.

It surprised Alec to learn that there were over a thousand head of deer in his park, and that this inheritance had come down through the ages, a gift from Henry the Eighth to an ancestor related to the Seymour family when Jane Seymour was Queen. It was a generous and highly unusual gift, because such parks and the right to hunt deer were the preserve of royalty. It would have suited Alec better had Henry kept his gift. The idea of hunting and killing anything for pleasure was abhorrent to him. As far as he was concerned, his deer were welcome to live out a peaceful existence without fear of being stalked and slaughtered by him or anyone else. He wanted his deer farmed in the same considered manner as were his cows and sheep, a death for good purpose. His uncle agreed. His steward kept his incredulity to himself.

He continued to stare out the window for a few more moments, hopeful that this time he would catch sight of a stag. He did not. So he quietly pulled the sash and padded back across the expanse of bedchamber to the undraped four-poster bed, where he found his wife awake. She was propped up against the bank of pillows, which kept her as comfortable as possible for her advanced stage of pregnancy. She was fiddling with the tied ends of her long, thick braid of pale apricot hair and smiling at him.

"Did I wake you?" he asked.

"No. I've been awake for a little while. And you know I can't sleep without you."

His brow furrowed. "You should've said something and I'd have come back to bed."

Selina's smile widened. He was even more darkly handsome when fretful. She knew his concern was all for her and the baby; she was due to give birth any day. Childbirth terrified them both. He could not hide his terror. She did, for him, and because she was philosophical; there was nothing she could do about the outcome now, except pray and hope she and the baby survived the ordeal, and unharmed.

"And spoil the only fifteen minutes of peace in His Lordship's day? I could not be so discourteous."

"Do I complain that often?" When she nodded, he burst into laughter. "Dear God, I've become such a bore!"

Selina tossed her thick braid over a shoulder and put out a hand. "But my handsome bore."

He came around to her side of the bed and sat close, on the edge of the mattress. He played with her fingers. He wanted to ask about the baby, but refrained from doing so because he knew he was being overly anxious, and because regardless of how she felt or how anxious she was, she would bravely tell him all was right with her and their child. Which was probably true, but it did not make him any more confident. So he did his best to keep the conversation light.

"I thought I might take the boys for a scamper through the wood after breakfast."

The "boys" were Alec's greyhounds, Marziran and Cromwell.

"Return in time to change for nuncheon. We have guests."

"Guests?"

"Sir Tinsley and Lady Ferris. Colonel Bailey and his wife. And the Reverend Purefoy. It will be our last social function before…before we become a family."

"Are we to dine amongst the rubble and the scaffolds?"

"In the loggia overlooking the bowling green. It's as far from the banging-in of nails as I could place the tables, and without our guests having to be seated out in the park with the deer."

"No doubt where my uncle would prefer to have them seated," Alec quipped.

"Yes. But he's promised to be on his best behavior, despite his aversion for Sir Tinsley."

"Oh, he'll be the model of restraint for you," Alec assured her with a grin. "Though I can't promise he won't goad our neighbor by flirting with his wife."

Selina cocked her head. "Is that what he was doing?" she asked, genuinely surprised. "I thought he was stopping her from making a fool of herself with you—"

"*Me?*"

"Yes. Surely you know Lady Ferris has a tendre for you? And if she were twenty years younger that would be cause for concern." She sighed, adding teasingly, "I shall do my best to bear it, but I will never get used to females making fools of themselves over you—even the females of your own family."

Alec hunched his shoulders with embarrassment. "The only family I need is here, here in this house. I knew so little about my mother, I had no idea she had a sister, least of all one who lived on the neighboring estate. What are the odds?"

"In the country?" Selina was incredulous at his naivety. "Every chance in the world! My brother married the girl from the neighboring farm, all so he could double his acreage. In exchange, Caro became Lady Cobham. Not a fair trade in my opinion. Clive has all the appeal of a dried-out barnacle. Still, Uncle Plant should have told you years ago that your mother had a sister. But I suspect he saw no reason to do so when your own parents had disowned you. Why would he think an aunt would care any differently? Oh! That was-was—"

"—the truth. It could also explain Lady Ferris's tendre, as you call it. Perhaps she's trying to make up for my parents' monumental neglect? No doubt it's as much a novelty to her to have a nephew, as it is for me to find I have an aunt."

"Yes, I'm sure that must be it," Selina said without conviction, because she did not believe it.

The last occasion she'd been in the company of Sir Tinsley and his wife, she'd received the distinct impression Alec's existence was no surprise to them. That Sir Tinsley and Lady Ferris were now eager to foster the family connection she cynically suspected had everything to do with the fact Alec had inherited the family estate. More importantly in the eyes of the socially-conscious Sir Tinsley, His Majesty had seen fit to bestow a marquessate upon her husband, and thus elevated him to dizzying heights within the nobility.

In any other circumstance Selina would have found a reason to distance herself from the likes of the toadying Sir Tinsley. But his wife was Alec's aunt, sister of Alec's mother, a woman who remained an enigma. And while Alec was able to dismiss his mother from his consciousness, Selina had a burning desire to know more about the Countess of Delvin, and the sort of woman she'd been. She wanted to understand what had driven her to risk an affair with a mulatto footman. But what astounded Selina more was that Alec's mother had then given up her infant as if he never existed. Selina could no more abandon the child she was carrying as stop breathing. To have the infant taken from her, never to be seen again, was surely an agony worse than death…

Sensing Alec was regarding her, she smiled reassuringly and changed the subject.

"While you were admiring the view, Jeffries stuck his nose into the room."

Alec frowned. Something must be up for his valet to trespass into the bedchamber. But he wasn't about to cut short his only time of the day spent alone with his wife. If there was a dire need for Jeffries to see him, he'd stick his nose in again. He leaned in and kissed her forehead, clearing his thoughts of all else but her.

"Let's have breakfast in here this morning."

She touched his cheek. "A splendid idea."

"You do know how much I love you, don't you?"

"I do." Sudden tears clouded her vision. "I just wish I wouldn't fall all to pieces every time you say it. I'm sure that's the fault of my *interesting condition*, as Evans stubbornly continues to refer to my pregnancy," she rattled on, all to stop the sudden tears from flowing. "And this despite me lecturing her that pregnancy is a perfectly normal and frequent condition for a married woman—so Aunt Olivia keeps reassuring me in her letters."

"It is. And I don't know what you've got to complain about. I'm the one Evans has damned, for putting you in this *interesting condition*. I frequently catch her dark, sidelong glances."

Selina chuckled, and felt better for it.

"The dark looks aren't because I'm pregnant, my darling. It's because we continue to share a bed. She's scandalized. And she not the only one. Yesterday Mrs. Turner asked me *again*, now the renovations are complete in this wing, when His Lordship would be occupying his own bedchamber. Her tone implied that there was now no excuse for you not to do so. And I'm sure if you did, it would make Jeffries' valeting duties and Evans' care of me so much the easier for them."

"God forbid I should inconvenience our personal servants!" he scoffed, and blushed in spite of himself. "But if my being here is a nuisance and you would prefer—"

"Nuisance? *Prefer?*"

Selina tried to sit up, but her belly stopped her from doing more than lifting her shoulders before she lay back against the bank of pillows.

"The question is not are you being a nuisance," she grumbled good naturedly. "But am I being selfish having you here when I'm the size of a-a cow? I may not be able to sleep, but that does not mean you must also have a sleepless night. And what with everything that is put upon you during the day, it's no small wonder you're tired and hear every noise as if it is the boom from a cannon." She took a deep breath. "So if His Lordship would prefer his own bedchamber—"

"No. Ordinary people share a bed, come what may. We will too."

"Ordinary people do not have the luxury of doing otherwise. Lord Halsey does. Besides which, most people expect us to have separate bedchambers. It is the 'done thing' amongst our kind. I can name only a handful of noble couples who share a bedchamber—one is your good friend Lord Salt and his countess, and with their infant son, too."

Alec was surprised. "He told you?"

Selina shook her head, amused. "Salt share such a confidence? The man is part ice block! No. She—Jane—did."

"You didn't tell me that."

"If I told you everything that is written in confidence between females, particularly those details which concern childbirth and the rearing of infants, you would be even more anxious than you already are."

"Thank you for sparing me. But I do want to share everything with you—even your bed." He squeezed her fingers. "Here—here in this bedchamber, we are like any other married couple in love, and everyone and everything else can go hang. No. I will stay, and through as many pregnancies as we are blessed with, and well into my dotage. It is all part of the grand adventure of being married, isn't it?" He looked into her dark eyes. "But only if that's what you want, too."

"It is what I want. Very much." And to stop herself bursting into tears at his loving sincerity, she added nonchalantly, "Besides, sharing a bed with a woman who is nine months pregnant is hardly the worse thing you've had to endure."

"Sleeping alone without you would be the second worse thing."

"Aha! So I was wrong!" she declared, continuing to tease him. Yet as soon as the words were out of her mouth she realized her mistake, and that she had undone all her good work in trying to keep his mind far from the perils of childbirth. "Sharing a bed with your pregnant wife *is* the worse thing!"

Alec lost his smile and the color drained from his face. He could barely say the words aloud. "No. Losing you...losing you both...that would be unbearable."

He turned his head to gently lay his cheek upon her belly, and there he stayed, still and quiet, reveling in the new life growing within her. And when she gently ran her fingers through his long black curls, he closed his eyes. Finally, he sat up. His eyes were glassy.

Selina drew in breath, mortified. "Oh, my dearest dear, I didn't mean to distress—"

"Darling, I'm—I'm so—*happy*. I've never been happier."

"Oh?" She blushed and beamed. "Nor I... Why don't you come back to bed for a little while longer? Evans won't be here with the tea things for another hour..." When he joined her and snuggled in, she reached for a bundle of letters on the bedside table. There was now enough morning light streaming through the mullioned windows to read. "Do you want to hear what Cosmo wrote to me? His letter arrived yesterday."

He nodded and burrowed under the covers, delighting in the warmth of her, and nestled in. He heard Selina's voice, and did his best to listen to what her cousin had to say about wandering the wilds of the Irish countryside. But soon he heard only one word in three and lost the will to concentrate. By the end of the first paragraph, Alec had fallen into a deep sleep.

⚭

THE TINKLE OF A SILVER SPOON AGAINST THE SIDE OF A porcelain tea cup woke him. But he was so heavy-headed he just lay there, sprawled out in the bed, of which he was now the only occupant. Finally, he sat up on an elbow and pulled the hair out of his eyes. He blinked into the sunlight streaming across the oriental rug.

His wife's lady's maid was fussing about the tea trolley. With Evans was one of the female attendants; a second lingered by the entrance to Selina's dressing room with an article of clothing draped over an arm. Both had their gaze to the floor. And then he was surprised when his valet stuck his head in from the hallway that connected this bedchamber to his apartment. Jeffries lingered, and when Alec met his gaze, his eyes widened and held for a moment, and then just as quickly he disappeared again.

Something must indeed be bothering Jeffries—or someone...

Selina, who was comfortably seated on the chaise by the fire with her slippered feet elevated on an ottoman, and balancing a cup of tea on her belly, answered the question without him having to ask. She spoke in French, the language they preferred if they were not entirely alone. It gave them the latitude to carry on an intimate conversation without fear of being overheard, or having their conversation repeated. That Evans and Jeffries understood the French language was beside the point; such devoted servants were deaf when required. And there was the small detail that she had never confided in him—Alec speaking in French gave her goose bumps—it always did.

"Your London foreman—Stephens? Yes! Stephens. He's asked for you. Something about a discovery under the flagstones in Stone Court. And that makes the third time Jeffries has shown himself. I'm sure your bathwater is now tepid."

"This—um—discovery requires my presence before breakfast?"

"It would seem so, yes. Workmen have downed tools and are refusing to pick them up again, for anyone—not even for Turner."

Alec pulled a face. "My taciturn steward won't be pleased. He and Stephens have already exchanged more than a few words upon occasion."

Selina sipped her tea. "I'm not surprised. Turner has lived on the estate all his life, and been steward for—how long? Twenty—"

"Five-and-twenty years."

"He's been steward for twenty-five years, and his father was steward before him. And you, my lord, have seen fit to not only import workers from the metropolis, but put them under the charge of a London foreman."

"A necessary evil if we are to ever have this house repaired and made livable."

"Oh, I'm not criticizing you, my darling." Selina dimpled. "But perhaps I need to remind His Lordship that when you first mooted the idea, it was while we were sailing back from Midanich, and I not only wholeheartedly agreed with you, I was the one who advised you to employ a foreman to supervise your foreign workforce."

"You did. Thank you. And you warned me that a man like Turner, who has had the run of this place for decades with little interference, would loathe the very idea of outside workers crawling all over the estate, though he would not tell me so to my face."

"Just as the housekeeper won't say to mine that she is unhappy we have brought our London servants to look after us." Selina smiled cheekily. "As our steward and housekeeper are married to one another, they at least have the consolation of grumbling to each other about their masters."

"There is that. We—and most particularly I—must provide a constant source of grumbling for the poor Turners."

Selina put aside her tea cup, and in an about-face said with a pout, "They really ought not to grumble. Our coming to live here must be the most interfering, and thus exciting thing to have happened on this estate in decades!"

At that, Alec laughed out loud. He finally slid out of bed, found his banyan amongst the crumpled covers, and shrugged it on.

"Must you?" she complained.

He pulled the banyan about his body as he crossed to the tea trolley, and waved aside the maid to pour himself out a cup of tea.

"Must I—what, my lady?" he asked, perplexed.

"I much prefer my Greek statue sans clothing."

Alec continued to pour the tea with a steady hand and with only the slightest of pauses. Without a look away from his teacup, he said very quietly, "Behave yourself, lady wife, or I will take to wearing one of those voluminous, shapeless nightshirts favored by gentlemen of a certain age."

"You don't own such a tiresome article. But perhaps you should," Selina pondered. "Until after my lying in... Aunt Olivia confided that did the trick in extinguishing the flame of her-her *cravings* for the Duke."

Alec gave a bark of laughter and almost overset his teacup. He never ceased to be delighted by Selina's directness. He sipped at his tea and came over to her as Evans moved away, the attendant in tow.

"Did it? Well, it was a very poorly-executed trick given Olivia had over a dozen lyings-in! I wouldn't wish that on you, but neither will I wear such a garment."

Selina tilted up her cheek. "So your threat was a hollow one, my lord?"

"You know it was. I will not be investing in a nightshirt—ever."

"Thank you. I'm pleased to hear it. Now kiss me and go and see what Jeffries wants before he paces the vanish off the boards. I know your mind won't rest until you've heard what he has to tell you. I will see you at nuncheon."

"Speaking of minds that won't rest," Alec said turning her chin to gently kiss her mouth, "shall I send Jeffries to the library after breakfast?"

Selina's dark eyes lit up.

"Can you spare him?"

"He would be disappointed if you did not need his assistance."

"Did he tell you we are making a search of the family records to draw up a family tree?"

Alec raised an eyebrow. "Still wanting to saddle our infant with a name from amongst my ancestors?"

Selina instinctively smoothed a hand over her roundness. "As is proper for the heir to a marquessate. I'm hoping that if I go back far enough, I'll find a string of names that we'll both find acceptable."

"I'll be happy with whatever names you choose, but not Roderick, Edward, or Joseph."

Selina frowned. "Roderick was your father. Edward was your brother... But Joseph...?"

"A retired Scottish advocate who was at one time employed in this house as a footman, and who, rumor has it, was very close to my mother."

Selina's eyes widened. The mulatto footman!

"And if we have a daughter—not Helen," Selina stated, mentioning the Countess of Delvin's Christian name.

Alec flicked her cheek. "Thank you. Not Helen."

On that sobering note, Alec left their bedchamber, Selina watching him go and wishing she had not mentioned his mother. Yet she had every intention of asking his uncle about Joseph, the retired advocate...

Alec, however, dismissed the Countess from his thoughts the instant he turned his back, wondering what it was the men had found under the flagstones in Stone Court to make them stop work. He hoped it was something to pique his interest.

He would never tell Selina, but keeping a mind active in the depths of the country was not only difficult for his valet with his particular set of skills, but for himself, who had given up a diplomatic career for life as a country gentleman. His days were always busy, but he missed what London and the Foreign Department had to offer. And he was looking forward to a time when they could return for at least part of the year to the townhouse in St. James's Place.

"So, Jeffries," Alec said, strolling into his dressing room, teacup in hand. "What's this about a discovery under the flagstones?"

TWO

"Sir! I need a word in private."

Alec shot a glance at his valet, and then turned to where a young man with red freckles and carrot-colored hair was framed in the doorway. He had one foot in the dressing room and the other in the passageway, as if he were unsure if he were coming or going, but very aware he was impinging.

"Has this something to do with the discovery in Stone Court?" Alec asked.

"Stone Court? I don't know about that, sir. This is about—"

"I requested Mr. Fisher wait until I had dressed you, my lord." The valet sniffed his displeasure, not a look at the intruder. "But he could not be prevailed upon to—"

"It's about my cousin Hugh, sir," Tam Fisher interrupted in a rush. "He's disappeared and his mother's worried sick, and I thought you—"

"Hugh?"

"Hugh Turner. Mr. Turner's son, sir.

"And he's disappeared? When?"

"Several days ago."

"Why the urgency now?"

"Precisely what I asked, my lord," Jeffries stated.

"It's not your place to ask, is it?" Tam sneered at the valet.

Alec's mouth pressed into a thin line. He resisted the urge to roll his eyes at Tam's continued resentment of Hadrian Jeffries, all because Hadrian had taken his place as valet. Particularly as Tam had no need to be resentful. He was no longer a servant but a much sought-after apothecary who could boast the patronage of members of the aristocracy—Alec and at least one duke amongst his clientele. He had also been welcomed into Alec's extended family. This should have been enough for him to feel valued, and to treat Hadrian Jeffries with the respect due a gentleman's gentleman. Alec did not want to state the obvious, but he did.

"Mr. Jeffries has only my best interests at heart, Tam. You of all people should know that. This is—"

"But—sir! I—"

"This is Jeffries' domain, not yours," Alec stated curtly. "Were my uncle to invade my dressing room, Jeffries would have every right to ask him to state his business, just as he did you."

"Yes, sir. Of course."

"So whatever you have to confide, you can say before both of us."

"Yes, sir," Tam repeated, not a glance at the valet. "It's only urgent now because Hugh's mother is in a panic. But she doesn't want a fuss. And she doesn't want Mr. Turner to know he's missing on account of him being your steward… It's thorny. So if it's all the same to you, I'll beg your pardon and request a word in private when we can be private."

"Very well. But as Hugh Turner has been gone for several days, an hour to make myself presentable and have breakfast won't make a difference—"

"My lord, Mr. Stephens and Mr. Turner are awaiting you in the Stone Court."

"Thank you for the reminder, Jeffries. So they are. Send word I'll be with them after I've had breakfast. No doubt whatever the workmen have discovered has been under those flag stones for decades, so it, too, can wait."

"Don't let on to the Turners I'm here," Tam ordered Jeffries.

"I would not presume to do so, Mr. Fisher," said the valet. "If you would care to await His Lordship in the sitting room, you will find the table set for breakfast."

Jeffries then bowed to the young man with a courteousness bordering on insolence. And when Alec turned his back and strolled through to his closet to be shaved, the valet took the opportunity to look Tam full in the face. He lifted his brows with the same insolence he had infused into his obsequious bow. And when Tam's hands clenched into fists Jeffries grinned. Having achieved his object, the valet turned and followed his noble employer with a lightness of step, and closed over the door.

⁊℣

"*VAUNTFUL PICKTHANK,*" TAM MUTTERED, BLOWING OUT HIS cheeks as he stomped into the sitting room, hands still balled.

"Have some egg. Nothin' like warm egg to settle an upset."

Tam stopped short and swiveled on a boot heel. Standing at the sideboard with a silver cover in one hand was Lord Halsey's grizzled-haired uncle, Plantagenet Halsey MP. All the fight went out of him. He blinked and flexed his fingers.

"Wonderin' why I'm not downstairs in the breakfast room?" the old man asked conversationally. "Suspect it's the same reason you're here too. 'Cause here's the only place we get His Lordship's undivided attention. Damme if I don't have to make an appointment to speak with my own nephew!"

That made Tam smile. When he went to the sideboard, Plantagenet Halsey handed him a plate.

"And with the egg, I recommend the venison in collops."

The old man filled his plate and took his place at the table with his back to the mullioned windows, long legs sprawled out. A nod to the footman and the servant filled his tankard with ale. And when Tam sat opposite, he set down his knife and fork and raised his tankard.

"Here's to your physic garden, Thomas. I took a stroll up through the kitchen gardens this mornin' and inspected the herb beds. They're all coming along nicely. One day it may rival the one at Chelsea."

Tam colored at such praise. "I've no expectations, sir, but if it can provide the medicinals this estate and the local village need, then I'll be more than satisfied."

"And so will His Lordship... I trust you've written up plenty of instructions for the gardeners, so they'll know how best to look after it all when you take your leave."

Tam swallowed a mouthful of egg whole. His brow furrowed.

"Take my leave, sir…?"

Plantagenet Halsey shoveled egg onto his fork. He looked across at Tam.

"You'll not be wantin' to kick your heels down here much after Her Ladyship is safely delivered. I suspect you're eager to return to St. James's Street. What with the patronage of Her Grace of Cleveley and the Duchess of Romney-St. Neots, my nephew tells me you have customers pressin' through the front door the moment the premises are unbolted. And those that don't come themselves, send their servants to queue down the street." He ate his egg with relish, then punctured the air with his raised fork. "Very proud of you, Thomas. Very proud indeed."

"Thank you, sir. In truth, I am keen to return to St. James's. Not to serve behind the counter. I leave that to my associate Mr. Clements. It's the patient visits which interest me. And since the Duchess of Cleveley has graciously appointed me her personal apothecary, I've gained a long list of clients who—" He stopped himself. "But none of that matters here. What does is Lady Halsey being safely delivered of her infant," he added earnestly. "And I've assured His Lordship I'll remain for as long as I'm needed."

Plantagenet Halsey nodded and went on eating, concentration seemingly on the thin slices of venison in a delicate parsley and cinnamon butter sauce.

"That's commendable, my boy. And I have every confidence in you—and so does His Lordship. Let's hope your assistance ain't required and the delivery is as uneventful as any first-time birth can be. Mind you, I have nothin' against man-midwives, and I'm no expert, but I can tell you I'll be feelin' a whole lot less nervy once Her Grace of Romney-St. Neots and the Lady Sybilla arrive to take charge of the nursery. Mother and daughter have more than a dozen births between 'em. In my books that's experience for which there is no substitute!"

The old man punctuated his declaration with a firm nod, then added with a seemingly cavalier air, "Still… I wouldn't blame you if you hadn't thought twice about returnin' here to Delvin, pardon, *Deer Park*, as it's to be known from now on."

Tam frowned and set down his coffee cup. "But I didn't think

twice. You know I'd do anything for Lord Halsey. Anything at all. As
soon as I got his letter I made arrangements for Mr. Clements to take
over my client list, and we put on an assistant, and I came straight
down to—"

Plantagenet Halsey put up a hand. "I believe you, Thomas. I
know you're devoted to His Lordship, and so does he. I only meant
that you may have had some misgivin's about comin' to this house. It
was only this time last year you were here with my nephew. Though,
what with our Continental jaunt and the sweethearts finally married
and a babe on the way almost immediately, not to mention you
finishin' off your apprenticeship, it does seem as if years, not months,
have gone by. But this time last year His Lordship was in a distracted
state. With his brother's untimely death and nothin' resolved then
with his sweetheart, he spent much of his time wrapped in a cloak of
self-pity. He didn't notice this place fallin' around his ears, and I'd
wager he had no notion of your apprehension. It musn't have been
easy for you…"

"I don't blame him, sir. It's not as if he had any idea of what my
life was like growing up at Delvin—excuse me, *Deer Park*. How could
he? He never lived here, and he never visited until just before his
mother's death. By that time I was long gone."

"That's a mature way of lookin' at it. No, he did not. I made sure
of that. I should've made sure you didn't either."

Tam paused and leaned in, curious, knife and fork poised in
midair.

"Me, sir? Could you? Could you have made sure I didn't?"

"Do you remember me visitin' when you were a very small lad,
just grown out of your pudding-cap?"

Tam sat back, wondering why the old man was inclined to remi-
nisce, and why now. Surely he knew all there was to know about his
life on the estate, and anything he didn't Tam had told him when
asked. But he humored him, and pondered his question as he sliced
up the venison on his plate.

"There was one time… You gave me a bag of sweetmeats. I'd
never had sugary confection before. None of us Fishers had. Which is
why I remember it. I ate the lot in one go and was ill afterwards. That
taught me not to be greedy. But I thought if I was caught with such
sugary treasure I'd be accused of stealing."

"Did you? Ha!" Plantagenet Halsey smiled and shook his head. He drank down his ale, and with it the smile was gone. "That was a very different time for both of us. Just as this is a very different time now... I don't mean because the buildin's are bein' turned inside out and set to rights again. But because my nephew and his wife are makin' this house a home. Somethin' it's never been—not since I was a child, and definitely not in your livin' memory. It certainly wasn't in the handful of years Edward was earl. But soon, God willin', there'll be a brood of children runnin' up and down these galleries, makin' all sorts of playful racket. And it'll be because they are loved and wanted that their laughter will chase away the gremlins of the past, and forever." He held Tam's gaze with an unblinking stare. "This is to be a place of cheeriness and optimism from now on, Thomas, and you and me are goin' to be part of it."

"I'd like that very much, sir."

"I'm glad to hear it..."

The old man sat back, a seemingly casual glance at the liveried footman standing to attention by the sideboard. He needed to satisfy himself that the servant was one of the two dozen his nephew had brought with him from his town residence. These servants, from footmen to maids, worked exclusively in the noble couple's private apartments. They had their own servant quarters, and as they considered themselves several notches above their country bumpkin associates, they had very little to do with the local servants, those who had come with the house or were employed from the village. That the footman by the sideboard was from the city gave Plantagenet Halsey the confidence to speak his mind knowing his words wouldn't be repeated in the servant hall presided over by the Turners.

"Just say, for argument's sake, if you were to hear any mutterings about what went on here in days gone by, when you were a small lad, or before then," he said conversationally. "If there were grumblings about the changes His Lordship is makin' here, there, and everywhere... If the Turners, or one of the old retainers such as Adams the gamekeeper—they've all been here since my late brother's time as earl —or even farther afield, say the neighborin' landowner Ferris and his ilk... If any of that lot were to take it upon themselves to mention some unpleasantness from the past—"

"They wouldn't want to say anything against His Lordship or-or you, sir, in my hearing, or they'd get an earful back!" Tam said fiercely. "Don't you worry. I'd soon put them in their place!"

"That's very commendable and loyal, Thomas. But I don't want you troublin' yourself to—"

"It's no trouble, sir! I'd want to say something!"

"Of course you would," Plantagenet Halsey agreed smoothly. "But, between you and me, I doubt the type of disagreeable gossip I'm talkin' about would be said to your face. You'd only hear it in passin', or when you weren't meant to hear it, or someone might tell you what they heard. If you get my meanin'."

Tam frowned and sipped at his coffee. He barely noticed it had gone cold.

"I understand. I just don't know what it is you want me to do about such disloyalty and tattle."

Plantagenet Halsey suppressed a smile at the young man's frown of earnestness, and schooled his features to appear unconcerned. "I don't want you to do anythin' about it."

"Pardon, sir? Why not?"

"If you heard or were told somethin' you thought disloyal or disparagin' *tattle* about His Lordship or his family, or about his ancestors, or-or about *me*… I'd be particularly grateful if you'd keep it to yourself until you could tell me about it."

The crease between Tam's brows deepened. "You want me to tell you if I hear any tattle?"

"Yes. So I can deal with it in my own way. We don't want to bother His Lordship with such nonsense, do we—"

"No, sir, we do not!"

"—because he has enough on his mind. What with pullin' these buildin's up out of last century and into this. The daily runnin' of the estate, and keepin' abreast of tenant concerns. And with an infant due any day, he don't need anythin' else addin' to his burden of worry, or castin' a cloud over his happiness."

"You can depend on me."

The old man leaned forward with a smile.

"Good lad. I knew I could."

"And I can tell you now, sir, that I haven't heard anything," Tam reassured him. "But that's probably because I spend my time in the gardens, or in the distillery making up remedies."

"That's an excellent use of your time. Best to keep busy and stay clear of all the fuss indoors. I do." Plantagenet Halsey pushed aside his tankard, adding in a light tone at odds with the frown lines across his brow, "But if you were to hear anythin', however trivial, bring it to me. Understand, my boy?"

"Yes, sir. Of course," Tam reassured him.

Though he wasn't sure why the old man was harping on, or needing his assurances, because he had already given them. No doubt Mr. Halsey had his reasons which he did not wish to divulge, and that was fine by Tam. If it meant the old man could sleep easy at night, and Lord Halsey was not bothered and could concentrate on what truly mattered, then he was more than happy to oblige them both. And then, with a sudden gulp, he realized he had just done exactly what the old man had asked him not to do.

He had barged into His Lordship's dressing room demanding to speak to him about Hugh Turner's disappearance. But he'd not had a chance to tell him the entire story, or why he was worried about his cousin. So perhaps it would be best to confide in the old man and not His Lordship. And if it kept that snot-nosed Jeffries in ignorance, then he was all for it. The more he thought about it, the more it made sense. Plantagenet Halsey had grown up on the estate. He'd known the Turners longer than anyone else, and he knew Hugh, too. So perhaps his cousin wouldn't mind if Mr. Halsey involved himself. And he'd also be able to figure a way of not involving His Lordship. It was worth a try...

Tam set his knife and fork on the empty plate and put it aside.

"Sir, if we'd had this conversation earlier, I'd have come to you first... Thing is, I tried to speak with His Lordship about Hugh Turner, just before I came in here. I didn't get to tell him much on account of Jeffries sticking his nose in where it's not wanted. So all His Lordship knows is that Mrs. Turner is worried about Hugh, but not why."

"So what's the rascal got himself entangled in this time?"

"To be honest, I don't know. Mrs. Turner says it's not unusual for Hugh to spend nights away and not tell her or his father. But she suspects he's gone poaching."

The old man sat up.

"Poachin'?" His lips twitched. "But everyone knows we don't have

poachers around here, Thomas. Our local high-and-bloody-mighty
magistrate Sir Tinsley will tell you so himself. Puffs out his chest
about it whenever he can, like a prized goose!"

Tam's face split into a grin. "So I've heard, sir."

"Why does Mrs. Turner think her boy's off poachin'?"

"His father's crossbow is gone. And Adams reported one of the
game nets is missing. And then there's the—"

"What's he tryin' to filch, d'you think? Hare? Deer? Partridge?"

"With a crossbow? Not partridge, sir."

"Ha! You're right. There'd be only feathers left to fly off the poor
birdie. And for Hugh's poor mother, a son with the threat of a rope
around his neck! Fool."

"But—is poaching a hanging offence?"

"Poachin'? He don't need to be doin' anythin' of the sort to find
himself on the wrong side of the law. Just bein' out with a crossbow,
or even that net, could have the lad transported. In fact, he don't need
to have anythin' on him to be prosecuted. Found in the wood after
dusk is enough grounds for any of us, except His Lordship to be
charged with intent to poach."

"Intent? That seems hardly fair, sir."

"When have laws ever taken fairness into account? Laws are
passed to protect the interests of those who make 'em. And woe
betide you tread on the interests of our parliamentarians!"

"You're a parliamentarian, sir."

The old man couldn't help a smile.

"Aye, I am, Thomas. And I'm there to keep my fellows honest. A
few of us think beyond fillin' our own pockets with coin and our
bellies with beef. Someone's got to try and prick the collective
conscience. Though... Even if I were to use a batterin' ram, it
wouldn't knock any sense into the heads of my fellow MPs to repeal
the Black Act—"

"Black Act?"

"Heinous piece of legislation that's slapped the death penalty on
more than fifty criminal offences." The old man huffed. "If you can
call it criminal for forest dwellers to scrounge for peat and kindling
for their fires. They've done so for generations, only takin' what they
need, and this Black Act comes along and makes it a hangin' offence!
I ask you, is that fair? Is it criminal to eke out an existence on scraps?"

He tapped his finger on the table. "I'll tell you what's criminal—takin' away the rights of the poor to keep themselves alive by honest means, that's what!"

"I've not heard of any forest dwellers or the poor from around here being prosecuted as wood thieves. Have you, sir?"

"No. And you're not likely to, or for poachin' either, not while I'm the local MP!"

Tam's eyes widened in understanding.

"Because Sir Tinsley would have to answer to you...?"

"Aye, Thomas. He would. Our local magistrate might be a prized goose who ruffles out his plumage at every opportunity, but I'm a Halsey. And we Halseys have been in Kent since forever, and ennobled at the conquest. That means a lot to a baronet such as Ferris. He's proud of the fact he's His Lordship's closest neighbor. He's prouder still that he's bound to us through kin. His wife's sister was countess here. Which means His Lordship is his nephew by marriage. And now that his nephew is Marquess Halsey, he can boast even more. And to be invited to dine at His Lordship's table, Ferris knows not to get on the wrong side of *me*. I can tell you, Thomas, I don't like to throw my name around, but if it means savin' our villagers from unjust laws and Crown stupidity, then needs must."

Tam thought about this for a moment, and then he grinned, saying confidently, "And Sir Tinsley gets to remain the local magistrate as long as no one gets transported or strung up."

"Aye, that's the way of it, Thomas. When the circumstance calls for it, he knows when to be blind, deaf, and unutterably mute. Besides it's to our mutual benefit."

Tam met his gaze.

"Do you mean that he can also boast that the locals respect him enough, or fear him enough, that they don't break the law?"

Plantagenet Halsey's eyes narrowed and he tapped his long nose at the young man's astuteness.

"Aye. I do."

Tam glanced at his empty coffee cup and then back up at the old man, and chose his words carefully.

"Then, would it be fair to say, sir, that others would know your views on this Black Act, and this understanding you have with Sir Tinsley?"

Plantagenet Halsey stuck out his bottom lip. "It would. Why do you ask?"

"Well, sir, it seems to me, if that's so, and now knowing how matters stand between you and the magistrate, I'd reckon the Turners would know that too—"

"And so you're wonderin' why Mrs. Turner is unnecessarily worried about her boy takin' a crossbow to the wood?"

"Yes, sir."

Plantagenet Halsey nodded at the young man's reasoned assumption.

"Fair point, Thomas… Hugh mightn't be transported or strung up, but Mrs. Turner knows it don't mean the magistrate won't make an example of him, to warn others not to be so foolish as to flout his authority as magistrate. That's an embarrassment Sir Tinsley won't suffer. And it's also an embarrassment the Turners don't want either. Ferris could slap Hugh with a hefty fine for just bein' in the wood. That's a cost his parents would have to bear, because Hugh don't have a coin of his own. Or if he's been caught more than once, then our magistrate might threaten him with the Assizes. Now no one wants to be carted off to stand before a judge, now do they?"

"Mrs. Turner says Hugh's done it before, but not been caught. But that this time it's different because he's been gone three nights. And he's not the only one missing."

"Who else was in on this foolhardy venture?"

"Two lads from the village. But what I think has got Mrs. Turner worried is that her dignity will be hurt if he's failed in his duty by Lady Ferris."

"What do you mean his duty by Lady Ferris?" Plantagenet Halsey asked more harshly than he intended. "What's he done to upset her?"

Tam baulked at the sudden change in the old man's demeanor. Gone was his conviviality. Tam wasn't sure how to respond. He was saved a reply.

Alec strolled into the sitting room flanked by his greyhounds, and in time to hear his uncle's growling demand. He sent the dogs to their rug by the fireplace and went to the sideboard to peer under the silver-domed dishes.

"Good morning. Has the egg disagreed with you, Uncle?"

"Eh? Egg? No. No. You have the egg. Thomas and I did," the old man muttered. He mentally shook his anger off and forced a smile. "And a good mornin' to you and your four-legged fiends! I trust Her Ladyship slept well?"

"As well as to be expected given she can neither lie down or sit up or truly be comfortable. At least our little monkey has settled, and no longer keeps her awake half the night with his somersaults."

"Monkey?" The old man was baffled. Then he chuckled, realizing Alec was referring to his unborn child. "The calm before the storm." He clapped and then rubbed his hands together with glee. "I can't wait!"

Alec took his place at the head of the table, dropping his gaze on a bashful smile, points of color in each cheek. He flicked out the skirts of his light-blue linen riding frock and sat. "Neither can I."

Plantagenet Halsey caught Tam's attention and jerked his head toward the door, signal he wanted him to take his leave, which had Tam scrambling out of his chair. Alec looked up and quietly told him to sit, adding mildly, as he spread a napkin across his lap,

"Tell me about Hugh Turner. Why his mother is—what did you say to me earlier—ah, yes! Why his mother is *in a panic?*"

THREE

"You don't need to spoil y' breakfast hearin' about a rascal like Hugh Turner," Plantagenet Halsey blustered. "The boy's always gettin' himself into scrapes. Never still. Can't fix on one thing. His parents despair of him settlin' into a vocation."

"That tells me something about the boy," Alec replied. "What it doesn't tell me is why his mother is particularly worried about him upon this occasion."

Plantagenet Halsey threw up a hand. He was dismissive.

"Mothers worry. And with a boy like Hugh, they worry even more."

Alec watched his uncle go to the sideboard and return with the coffee pot. He put out his cup. He nodded for Tam to do the same.

"I've given the Turners enough to worry about in their respective roles in my household without an errant son adding to it. But you know Mrs. Turner better than I, so you can correct me if I'm wrong. She doesn't come across as the sort who would be alarmed without good reason, particularly about a son who is always *getting himself into scrapes*."

"Aye, I can't argue with you on that score," his uncle agreed, resuming his seat. He pushed the sugar bowl towards Tam and held his gaze. "It may have somethin' to do with Hugh not keepin' his appointment with Lady Ferris. Would that account for Mrs. Turner's worry, Thomas?"

Tam took the hint. He was to stick to talk about Hugh's truancy with Lady Ferris, and not mention his cousin's poaching in the wood. But he wouldn't lie to Lord Halsey, and to make certain he remained on topic he kept his eyes on the old man. "I dare say that's it, sir. Hugh helps out in Lady Ferris's garden in the summer. Sometimes he goes over to the Baileys', and helps out Mrs. Bailey too. He's been going between the two for a few years now. A lot of the village lads will work in their fields, or when there are odd jobs need doing about their farms, but Hugh was the only one who took an interest in the flower beds." Tam glanced at Alec and seeing he was busy with what was on his plate, and not looking at him, relaxed. "Mrs. Turner said the last time Hugh returned from one of his gardening expeditions, he mentioned that Lady Ferris had asked him for an assurance he meant to return, and that when he readily gave it, she told him Sir Tinsley would be pleased to hear it, too."

"Why did Lady Ferris need such an assurance?" asked Alec.

When Plantagenet Halsey nodded at him, Tam explained, "Mrs. Turner said Lady Ferris was worried that as most of the village now worked here, here at Deer Park, Hugh meant to do so, too. And he wouldn't have the time for her garden, that he might only go over to help Mrs. Bailey and not her. Hugh told his mother that Lady Ferris was very upset about that possibility, and only calmed when he, Hugh, gave her a solemn promise."

"And despite being a rascal and getting himself into scrapes, he is wanted in the gardens of two of our most prominent landowning neighbors? Is he the type of boy to offer solemn promises, and to keep them?"

When both the old man and Tam looked at one another and then at Alec and nodded, he found himself smiling to himself at their complicity. Still, he did not let on he was aware of this, and said, looking from his uncle to Tam, and then back down at his plate,

"Then I see why Mrs. Turner is worried about her son's whereabouts. Any thoughts, Uncle?"

Plantagenet Halsey pulled a face and was about to shake his head, then said conversationally, as if the thought had just occurred to him, "I'll tell you what. Why don't I have a word with Mrs. Turner. See if I can find out anythin' more about Hugh, and let you know at nuncheon."

"Thank you. An excellent idea." Alec pushed back his chair and put his napkin on the table. "And while you're doing that, Tam can accompany me for a ride across the park. I promised Cromwell and Marziran a good run this morning."

At mention of their names, the greyhounds pricked up their ears and lifted their muzzles off a paw.

"I was to meet Roger in the distillery…" Tam started to explain, a glance at the old man.

"Go there first. I need more eye drops," Alec said, fishing out a small blue bottle from his frock coat pocket and giving it to Tam. "I have a small detour to Stone Court, to see what they've found under the flagging." He gave the signal for his dogs to come to heel and looked up to find his uncle making shooing motions at Tam. "Perhaps you'd like to come with us, Uncle, and find out why the workers have downed tools?"

"I'll let you deal with that lot," the old man answered, following his nephew and Tam across the room to the door, careful not to come between master and four-legged companions. "My guess is they've hit a pipe in one of the old drains that run across the courtyard and made a mess of things. Or perhaps they've dug up some old pig and sheep bones and don't know what to make of 'em? Before the Nursery gallery went up, that side was open to the kitchen gardens and the brewers house."

Alec paused in the doorway.

"I'd have thought Turner would know at least as much as you, if not more—having access to all the plans and surveyor's maps—to inform Stephens and his men what was under the flagging, and what to expect?"

"Aye, he does and he should," the old man agreed, adding with a huff, "But if your steward and your foreman don't see eye to eye, who's to say what Turner's seen fit to withhold from a *foreigner*."

Alec was taken aback. "Foreigner?"

"Aye. A stranger. What Kentish men call a man who's not from around here."

"I know the term, Uncle. My surprise is not that my steward thinks Stephens a foreigner, but that he would deliberately withhold information from him which might hamper the work being undertaken, all because the man is not a local."

Plantagenet Halsey looked uncomfortable. "I'm not sayin' he would. Just that he might. These people aren't used to their lives bein' turned upside down and their place invaded by a lot of foreigners. It's unsettlin'. And for a man like Turner, who's had the run of this place for decades, he'd feel his authority was under threat. He'd not take kindly to being advised by men who've been here all of five minutes." He smiled thinly. "But I'm not tellin' you somethin' you don't already know. And I know you'll deal with it in your usual tactful way."

Alec leaned in the doorway, hands deep in the pockets of his frock coat. It was the first time his uncle had voiced any concerns about the importation of a labor force from outside the district.

"Has Turner said something to you?"

"Why would he do that?" the old man blustered. "He don't need to say anythin' for me to give an opinion on why I think your steward and your foreman are less than cooperative."

Alec was unconvinced. When he thought about it, it was just the sort of thing Turner would do—confide in a senior member of the family who knew the estate and its workers intimately, and for more years than he did himself. And he would do so in preference to voicing his concerns to Alec, who, despite inheriting the estate on the death of his brother and being ennobled, was, in Turner's eyes, as much a foreigner as Stephens. But he kept his thoughts to himself, saying flatly,

"Perhaps my steward has lost his way and forgotten he has an employer? Bringing in workers from London can only be a good thing, for him, and for me. For him to know that Deer Park is not his to rule as he sees fit, and for me to receive opinions independent of his, so that I know I am getting the best advice." He met his uncle's blue eyes. "Everyone from my steward to the laundress needs to know I am master in my home. That can only happen if my steward and I speak with the one voice—mine. Would you agree?

"Aye, my lord," the old man replied with a soft smile. "He does, and I do."

The smile died watching his nephew disappear down the corridor, Tam and the greyhounds following. Plantagenet Halsey turned and went another way. Down the back stairs, and through passages known only to those who had lived in the house for as long as he had. He did not seek out Mrs. Turner. Enquiring into her son's absconding could wait. He had a much more pressing need to visit the library. He wanted to find those maps and surveyor's plans of the house, and in particular one of the Stone Court, his nephew had mentioned. He'd had a presentiment of precisely what it was the workers had found under the flagging, and it filled him with dread.

𝓦

ALEC STRODE ON UNTIL HE REACHED THE TOP OF THE WIDE staircase. It went up to the long Picture Gallery that overlooked the Stone Court, and down to the Great Hall, which backed on to the same courtyard. Here he brought the greyhounds to heel and turned to Tam.

"I would never ask you to break any promises made to my uncle, but what is it about Hugh Turner's disappearance that is worrying him?"

Tam swallowed hard. He did his best by the old man, but in the end he told Alec everything.

𝓦

HALF A DOZEN WORKMEN STOOD IDLE IN THE SHADE OF THE wide arcade that ran the length of Stone Court and abutted the Great Hall. The same number of workers were diagonally opposite, on their haunches or sprawled out at the entrance of a deep archway. This cut through the ground floor of the three-story Nursery gallery to an expanse of lawn which sloped away to the brewers house, dairy, and laundry, all visible from the mullioned windows above.

Generations of Halseys had been born, cared for and fussed over by a battalion of nursery attendants in this gallery. And as children, before being breeched and taken in hand by tutors, they had played on the lawn. That is, every Halsey except Alec. He had been born here, but was never fussed over or cared for or had run about on the lawn. He had been sent away while still in swaddling. But he intended to run about on this lawn with his own children, his father be damned; he was determined. He looked away from the archway and returned his attention to the present.

Tools of trade and a pile of up-earthed flagstones had been abandoned by the workmen between the archway and the arcade. This was the final area of Stone Court to have the flagging taken up and re-laid. The rest of the enclosed courtyard was now a perfectly smooth edge-to-edge surface of sandstone blocks in tones of gray and white. Stark and rather sterile, with tall buildings on all four sides, Stone Court reminded Alec of one of the palace yards at Herzfeld Castle in the far-off European principality of Midanich.

That castle courtyard was a bleak place where prisoners of the Margrave were permitted out of their cells to walk its perimeter for one hour a week. Alec had been such a prisoner a very long time ago, and so too had his best friend Cosmo, but more recently, during the civil war. Poor Cosmo had suffered terribly from his incarceration, and was still suffering. Alec had wanted him to continue his recovery at Deer Park. But Cosmo had not forgiven him for his part in that war. And nothing anyone said could change Cosmo's belief that his imprisonment and torture were Alec's fault. Thus he had not come into Kent but gone off to Ireland, hoping the wide-open spaces would cure him of his nightmares. Selina was convinced time would heal Cosmo, and he would return to his old self. Alec was not so certain.

What he was certain of was that upon reflection, it was a good thing Cosmo had not come to Deer Park. He'd have stepped into Stone Court and all the old nightmares of his captivity would've come hurtling to the fore. He would indeed have wondered if he had stepped back into Herzfeld Castle. The Stone Court had all the charm of a prison yard. Yet, according to all who saw it that first time, it was just one of the many impressive reminders throughout this house of the Halsey family's years of privilege and service to their Sovereign.

But to Alec, Stone Court and the many long galleries were a constant reminder that this manor had been added to by successive generations of Halseys with little thought to the architectural merit of the additions. So that from the first medieval house on this site to the clock tower erected by his father a few decades earlier, Deer Park was an architectural hotchpotch.

After several centuries of his ancestors building to impress, he was now left to fix and prop everything up. Sometimes he wondered—and today was a good example of that—if it might not have been easier—and he knew it would have been far less expensive—to let the place fall into ruin. He could build something new up on the hill.

Something in the Palladian manner, more functional and family orientated, and less an ostentatious ramshackle. Freshly painted and newly furnished, a Palladian villa would have suited him.

But Selina loved Deer Park and all its architectural eccentricities. She thought it magical and the perfect place to raise and watch children grow. *Think of all the hide-and-go-seek places they'll find around every corner.* And with so many courtyards and a high, thick wall surrounding the entire house and gardens, there wasn't any fear of the children wandering off until they were old enough to do so unchaperoned. They could then scamper across the park, venture into the woodland, and ride about the estate to their hearts' content. Her enthusiasm was infectious. So much so he wished he'd not only been born here, but had been given the opportunity to explore the house and estate as a boy.

His uncle had grown up here; so too had his estranged brother. And however much his uncle decried the ancestral wastefulness and grandiose nature of the spending on a *barnacle on the Kentish landscape*, it was obvious he loved the place as much as Selina did.

So while his children were small, and his uncle lived, this medieval and Jacobean conglomeration would remain home to the Marquess Halsey and his marchioness, and their family. Which meant dealing with the centuries of architectural pretension, and as a result, the structural discoveries to be had in the attics, behind the plastered walls, and now, it seemed, under the flagstones of Stone Court.

⚭

ALEC EMERGED FROM THE PASSAGEWAY THAT LED FROM THE Great Hall into the shade of the arcade, walked out into the courtyard and stopped. He looked about him. Conversations abruptly ceased. Every man rose to his feet, and those slouching against the brickwork stood tall. Arms were respectfully dangled at sides, and gazes dropped to the ground.

Two men of similar height and build came forward to meet him. Both wore the neutral tones and hard-wearing fabrics of their chosen vocations. Both politely doffed their hats. But when the elder man spoke without first being addressed, a ripple of annoyed surprise went through the workers, who looked at one another and then to Alec to see his reaction to such discourtesy. But Alec encouraged his steward to speak plainly, and he had expressed the same to the building foreman when he had given him the position of overseeing the entire restoration project. So he was not surprised or annoyed at either man's forwardness. What disturbed him was their animosity towards one another.

"Good morning, my lord. I apologise you've been needlessly disturbed," Paul Turner said with a glance of annoyance at the man next to him. "Had Mr. Stephens listened to reason, this matter would have been resolved, with you none the wiser."

Alec looked to the foreman for a response.

"I respectfully disagree, my lord," Saul Stephens said placidly, adding with enough casual malice in his tone to put his colleague on edge, "His Lordship being *none the wiser* is what worries me, Mr. Turner."

"As steward, it is for me to decide what His Lordship does and does not need to be worried about, not you, Mr. Stephens," Paul Turner enunciated coldly.

"And as head foreman and engineer, I would be failing in my responsibility if I did not inform Lord Halsey of the magnitude of the problem—"

"*Magnitude?*" blustered the steward, a glance at Alec. "If you'd instructed your men to leave the flagging untouched in this quadrant, as I had ordered, there would not now be a problem—"

"Turner, perhaps I should see this problem for myself," Alec interrupted quietly. "And then you may both explain your positions."

"Very well, my lord. But—and Mr. Stephens and I are in accord on this—the area is too unstable to step closer."

"Aye. It is, my lord," agreed the foreman. "We'll need to assess the hole from another access point—"

"Hole?" Alec asked, looking between the shoulders of both men to the abandoned pile of tools.

Steward and foreman looked at one another, and when the steward remained tight-lipped, the foreman responded.

"More a cavern than a hole."

Alec couldn't hide his astonishment. "You've discovered a cavern under the flagstones?"

"Aye, my lord. But it is not a natural feature placed there by

God," the foreman explained. "And it did not appear from nowhere, like a volcano or a well sprung from the earth. It's man made. We stuck a taper into the darkness to see what we could. The light cast was dim at best from such a height. And I was worried lest the entire roof collapse, so we were quick about it. In those few seconds, I saw white-washed walls, so it is a room built to purpose, but I couldn't say for certain its depth or width."

"Built to purpose? As I understand it," Alec continued, "the cellars are situated under the Nursery Gallery and run part of the way under this court. So could this hole have opened up over one of the cellar rooms?"

"It is too far south, my lord," the steward responded quickly. "The main cellar is under the Nursery Gallery, that's true. And the two smaller cellar rooms are under the flagstones in the northern-most quadrant. The cellar wall is perpendicular to the Nursery Gallery for about twenty feet before making a right angle, away from this quadrant and running all the way to the Clock Tower Gallery."

Alec took a moment to visualize this arrangement. He had only been down in the cellar once. He was shown a large, long room full of racks of bottles and barrels and some equipment he had only glanced at. But he did remember the impressive vaulted brick ceiling, and that covering the farthest wall was a carpet. He went to step up to it and was warned to stay back. The carpet was pungent with mould, and who knew what lived in it and behind it. He had also studied the plans to every building of his house many times, while discussing the renovations and additions and modifications with his architect, fore-man, steward, and also with Selina and his uncle. So he had a reason-able idea of what the steward described was under their feet directly ahead. But it was not unreasonable to suppose he had overlooked any number of rooms, particularly when they were below ground level, and utilitarian in nature. He did however expect his steward and his foreman to have done so, and something in their hostility to one another made him ask,

"Was the discovery of this room a complete surprise to you both?"

"Surprise?" The steward jumped on the word and was defensive. "Most certainly it was a surprise, my lord. In all my years, there was never mention of a room under this quadrant of Stone Court."

"Which is why my men went about taking up the flagstones as if all that they would encounter beneath would be earth, and muddy at that, what with the wet summer we've been having," added the foreman.

Alec recalled something his steward had said earlier. "You did not want Stephens and his men to disturb the flagstones in this quadrant, Mr. Turner…Why?"

"An unnecessary expense in time and money to take up what was already perfectly laid. I stand by that decision, my lord."

"You can do so, Mr. Turner. That is your right," said the foreman. "And I'll stand by mine to do what is fit and proper. And it's as well we did start to take up the flagging, because the ceiling of that room beneath them was bound to fall in sooner rather than later. It might not have happened today or tomorrow, but it would've happened. And if someone had walked across it after a heavy downpour, the lot might've caved in. And that man, woman, or child would've dropped ten or more feet, broken a leg or an arm or cracked their skull."

"Melodramatic nonsense!" the steward said dismissively. "The flagging in this courtyard has stood the test of time for hundreds of years. It is only with your interference that the roof of that room collapsed and we now have a gaping hole."

"It was my wish all the flagstones be lifted up and re-laid," Alec stated. "Perhaps it is serendipity this happened now, while Mr. Stephens and his men are here on site to repair the damage."

"I cannot disagree with you, my lord," grumbled the steward. "And the sooner it is fixed the better. There's a storm coming. I advised Mr. Stephens to board up that hole as quickly as possible. But his men have downed tools and refuse to take them up again. So here we are…with Your Lordship needlessly involved."

Alec looked to the foreman.

"Contrary to what Mr. Turner thinks, my lord, I want the same outcome—to have that hole patched and the flagging re-laid and the surface water-tight before the next deluge. But as I explained to him, it's not a simple matter of closing up the hole by running boards across what is left of the brick ceiling and re-laying the flagstones over those boards. If we do that, I'd give it three months at best before we were back at this juncture. What I said would happen, will happen. Bones will be broken."

"What do you suggest?"

"We need to get into that room and look at the problem from below. The ceiling will need to be taken down brick by brick and rebuilt before we can re-lay the flagstones."

"Extra work. Extra time. And extra expense!" Paul Turner protested with a huff of dismissal.

"Yes. But necessary," Alec replied smoothly, punctuating this with a quick smile, a smile his steward had come to know well.

It was a warning. His noble employer was patient and understanding to a point, but when it came to emotive half-truths and speculation, he was less tolerant. It was a signal for Turner to end his opposition or face open criticism, not only before a pack of foreign workers, but the half a dozen local men up on scaffolding working on the windows of the opposite gallery, and who had an ear to the conversation taking place below them. It was a humiliation he was not willing to risk, so he nodded his acquiescence, adding to reassert his position,

"Very well, my lord. Mr. Stephens will be accorded every assistance in the repair. But I must insist that before work commences, there be a thorough survey of the cellars. My men will do that. I'll let Mr. Stephens know what we find. We can then decide upon recommendations to rectify the damage done. It will mean a delay in finishing this courtyard, but perhaps no extra expense will be involved, given Stephen's men caused the initial damage..."

The foreman gave a start. "Damage? We were unaware we were creating damage in the first place because you, Mr. Turner, failed to inform us of the—"

"There is no need to cast blame in either direction," Alec stated firmly. "I want the cellars thoroughly surveyed and the damage repaired. That's all there is to it. The expense is immaterial."

He looked from his steward to the foreman, and both nodded.

"Aye, my lord. I'll have the hole covered with a tarpaulin in the meantime," Stephens said. "It will help make the site watertight. But I can't guarantee we'll manage to keep out all the rain, given the recent wet weather."

"Then let's trust in Mr. Turner's efficiency in having the survey done as expeditiously as possible."

"I'll get right on it, my lord," the steward announced with a cheerfulness he had not exhibited up until now. "And to make certain no one takes a misstep onto the tarpaulin and drops into the void, I'll post men to guard the site. And at the entrance to the cellars, too. That should stop any unwanted noses from poking into places they shouldn't."

Something about his steward's sudden exuberance intrigued Alec.

"Before you step into that room, let me know," he said quietly. "I want to be there when you do."

The steward's face fell.

"Surely Your Lordship has more important matters to attend to than waste time on the musty contents shelved in a room that hasn't been aired in decades?"

Alec smiled. "I never pass up the opportunity to see a mystery solved." He nodded to the foreman, who stepped back and away, and added flatly, "Walk with me, Mr. Turner."

The steward obediently followed Alec through the Nursery Court archway and out onto the sloping lawn, taking the path to the stable block. They had not gone many strides when Alec stopped and turned. There wasn't a person in sight. Which was his object. He did not want their conversation overheard, by anyone.

"I had venison for breakfast this morning."

"Very good, my lord. I hope you enjoyed it. This estate has the best venison in Kent."

"So I am told, which is very gratifying but…the cull isn't scheduled until August, is it?"

The steward was puzzled. "My lord…?"

"It's what was agreed upon with Adams. That my deer would not be hunted, but culled in August, and not before."

"The gamekeeper and his assistants know your wishes, my lord."

"Then how do you account for the venison on my plate at breakfast?"

"I could not say, my lord. This is the traditional time of year when the stags are hunted. But as Your Lordship has put a stop to that sport, then one would assume the venison came from an injured animal that had to be put down. Or perhaps it was an illegal kill by a couple of poachers, and confiscated by Adams. He would not have wanted to waste such a beast, so would've offered it up to Cook, for your plate."

"All plausible explanations. Though…my gamekeeper assures me we do not have poaching or poachers on my estate."

The steward met Alec's gaze. He did not blink.

"That is quite right, my lord. The only explanation must then be that Adams came across an injured animal and put it out of its misery."

"Ask him. I want to know the origin of my meat—accidental death, poaching, or otherwise."

"Yes, my lord. Will that be all?"

When Alec nodded his dismissal Paul Turner bowed, swiveled on a boot heel and slowly retraced his steps along the crushed stone path to the Nursery Gallery.

ЖС

THE STEWARD MADE SURE TO APPEAR UNHURRIED. HE WAS thankful to be outdoors and alone. No one would hear him swear out his frustration long and hard under his breath, about his noble employer. He considered the Marquess Halsey's interference in his day-to-day running of the estate a complication he could live without.

The Turners had loyally served the Halsey family for five generations. He, his father, and his father's father had all been stewards to the earls of Delvin. And he hoped one of his sons would follow on after him in the position. But that certainty was challenged with the sudden death of the last earl of Delvin, and the estate passing into the hands of His Lordship's brother, the most noble Marquess Halsey. As Alec Halsey, he had come into his inheritance a little over a year ago. But given the long tenure of the Turner family as stewards of the estate, as far as Paul Turner was concerned, His Lordship had been master for all of five minutes!

Yet, in those five minutes, the Marquess Halsey had asked enough difficult questions, and was intent on implementing so many changes that the steward was beginning to doubt the reassurances he'd been given: That his present master, as a newly-married man about to become a father, would be too caught up in the birth of his first child to delve too deeply into estate affairs. That soon after the birth of an heir, the noble couple meant to return to London and their life there.

After all, His Lordship had a career as a diplomatist, and His Majesty expected him to continue on in this role. So what was required of the steward, his wife the housekeeper, and the rest of the servants who lived locally, was to keep their mouths shut, be patient, and wait it out until life returned to how it had always been for centuries past.

But Paul Turner was no fool. And Lord Halsey was no fool either. The nobleman was too honest and too clever for his own good. It was the steward's opinion, and so he'd confided in his wife, that it was only a matter of time before His Lordship discovered that his steward, his housekeeper, his gamekeeper, and all those servants who came under the Turners' jurisdiction, were forestalling on their employer's requests for change while pretending to carry out his wishes. And while it wouldn't take long before His Lordship found this out for himself, there were plenty of foreign workers crawling all over the place who were only too willing to whisper in his ear, Saul Stephens principal amongst that number.

What ill luck the cellar's vaulted ceiling had collapsed! Misdirecting the foreman and his workforce would take ingenuity. But it wasn't ill-luck that had brought venison to His Lordship's table. The steward put that down to sheer negligent stupidity. And that he could do something about, and quickly.

With a purposeful stride, Paul Turner returned to the Stone Court. But he did not stop to speak with the foreman, nor did he go to his office, or send for Adams the gamekeeper. He went in search of the one person he trusted above all others, and who he knew would be able to advise him on the best course of action to ensure the Marquess Halsey continued in his ignorance—His Lordship's uncle, Plantagenet Halsey.

FOUR

When Selina entered the library with her lady's maid and Hadrian Jeffries, Plantagenet Halsey was discovered up one of the ladders. His shoulder leaned against the frame of a bookcase and his long nose was stuck between several leaves of parchment. He was so engrossed in his reading they had time to walk the length of the room without disturbing him.

Arriving at the foot of the ladder, Hadrian Jeffries immediately crouched to pick up the rolls of paper littering the floor.

"Don't do that!" came the command from behind the parchment. "There's method in m'mess."

Instantly, Hadrian Jeffries set down precisely where he had found them the three rolls he had hugged to his waistcoat. He straightened and looked up at the old man.

"Why don't you continue where we left off yesterday?" Selina suggested with a smile to the valet. When Hadrian Jeffries brought his nose down, nodded and stepped away from the ladder, she turned and peered up at the old man. "May I ask what you're searching for?"

Selina's question got her all his attention. He lowered the diagram he was studying and smiled down into her upturned face.

"How is my favorite niece this mornin'?"

"I am your only niece, Uncle."

"And my favorite." He came jauntily down the rungs and put aside the parchment. He smiled into her dark eyes. "Are you well?"

"Very well. We both are." She kissed his cheek. "Thank you for looking at me and not my bump! Everyone looks there first and then asks how I am. I know they are really asking after the baby."

"Everyone except Alec," he said tenderly, gaze sweeping over her abundance of apricot curls tamed into several braids coiled close to her head. Her face was fuller than usual due to her advanced pregnancy, but that did not detract from her unblemished beauty. She had a healthy glow and her dark eyes were bright. For all that, he sensed her anxiety, and knew she was not being flippant. "He will always see you first. You do know that, don't you?"

That brought instant tears. She nodded and quickly dabbed at her eyes. "Yes. Yes. I do. Evans? Have tea fetched," she said over her shoulder to her lady's maid before taking the old man by the arm. "Shall we stroll while we wait—or perhaps you need to continue with your methodical mess so you don't lose a place?"

"What? Miss an opportunity to promenade with you amongst these fusty books? This lot can wait."

"I thought we could stroll the loggia," she suggested lightly. "We won't trip over any books there."

The old man understood. She wanted to have a private word. After all, there were no books to trip over here in the library, despite her claim. Every volume had been accounted for, up on the shelves or in neat piles on tables or by sofas. Hadrian Jeffries, with the help of two footmen, had made quick work of tidying the shelves. Now the valet and Selina were in the process of methodically reorganizing the volumes. Which was why he'd had difficulty locating what he was looking for. But once located, every map and diagram, every piece of correspondence pertaining to the layout of the house and gardens, and parklands, were all to be found in the one place.

He was all admiration for the valet's compulsive need for order and organization. It made him feel guilty for making a mess. That quickly vanished at the prospect of what the Marchioness wished to discuss with him that she did not want overheard by the footmen by the double doors and, most surprisingly, by the family's two most trusted servants.

"Fresh air will do us both good," he replied. "Don't you worry. I'll take good care of her," he said to Evans, when she made motions to follow. "By the time you have that tea fetched, we'll have returned."

Evans was so startled to be personally addressed by Plantagenet Halsey that she bobbed a curtsey and bustled away.

"She means well," Selina assured him. "But the closer I am to my confinement the closer she is to my back." She glanced up at the old man with a wry smile and changed the subject. "You are going to be brave today and join us for nuncheon, aren't you? For my sake."

Plantagenet Halsey chuckled. "Being brave is one way of puttin' it. Havin' to listen to the likes of Ferris, Bailey, and our dear Reverend Purefoy pontificating requires more than bravery. But I'll be there, for you. You'll need someone to keep you entertained."

Selina beamed. "That makes me happy."

He let Selina go out of the library doors before him, and they crossed the passageway to another set of doors which opened out onto the loggia. A long arcade propped up by Roman columns and housing marble statues of Roman emperors on tall pediments, the loggia ran the length of Green Court, a wide expanse of rolling lawn used by the family for playing bowls. At the front of the house, and the entrance used by guests, this was the quietest place within the manor house complex, particularly with all the renovations taking place. That is, if one discounted the Clock Tower bell over the entrance archway, which chimed the hour.

In the cool shade of the loggia was where Selina had decided they would have nuncheon. Tapestry carpets had been moved from indoors, beaten free of dust and then laid over the black-and-white checkerboard tiles. Placed upon them was a long mahogany table and a set of dark mahogany chairs with red velvet tasseled cushions. The table was set with the second-best porcelain dinner service, etched crystal glasses, silver cutlery, and three low-set silver epergnes, the bowls filled with summer fruits. Everything was in readiness for the guests' arrival, but presently the arcade was deserted of servants, except for the two footmen at the far end standing to attention and out of earshot.

Her guests were due within the hour, giving her plenty of time and the opportunity to have a private word with Alec's uncle. And as she was not one for dissimulation and the old man preferred plain speaking, she came straight to the point. Walking arm and arm with him in the shade, she stopped abruptly by the bust of Augustus Caesar and turned to face him.

"I want to talk to you about the birth…and about Alec…and if the unthinkable were to happen—"

"It won't," he cut in flatly. "Everythin' about this birth will be fine. *Everythin'*."

Selina was so surprised by the suppressed emotion in his tone that she unconsciously reassured him. "Oh, I am sure it will be. It's just that if there were—"

"You can't think about *if*. Why would you?"

"Why would I *not* think of what might go wrong? Females die in childbirth every day. There is a grave and real risk of mother or child or both dying during labor for any number of reasons. For both to live through the ordeal is not a certainty. I'm not being overly dramatic. It is a fact of life."

"I know you're not. What you say is true. But it ain't goin' to happen to *you*."

"Thank you for your confidence. I do not want to worry you unnecessarily. But one of us has to face the very real likelihood of there being—*complications*."

The old man eyed her speculatively. "Alec not able to?"

"We have touched lightly on the possibility… But no, not about a future without—without *me*. But I know it is not far from his thoughts. He is not sleeping well. I find him staring out of windows, preoccupied, and he can't always be admiring the scenery!" When Plantagenet Halsey chuckled, she gave his arm a squeeze. "Has he said anything to you?"

"Not a word." He patted her hand. "You'll both be less apprehensive and more confident when Her Grace and her daughter finally get here."

"That's true. I will. Though I doubt anything Aunt Olivia or Cousin Sybilla could say will lessen *his* worry."

"Y'know, it won't harm him to stew. That's what men do best when they ain't able to do somethin' about a situation that's out of their control. And childbirth is certainly one of those times, ain't it?" He smiled down at her. "It will make the moment that much more joyful when he hears the news you and the babe came through the ordeal safe and well. But he won't feel true relief until he actually sees you with his child in your arms. Now that's a glorious sight. And one he'll never forget for the rest of his days. So don't you worry about him. He'll be all right. And I'll be right by his side pacing the boards to paper with him!"

It was meant to rally her, to make her smile and feel at ease. But when Selina only nodded and took a deep shuddering breath, he gently cupped her face in his long fingers and smiled down at her.

"Everythin' about this birth is goin' to turn out splendidly for you and Alec. And very soon you'll be a family. And there ain't nothin' more precious and satisfyin' than watchin' your infant grow, and you will do that together. That is what I believe, and what you must believe."

Despite his confident tone, she saw a sadness in his expression and it gave her pause. She did not want him to be sad or worried, but she needed to make him understand. So she took his hand and gently placed it on the painted cotton of her maternity gown where her belly was roundest. She then put her hand over his. She was pleased when he did not pull away, for it was the first time she had invited him to feel her pregnancy, and it must have felt strange indeed. She wondered if he had ever been given such an opportunity before, and guessed not. And when he let his long fingers relax and lightly spread to gently press against her, as if this would allow him to feel the child within, she smiled up at him.

"He doesn't move anymore. At first that worried me. But Aunt Olivia tells me it is perfectly normal in the final weeks."

"Aye, so I'm told... He?"

"Oh, I do not know for certain. Who can?" she answered with a smile at the expectation in his voice. "But if I think it will be a boy, I am hoping that will be enough to make it come true. I want Alec to have an heir. For this estate to have an heir. It's what you want too, isn't it?"

"Yes. But I'd have been happy with a boy or girl. And he will be too."

Selina's fingers curled about his.

"Uncle...promise me...promise me that if...that when my time comes and if there is a complication in the birth and there is a choice to make...promise me...promise me that you'll save this child."

"I can't do that," he said on a hard swallow, voice barely audible.

"You must—for me, and for Alec."

He shook his head, and reluctantly slid his hand out from under hers. He brought his gaze up to her eyes. Hers were brimming with tears. He felt wretched. But he still could not make himself agree to her promise.

"Only Alec has the right. Only he can make that choice. And he'll choose you."

"Yes. That's what I'm afraid of and why you must make him choose the child. Our child. His son. For his sake. He deserves to have a son and heir. He is a good man. A loving man. He is like you. He will make the most wonderful father. There are no two better men in all the world who I would want to raise my child."

The old man scooped up her fingers and pressed his lips to the back of her hand. His voice shook with emotion.

"My dearest girl, that is the grandest compliment I've ever had. I thank you for it. But why this worry? Surely it is mere fear of the unknown that has pushed your thoughts in this morbid direction? It is your first, after all." He smiled down at her. "Let me tell you—just between you and me—Alec's mama was as worried as you are now. All nervy and jittery with a head full of gloomy thoughts as the day approached for her confinement. I was forever reassurin' her everythin' would turn out well, that she would live, and so would her child." He shook his head on a memory and huffed. "And where did all that needless worry end up? With me havin' thirty-six years of worry in its place!" He flicked her cheek. "You never stop worryin' once your child arrives into the world. That's only the beginnin'. You'll see…"

Selina tried to rally but her smile was forced. She was desperate for him to understand what was troubling her, so that he would do as she wished in the event there was a decision to be made between saving her life, or the life of her baby.

"I have no right to cast blame, and I do not," she assured him. "Alec's mother may have been an adulteress, and her unborn child not her husband's offspring, but she never tried to stop a pregnancy, to make it go away—"

"Why would she do such a heinous thing?" the old man asked, a deep frown between his brows. "The child was conceived in love, and very much wanted by both parents."

"I believe you, Uncle. But I am not talking about her," Selina confided, almost in a whisper. "I prevented myself from becoming pregnant by George, and thus I prevented him from having the son he so desperately wanted. I must atone for my sins, if this child is to have any chance in life—"

"Poppycock! Your first husband was a pitiless brute. Jamison-Lewis didn't deserve you. And he didn't deserve for you to give him children! Sins? Pah! There weren't nothin' sinful in what you did. It's called self-preservation. What you did was for the best—for you, and for the prospects of any unborn child forced on you by that monster."

"Who's to say that just because he was a monster to me, he would have been a bad father?"

"Who's to say…?" Plantagenet Halsey goggled at her. Now he truly did think her pregnancy was addling her brain. "I say it! *Everyone* says it! Ye Gods, Selina, I don't give two tuppence for what you did to survive that hell of a marriage. Alec don't care either. We've all made choices in life that we find repugnant, or which we regret, and are not proud of. But we must hold to the belief that we did what we did for the *right* reasons."

He put her arm through his and drew her close, and she let him stroll with her farther up the loggia.

"Let me tell you somethin' I've never told another," he confided, leaning into her so he could talk softly. "I was once forced to make a choice no man should ever have to make. That choice still haunts me. But I made it and I stuck by it—for Alec's sake." He stopped, turned, and looked down at her. The light had gone out of his blue eyes. "I broke his mother's heart. I'm not proud of that but one of us had to be hard hearted. And then I made matters worse for her, and for a time she hated me, because I agreed to m'brother's terms and conditions. I had to. He'd not compromise, but I never expected he would. He'd not have given me Alec otherwise. Poor Helen had her infant taken from her before he'd even had time to suckle… But she understood there was no other way, not if we wanted the boy to live. Now that's between us. And I tell you all this because you and Alec will never have to make such God-awful choices. The unthinkable ain't goin' to happen to you or your infant. Understand me? We'll all get through this—*together*."

"Thank you for confiding in me… And I will try my best to think only good thoughts about what is to come."

He put his hands lightly on her shoulders and kissed her forehead.

"Good girl. The only thoughts you need to be fillin' that beautiful head with is a list of names for your infant that you and Alec can choose from. But if it will give you peace of mind, I give you my pledge of honor to do everythin' in my power to look after Alec and your infant should—should that be necessary. Now—"

"Thank you. Thank you from the bottom of my heart!" Selina declared on a sob of relief.

"—let's have that cup of tea. You must be parched. Ah! Your shadow has read m'mind" he muttered, Evans bustling towards them with a maid in tow, carrying the tray of tea things; behind her was a footman with the silver teapot and its warmer.

What was unexpected was seeing the steward a few steps behind the tea convoy. When the servants stopped at one end of the table and began setting up the tea pot and cups, Paul Turner continued on and waylaid the strolling couple. A bow to Selina, and he addressed them both.

"If you will excuse us, my lady. I have an urgent matter to discuss with Mr. Halsey."

"Can't it wait until we've had our tea?" grumbled the old man.

"Unfortunately not, sir. I must insist that it be at once."

"Then off to the library we go, Mr. Turner."

Plantagenet Halsey rolled his eyes at Selina, and stomped away, the steward following, hands clasped behind his back. A little too tightly, in Selina's opinion, which meant the dour man was in an even gloomier mood than usual. She wondered what he wanted with Alec's uncle, when surely if the matter was urgent, it should be discussed with her husband present. She wished herself a bee buzzing at the window to overhear what she did not doubt would be a most interesting conversation.

A foot inside the library, and the steward ordered the footmen out with a jerk of his thumb. With the double doors closed on their backs, he rounded on the old man.

"Sir! I implore you! You've got to put a stop to his meddling before it's too late."

FIVE

Hadrian Jeffries had a footman position the ladder before a bookcase that had upon its shelves the Halsey family diaries, estate account books, and various histories and biographies about prominent family members and their connections in the district. Close by was a group of sofas arranged before a fireplace. At the back of one of these sofas was a long narrow table with a chair drawn up to it. Here Hadrian would sit while the Marchioness was comfortable on the sofa, propped on pillows, with her feet up. They were seated close enough to be able to pass documents and books back and forth without the valet having to rise from his chair. They often spent an agreeable couple of hours going through the archive of family papers, searching for family names and dates, and he writing up a list, which would eventually be turned into a family tree. He had started drafting one already, and it lay on the table by a stack of books, the ink drying where he had recently ruled up another sheet of family connections. He was also compiling a list from which his noble employers would choose the string of Christian names suitable for the infant who would one day inherit a marquessate.

Hadrian had been up the library ladder searching for a particular diary when a sheaf of papers slipped out from between the covers of a slim volume he had just flicked open. The papers fluttered in the air, then fell, a few sheets settling across the table, the rest to the polished parquetry. He quickly went to retrieve them. But when the opening and closing of the double doors brought with it a gust of wind, several of the papers whipped into the air and blew under the table.

He crawled on all fours, then sprawled out to reach one particular piece that had slid under the sofa. It was just out of touch. Prone, legs sticking out from under the table, and with his arm halfway under the sofa, fingertips to the flyaway paper, he heard the steward's voice. At first he thought he was being addressed. But the steward was answered, and by none other than Mr. Halsey.

The valet's instinctive response was to scramble up, brush his waistcoat and breeches free of dust, and either sit at the table and appear as unobtrusive as possible, or stand and wait to be noticed. But something, intuition perhaps, made him pause. Hearing Plantagenet Halsey's terse reply to the steward, he froze. And because he did not move he delayed making his presence known. Which meant he overheard more of the heated exchange than he should have. And it soon became apparent he no longer had the option to show himself.

Silently, and with extreme care, he drew up his legs so that he was fully concealed under the table. And to make certain he was not seen, he pushed his back up against the sofa, hugged his stockinged legs to his chest, and rested his chin on his knees. He had no idea what he would say if he were caught, or if he would even attempt to lie about eavesdropping on the steward and the old man. But those fears vanished listening to their conversation, which was clearly audible in such a silent cavernous space. And with mention of His Lordship, the valet was soon hanging on every word; with his exceptional retentive memory, he could not help but remember it all.

⚘

"MEDDLIN'? WHO'S MEDDLIN'?" PLANTAGENET HALSEY demanded.

"You know very well to whom I'm referring, sir."

The old man's bushy brows shot up. He was curt.

"Not when you speak of him in that impertinent tone!"

The steward instantly came to a sense of his position and bowed his head.

"I beg your pardon, sir. I meant no disrespect to His Lordship."

He stripped the frustrated bitterness from his voice to say evenly, "I fear His Lordship is interfering in matters that do not concern him."

Plantagenet Halsey looked suitably baffled. "I don't understand what you're gettin' at."

"His Lordship enquired of me this morning as to the origin of his venison, and I told him—"

"—it came from his own deer park. Don't take a genius to figure that out!"

The steward forced himself to pause and take a deep breath for he knew Plantagenet Halsey was no fool, whatever his blustering exterior. He also knew to whom he owed his allegiance, so he ignored the old man's flippancy to explain smoothly,

"I told His Lordship I had no notion how venison ended up on his plate. And now he has charged me with discovering from Adams how the beast met its demise, and whether it was the result of thievery, or an accidental injury."

"What's the concern? Adams will tell you it was an accidental injury and there's an end to the matter."

"I wish it were that simple but—"

"You just tell His Lordship what Adams tells you. How much simpler can it be?"

"But you and I know there's a good chance that what Adams tells me and what is the truth are two different things entirely."

Plantagenet Halsey huffed his annoyance. He was losing patience.

"Listen, Turner. If His Lordship's gamekeeper tells you the venison came from an injured animal he put out of its misery, then that's what happened. All you have to do is relay that to His Lordship. Whether you believe it or not is of no consequence, and you need not concern yourself. Your conscience is clear because you're just repeatin' what's been told to you. Understand?"

The steward held Plantagenet Halsey's gaze. There was a stubbornness and determination about the old man's mouth, and a cold light in the pale eyes. He knew when to bow to authority, and was the first to blink

"Yes, sir. I do. Like my father before me, my allegiance is, and always will be, to the master of Delvin—I beg your pardon—*Deer Park*."

"Got a nice ring to it—*Deer Park*. I like it."

"If you say so."

"I do." Plantagenet Halsey tried to cajole the dour steward. "Why the long face? I wasn't castin' aspersions on your character or your loyalty. Just do as you've always done and everythin' will be fine. It always is."

"I am trying my best, sir. Believe me. I just wish I had your optimism that matters will right themselves."

"They will. His Lordship is not unreasonable, and if you sound convincin' he'll believe you."

"Sir, I do not doubt that Lord Halsey will be polite enough to accept my explanation, but I beg to differ. He won't believe me, or Adams."

"Why not?"

"Because His Lordship is astute. He notices—*everything*."

The old man gave a crack of laughter. His voice held a note of undisguised pride.

"He does, doesn't he? Got a sharp mind… Sometimes it's too sharp for his own good. I ate venison with him this mornin'—which was very good by the way—and the thing of it is, I didn't think twice how that meat came to be on m'plate." He shook his head. "But of course, he would. Been inquisitive since a tot. Always askin' questions about this and that, and how it worked, or where it came from, and how did it get there! Used to fair exhaust me sometimes…" He rubbed the stubble on his jaw. "Wonder why he noticed the venison in particular?"

Anticipating the old man's question, the steward said flatly, "His Lordship has put a stop to hunting deer for sport. And as the cull isn't until August, to have venison served up two months before is unusual."

"Good for him! Hate deer huntin'. Loathed it since I was a lad. You must remember that I would do everythin' I could to avoid goin' out with m'father and brother."

"I do, sir. I also remember you once destroyed their crossbows in the hopes that would put an end to the hunting season. My father was furious with you."

The old man chuckled. "But he couldn't do anythin' about that could he? And my father never found out it was me. He and Rod were as mad as hell fire. Ha!"

"That would be because my father made *me* take the blame, and I received the beating meant for you."

"He did? You did?" The old man lost his smile. He was shocked. "I had no idea. Damme!" He patted the steward's shoulder. "I'm sorry, Paul. I'll wager that wasn't your only beatin', if your father was makin' you pay for my waywardness."

The steward again met the old man's gaze.

"There is no need to apologize, sir. Our fathers did what they thought was for the best. Just as I do for my own sons."

"How are Roger and Hugh…?" Plantagenet Halsey asked as casually as he could manage. "Roger went up to Oxford, didn't he?"

"Thank you for asking, sir. He did, and I am proud to say completed his degree. He's now returned and is under my tutelage."

"Goin' to follow in your footsteps? Good for him! But he's got big shoes to fill."

"Thank you, sir."

"So why isn't he your shadow? I seem to recall you were always followin' your pater about when he was steward."

"I did, but I was receptive to my father's guidance. Newly returned from university, Roger has his own—ideas—ideas he thinks are better than a steward with twenty years' experience."

The old man gave a grunt. "An obdurate son bookful of thoughts, who ain't willin' to listen to a steward's advice because you're his father also, eh?"

"Yes, sir. I see that you do understand the situation."

"We can't have a steward who ain't up to the task, or one who questions how things are done around here, now can we?"

"No, sir. I am well aware of my obligations, and his. Although he is apprenticed to me and has the expectation of becoming steward one day, I won't allow him to be privy to any particulars until I am confident of his understanding, and his loyalty."

"Good. I have every confidence you'll set him straight."

Paul Turner couldn't help a crooked smile. "I am doing my best. He needs to have the ignorance knocked back into him. If you understand my meaning. So I've apprenticed him on rotation to the various trades on the estate, to learn firsthand from those who can teach him—"

"—and to whom he'll listen more willin'ly than his father?" The old man gave a bark of laughter and shook his head. "Well ain't that marvelous! I pity the poor souls who have to wrangle with such youthful pigheadedness. But I have every confidence in Adams and his ilk bringin' him to heel. Who's dealin' with him presently?"

"He was with Adams for two months, and now I've sent him to Mr. Fisher, where he'll be learning about the wonders, if not the mysteries, of the apothecary."

"After two months traipsing the woods behind our gamekeeper, pullin' nettles off weeds, distillin' all manner of concoctions in Tam's dispensary will be heaven! And what about your younger boy Hugh?" Plantagenet Halsey continued smoothly. "What's your other lad been up to? Hopefully he's less trouble than Roger…?"

"I wish that were true, sir. Hugh is a worry to his mother and me in a different way, but I need not bother you with—"

Plantagenet Halsey crossed his arms. "No bother. I asked about Roger. So tell me about Hugh."

"I had hoped to apprentice Hugh to Adams, because he prefers to be out-of-doors. He was never one for learning from books."

"Sounds a wise choice."

"I thought so too. But I have yet to convince Adams to take him on."

"Had enough of Roger, so don't want to take on another of your sons? Want me to have a word with our gamekeeper?"

"Thank you, sir. But no. I'll handle it. Once I can get Hugh home."

"Where is he?"

"He's out in the wood. He's been gone three nights. His mother is worried. I'm not."

"Why not?"

"It's not uncommon for him to stay away while he's licking his wounds." The steward felt heat in his cheeks. "We—Hugh and I—we exchanged heated words."

"About what?"

"Poaching."

Plantagenet Halsey frowned. "What's he doin' poachin' deer?"

"He's not poaching, sir. He's against it. That's why he went off into the wood with two of his friends from the village. Not to catch deer, but to stop poachers."

The old man lost his frown. He was adamant.

"We don't have poachers. Everyone knows that. He should know that. Did you tell him?"

"I did. He doesn't believe me." The steward shrugged. "And rightly so. He knows his father lied, and to his face, but he doesn't know why I did. I'm not proud I did. As a father, that's contemptible. But as steward, I did what I had to do. I always do... *Ut prodessem multis.*"

"It is for the benefit of the many." Plantagenet Halsey narrowed his eyes and leaned in. "You believe that to still hold true, don't you? That what I—we—do is for the benefit of the many?"

"Yes, sir. You can count on me."

The old man stood tall and relaxed a little. "Don't you worry about Hugh. He'll come home when he's run out of food to forage! Adams may well find them before that happens. Have you thought he might be over at the Ferris's farm helpin' Lady Ferris with her flowers?"

"Hugh helps Lady Ferris in her garden?" The steward was incredulous.

"Aye, and from what I hear, he sometimes helps out Mrs. Bailey in her garden, too. If I know anythin' of those two, they're in competition for Hugh's time. Ha! Nothin' better to fill their days... But is it a bad thing the lad likes to do a bit of gardenin'? You look unconvinced."

"I am not against it, sir. Roger used to help out in the Ferris garden in his summer term breaks. That is, until there was an incident with Lady Ferris—"

"Incident?" the old man snapped. "With Lady Ferris?"

"Yes, sir. Her-her—*anility* has—"

"*What?* I know her mind ain't what it used to be but there's no harm in her."

"I beg to differ, sir, if Roger is to be believed. And my son would not lie about such a thing."

"Eh?"

"Roger says Lady Ferris is prone to moments where she is not herself—where she becomes distracted. Praise be Her Ladyship was reasonable when last here to nuncheon with Lord and Lady Halsey. But—"

"How *unreasonable* do you think a tiny lady could possibly be to a couple of strappin' lads like Roger and Hugh, or anyone else for that matter? What's this incident, and when did it happen?"

"While you were abroad. I do not know precise details, but Roger does. He says Her Ladyship lunged at a footman with her sewing scissors, thinking him an intruder. The servant gossip is it's happened more than once."

Plantagenet Halsey snorted his skepticism. "*Servant gossip? Lunged* at a-a *footman?* With her—with her *sewin' scissors?* For God's sake! The woman's five feet tall at a stretch, and weighs less than a half-drowned cat!"

"Yes, sir. I realize that, but witnessing such a shocking episode was enough for Roger not to want to return to the Ferris farm—"

"—but not enough to stop Hugh helpin' an old lady with her roses? Hugh just went up in my estimation. Look, Turner. You'd have to agree that mistakin' a footman for an intruder don't make her unsafe. Good for her for having the gumption to defend herself. Not that she'd be the least obstacle to a brute of a footman, but she made the effort. I'll wager he wasn't even scratched in the scuffle!"

"As Roger tells it, no, he wasn't. It did occur to me that perhaps with her mind not what it once was, she may not have recognized her own servant, and in her panic defended herself with the scissors. And she may be small and look frail, but Roger said it took two footmen to restrain her and remove the sewing scissors from her grasp."

"Did it?" The old man was unconvinced, but he allowed the steward a concession by saying, "I'll keep an eye on her while she's here… Let you know what I think." Adding abruptly, "I must away. The neighbors are due here any hour. If that's all—"

"Sorry, sir, but there is an even more pressing dilemma."

The old man turned his shoulder but stood his ground. His bright eyes went dull.

"And what dilemma is too onerous for the steward of Deer Park?"

"I need to know what I'm to do about the hole that's opened up in Stone Court."

SIX

THE STEWARD LOWERED HIS VOICE, AS IF HE FEARED BEING overheard. Which, unbeknownst to him, he was. The drop in the conversation had Hadrian Jeffries shuffling forwards on his buttocks. He was so intent on catching every word that he almost forgot he needed to remain concealed under the table.

Plantagenet Halsey did not hesitate in his reply. "Fix it."

"Were it as simple as those two words. The only way to repair the ceiling is from within the room itself."

"Why can't you patch it from up top?"

"I did suggest that. I was all for boarding over the hole, then dropping the flagstones directly onto the boarding. But the foreman employed by His Lordship was adamant that was no remedy at all, and was most certainly not a long-term solution. In fact, attempting to board it up would, in all likelihood, lead to further collapse. I have to agree with his assessment, though I did not say so at the time."

Plantagenet Halsey took a step closer to the steward.

"Tell me, Turner: Why doesn't that room appear on any of the estate plans?"

The steward wondered if the old man was asking him a trick question. But he didn't have the energy to spar with him, so said flatly, "So it remains a secret."

The old man tapped his long nose, then pointed a finger at the steward and grinned.

"Precisely! But with the ceilin' collapsed, it ain't goin' to remain a secret for much longer, is it?"

"No, sir."

"So I want you to do somethin' to repair it any way you can, before questions are asked."

"I'm afraid those questions have already started. The foreman is keen to send his men into the cellar to ascertain the damage done, and to see to repairs."

"You of course put a stop to that."

"I did. For the time being."

"The time being ain't good enough. No one is goin' into that vault —let's call it what it is—ever. That was the point of havin' it sealed up and purposely left off estate plans, so it would never be opened again." The old man peered at the steward. "You know what that vault contains, Turner?"

"No, sir. But I've heard the rumors—"

"How can there be rumors when no one knows of its existence?"

"Very true, sir. My father told me about the vault just before he died and I took over as steward."

"So what do you know, eh?"

The steward did not prevaricate. He was precise and to the point.

"That the vault was used by various heads of the Halsey family, and for generations. It was your father who had it sealed up. Lord Delvin gave instructions it was to remain closed forevermore. But your brother, when he was earl, had it reopened..." The steward's gaze flickered up to meet the old man's eyes, and he chose his next words carefully. "He said he wanted to honor the ancient family practice of interment."

Plantagenet Halsey sniffed contemptuously and threw up a hand in dismissal.

"*Honor?*" he repeated, as if he'd tasted something sour. "What a pile of horse manure! You must know that ain't true, so why shovel it at me, eh? That line was used by my brother to excuse our ancestors' appallin' behavior. It's just as well he only preached what our murderous relatives practiced!"

"Thankfully for you, sir."

The old man sighed heavily, pulled a face in thought, then huffed. "And when you think on it, had m'father not broken that murderous chain I'd not be here, and in turn, nor would His Lordship."

The steward wasn't sure if he was supposed to respond but he did.

"But surely it is not for us to judge them—your illustrious relatives, or for that matter any Kentish landowning family who wish to preserve their estate intact. It was—*it is*—their only recourse if they hope to flout a law which has been in place since before the Conqueror's invasion."

"You can think that, and most around here do. But what I say is that nothin'—and I do mean nothin'—justifies murder. And my relatives engaged in murder for centuries, and so have others who own a clod of Kentish earth. For all I know they're still *honorin'* that ancient family practice. It's cold-blooded and calculated, and it ain't right. And it ain't happenin' here!" When the steward remained silent, he squinted down at him, adding in a low voice, "And it wouldn't be speculation if I said because you know all about m'family's ancient practice of *interment*, then you don't need to bloody well guess what's interred in that vault, do you, Turner?"

The steward dared not look away and did his best to keep the emotion from his voice. But he couldn't stop his face burning red with mortification.

"As I know about the practice, it would be disingenuous of me to claim ignorance," he answered quietly. "But the truth is I've not given the matter a day's thought since my father told me about it, until today, with this calamity in Stone Court."

"Your honesty and shame is gratifying. And to return the favor, to tell you a truth, I've done my darnedest my entire life to forget that vault exists. But it's there and there ain't nothin' we can do about it, except keep it sealed and a secret. And that's what we're goin' to do. Understand?"

"I do."

"Good. So what we now need to do is concentrate on gettin' that hole patched up as quickly as possible, which should stop all the speculatin', and put a stop to His Lordship bein' anymore involved than he already is."

"I agree with you, sir."

"You know what's got me flummoxed after perusin' the house plans, Turner—Why m'murderous forebears built a family vault under Stone Court. I'd assumed all along it was under the Nursery gallery like the rest of the cellars."

"I wondered that too," mused the steward. "I venture to suggest that perhaps at the time it was constructed, which was when the Nursery gallery was built in the fourth decade of the fifteen hundreds, the workers were unable to tunnel further under the building because of a geological obstruction. Rock too hard to crack and take away, perhaps. So it was easier and quicker to tunnel under the courtyard."

"You may well be right... *Damme*. Of all the ill luck for this to happen now. We don't need bad luck at a time like this, Turner. Not with His Lordship's infant due in a matter of days..."

The old man chewed a thumb in thought, and the steward took the pause as an opportunity to reassure him.

"A tarpaulin has been placed over the collapsed roof to stop the weather entering, and from prying eyes venturing to take a look into the void via the upper stories of the galleries. I have also had men posted to the Stone Court, day and night."

"How do you propose to put a stop to His Lordship's foreman and his men tryin' to enter the vault via the cellars?"

"As I understand it, there is a vestibule to the vault, so that one has to go through that to reach the interior of the vault proper. It was the entrance to the vestibule that was bricked up by your father, but then these bricks were pulled out again by your brother. When it was bricked up a second time, the new brick work was concealed behind a tapestry. It still is. And even if the foreman and his men were to enter the cellars in search of an entrance to the vault, they would need to know where to look, and what to look for."

"And if they peered behind the tapestry, what then?"

"They might have an eye to seeing that the brickwork does not match the rest of the cellar's brickwork. And if they then decided to tear out those bricks and came across the vestibule, they would still be no nearer to opening the vault."

"Why not?"

"Because between the vestibule and the vault there is a heavy oak door. And this door is chained and padlocked. One needs the key to open the padlock, and then another to unlock the door before one can enter the vault itself."

Plantagenet Halsey squinted at Paul Turner. "For someone who has tried to forget a vaulted even existed, you know a hell of a lot about how to get into it!"

The steward swallowed and smiled crookedly. "The vault and its vestibule may not be on any plans of the house, sir, but that's not to say it hasn't been written about—"

"What? *Written about*? Who wrote about it? Not my father, that's certain! Was my brother stupid enough to write about it in *letters*? And to whom did he—"

"No, sir! Not that I am aware. Not letters. There's a document, a document about the vault. What to do in the event of wanting to open it. What I just told you. No one else knows about it—not even His Lordship. And his brother certainly did not."

"I didn't know it existed until you just told me! Does it say anythin' else?"

"It's been years since I've had reason to take that document from the safe. What I do remember is that the keys, to the padlock and to the door of the vault, are not kept here but are held in trust by the Halsey family attorneys in London."

"What the hell for?! So you're tellin' me that even if we were to tear down the bricks behind the tapestry and get into the vestibule, we'd still need to send to London for keys to be able to open the damn door to the vault?"

"Yes, sir. I am."

The old man rolled his eyes and wiped a hand down his face in frustration. He took a deep breath. "Whose idea was this? Not m'brother's I'll wager."

"I'd have to refer to the document, but I believe it was dated after Lord Delvin's death, but before his son—your nephew—took possession of the estate."

Plantagenet Halsey's eyebrows shot up. "While the Countess was still alive?"

"Yes, sir… Sir, I realize this is not what you wanted to hear, but the keys being in London, and having to send for them, and I do not doubt the family lawyer will accompany them into Kent, does mean we have time on our side."

"Meanin'?"

"Even if His Lordship were to send the foreman and his men into the cellars, they first need to search for where the vestibule entrance is bricked up. And even if they were to tear down those bricks on His Lordship's orders, and enter the vestibule, they still have to confront a padlocked and locked door—"

"—which they could just axe and splinter and force their way in!"

The steward dared to smile.

"I beg your pardon, sir, but do you think it likely that His Lordship, who is going out of his way to restore this house with all the sensitivity of one wishing to preserve its history, would allow the foreman and his men to act as ruffians towards a door to a room that has been there for the better part of three hundred years?"

Plantagenet Halsey gave a huff of laughter. "Ha! You're right! No. He would not." His smile dropped into a frown. "But he ain't goin' to get as far as that door, is he, Turner? You'll do somethin' to put him off. Say the ground is unstable. Say the roof could collapse on his head. Say whatever you damn-well like, but put him off you will!"

"I wish it were that simple—"

"There's that word again—*simple*. You should know by now that nothin' is simple with His Lordship. Get used to it."

"I am doing my best, sir. It's just that His Lordship has requested to be present so he can assess the damage with his foreman."

"Has he? Well that ain't happenin'"

"But—"

"No, Turner. 'Buts' won't do. No one else, most particularly the young Marchioness in her present state, needs to have their dreams forever disturbed. Understand me?"

"Yes, sir." The steward thought a moment, took a deep breath and said, "Then I foresee it will take me and my men some considerable time to find a way to reach that hole in Stone Court from below, given there is no mention of there being an additional room to the cellars on any of the estate plans. And as there is the prospect of further collapse, and men being injured, it will be a slow and laborious process to begin with... I'm certain His Lordship would want me to err on the side of caution. Should the vestibule be discovered because of His Lordship's persistent inquisitiveness, there is still the oak door barring further progress. And when it is discovered this is bolted and padlocked, I do not doubt His Lordship will request the keys. Keys I do not have, and which it will take a considerable search of the family archives to find—"

"—and even when you do find 'em—because His Lordship won't give up on you findin' a key, that's certain!—we'll need to send to London," the old man added with satisfaction. "And those keys will need to be accompanied by the family's attorney. And the chambers of Yarrborough and Yarrborough is a busy city practice. I suspect none of the Yarrborough brothers, or their associates, can just down court papers to come scurrying here on a moment's notice. It could take weeks before they have a suitable opportunity to be at His Lordship's beck and call."

The old man clapped and then rubbed his hands together with satisfaction.

"That should delay the matter sufficiently, I should think. The infant will've arrived by then, and His Lordship will be too caught up in being a new papa to be bothered with courtyard repairs. And that's when you and your men can go to work patchin' up the roof from above. God-willin' you'll have it sealed nice and tight before His Lordship gives that hole in Stone Court another thought. He'll just be happy to have the job done and the problem solved. It's not as if he don't have enough other problems with this crumblin' pile of old bricks and splintered wood to keep him and his foreign workforce occupied in the meantime, is it?"

The steward agreed with an uncharacteristic grin.

"No, sir. And you can be assured me and my men will be unable to find any plausible way into that vault from the cellars. Or if we do, as I said, it will take us considerable time and effort to get beyond the brickwork."

"Thank you, Turner. Your assurances have eased m'mind."

The steward nodded and bowed his head for a moment before meeting the old man's gaze.

"You can always count on my loyalty, sir. You do know that, don't you?"

"I do, Paul. I've counted on you more times than I care to count." Plantagenet Halsey took a breath, suddenly overcome, and placed his hand on the steward's shoulder. He gripped it briefly. And with a final pat to the steward's arm, let drop his arm. "Your loyalty is beyond price. I'll never be able to thank you for—"

"Please, sir. Let's leave it there. I'd best get on. There's much to do, and Mrs. Turner will be wondering where I am. His Lordship has guests—but you know that."

"Aye, I do." The old man took another deep breath and said with a click of his tongue, "And remember, if you have any further difficulties with that pack of foreign workers, you come to me. I'll deal with that lot. Now off you go before Her Ladyship wonders what we're up to in here that I've let my tea go cold on the terrace." He gave a crack of laughter and shook his head. "And you think His Lordship sees everythin'? Ha!"

THE LIBRARY DOOR CLOSED, AND HADRIAN JEFFRIES forced himself to count to ten. The continued silence had him scrambling out from under the table without fear of being discovered. He had pins and needles in both legs and trembled all over. He wasn't sure what disturbed him most—that he had eavesdropped on a deeply private conversation between master and servant, or what the content of that conversation meant for his master. He felt sick to his stomach and craved fresh air. But before he could dash outdoors, his overwhelming need to leave everything he touched neat and orderly, compelled him to tidy up.

Hands shaking, he retrieved the papers which had fluttered to the carpet and forced him to crawl under the table in the first place. He unconsciously shuffled, then tapped them into a pile so the edges were all squared, then placed them atop his opened diary. He would read them later, when he could think straight.

Mind racing with everything he had heard and memorized between the steward and His Lordship's uncle, he wondered what he needed to do about it, now that he was in possession of such astounding information. What was certain was that he could not keep it to himself. His Lordship had a right to know, and he had a duty to tell him. But how and when to do so without causing discord between beloved uncle and nephew? He needed advice, advice on how to proceed, and how to approach His Lordship. And he needed it now.

He left the library, mind buzzing and heart pumping. His feet took him into the warren of narrow passageways used by the servants, out of one building, across a courtyard, and into the next, until he was in the cool dark depths of the house where only servants, menials, and tradesmen loitered. But he did not stop nor engage anyone in conversation. He barely made eye contact. No one thought this strange. After all, His Lordship's valet could go where he pleased. And being His Lordship's valet meant he was the eyes and ears of the master as far as the other servants were concerned. So they were always on alert in his presence, or did their best to avoid him for fear of coming to the attention of the Marquess Halsey.

Hadrian barely noticed anyone or anything. His mind was buzzing with Plantagenet Halsey's words—*my relatives engaged in murder for centuries*. What was hidden away in a secret vault that related to the family's murderous activities must surely be the stuff of nightmares. And he wasn't surprised the old man had no wish for his nephew and his wife to make such a discovery.

It was all very puzzling and alarming. With a rising panic, a distracted Hadrian pushed wide the kitchen door and strode out through the cobbled courtyard to the walled vegetable garden beyond. Here he stopped, to finally draw a deep breath, squinting in the summer light. He inhaled fresh air pungent with honeysuckle, and with the breeze in his face and the sun on his back, he took a moment to look about him. Just through the garden gate was the orderly tilled and planted beds of the recently established Physic garden. Beyond, a winding path bordered by shade trees led to a distillery and the preparation rooms any apothecary would be proud to call his own.

Hadrian went through the gate and took the shaded path, hardly knowing his immediate intentions. Coming out into the sun again he found himself at the steps of the preparation rooms. He blinked with surprise. Watching him from the doorway was Mr. Thomas Fisher, and at the window, with his elbows on the sill and his face in his hands, his surly assistant Roger Turner. Neither were welcoming.

SEVEN

"State your business, Jeffries," Tam said stiffly, taking his shoulder off the door jamb.

The valet slowly approached the apothecary. He wasn't precisely sure what it was he wanted, or what had brought him here, into the domain of the freckle-faced Thomas Fisher. The one-time valet to His Lordship looked more youth than man, despite being apothecary to the great and titled. But what mattered to Hadrian was that Fisher was no longer a servant in His Lordship's household, but had been elevated to favored family friend. Perhaps it was serendipity that had brought him here…

"I—I'd like a word, Mr. Fisher." He glanced at the surly assistant still framed in the window. "In private, if I may…"

Tam's instinctive response was to tell the uppity valet that if he hadn't come on an errand for his master, then to go on his way. Jeffries had made Tam's life a misery when he'd been valet to Alec Halsey. He'd considered Tam unworthy of being a gentleman's gentleman, and with the collusion of the butler, had hindered Tam's efforts at every turn. Jeffries had made him appear incompetent in the hopes of having him dismissed so that he could take on the position. And here they were now, a twelvemonth later, with Jeffries getting his wish.

But much water had washed over the river stones since those days, and while Hadrian Jeffries may have achieved his object of taking over the role of Lord Halsey's valet, Tam had shot into the stratosphere as far as every servant was concerned. Not only had he inherited a thousand-pound legacy, a legacy he had plowed into his own apothecary's business on St. James's Street in Westminster, but he now sat at His Lordship's table as his friend. Mr. Hadrian Jeffries would remain a gentleman's gentleman for the rest of his days.

Knowing this gave Tam a temporary satisfaction. But he was incapable of being vindictive. So he shoved back down deep within him the memories of his humiliation when a servant, and instead of dismissing the valet and telling him to go on his way—that they had nothing to say to one another—he gave him a nod.

"Say your piece, Jeffries. I'm listening."

Hadrian was suddenly dry in the back of his throat. He glanced again at the assistant, this time gaze lingering in the hopes Thomas Fisher would notice without him having to state the obvious.

"It would be better said indoors, Mr. Fisher…"

Tam had seen the sidelong glance at Roger the first time, and like that first time he chose to ignore it.

"Here will do nicely."

The valet tried not to show his disappointment. He deserved the apothecary's hostility. Until that morning, indeed until his time under the table eavesdropping on the conversation between Mr. Halsey and the steward, he would have continued to regard Thomas Fisher in the same manner. But if there was one thing he knew for certain, it was that the youth was devoted to the Marquess. Like him, the apothecary would do anything to help His Lordship. In that they were in accord. And so holding to this belief, he hoped he might be able to help him out of his dilemma.

"If it were that simple, I would tell you here. But it is not and—and, if you would allow me to move out of the sun… I am—I am not entirely well, Mr. Fisher."

Tam's brow furrowed. "Not well?"

"I am sorry for it, but I fear I am decidedly unwell," admitted the valet. "I will be better directly… If I could sit a moment in the shade, perhaps that would help… Again, I am sorry…"

Tam came swiftly down the steps to take a closer look. The valet had a chalk-like pallor, and sweat beaded his forehead. He took Jeffries' pulse at the wrist and noted it was racing. Not only that but he was also swaying. Tam's instincts as a healer took over. Any animosity towards Hadrian Jeffries vanished. Here now was a patient in need of his care. Without a second thought, he put an arm across the valet's shoulders to keep him upright, and called out to his assistant.

Roger appeared in the doorway but he made no effort to bestir himself. He leaned against the door jamb and watched Tam help the valet up the steps. It was only when he was in the way of the two men that he finally moved aside.

Hadrian Jeffries slumped forward, giddy. Tam hauled him upright and barked out for a chair. This time Roger moved and did as he was ordered. But he was slow, too slow for Tam, who snatched the chair from him, thumped it down on all four legs and eased the valet onto it.

"Don't move!" Tam demanded of Roger. "Stay next to him, and if he starts to lean, push him upright."

Roger let it be known by a roll of his eyes that he was taking orders under sufferance. Tam ignored him and crossed to the work bench, where he quickly rummaged through an assortment of labeled bottles. He found what he was looking for, uncorked it, grabbed a small cloth, and returned to the valet. He put the cloth over the open mouth of the bottle, upended it and let the liquid soak into the material.

When a pungent and unmistakable aroma filled the air, Roger pinched his nostrils and made a face. If he had not been concerned for the valet, Tam would've laughed at such posturing, then given him a lecture on how to behave before a patient. He tried to instruct Roger in what he was doing.

"Lavender oil applied to the temples helps to ease headaches, and soothes agitation—"

"Knocking him out more belike!" Roger scoffed. "It's a God-awful stench, Cous—"

"I'm not your cousin here, Roger Turner," Tam said through his teeth.

Roger shrugged a shoulder, unconcerned. "As you please. But your hocus pocus doesn't change the fact we're cousins, does it?"

"I will please myself, and you will please me too while you're under my direction!"

"If I must—Oi! Isn't this fellow His Lordship's whipping boy—"

"Jeffries is Lord Halsey's valet," Tam stated, the harsh tone belying the gentleness in his application of the lavender drops to Hadrian's temples. He stood and stepped away, a concerned frown leveled at the valet as he said more calmly, "Close your eyes, Jeffries. Take a few deep breaths. You'll feel better directly."

With the valet doing as he was told, he turned his attention to Roger Turner. Mentally his shoulders slumped. Tam had only agreed to take him on to appease Roger's mother. There was no teaching a reluctant mind, and there was no hope of knocking any humility into one who considered himself above the drudgery of the everyday. Whatever the Turners hoped to the contrary, their eldest son Roger thought too much of himself to be of use to anyone.

"While Jeffries is regaining his equilibrium, you can fetch up a jug of small beer," Tam ordered. "Don't get it from the house. Go down to the village. You needn't hurry back."

Roger was about to retort he hadn't spent three years at university to take up a position as lackey. And as he was no man's servant, he didn't fetch and carry for anyone, and most certainly not for a valet however grand his employer, and even if that employer was master of this estate. And then he remembered that it being Tuesday it was wash day. And that the laundry buildings were part of the cluster of low-set buildings known on the estate as the village. It included not only the blacksmith, the carpenter, and the wheelwright, but the brew house and oast house. And to get beer meant having to pass by the laundry.

And today being wash day, all the young laundry maids would be ankle deep in the washing tubs of sudsy water, petticoats tucked up to their thighs so as not to get them wet, long shapely legs without their stockings, and bare feet pounding away at the dirty linens and sheets underfoot. They were a cheerful lot, giggling away as they stomped the washing clean. They didn't even seem to mind the astringent foul smell of the soap that hung low in the hot humid air, and not only made Roger's nose sting and his throat ache, but also want to retch. But he'd put up with the stench and a sore nose and throat, all for the thrill of being the singular male witness in this all female bastion of naked thighs and jiggling breasts.

And with Hugh out of the way, there was no possibility of finding his brother in the darkness of the mangle room, hiding amongst the machinery but in line of sight of the girls in their tubs. He'd have the room all to himself, with no fear of having his enjoyment interrupted. No one came into the mangle room except on the Friday after wash day.

With thoughts of a bevy of giggling jiggling laundry maids in his mind's eye, Roger dawdled out of the preparation room as if he had all the time in the world. But once beyond the gate he lengthened his stride. Fetching a jug of beer was the last thing on his mind.

⚚

WITH ROGER GONE, TAM BUSIED HIMSELF AT THE WORK BENCH, one eye on Hadrian Jeffries who he had ordered to keep his eyes closed until he no longer felt anxious and unsteady.

Hadrian did as he was told, sitting back in the chair with shoulders squared. He took a few deep breaths, the scent of lavender surprisingly soothing. His mind became less clouded, less crammed with words, and his heart didn't feel as if it were thumping in his ears. Keeping his eyes closed he tried to remember what he had first seen upon entering this space. There were shelves of bottles, all labeled, and under a row of windows a long table that had upon it all manner of bundled herbs and foliage. At the fireplace, two kettles sat on the hob. And while his mind's eye tried to recall the inner space, his hearing pricked at the sounds beyond the window. Somewhere nearby a dog barked. Men in conversation passed by the gate, their boots crunching on the gravel path. Accompanying them was the trundle of wheels. Perhaps it was several of the gardeners with wheelbarrows. And then there was girlish giggling and a short sharp response from an authoritarian female telling her charges to keep their eyes front and their mouths shut... Maids with bundles of washing being herded by a female superior from the house and down to the laundry.

⚚

WITH THE COLOR RETURNED TO HADRIAN JEFFRIES'S CHEEKS and his shoulders relaxed, Tam went through to the back room. He returned with two tumblers of lemon water. He waited for the valet to open his eyes, then held out a tumbler, making certain the valet had it securely in hand before stepping away. He then grabbed a chair and sat facing him.

When Hadrian sniffed into his tumbler, Tam smiled crookedly.

"I'm not about to poison you! It tastes as it smells, of lemons. You're welcome to the beer, but that's likely to arrive this side of never, knowing Roger. I sent him to fetch it to get rid of him." Tam sipped from his tumbler. "The lemon water will help the giddiness."

Hadrian sipped gratefully. "Thank you. I am parched." After taking a few more sips he asked diffidently with a frown, "Is Roger in the habit of not doing as you tell him, Mr. Fisher?"

"Because we're cousins and he's older than me?" Tam voiced what the valet was thinking. "That's a fair estimation. But Roger does as he pleases, wherever he is and with whomever. I only took him on as a favor to Mrs. Turner."

"Is he not too old to be an apprentice?"

"He is. And he isn't my apprentice. He's supposed to be helping me out while I'm down here establishing the physic garden for His Lordship, so he has some notion of an apothecary's duties and responsibilities on the estate. It's all part of his training—"

"Training?"

"—to follow in his father's footsteps and be steward of Deer Park one day."

Hadrian could not hide his astonishment. But he managed to say evenly, "And being of assistance to you will help him in this endeavor?"

Tam shrugged. "If it were anyone but Roger it would. But a Turner has been steward here for at least five generations. And Roger being the eldest, he'll take over from his father when the time comes… So Mr. Turner is determined he should know how an estate is run from every quarter, or he won't be able to do his job properly. That means spending time with me. But you'd know all about estates and—"

"No. No, I don't. This is my first stay in the country. My family were—are—city dwellers. So my knowledge is sadly lacking about estates and how they are run."

"What a high treat for you then to be stuck in the wilds of Kent!

But you didn't come to see me for the pleasure of my conversation. So why are you here?"

Hadrian finished off the last drop of lemon water in the tumbler and holding it a little too firmly he looked Tam full in the face and said, "Firstly, allow me to apologize for my abhorrent behavior towards you when you first came to St. James's Place—"

"No. Don't. I don't want your apology! Just because I came to your aid doesn't mean I don't still hold you in contempt! I am duty-bound as an apothecary to treat the ill. You needed treatment and I provided it. There's an end to the matter."

"I must respectfully disagree, Mr. Fisher. You do not have to accept my apology. Nor do I expect you to show me anything but the contempt I showed you. But I offer you my sincere apology, and tell you I was in the wrong—"

"Yes. Yes. You were!" Tam spat out before he could stop himself, the memories of his mistreatment at the hands of this man and the butler at St. James's place getting the better of him. "You and Mr. Wantage made my life belowstairs unbearable. But I don't dwell. And I don't want to talk about it again. Leave it there."

Hadrian made Tam a quaint little bow of his head. "Yes, sir. If that is your wish. But I am sorry."

That bow, and calling him 'sir' brought home to Tam that their circumstances were now very different. He was now the one in authority. He could, if he so wished, do Jeffries a disservice, if it was in his nature to do so; the valet was letting him know that he could. Though he was far from trusting him, it put Tam more in charity with the valet than he had ever been before.

"I'll accept your apology," Tam replied, adding in a rush because his emotions were still raw, "But that don't make us friends! Got it?"

Hadrian Jeffries nodded, and was careful not to smile so as not to appear insincere. He was not smiling at Tam, but at the boy Tam still was, because for all his learning and experience as an apothecary to the great and titled, just under the surface there still lurked the boy, unsure of himself and his place in the world.

"Yes, Mr. Fisher. I—"

"And you can stop with the Mister Fisher," Tam grumbled. "It's Fisher or Thomas or Tam. No one calls me Mr. Fisher, only

customers. Even Her Grace of Clevely calls me Thomas. So call me
what you will but drop the 'mister' while we're being private."

"Very well—Thomas. Though in calling you by your name you
accord me the honor of an equal—"

"Mr. Halsey rightly says we're all equal, just as the vicar preaches
it, that no servant is greater than his master, nor—"

"—is a messenger greater than the one who sent him," Hadrian
interrupted. "From the Book of John, I believe."

Tam nodded. "It is. Mr. Halsey says it's only luck of birth that's
put some higher up the ladder of life than others. And the vicar says
that how we treat each other in this life will determine how we are
treated in the next. But you didn't come here for one of Mr. Halsey's
homilies or the vicar's sermons. So why did you come?"

"Truthfully, I don't know what lead me to your door," Hadrian
confessed. "But now that I sit here with a calmer heart and a clearer
head, I am convinced I could not wish to confide in a better man
than you, Thomas."

Skeptical at such praise, Tam crossed his arms and sat back and
waited.

"It's about His Lordship—"

"I won't break any confidences. You shouldn't neither."

"That is as it should be. I'm not asking you to, and I would not
do so. I wish to seek your advice on how best to help him."

"Help him?" Tam drew his chair closer, belligerence turning to
concern. "How?"

Hadrian Jeffries sat forward and lowering his voice looked into
Tam's eyes. "Can I trust you, Thomas?"

"Where His Lordship is concerned? With anything! But can His
Lordship trust you, Jeffries?"

"He has my utmost devotion, as I know he has yours. And
nothing I say here, within these walls, will go further than we two,
unless you deem it otherwise. I give you my word."

Hadrian stuck out his hand.

Tam looked at that hand extended in mid-air and hesitated.
Hadrian's face stained red with the fear of rejection. But Tam's hesitation was but for a moment. He took Hadrian's hand in a firm grip
and they shook hands. Hadrian mentally sighed with relief. Both
then sat back, silent; the only sound coming from beyond the

window was of bees, heavy with pollen, buzzing in and out of the flowerbeds.

"To own to a truth, I don't know why I am so much affected by what I overheard," Hadrian confessed. "When one considers what we —His Lordship and I—went through in Midanich, being caught up in that country's civil war. It was dangerous, and more than once I wondered if we might find ourselves put up against a wall and shot…"

When the valet fell silent and that silence continued, Tam tried to temper the impatience in his tone. "I can't help you or His Lordship if you don't first tell me what this is all about—"

"Yes. Yes! I beg your pardon, Mr.—Thomas. It happened in the library just now. I overheard Mr. Halsey and Mr. Turner in conversation…"

And so Hadrian gave Tam an account of the conversation between the steward and His Lordship's uncle. He did so calmly, but with a frown between his brows and a distant look in his eyes as he was reliving the experience in his mind's eye. By the time he had finished, his face was not the only one that was chalk white. Tam stared at him in amazement. It was not so much that he disbelieved Hadrian, but that there must be some misunderstanding in what the valet thought he had overheard, particularly as he was under a table at the time.

"Are you certain that when Mr. Halsey used the words *murderous forebears* he wasn't exaggerating? He does have a tendency to over-butter his bread sometimes. And I mean no disrespect when I say that!" Tam added darkly, as if he had somehow been disloyal to the old man.

"I know you do, Thomas. I did not take it any other way. And it did cross my mind that Mr. Halsey was, as you say, over-buttering his bread," Hadrian agreed. "But it wasn't a throw-away comment in the usual manner of throw-away comments. And it wasn't said in Mr. Halsey's usual blustering manner, of which I am well aware. And he was at pains to make certain Mr. Turner understood that His Lordship should never come to hear about the family's murderous past."

"I don't understand why Mr. Halsey would want to talk about his family's murderous past, as he calls it, with Mr. Turner, but not want Lord Halsey to know."

"I think it has everything to do with the hole that's opened up in Stone Court."

"Why? How? I don't understand."

"Because beneath Stone Court there's a vault."

"And you think this vault and His Lordship's murderous ancestors are in someway connected?"

"I do not think it, Thomas. I know so, because Mr. Halsey and Mr. Turner discussed the connection. Heads of the Halsey family used the vault for generations for the—let me remember correctly the exact words—ah yes! The vault was used for generations to *honor the ancient family practice of interment*—"

"Interment?" Tam blurted out the word for he knew its meaning and it disturbed him. "Are you certain?"

When the valet nodded. "A sinister place of interment, Mr. Fisher."

Tam sat up straight. He did not like the word sinister. It implied the steward and Plantagenet Halsey were attempting to hide something disturbing and possibly evil. But then again, if the old man had uttered the words *murderous forebears,* and had co-opted Mr. Turner to keep Lord Halsey in ignorance about a secret vault under Stone Court, then perhaps Hadrian Jeffries was well within his rights in using the word sinister.

"But if it is secret and you think it sinister, then that vault is-is—" Tam stopped himself and met Hadrian's gaze, hoping he would finish the sentence for him. When he did not he asked, putting off the inevitable, "What are you going to do with what you know, Mr. Jeffries?"

"That is why I came to you. To ask what I should do."

Without hesitation, Tam said, "Tell His Lordship. Tell him everything you've told me, and more, if there is more to tell. I don't know why Mr. Halsey and Mr. Turner think it best to keep His Lordship in ignorance, but if I know one thing about Lord Halsey it's that he'd want to know the truth, whatever it is, regardless if it is all in the past or happened yesterday. So that is my advice to you, Hadrian."

The valet smiled. "Thank you, Thomas. I hoped you would give me such advice. It is what I want to do, too. And I will. This evening. And now I had best return to the house. His Lordship has guests this afternoon."

When Hadrian stood, so did Tam, and yet neither moved away from the chairs.

Tam swallowed, suddenly dry in the throat. "Did—did Mr. Halsey or Mr. Turner mention what's in this family vault that they don't want Lord Halsey to discover?"

Hadrian shook his head. "No. But as we both know what interment means, we can guess, can't we?"

Tam frowned and crossed the room to the door. He did not want to say it out loud. He made Hadrian do that by demanding, "So? What is your best guess, Mr. Jeffries, as to what is in that vault?"

"Bodies, Mr. Fisher. The bodies of men murdered by Lord Halsey's ancestors."

EIGHT

ALEC ARRIVED LATE TO THE NUNCHEON.

He had returned from the ride through the wood with his greyhounds to find a change of clothes laid out, but his bathtub empty, and his valet absent. Neither of the two attendants could tell him Jeffries' whereabouts, and when the butler was called, neither could he.

Alec was at his dressing table in his shirtsleeves when Hadrian Jeffries finally appeared. If he hadn't been pressed for time, he would have asked his valet what was the matter—the man was distant, all thumbs, and couldn't look him in the eye. In fact such was his valet's preoccupation that he didn't even attempt to give Alec an excuse for his tardiness. But as Alec was pushed for time, he let Jeffries finish dressing him in silence, and left his apartment none the wiser.

He was still pondering Jeffries' uncharacteristic behavior when he stepped out into the shade of the loggia wearing a light-blue linen frock coat with matching breeches, and a waistcoat embroidered with sprays of lily of the valley, strawberry flowers, and acanthus leaves. A large, white silk bow at his nape, and diamond shoe buckles completed his toilette. It was a far cry from the buckskin breeches and brown riding frock of earlier in the day, attire in which he was most comfortable. His present outfit was more suited to a stroll through London's Green Park with his noble peers. But Selina had confided that their country neighbors were rather disappointed in his lack of sartorial splendor upon their previous visit. So for this occasion he must dress the part of the Marquess Halsey, or an approximation of what they thought a member of the aristocracy would wear when entertaining. She, however, would dress for comfort. And in her present condition she refused to wear anything more restrictive than a pair of jumps under her light cotton maternity gown. He would have to be splendid for both of them.

And he did indeed look splendid, thought Selina with a mental sigh, watching him squint in the sunlight that bounced off the gravel path bordering the bowling green. She was certain the two women at her back were also sighing their satisfaction, and possibly his uncle, too. While the rotund, the barrel-chested, and the round-shouldered gentlemen guests would be more envious of the expense in the fabric than they would be aware of the effect her handsome lord had on females. As for the youngest man present... The reed-thin Mr. Ferris might be at her back, and thus she could not see him, but Selina was certain he had whipped out his quizzing glass and made an affectatious display of putting it up to his eye the moment Alec appeared. She wondered how often he practiced such a move before his looking-glass.

"Here you are at last, my lord!" she announced with a bright smile, as she came through the group with hand outstretched. "And not a minute too soon."

Alec bowed over her fingers, one hand held behind his back, and then glanced over her shoulder at his guests, all of whom had arrived. They milled about a trolley, from where a liveried footman under direction of the butler was dispensing glasses of wine. They all turned as one, and conversations paused mid-sentence. But it was at the long table set for nuncheon that Alec stared longest. For in amongst the silver, porcelain and crystal was a large bunch of white roses. He brought his gaze back to his wife and smiled.

"Forgive my tardiness, my lady. I had hoped this small token would make up for it. From the wood. I can't take all the credit. Cromwell and Marziran were with me." From behind his back he produced a fragrant posy of lily of the valley. Again he glanced at the table. "But I see Her Ladyship has already received a beautiful bounty..."

Selina blushed in surprise and unconsciously sniffed at the posy.

"They're delightful. *You're* delightful, you darling man," she said under her breath, briefly touching his cheek. "Now please speak to your aunt. She needs soothing. We do not want a scene before we've even sat at table." She stepped back and said audibly, "They're delightful, aren't they? They're from a garden I never knew we had. Imagine! Lady Ferris tells me it is a rose garden planted by your mother, and long-since neglected. So by way of letting us know it is there, she took the liberty of having these picked. They are beautiful, and fragrant, too."

"Let's have this put in water and on the table at Her Ladyship's place," Alec instructed the footman when Selina handed the posy to the nearest servant. He made no comment about his mother's rose garden, and with a wink and a smile at his wife, went to join his guests. His uncle came and took his place, and handed Selina a glass of wine.

There were two couples, Sir Tinsley and Lady Ferris, and Colonel and Mrs. Bailey, the largest landowners in the Fivetrees district after Alec. He did not know precisely where their lands bordered his, but his steward informed him that they did, and thus they were his closest neighbors. The other guests were the unmarried Reverend Purefoy, who held the living at Fivetrees, and was the wide-shouldered brother of Mrs. Bailey, and a thin young man with a jutting jaw by the name of Mr. Ralph Ferris, who, Alec was informed upon being introduced, was Sir Tinsley's cousin and heir.

Alec had only time to welcome everyone before Lady Ferris pushed her wine glass on her husband and stood before him. A small attractive woman with large dark eyes and a head of black curly hair generously streaked with silver, she resembled his estranged mother enough to make Alec uncomfortable. Yet, he did his best to hide this irrational feeling, and welcomed her with a lovely smile. She bobbed a curtsey, which was his due as Marquess, and then held out her hand to him.

He bowed over it saying conversationally, "Thank you for alerting us to the rose garden we never knew we had, my lady. There is so much of this estate I have yet to explore."

"I do not doubt that. I made the grand presumption that you would not have known about this particular garden because it is out of the way, in the far corner of the walled gardens on the other side of these buildings." She gave a little sigh. "Not the ideal place to plant rose bushes, and so I told your mother, but she was determined, and how they have thrived! There must be something particular in the soil in that far corner—And it's not *my lady* but *aunt*."

"Forgive me. I have only ever had an uncle. So having an aunt is novel, and takes some getting used to."

Lady Ferris wrapped her arm around Alec's linen sleeve, and he let her take him for a stroll down the loggia, away from his other guests.

"My sister—your mother—and I were orphans, so we had no one to call aunt or uncle."

Alec was surprised. "I'm sorry to hear it. I did not know."

She peeped up at him. "I do not doubt it. Sadly, it's not only this estate but your family history of which you have been kept ignorant. Your Uncle Plantagenet—Tagent to me, because I never could pronounce his frightful name as a child—he tells me you have no interest in family history and I should not bother you with it. But I think you should know as not—about your mother's family, and about your father. If not for your sake, then for the sake of your children."

He could sense she was eager to confide, so let her by asking casually, "How old were you when you were orphaned?"

"Your mother was four. Our brother was six, or was he seven? I was an infant. Our mother died in childbirth having me. We became wards of your grandfather, who we were told was a distant relation— All this work you're having done inside and out, all the hammering and sawing and activity of men coming and going, has brought back so many memories for me—"

"I do apologize for the noise. This spot is as quiet as it gets. Lady Halsey went to great effort to ensure—"

"Please, no apology is required. And I am certain your lovely wife was at pains to make our visit as pleasant as possible. But I like the upheaval and the clatter. Country living is such a dull affair without it. And God knows this crumbling pile needs renovation! Tagent's father was the last Halsey to invest any funds in its upkeep. He spent inordinate sums having plaster work redone and woodwork fixed. It was he who put in the second staircase at the back of the Great Hall…"

"Did he indeed?" Alec responded when his aunt's voice trailed off and she stared into the middle distance. "I had wondered what—"

"We often played hide-and-go-seek and would get in the way of the carpenters and the plasterers," she continued as if Alec had not spoken, becoming animated the more she reminisced. "To give our hiding and our seeking a degree of difficulty, when the boys discovered our hiding spots, Helen and I had to say which one of them had found us. Helen wasn't terribly good at telling the brothers apart. Your mother always guessed, and mostly got it wrong. I, on the other hand, never failed to know one from the other," she added proudly, then sighed and shrugged her shoulders. "The pranks boys will get up to!"

They had walked the length of the Doric columns of the first section of the loggia, and Alec was keenly aware he had left Selina and his uncle with the rest of the guests, who would all be eager by now to sit to nuncheon. So he turned and headed back towards the table, Lady Ferris still clinging to his arm. He walked slowly because he wanted to know more about the brothers. He voiced his inkling.

"Were the brothers that similar in height and looks?"

Lady Ferris gave a start and stopped. "What? You don't know?"

"Know? What don't I know, Aunt?"

With an unladylike snort of disbelief, she patted his arm as if he needed her sympathy. "My dear boy, you are sadly lacking in family history aren't you if Tagent didn't even offer you that kernel about him and Rod!"

"To be fair to my uncle, I never asked."

She looked to the far end of the loggia, where Plantagenet Halsey was holding his glass in one hand and gesticulating with the other, Colonel and Mrs. Bailey his rapt audience. "That would have suited him," she mused. "I do not doubt he contrived it so you wouldn't… You cannot ask about what you do not know."

"That is very true. Would there have been any reason for me *not* to know this information about my uncle and his brother?"

That made Lady Ferris glance back up at Alec. The faraway look returned, and when she again fixed on his uncle, he thought her about to respond to his question. Instead she abruptly changed the subject, saying distractedly and with annoyance,

"Hugh Turner has not been to work in my garden this entire

week. I would understand it if he had stayed away because of the rain, but the last three days have been gloriously sunny... And I still can't find my sewing scissors!"

"Do you think Hugh has your sewing scissors?" Alec asked lamely, not knowing where the conversation was heading.

Lady Ferris stared at him, baffled.

"Why? Why would that boy have my scissors? No! No! No! I put them somewhere safe and now I can't find them. Hugh was to help cut my rose bushes—"

"—with the sewing scissors?"

Lady Ferris burst into a trill of laughter, laughter she quickly stifled behind her hand. "Dearest boy, you are out of your depth here in the country, aren't you!"

Alec blushed and began to explain that he knew perfectly well that Hugh could not cut the stems of rose bushes with sewing scissors when she continued, a wave of her hand in dismissal.

"Let's not bother ourselves about that silly boy. Sir Tinsley says I am being overly sensitive because he sometimes sneaks off to work in Mrs. Bailey's garden too, and I am just jealous." She smiled. "There's a grain of truth in that! But Sir Tinsley also said that boys will be boys. Hugh's brother Roger used to help out in my rose garden too, but he was far less reliable than Hugh. Roger did so out of an obligation, and because Sir Tinsley bribed him with joining the hunt for his services to my roses. Whereas Hugh liked gardening for its own sake... Or at least I thought he did..."

"Hugh's absence must be uncustomary, or you wouldn't be upset by it," Alec ventured gently.

Lady Ferris lost her smile, nodded, and teared up. She quickly dabbed at her eyes, and as abruptly as she had changed the topic of conversation to speak of the Turner boys, she now did so again and returned to her original thoughts. She spoke as if she had not mentioned Hugh and Roger at all.

"I'm not surprised Tagent has kept you in ignorance," she complained. "As with everything to do with you, he is deliberate." She smiled and said cheekily, as if she were the possessor of a great secret, "I am very sure he would not appreciate me confiding in you, if he has kept it from you for all these years—How old are you?"

"Thirty-six."

"Thirty-six?" Lady Ferris was shocked. "Where have all those years gone..." She glanced down the loggia at the Marchioness who was now in conversation with the Reverend Purefoy and spoke her thoughts out loud, "She's much younger than you, isn't she—"

"Yes," Alec interrupted curtly. "Eleven years younger, to be precise."

Lady Ferris patted his sleeve. "Good. Plenty of breeding years to give you a brood of children, something the Halseys were never good at. But not only the Halseys. The first families in this small corner of England have singular heirs, singular *sons*, that is, and no daughters whatsoever. That made Helen and me a novelty. Then again, Rod and Tagent were a novelty, too. Even more so, as they provided the Halsey lands with two male heirs. There's an old Fivetrees Blessing chiseled into the market square stonework. It's in Latin but translates as *May you be blessed with one son only, and have no daughters to your name.*"

"*Et benedicta tu quae uno filio tantum, non et filiabus nomen tuum.* A rather odd blessing," Alec remarked with a frown.

Lady Ferris gave a shrug, as if there was nothing more to say on the matter, adding cryptically, "Everything about Fivetrees is odd. That blessing may be the least odd thing about it."

"But to be so specific in its requirements..."

"Poor Sir Tinsley is saddled with that preposterous creature and his eyeglass who is presently boring your dear wife senseless," she said on a sigh, distracted by Mr. Ralph Ferris, who was in animated conversation with the Marchioness and the vicar, quizzing glass moving rapidly about his face, as if he were swatting a gnat. "We had two sons but both died young, and we had no daughters to disown... But you haven't the least notion of what I'm talking about, do you, so you think I'm a babbling brook of inconsequentialities!"

"I don't, but that doesn't mean I mind you babbling," Alec replied kindly. "Better to have a babbling aunt than no aunt at all."

"Oh! You dear, dear boy! What a lovely thing to say! Though I doubt your uncle would see it the same way. I'm certain he wishes me a thousand miles away, worried I may, at any moment, divulge the family secrets."

Alec leaned into her. "I sense that you've never let my uncle's displeasure stop you in the past from doing just as you wished."

Her hand shot up to her cheek, as if she were shocked. But her eyes sparkled mischief.

"Clever boy! Too true! I do believe I shall tell you what your uncle did not want you to know. And I am very sure you *will* be shocked, regardless of what you think to the contrary." She leaned in, the smile and laughter gone, but with the twinkle still in her eye. "Roderick and Plantagenet—to give them their birth names—were born on the same day, to the same mother, just minutes apart."

"Tw—*twins*? My uncle and my father were twins?"

"Aha! You *are* shocked."

"I own to it, Aunt. I had no idea."

"Of course you didn't. Why would you, if Tagent had not told you? I fear I shall shock you further by telling you that the brothers were two of the same person. Born selfsame twins. No one could tell them apart from birth."

Alec was rarely speechless, but he was now. He stared, not at Lady Ferris, but down the length of the loggia at his uncle. He could not comprehend that his uncle and his father were, for all intents and purposes, one and the same person but walking about as two different individuals. Why had no one mentioned this to him? He had never met his father. The earl had died without ever seeing him, casting him out at birth—the product of his wife's affair with a mulatto footman, so went the tale. And Alec had lived all his life with his uncle, the earl dying before Alec's twentieth year. He did not mourn his passing.

Yet now he was to look upon his uncle and see his estranged father? And if both men were alike in form as to be interchangeable, were they just as identical in personality, too? If he found it almost impossible to believe the former, he almost certainly found it unbelievable, and intolerable, to contemplate the latter. His uncle and his father could never share the same traits. One had abandoned him. The other had loved and nurtured him. One was known to be an arrogant, vainglorious champion of the nobility. The other was an outspoken parliamentarian who fought to gain rights for those who could not fight for them themselves. One he had loathed. The other he loved.

Surprisingly, the first question that popped into his head was where were the paintings of his father, the earl?

The Picture Gallery contained only one likeness, and that was of the brothers as boys. He'd stood before a large canvas of the Earl and Countess of Delvin with their two sons when just breeched, peering through his lenses and trying to feel some connection to grandparents he had never known, and two boys he knew so little about. He remembered his surprise at the similarity in age between the brothers, but that their hair color was different, one brown, the other blonde. It had never occurred to him to think them twins.

There were no portraits of his father as a young man, or indeed as an old one. And none of his uncle either. There was a painting, a full-length, of his mother as countess in all her ermine finery, but no matching portrait of her husband the earl, which was decidedly unusual. Alec reasoned his father would most definitely have been painted for posterity. And more than once. Such paintings must exist. That they were not upon the walls of the ancestral home made Alec now wonder, given what his aunt had just revealed to him, if they had been deliberately removed so he would never see them, and thus ask questions his uncle did not wish to answer.

Such was his continued shock that he did not know how to respond to his aunt's revelation. He was staring at his uncle, and said the first thing that popped into his head which was wondering at the different hair coloring of the two boys in the family portrait. Lady Ferris had an immediate and simple explanation.

"They were painted that way to tell them apart, and so future generations could also know one from the other. In truth, both boys were white blonde until well into their teens." She squeezed Alec's arm, looking up at him with a concerned frown when he finally tore his gaze from his uncle to meet hers. "I fear this discovery is an unpleasant one for you. I wish it were not so. Perhaps your uncle was right to keep you in ignorance. Though I always maintained you deserved the truth about your birth, and everything that came before it. Sadly, the brothers—and I must presume your mother by her silence—did not agree." She cocked her head. "Your future was possibly the only thing that all three did agree upon... But I have said enough! Tagent would say I have said far too much. Come. Let us rejoin your little party. I am very sure Sir Tinsley and the Colonel cannot wait to devour the culinary creations of your cook. Lady Halsey tells me you brought your own chef with you from London...?"

Alec returned with his aunt to the nuncheon table, but he was in no great hurry, and he found he had lost his appetite. As they strolled up the loggia, he heard only one word in three of Lady Ferris's dealings with a temperamental cook. His gaze, and his thoughts, were on his uncle.

His guests were in a semi-circle, a rapt audience to one of Plantagenet Halsey's anecdotes. They chortled and commented, and Selina made a quip, her hand affectionately on his uncle's upturned cuff, gazing up at the old man. He patted her hand and returned her loving expression, and made some remark that had everyone laughing. It was evident he was holding court and enjoying every minute of it. With the new-found knowledge Alec now had about the man who had raised him, to whom he owed his life, and whom he loved above all others except Selina, he came to a most disturbing realization: He knew nothing about the first twenty-five years of his uncle's life, those years before he had taken on the sole responsibility for Alec's welfare. It was a quarter of a century Plantagenet Halsey had kept to himself. If asked, he always brushed aside those years as unimportant. But now Alec wondered about those twenty-five years, why his uncle deemed them irrelevant, and why he wanted to keep Alec in ignorance. What was it about those years? What had happened then to make his uncle want to keep a curtain pulled on Alec ever knowing about them, as if he were keeping from him a closely-guarded secret. It begged the question if he truly knew his uncle at all.

NINE

ALEC WAS IN SOME SORT OF STUPOR FOR THE FIRST HALF OF THE meal. He made selections from the dishes passed about the table, ate what was on his plate, and sipped at the wine in his glass. He even made small talk with Mrs. Bailey, recounted an anecdote from his time abroad, responded to his uncle's question about the name given to the barges used for transportation along the canals in Midanich —*treckschuiten*—and even managed to smile and wink at his wife when she made a quip about who between them was the most excited at the prospect of becoming a parent. But a thick fog of unanswered questions and speculation swirled about in his head the entire meal. All he could think about was the revelation that his uncle and his father were selfsame twins. And the question he most wanted answering was why his uncle had felt the need to keep this from him. That led him to wonder who else in the family knew. Had they been forewarned not to tell him? Did his godmother Olivia, Duchess of Romney-St. Neots know? Did Selina's brother, Lord Cobham? And what of the family lawyers, the retainers, his steward, and game-keeper, and the neighbors here down in Kent?

It was incredible to him that he did not know. Then again, he had learned from an early age not to ask about his parentage, about this estate, and most particularly about his uncle's past. But if his uncle wanted to keep him in ignorance, then there had to be others who had colluded with him to make this possible. Equally, there must be those in a similar state of ignorance. He was confident Selina had no idea about his uncle and his father being twins. She would not keep such a startling piece of family history from him. And she was digging deep into his family's archives, but apparently not deep enough if there was no written record of this birth. And if there was no record, that in itself begged the question, why not? But perhaps she had not come across the relevant information yet.

And here was his wife sharing what she had thus far discovered buried in the library shelves with those at the nuncheon table. And she had done so on the prompting of his aunt. So he forced himself to set aside his mental musings for a later time, momentarily shaking off his preoccupation with his uncle's past for when he could confront him in private and hopefully learn the truth. He rejoined the conversation, though he had no idea the precise point which was being discussed. Lady Halsey had the attention of the entire table.

"I have a particular interest in numbers and patterns," Selina was saying. "So my discovery amongst the Halsey papers came as quite a surprise. In fact I was astonished. While on the face of it, it appears banal, the odds of it occurring tells me it possibly can't ring true."

"I do not doubt your astonishment, my lady," Sir Tinsley agreed, leaping into the conversation with a patronizing smile of reassurance. He took a swift glance about the table, fleshy face split into a smug smile, silver knife and fork held either side of a patterned porcelain plate onto which a footman was ladling mushrooms. "But to those born and bred in this corner of the county it is a common enough occurrence as to be considered everyday. Would you not agree, Colonel? Sir?" he added, a look at Colonel Bailey, and then at Plantagenet Halsey.

Neither were given the opportunity to comment when Lady Ferris chimed in.

"Common indeed, Sir Tinsley," his wife affirmed. "So common, in fact, that there is an ancient inscription engraved in stone in the market square." She smiled at Alec. "I was just telling my nephew about this upon our stroll. He has a far better grasp on Latin than I ever will, though Sir Tinsley knows it well enough—"

"*Et benedicta tu quae uno filio tantum, non et filiabus nomen tuum.* May you be blessed with one son only, and have no daughters to your name."

"Thank you, my dear," Lady Ferris said to her husband.

"What an odd inscription and to be placed in a market square," Selina remarked. "Why in Latin, for who can read that ancient tongue but scholars and the sons of gentlemen? Certainly not the villagers or those who come to market to sell their wares."

"Very true, my lady," agreed Sir Tinsley. "The intention is clear. It is inscribed in that scholarly tongue, not for the common folk, the tenant farmer or the shopkeeper, but for those in the district who were born to rule them. The masters of their family's fate and fortune—"

"—and their wives," Selina interrupted. "The masters and their wives, for there cannot be a family without both."

When the magistrate chuckled and slowly shook his head Alec mentally winced at the man's condescension. He remained mute, and ignored the furtive looks of his guests who no doubt expected him to step in and turn a conversation from a decidedly combative path. But he knew his wife would not appreciate his interference, and rightly so. She could take care of herself in any argument, so he continued to sit back and sip his wine. He hoped Sir Tinsley had the wherewithal to realize he would not be the victor in any verbal sparring with the Marchioness. He would be best acquiescing to Her Ladyship's point, if for no other reason than it was her table, and he her guest. But that was too much to ask for. The magistrate's next words sank all hope.

"Wives?" He scoffed. "My dear Lady Halsey, it is not for the wives, or indeed the mothers, sisters, or daughters, of these masters to worry their pretty heads about fate and fortune—"

"Pretty heads? Is that what females are, sir? Mere ornaments?"

"There is nothing mere about you, my dear Lady Halsey," the magistrate replied with a smile that told Selina he thought he had offered her a salve to soothe whatever her affront. "I speak for everyone here, and I trust His Lordship won't take offence, for I do not say it as mere flattery but as fact, that you are not pretty, you are divinely beautiful. But alas beauty is no qualification in matters of inheritance. The decision-making must be left to those best equipped to decide the future."

"And those 'best equipped' is but half the equation—for what is a husband without his wife...?" Selina asked with a quick smile.

When she followed this up with an enquiring tilt of her head and wide dark eyes, drawing in breath on a swift gulp was all Alec could do to stop himself laughing out loud and spitting wine in the process. Oh, Sir Tinsley had chosen his combatant most unwisely.

"Indeed! I see that you do understand, my lady," the magistrate said with a satisfied grin, completely misreading his hostess. "The inscription is in Latin for a purpose. You said it yourself: For the *sons* of gentlemen. It serves as a reminder. A family's fate, and its fortune, is entirely in the hands of the husband. That circumstance is even more important when one considers the vagaries of this little corner of England and His Lordship's place in it—"

"That's enough about fate and fortune, Ferris," Plantagenet Halsey growled, half out of his chair to reach for a peach from the epergne. "You're ruinin' m'appetite, and everyone else's too, I'll wager."

"Eh? Oh! Ah! Quite! Quite! I take your point, sir," Sir Tinsley muttered, entirely deflated. He coughed into his fist and snatched up his wine glass to drink deeply.

The old man put his buttocks back on the tapestry cushion and lost the dark look. He smiled at Selina, adding in an altogether different voice, "M'mathematical musings are rudimentary at best, so if you'd care to explain your discovery in the family archive so an old man can understand, I'd appreciate it."

"I will do my best," Selina responded in kind, a glance at Alec to see if he had heard his uncle's order to the magistrate. The raise of an eyebrow told her he had. So had everyone else, for their eyes shot to the linen napkins across their laps and stayed there. "But after what Sir Tinsley has just told us about an inscription in the market square, I think what I've discovered is perhaps not as astonishing as I first supposed. Particularly as it seems it is not restricted to the Halsey family."

"Perhaps it is the wine, or the summer heat or both, but I am none the wiser, my lady," Alec said politely, and with a slight widening of his eyes confirming Selina's suspicion that he had not been listening to the earlier discussion at all, but had been off on some private reverie. So she patiently repeated what she had already told their guests, all of whom were either too polite not to look surprised, or were already aware of what she had only recently discovered for herself.

"It seems your ancestors have a propensity to produce only one male child per generation, and have been doing so for over two hundred years. To think a family has a run of single male children, with no brothers or sisters, not even any that tragically died in childbirth, or at a young age from some ailment or other—well, none that were considered significant enough to be recorded in the family history, or noted in the family Bible—is, quite simply, astonishing."

"There is nothing simple about it, my lady," Alec agreed, sitting up with a glance at his uncle who was not looking his way. "That is remarkable. I am sure you must be correct in your calculations, but I will ask it anyway—You are certain?"

"I am. Though I shouldn't be, should I, if one can confidently say that whether a male or female child is produced is as probable as the outcome of a flip of a coin. So having just one child, and that one child being male for five generations, it is not only astounding, but wholly improbable—"

"I'm not sure I follow..." interrupted Plantagenet Halsey with a frown of incomprehension.

"I beg your pardon, Uncle," Selina said with a smile. "Let me explain it this way: If we assume the likelihood of a male or female being born is equal then we can compare it to the flipping of a coin. Each conception has a fifty-fifty chance of the infant being a boy or a girl, a tail or a head. And yet, with the Halsey family, it would be the same odds as landing five tails in a row, which is highly unlikely indeed. It's as if the family were in possession of a coin with two tails and no heads, so that regardless of the flip, the coin is guaranteed to land on a tail and produce a boy every time."

Plantagenet Halsey rubbed his hands together. "Bravo! Then by your calculations I'm expectin' a grand-nephew any day now!"

Everyone smiled and clapped.

"A coin with two tails and no head suggests interference of some kind to ensure a desired outcome, does it not, my lady?" Alec asked his wife, ignoring his uncle's exuberance and the congratulatory smiles of his guests.

Selina nodded, so wrapped up in the mathematical problem that she remained unaware of what her husband was suggesting, eager to explain. "It is a mathematical conundrum for a family to produce only one child and that a boy, for so many generations. And being such outrageous odds I am skeptical of it being mere chance…"

Alec shifted his gaze from his wife to his uncle and raised his brows. "Any thoughts, Uncle?"

The old man shrugged and pulled a face, bewildered. "Only that I'm as bedazzled as the rest of the table as to Her Ladyship's mathematical mind. I'd have thought you'd be pleased the odds are in favor of a son and heir."

Alec held the old man's gaze, as if he expected him to say something entirely different.

"The only odds I'm interested in are those that favor the birth of a healthy child and for my wife to survive the ordeal." He then asked Selina, "I presume this improbable run of male-only children came to a halt with the birth of my uncle and his brother?"

Selina pondered this a moment as she selected a succulent strawberry from the bowl put in front to her by a footman. What she said did not surprise Alec, though he wished she had. "You must be right, though I have yet to come across the records of their birth… I had supposed to find them in amongst the family papers—"

"There are no such papers?"

Selina shook her head. "Not that I have discovered—yet."

"How odd that the first recorded births of male siblings in over two hundred years seem to have been misplaced. What do you think happened to them, Uncle?"

Again, Plantagenet Halsey shrugged, unconcerned. "The document must exist. Her Ladyship just needs to dig a bit deeper."

"Perhaps there was something about your birth and the birth of your brother that was not like the others…?" Alec suggested, gaze on his uncle, not a glance at Lady Ferris.

The old man did not hesitate to respond. He gave a bark of laughter and slapped the table. "Aye! Well that's obvious! There were two of us!"

The guests chortled in return. Alec received the distinct impression it was forced laughter. He said to Sir Tinsley,

"Her Ladyship is confounded by the mathematical improbability of such an outcome and yet, you, sir, were not surprised at all. In fact you called it a *common enough occurrence*. Would you care to tell me why?"

"Yes, Ferris," Plantagenet Halsey added, the growl and the frown returned. "Now that you've opened your trap as wide as it'll go, why don't you give His Lordship your expert opinion on my family's male lineage?"

Sir Tinsley stuck out his bottom lip, coloring painfully. "I—I am not a mathematician. Nor do I purport to have any expertise on your noble family, sir. Therefore, my lord, I would prefer not to venture an opinion."

"That's the wisest pronouncement you've made today, Ferris," the old man stated with finality. He downed the last of the wine and held out his glass to a footman to refill without taking his eyes off the magistrate. "No one with eyes can dispute Her Ladyship's beauty, but she is far more than just a pretty face, and there ain't a mathematician in this country who'd disagree with that. But if it's all the same to His Lordship and the assembled company I'd rather change the subject. M'relatives bore me at the best of times, present company excluded."

There was an extended silence as the guests glanced furtively at the Marquess to seek his reaction to his uncle's proclamation. Alec was thinking how deftly his uncle had managed to steer the conversation away from Ferris answering the question as to why he had stated male-only children a common occurrence, not restricted to the Halsey family. So be it. He would let the matter drop for now.

In the silence which followed the old man's pronouncement, the Reverend Purefoy saw it as an opportunity to provide an explanation that was the only one worthy of consideration.

"I believe," he said diffidently, patting the corners of his wet mouth with the point of a linen napkin, then peering about the table to make sure he had everyone's attention, "that the answer, not only to Her Ladyship's mathematical conundrum but the presence of such an inscription in the market square, is a simple one. It is God's will. Just as God has blessed the Lady Halsey with a mathematical brain worthy of her beauty, so too has He blessed the Halsey family with a healthy son for each successive generation. I pray He will do so again with your own precious offspring, my dear Lady Halsey."

"God's will? Oh yes," Mrs. Bailey agreed breathlessly. "It can be the only explanation! And I humbly add my voice to my brother's. Everyone here is praying you are delivered of a healthy son, my lady. I myself take solace in His divine will for the tragedy of our own circumstances. The Colonel and I have one treasured son. We had two other infants… But sadly they were not long with us. But we have our precious Daniel, and I must be grateful to Him for allowing me the one son."

"My dearest sister, we have spoken many times over the years, and at length about the loss of your little ones," the Reverend Purefoy said soothingly. He put his handkerchief into his sister's hand. "No doubt Her Ladyship's forthcoming happy event has brought back painful memories for you. Though I counsel you to think of happier times, of Daniel's birth and how he has grown into a fine young man—"

"Yes. Oh, yes, you are right. So right," Mrs. Bailey responded in a whisper, nodding vigorously and blowing her nose at the same time. She scrunched the damp handkerchief tightly in her fist. "I must think of Daniel, *not* of the two little ones lost to us, but of him."

"God is holy, righteous, and just," continued her brother. "Thus we must trust in His judgment. By taking your infants at birth, He allowed them to escape the trials and pain of an earthly existence. None amongst my flock are as fortunate. They may crawl the earth but the sinful nature of their existence denies them everlasting life. You, my dear sister, will see your little ones again in Heaven. Rest assured."

"Yes. Yes. I am so blessed. Thank you, Adolphus." Mrs. Bailey looked about the silent table with a sniff and a smile, and her damp eyes fixed on Selina. "Please do forgive my ill manners for voicing my distress at your table, my lady. It was a momentary lapse. I do assure you it won't happen again."

"Mrs. Bailey, there is no need for you to apologise," Selina replied with a calmness that belied her anguish at hearing of the woman's loss. Instinctively, she cradled her roundness, as if protecting the child within from such sad news. "To lose a child is something from which a parent never recovers. To lose two infants…" She glanced down the table at Alec and suppressed a shiver of sadness. "That is unimaginable sorrow. You have every right to your grief."

"Your Ladyship is most kind," stuck in Colonel Bailey. "As the Reverend says, we have a fine son in Daniel. And when all is said and done, and one must be pragmatic, as we farmers always are, we are doubly blessed to have an only son, for he will inherit an estate intact with no possible division."

"A most serendipitous and blessed outcome for you, Colonel," the Reverend Purefoy said with a tight smile. "A circumstance I am certain your dear wife, my dearest sister, takes great comfort in, too."

"I do! Oh, I do" agreed Mrs. Bailey. "Every single day…"

There followed a heavy silence, with the guests either looking at their laps or glancing about at their fellow diners under their lashes. Alec exchanged an understanding smile with his wife, and was inclined to let the silence continue for a respectful moment before suggesting everyone adjourn to the assortment of chairs further along the loggia for tea and a game of bowls. But Mr. Ralph Ferris took it upon himself to presume the silence was an opportunity for him to finally make his mark on the conversation, and in turn come to the notice of his noble host.

He coughed into his closed fist, and proceeded to address Alec, punctuating his conversation with a succession of nervous snorts, while barely drawing breath.

"I, too, am grateful to providence, my lord, and to Him, for bestowing upon me the great privilege of being Sir Tinsley's heir apparent. And as I too am an only child, my cousin's estate will, just like Colonel Bailey's, remain intact and not be broken up as would have happened had I siblings to squabble over the inheritance. Such an outcome for those with property in other counties need not have the burden, relying as they do on the law of primogeniture. But as Your Lordship knows only too well, here in Kent, inheritance for those with property is a singularly curious matter. It is one I have had the privilege to study at close quarters, my father being in chambers, and—"

"Thank you, Ralph," Sir Tinsley interrupted tersely. "You have provided His Lordship with more than he cares to know about our family, and managed to shine a candle on my own dear wife's and my sorrow at not having a living son of our own to inherit the Ferris lands."

Mr. Ralph Ferris would have swallowed his tongue could he have done so. His cheeks burned and his Adam's apple went up and down. "Sir! I—I did not mean—I was only trying to—my dear Lady Ferris forgive—"

"Please do not blame Mr. Ferris, Sir Tinsley," argued Mrs. Bailey cheeks stained red with embarrassment. "It is my own selfish sadness that has caused this entire conversation to plummet into the depths of bad-mannered gloom. Dear me! How insensitive of me to think only of my own feelings and dare to mention my loss, when poor Lady Ferris—"

"Hush! Silly woman," Lady Ferris demanded with a dismissive wave. "I was reconciled to my fate decades ago. Nor have I given it a thought in years. So we will say no more on a subject that clearly upsets you, not me. Besides," she added, bestowing upon Alec a smile of genuine warmth, "I now find myself with a nephew as my neighbor, and his dear wife is about to deliver their first child, which will make me a great-aunt. A prospect I am looking forward to with relish!"

"Hear! Hear! Well said, my dear," Sir Tinsley agreed, tapping the table with the tips of his broad fingers. "This is not a time to bore our hosts with such sad ancient history. It is their time, a time when we can all look to a bright future. I am sure we are all agreed upon that!"

There was a murmur of consensus and Alec pounced on the moment to adjourn from the table, and with a change of scenery he hoped there would also be a change of mood. "If Her Ladyship is in agreement, I suggest we move to the chairs by the tea trolley to watch those of us who wish to play at bowls?"

TEN

PLANTAGENET HALSEY GLANCED OVER HIS SHOULDER AND SAW
Alec was at the tea trolley in conversation with Mrs. Bailey. He calculated this gave him a few minutes to have words with his fellow
bowlers Colonel Bailey and Sir Tinsley before Alec joined them. They
were on the opposite side of the green, inspecting which of the
bowling balls had come to rest closest the jack. So he left the
Reverend Purefoy giving Ralph Ferris an excruciatingly detailed
history of the game of bowls, and stomped out into the sunshine,
bowling ball in hand.

There was no time for prevarication.

"What the deuce was all that about at table, eh?" he hissed. "Latin
inscriptions and common occurrences and the like! I said I'd tell him
in my own good time. And I will. In *my* time. Not yours. And don't
think you can force m'hand in this! Either of you!"

The Colonel and the magistrate both slowly got up off their
haunches and looked at one another. If they were rattled by the old
man's bluster they didn't show it. It was the magistrate who spoke for
them both.

"You were warned this time last year, dear fellow. With the unfor-
tunate death of His Lordship's brother and that portion of the estate
passing to him, you were to tell him the truth about his inheritance.
But you didn't then, and you haven't now. So it is not you, but the
Fivetrees Five, who is having its hand forced."

"I still don't see why he needs to know everythin'! Nothin's changed."

The two men exchanged an eye roll, Sir Tinsley saying, "But it has changed. And you know it has. Adams tells me His Lordship proposes to ban the hunt—"

"He's just puttin' into practice what I've been preachin' in the Commons for the last thirty-odd years."

"And as our MP we've never told you not to stand by your convictions, however harebrained," Sir Tinsley replied patiently. "But championing a lost cause in the Parliament is a world away from the practicalities of life here—"

"And that's why I—*he*—needs time to grow into the place," Plantagenet Halsey argued, unconsciously moving the bowling ball from hand to hand. "He grew up in the city. All this is new to him. How things are managed in the country—"

"We don't take kindly to interference," warned the Colonel. "The previous incumbent knew how to keep his nose out of our affairs."

"He kept his nose out of your affairs because I bloody well made sure he knew nothin' in the first place! Edward was a vainglorious jolthead. He didn't give a tester for the country or the estate, and he certainly didn't give a brass farthin' for its people. All he cared about was that it brought in an income—"

"Much like yourself."

Plantagenet Halsey dropped the bowling ball, shocked. In the next instant he grabbed the Colonel by the front of his waistcoat and stuck his face in his, teeth gritted. "Take. That. Back."

"For God's sake, keep it civil," Sir Tinsley hissed. "Wives present. And the Marchioness is looking our way…"

With a shove, the old man let go of the Colonel, who lost his footing, boot heel coming down awkwardly on one of the bowling balls, twisting his ankle. He stumbled and would have fallen hard had not Plantagenet Halsey grabbed him again by the coat sleeve, the magistrate doing likewise, and both hauling the Colonel to stand tall. All three looked immediately down the green to see if their antics were noted. But the ladies were seated about the tea trolley in the shade, Mrs. Bailey was still giving Alec an earful of her conversation, and the Reverend and Mr. Ferris were occupied with practicing rolling a ball. The three gentlemen breathed a sigh of relief.

Plantagenet Halsey's shoulders relaxed, and he gave a bark of laughter that their comedic performance had no audience. He wasn't laughing when the magistrate gave the Colonel's arm a shake.

"Apologize, Bailey. Halsey may crow his causes in the Commons, but he's always done right by us, and by Fivetrees. Always."

"Oh, aye. He has done that," grumbled the Colonel, a resentful glance up at the old man. He stuck out his hand. "Accept my apology. Can't be enemies. Must remember what we do we do for the common good."

The old man gripped his hand. "Aye, that's right. I'm continually remindin' myself that it's better to be a hypocrite than what you lot've done, all in the name of the common good. No one could ever accuse me of interrerin' in what nature intended—"

"What? Now steady on!" blustered the Colonel, a sharp glance at the magistrate. "Retract your slander, sir, or I'll march straight up to His Lordship and tell him all about your nefarious activities—"

"No you won't," Plantagenet Halsey replied silkily with a confident up-tilt of his square chin. "You won't say a word. Wives present, as Ferris just reminded us. And your dear wife's mental state is fragile enough without her knowin' what you did in the name of preservin' your boundaries for an only son."

The Colonel brushed imaginary creases from the sleeves of his best black wool-worsted frock coat. It was far too warm to be wearing such an article on this summer's day, but his wife had insisted he don his Sunday best to dine with a marquess. He counted to ten. Sweat beaded his flat forehead. It had nothing to do with the heat. He always broke out in a sweat when the past was mentioned, and what was forced upon him to keep his estate intact. He'd been appalled when his father confided how matters stood, and had stood for generations. It was the day his first child, a daughter, had been born. He was overjoyed. It should have been a day of celebration. But he was never more miserable in his entire life than on that day. His father reminded him he wasn't alone in his sacrifice, that he wasn't the only one who suffered in the name of family. He had to do his duty by his ancestors. It was the way things were done at Fivetrees. That's what he'd been told, and what the Fivetrees Five believed and honored. Eventually he would have a son to inherit after him and life would go on as it always had. Sacrifice, soul searching, and near-madness, it was all for the greater good…

And so he said confidently, and with sincerity, "I'm not the only one to have made sacrifices, and I'd do it all again for my son. It's a burden we fellows have to shoulder. Don't dare threaten the weaker sex with this! Leave our wives out of it. It's none of their concern. Never will be. Besides, you'd have done the same in our position, Halsey. Own to it."

"No. I won't. I wouldn't. And I didn't."

"What sanctimonious piffle!" Sir Tinsley scoffed. "The Halseys are as neck-deep in this gavelkind conundrum as the rest of us."

"Not this Halsey, and not m'father, and not the next Halsey either, if I know anythin' of His Lordship," the old man stated confidently. "That's three generations with a clear conscience."

"Who's to say His Lordship will act any differently once he's fully apprised of the inheritance laws in this little quarter of England?" the Colonel argued.

"Who's to say…?" The old man looked at the Colonel as if he'd sprouted a second head. "*I* say it! I say he don't need to know about the appallin' history of Fivetrees and what his forebears did all in the name of inheritance. And I'm goin' to make damn sure he never finds out!"

"And how do you propose to keep him ignorant of the law when—"

"It ain't the law which concerns us, but what our ancestors did to flout it. Not on my great-grandfather's fartleberries would I want him to discover just how low that lot sank into the manure! His Lordship is more like me than you'll ever know, and if he starts askin' questions, believe me, he won't stop until he has the answers. And then you lot will be for it." The old man huffed and smiled crookedly. "You think this old windbag is a pious hypocrite, but His Lordship ain't a moral charlatan. His conscience is clear, and his soul untainted. And he's young enough to have the energy to run to ground sanctimonious fiends like you!"

When the magistrate and the Colonel glanced at one another in alarm, Plantagenet Halsey added on a more conciliatory note, "As soon as you two get out of the sun and cool your brainboxes, you'll realize you're panickin' to no purpose. Nothin' around here will be any different, whether His Lordship is in charge of this estate or I am."

"What about the hunt?" the Colonel grumbled.

The old man rolled his eyes and shook his head. "I should think that the least of your concerns."

"This concerns us all, Halsey," said the Colonel. "And Adams says His Lordship has ordered a stop to it."

Plantagenet Halsey waved a long hand, as if swatting a gnat.

"Let him have his way this season and next you'll see your privileges reinstated. Besides, it's not as if Adams will report you for trespassin' on His Lordship's lands. Has he ever?"

This time the Colonel and Sir Tinsley exchanged a hopeful glance, the magistrate asking, "You want us to carry on as usual, and disregard His Lordship's edict revoking our right to course across his lands?"

"Disregard is a strong word, and it's not as if you can ignore it, you being our local magistrate. And he said nothin' about hare coursin', just huntin' deer. If, for argument's sake, deer happened to wander across the boundary of this property and on to yours, you'd have a right to stop 'em by whatever means necessary so they don't destroy your crops, wouldn't you?"

Sir Tinsley blew out his cheeks and shook his head.

"No. I wouldn't. Therein lies the dilemma. The deer remain His Lordship's property, whether they are on his lands, or mine. And we can't do a damn thing about the deer, or hare, or whatever else belongs to Lord Halsey that crawls, flies or burrows beyond his boundaries. We need his permission to eradicate vermin that trespass, and I doubt very much he sees his deer as vermin. Not when he's stopped the hunt."

"Well then," Plantagenet Halsey replied chewing on his lip in thought. "If that's your considered opinion as magistrate, then there's only one option left to us."

"That being?" asked Sir Tinsely.

"I'll give you permission, but you're not to say a word to Lord Halsey. Understood?"

"Can he do that?" Colonel Bailey asked Sir Tinsley.

The magistrate thought a moment and then nodded slowly. "As

he has a stake in this estate, yes. If a deer wandered onto your land and you shot and killed it, it would come down to a petty legality of who owns the particular deer that trespassed in the first place—His Lordship or his uncle. And given Halsey here inherited a sizeable portion of the estate before Lord Halsey was even born, it could be argued that he had claim to the deer before his nephew."

"But it won't come to that because there won't be any argument from me. As far as I'm concerned he owns the lot. And that's all anyone is ever goin' to know, right?"

"Right." The two men replied in unison to the old man's threatening tone, Colonel Bailey adding, "And you'll get no argument from us! Though I've always been mystified as to why you'd give up claim to what's rightly your—"

"It's goin' to remain a mystery, Bailey. Keep your nose out of m'business, and I'll keep mine out of yours."

"Fair's fair," the Colonel agreed, pulling his chin into his stock. "What is it, Ferris? You don't look convinced."

"The estate's gamekeeper still in your pay?"

"When hasn't he been? I told you. Nothin's changed."

"So no disruption to the supply of venison to the usual markets?"

"Why would there be? You'll both still get your cut, pardon the pun, ha!, as will everyone else involved."

The magistrate took a deep breath, but the crease remained between his brows.

"We may have a problem. A small one, but a problem nonetheless, particularly if you're intent on keeping His Lordship none the wiser—"

"What's the problem?"

"Young Hugh. Turner's son."

"And how is the son of our steward a problem?" Plantagenet Halsey asked, surprised.

"While helping Lady Ferris in the garden, he's been filling her ear with the nonsense you've been saying in the Commons," the magistrate told him. "It appears he reads his father's newssheets. Your opinions about the Black Act and it robbing villagers of their livelihood—"

"But your wife knows my opinions, so it won't come as a shock to her."

"She does, and she isn't," the magistrate replied curtly. "What is, and what upset Lady Ferris is that not only is that boy spreading your nonsense amongst the village lads—"

"Those Turner boys are a menace. Always thought so," interrupted the Colonel, though there was no heat in his tone, so was unconvincing. "He should keep his radical and nonsensical opinions to himself. If the poor want to own pigs, they can bloody well find the wherewithal to feed 'em—"

"It's not the poor that concern me—" began the magistrate.

"Not a truer word spoken, by either of you," muttered the old man.

"—but what that whelp has been telling my wife about us," continued the magistrate as if Plantagenet Halsey had not spoken. "He asked her in the most polite manner imaginable if she thought Lord Halsey knows about the poaching that goes on in his wood, and —you'll both be amused by this I'm certain—done by gentlemen who *ought to know better.*"

"The impertinence!" snorted the Colonel. "The lad needs sense whipped into him. Lord Halsey is one of us, so there's no point—"

"But that's just it, Bailey. His Lordship isn't one of us, is he?" Sir Tinsley said evenly, all the while with his gaze on Plantagenet Halsey. "I think we should leave it to you to deal with young Hugh, Halsey. That is, unless you want your nephew to—"

"No. I'll have a word—"

"If they ever find him. He's gone missing y'know."

"I do know that, Bailey. So does Turner. If he's not returned by mornin', men will be sent out to beat the bracken."

"He can stay missing, for all we care!"

"But we do care, George," the magistrate said quietly. "Lest you've forgotten, the Turner family is one of the five, regardless of the fact they squandered their opportunities—"

"Meanin' they didn't follow our ancestors down a murderous rabbit hole," Plantagenet Halsey stuck in.

"Which is why they have little of their lands left and were forced to become stewards to your family," argued the magistrate.

"Nothin' wrong with an honest day's work," muttered the Colonel, abashed. "And of course I don't want harm to come to the lad, even if he is a whelp, because it will break his poor mother's heart. And none of us want that, do we?"

"No. None of us. Though mayhap you have more reason than most to not want to see Mrs. Turner suffer unduly?" Plantagenet Halsey asked, directing his unblinking gaze at the Colonel with a raise of his bushy brows. When Bailey's complexion turned beet red, the old man lowered his brows and continued evenly, addressing them both, "So it's agreed? We carry on as we've always done. With you keeping your part of the bargain, Ferris, Fivetrees will continue to have the lowest level of poachin' in the country."

"By which you mean Ferris here continues to allow the local poor to fetch kindling, graze pigs, and kill a hare or three from His Lordship's wood—"

"God forbid the poor should have the right to eke out a paltry existence!" scoffed the old man.

"Bailey, remember it's Halsey's wood too," interrupted Sir Tinsely.

"Oh, aye, I do. And I'm willing to turn a blind eye to it, too."

"And in return for you turnin' a blind eye and our magistrate here not enforcin' the letter of the law, you both get to hunt and course across this estate to your heart's content," Plantagenet Halsey stated. "Which to my mind is more than a fair deal. But even if you don't think it fair, they're m'terms. Accept 'em, or I step away and you can deal with His Lordship's edicts as best you can."

"What surprises me, Halsey, is that you're still able to offer terms. But how you manage His Lordship is none of our affair, or anyone else's. As long as you continue to manage him," Sir Tinsley warned. He picked up his bowling ball and turned about to face down the green, saying as he did so, "Now let's get back to this game before—Ah! And here is His Lordship come to join us. My lord!" he said more loudly and stepped forward to meet Alec with a smile. "As you can see by our procrastination, we're none the wiser as to whose ball was closest the jack, so we've stopped arguing and called it a draw. Did we not, Colonel? Halsey?"

When the two men nodded in agreement and looked sheepish Alec wondered what the three older men were up to, such was his uncle's guilty look. But he kept that to himself for another time, and was about to suggest they begin a new game to include the Reverend and Mr. Ferris, when raised voices at his back made him turn to face the loggia.

Coming up the gravel path beside the green as fast as she could walk without running was his housekeeper, Mrs. Turner. Her fingers were scrunched in the folds of her gown. A few strides behind her was her husband, Alec's steward, and with his arm outstretched. Turner was entreating his wife to stop and listen. But she was not listening. And she was not stopping. Following behind the Turners was Adams the gamekeeper.

Alec and the three bowlers watched in silence as this extraordinary scene played out before them, not knowing what to expect, and not wanting to interfere.

The steward got to his wife before she was halfway down the green and pulled her to him. She struggled to be let go, but he held her more tightly, face in her hair, talking rapidly, and trying to console her. Finally she stopped struggling, and went still in his arms. The stillness lasted but a moment. She slumped against his chest, sobbing. She would have collapsed at his feet, knees buckling under the weight of her grief, had he not quickly propped her up. And then the gamekeeper came to his aid.

Adams saw what was about to happen, and in three strides he was beside the steward. He scooped up the housekeeper, and this time she did not struggle but lay limp, all the fight gone out of her. With Mrs. Turner in his arms, and Turner beside him, Adams headed back to the shade of the loggia. The housekeeper was gently set on one of the chairs by the tea trolley. Turner went down beside the chair, and caught up his wife's hand in his. Adams hesitated a moment, looking down on them both, and then he left the housekeeper to her husband's ministrations and returned to the green.

Adams bowed before Alec, hat crushed in both hands.

Over the gamekeeper's uncovered head, Alec watched as Selina took control of the situation from her chaise. She pointed to a footman, spoke to Evans, and then to the two women sitting near to her. There then came an eruption of activity around the tea trolley. Mrs. Bailey and Lady Ferris were up off their chairs, and hovering over the couple. Evans brought the housekeeper a cup of tea, and a footman dashed indoors, no doubt to fetch the housekeeper what she needed to make her more comfortable. Alec hoped Selina had also sent for Tam. Confident his wife had everything under control and he was not needed, Alec looked back to his gamekeeper, who was now standing before him, moving from foot to foot with his eyes lowered.

"What's happened, Adams?" he asked, Plantagenet Halsey, Colonel Bailey, and Sir Tinsley at his back.

"It's young Hugh, my lord. The Turners' youngest boy. We've found him. He's-he's—dead."

ELEVEN

"*Dead?*"

"Yes, my lord. We found him not far from Old Bill's hut."

Alec looked across at the Turners. "Those poor parents..." He mentally shook himself and brought his gaze back to Adams. "Old Bill?"

"Been livin' in the wood since I can remember," Plantagenet Halsey cut in when the gamekeeper glanced his way. "Harmless. Wouldn't hurt a beetle, least of all young Hugh—"

"I wasn't suggesting he would," Alec said evenly, noting the sidelong glance directed at his uncle, and that Adams had waited for him to respond. "Old Bill will be glad of your character reference, particularly as Sir Tinsley will want to speak with him about the boy's death—"

"My lord, as Halsey just said," Sir Tinsley cut in, flustered. "I can't imagine Old Bill had anything to do with—"

"If he saw anything unusual. If he saw Hugh," Alec explained, half-turning to look at the magistrate. "We don't know how the boy died, if it was from natural causes, say an accident, or something else, you'd want to know, we all would."

"Yes! Yes! I see your point," muttered Sir Tinsley and fell silent.

"Who's to say he didn't die of natural causes?" argued the old man. "We don't know yet what happened to him. He could've had an accident. Tripped, fell, and hit his head on a log. He could've got himself caught in one of the mantraps, or eaten a poison berry or—"

"Adams?" Alec cut in. "Are you able to tell us anything?"

All four gentlemen looked to the gamekeeper. Despite Plantagenet Halsey's pronouncement, none thought Hugh Turner's death accidental, though all hoped it to be true.

"I wish it had been an accident, my lord," Adams replied solemnly. "Not that I told his parents one way or t'other. All I said was that we found their boy in the wood, and that he was dead."

"What didn't you tell them?" asked Alec. "And you'd best start at the beginning so you need not repeat yourself to Sir Tinsley. Though he may have questions for you later."

"I was doing the rounds with Peter and John over by Old Bill's hut," the gamekeeper explained, a sweeping glance at all four gentlemen before focusing on Alec. "About twenty yards or so from there, the hounds went off into the undergrowth. We at first thought they'd found the remains of a kill, entrails of a hare or a wild boar left behind by poach—vagrants passing through the wood. This time of year we get gypsies and the like looking for a place to set up camp. But the mantraps should see them off—"

"I thought Turner had discussed with you my views on mantraps —but we'll leave that for another time. What did the hounds find?" Alec prompted when the gamekeeper fell silent.

"As it turns out, it wasn't a wild boar, but the usual signs that come when a deer is brought down without permission—"

"You mean a deer killed by a poacher?"

"Yes, my lord. Not that we have regular poachers, as I said—"

"And the usual signs? What are they?"

Adams looked past Alec's shoulder and let his gaze rest on the magistrate. But when he remained mute the gamekeeper continued, bringing his focus back to Alec. "We found the rack, removed from the skull and out of sight. It'd been dragged behind a log. By the number of points, I'd reckon it to be one of your prize stags, my lord. I'm sorry to say—"

"A prize stag? The damn cheek of these villains!" the Colonel declared angrily. "How many points are we talking, Adams?"

"Fourteen—"

"*Fourteen*? Good Lord! That's not a stag, that's a mighty beast!" Sir Tinsley burst out in awe.

"I presume the rack was left behind because it was far too heavy to move with the rest of the carcass," Alec stated rather than asked.

"It is, my lord. It's usually retrieved once the meat—carcass—is disposed of using the usual channels. Perhaps this time they meant to leave it all along because they used it to hide the boy's body behind it, and tossed leaves on top of him for good measure. We saw the rack first, and when we dragged it out from behind the log, that's when we found the boy. We also found a crossbow and quiver."

"His?"

"More likely it belongs to his father," answered the gamekeeper.

"No chance he crawled in there behind the log after being injured, perhaps by the stag?"

"He could've been injured when the beast was brought down," conceded Adams. "And the rack is heavy. So if that had fallen on him... But, no. The stag didn't kill him."

"Get to the point, Adams," Sir Tinsley demanded, exasperated. "What do you think happened to the lad? The Turners will want answers, and what can we tell them if you don't tell us!"

"Yes, sir. It's just that His Lordship asked..."

"Yes! Yes! Do go on," the magistrate ordered with a dismissive huff, saying in an altogether different voice to Alec, "Apologies, my lord. I don't like to see any mother lose a son... Seeing your house-keeper in such distress... The Turners have been at Fivetrees almost as long as the Ferris and Bailey families."

"One of the original five families in this part of Kent," stuck in the Colonel. "Got an oak named after him, like the rest of us. Been here since before the Conqueror."

"Thank you for the history lesson—both of you—but it ain't what His Lordship needs right now," the old man chastised, which closed their mouths tight.

"Do you know how the boy died, Adams?" Alec asked. "Or do we need a physician first before—"

"I can tell you how we found him, my lord. With his throat cut. He would've drowned in his own blood, and it would've been quick but—"

"Good God!" muttered Plantagenet Halsey, astonished in equal measure by the bluntness in the delivery as to what had happened to the boy.

"—that wasn't our only grisly find," apologized the gamekeeper. "With the boy's body were—parts."

"Parts?" Alec was mystified. "What sort of parts?"

"Human parts, my lord. Two severed hands."

"The boy's hands were *severed*?"

"Yes and no."

"Confound it, man!" blustered the Colonel. "They either were or they weren't!"

"The boy's right hand was severed," explained the gamekeeper.

"Only one hand?" asked the magistrate.

"By man or beast?" asked the Colonel.

The gamekeeper looked from the magistrate to the Colonel, and then at Alec.

"I'd say it was with a blade."

"Did you look for a knife?" asked Alec.

"We did, my lord, but didn't find one. Or haven't yet. We'll return there on the morrow for a thorough search. The weather is closing in."

"You said two severed hands," stated Alec and waited.

"But if there are two hands surely they both belong to Hugh Turner," argued the magistrate, unperturbed by such a gruesome discovery. "His throat was cut to kill him, and then his hands were cut off as a warning to others not to poach."

"Is that a common practice?" Alec asked, surprised. "To remove hands as a warning to other poachers?

"Not common, but it has happened before," explained the magistrate. "What is common is removing the hoofs and head of a poached deer. Makes it easy to transport the carcass. Isn't that so, Adams?"

"Just so, sir," agreed the gamekeeper. "But only one of the hands belonged to Hugh Turner."

Alec had a fair idea what the gamekeeper was about to say, and could have said so himself, though Selina would have said he had a toss of the coin as to being correct. So he let the gamekeeper have the satisfaction of informing them.

"And how do you know that, Adams?"

"Because what we found were two right hands."

"Two *right* hands?" repeated Plantagenet Halsey, aghast. "That means—"

"—there are two boys with mortal wounds," the magistrate concluded.

"But no second body?" Alec asked the gamekeeper.

"Not that we've found yet, my lord. Although tomorrow may prove different…"

"Don't mention the hands for now," Alec ordered. "Let's keep that between us…until we know more. We need a proper search of the wood. You can take as many men as you need with you, Adams. I'm sure my foreman will release to you those men who've downed tools waiting for the hole in Stone Court to be investigated."

"Very good, my lord. That will be a great help. We'll leave at first light."

"I'll join you," said Alec.

"I can offer a few of my men. We can meet up near Old Bill's."

"Thank you, Bailey," said Alec. He turned to the magistrate. "I presume you'll have enough to do, waiting for the physician to examine the boy, and then there's the families, and others you will need to interview."

"Interview?" Sir Tinsley appeared nonplussed.

Alec was direct. "You have a murder inquiry on your hands, Sir Tinsley."

"Poor Hugh Turner and one severed right hand, owner yet unknown," Plantagenet Halsey announced grimly. He gave the magistrate's shoulder a squeeze and said in his ear, "I trust that's all your inquiries uncover…"

The old man then turned to greet the Turners who were again making their way up the path alongside the bowling green. A few steps behind them was the Reverend Purefoy, ashen-faced and rubbing his hands together as if washing them clean. The rest of the party by the tea trolley were watching on, silent and anxious.

Out of the corner of his eye Alec had seen them approaching, too. And now all five men turned to greet them, expressions suitably grave. Just as the couple arrived at the top of the green, Mrs. Turner broke from her husband, which surprised him. She marched straight up and confronted these solemn faces. Her eyes were red, her face damp and swollen from her sobbing. But she had no more tears to shed and when she spoke it was not profound sadness that broke her voice but unmitigated fury, which she unleashed on those standing before her.

"You're all to blame!" she shrieked. "Every *damned* one of you!"

ꝏ

SELINA COULD NOT HEAR MRS. TURNER'S WORDS BUT THERE was no mistaking her howls of despair. And when she lunged at the group of gentlemen, it was Colonel Bailey who went forward. He caught her about the wrists, pushed her arms to the small of her back and held her tight so she could not move, leg pressed into her petticoats and chest up against her heaving breasts. He put his cheek to her hair and whispered in her ear. She continued to sob. Finally, she pulled away. The gentlemen surged forward, surrounding them, obscuring Selina's line of vision. And when they parted, the Colonel and Mrs. Turner had disengaged. He returned to the circle of men, and she fell sobbing into her husband's comforting embrace.

The interaction between the Colonel and Mrs. Turner lasted mere moments but it left an ineffaceable impression on Selina. She knew pent-up emotional aggression unleashed when she saw it. It made her wince and draw in breath. Taking an involuntary step away from the edge of the green, her hand unconsciously smoothed across her rounded belly and stayed there. She instantly understood that the woman's anguish had prompted her to lash out, but the way in which the Colonel had reacted—how his meaty hands had grabbed her thin wrists, the way he had shoved his large body up to hers and then held her captive—were all hallmarks of an abusive relationship. And when he had whispered in the housekeeper's ear, Selina shuddered, feeling his hot breath on her own neck. With that intimate action came unwanted flashes of memory of the unspeakable cruelty she had suffered at the caprice of her sadistic first husband.

Flustered, nauseous, and overwhelmed, Selina fought to keep a grip on her dignity. And then Evans was at her side, suggesting in a measured undervoice that she return to the chaise longue, or, if she so wished, she could retire for the afternoon; no one would blame her for calling it a day after such difficult circumstances, and in her condition. Selina thanked God for her lady's maid, who had lived through the nightmare of her first marriage with her, and was possibly the only other person, Alec notwithstanding, who knew precisely what hell she had endured.

Determined to be stronger than she was, she took a deep breath and shook her head. She could not leave Alec at a time like this, nor was she prepared to neglect her duties as mistress of this household. And then there were the Turners and the loss of their son...

"I will be fine directly," she replied in an undervoice. "Would you have someone sent to see that the Turners have everything they need? I'm certain His Lordship has the situation in hand, but I do not want them to think they must carry on. They need to be at their home, and with their other son. Mrs. Wilson can step into Mrs. Turner's shoes for the time being."

"Yes, my lady. I'll see to it myself."

When Evans hesitated, Selina met her gaze. She did not need to ask to know her thoughts. She briefly closed her eyes and said softly, so only Evans could hear, "I saw it too—the-the—*possessiveness*—"

"That can never happen to you again. You know that. But that poor woman—My lady, something must be done."

"Yes. Yes. I will speak with His Lordship... A fresh pot of tea and perhaps coffee for the gentlemen," she added audibly because Mrs. Bailey was hovering nearby, ostensibly sipping tea from her cup. "If you would first give me your arm, to see me to the chaise—"

"Oh, do allow me, my lady!" said Mrs. Bailey, stepping up. She shoved her teacup and saucer at Evans without looking at her. "It's at such times as these that I am fortunate to be big-boned and strong. I can most certainly take your weight..."

Evans stared into the cup she now held and found it clean. Without another word she bobbed a curtsey, returned the unused teacup and saucer to the tea trolley and bustled away.

"How kind," Selina replied blandly, and leaned on Mrs. Bailey's crooked arm.

But she did not move off at once. The gentlemen still milled about at the top of the green in conversation with the gamekeeper, but she was pleased to see that the Reverend Purefoy had gone with the Turners. All three were headed along the path in the opposite direction to the loggia. That way led to the stables, and just beyond the stables, in a walled garden of its own, stood the steward's substantial residence.

Mrs. Bailey wasted no time in being forthright, and what she confided brought Selina out of any private reverie. The woman had all her attention.

"I've no doubt you were surprised by my dear husband's reaction to poor Mrs. Turner's desolation," she said in her characteristic breathless tone. "As one new to Fivetrees you may be wondering how it is he could be so familiar with her—"

"Mrs. Bailey, I admit I did have such a thought, but it is not my—"

"But it is *my* business, and I wish to share it with you, lest you think my dear colonel a brute and a fiend. Shall we walk on a little? I see Lady Ferris has dozed in her chair, despite the high drama of the past half hour." She sighed, adding confidentially, "Though I do not believe her to be asleep. She has done this before in company. When matters take a turn not to her liking, she simply closes her eyes."

Selina wasn't sure what shocked her more, the woman's matter of fact acceptance of Lady Ferris's behavior or the behavior itself.

"*Not to her liking?* A boy she knew well has been found dead in the wood. That is not unpleasant, it is tragic!"

"We all have our ways of coping with loss," Mrs. Bailey replied matter-of-factly. "But I do believe Lady Ferris lost her motherly instincts years ago…"

When she dared to put her hand to Selina's elbow, indication they should walk on past the tea trolley, Selina remained rooted to the spot. Something about Lady Ferris sitting in the chair with her eyes closed had caught her attention. Twinkles of light glistened on the woman's cheek. Her face was wet… Tears were coursing down her cheeks. Far from being devoid of emotion as Mrs. Bailey suggested, Selina could see that Lady Ferris was grieving in her own way, shutting out the world and its sorrows by closing her eyes. Dry in the throat and shaking, Selina finally turned away, allowing Mrs. Bailey to escort her to the shade of the loggia.

"Please do not fret about Lady Ferris's cold nature, my lady," counseled Mrs. Bailey. "In your condition any upset at this delicate stage could lead to-to complications, or worse, an early delivery, and I do not want that on my conscience! If you please, let us ignore Lady

Ferris's feelings for the moment, because I need to explain how matters stand between the Colonel and Mrs. Turner—"

"It is none of my—"

Selina was about to say again that is it was none of her concern, and then thought better of it. Because what everyone had just witnessed she decided was very much her concern. Not only because Mrs. Turner was her housekeeper, but as a female who had experienced the sadistic violence of a jealous husband and had vowed to make certain other females did not suffer at the hands of an abuser, she felt responsible for her well-being. That the Colonel's wife did not seem alarmed by her husband's violent possessiveness defied reasoning. She wondered if advanced pregnancy had addled her brain. Still, she managed to remain calm and expressionless, and say evenly,

"As you wish, Mrs. Bailey. You have my full attention. And do not worry yourself about me. I am far stronger than I appear, so I shall be perfectly all right, and so, too, will my baby, whatever you care to confide. In fact this little stroll has done wonders to restore my constitution."

Mrs. Bailey gave her hostess a sidelong appraisal and nodded slowly. The Marchioness might present as a delicate porcelain figurine with a mass of curls spun from old gold, but there was something about her—mayhap it was her dark eyes and forthright speech—that told her here was a woman of quiet determination, of resilience, who could not easily be broken, nor fooled. So she came straight to the point in a most roundabout way.

"My husband and Mrs. Turner are known to one another."

"I do not think I understand you, Mrs. Bailey."

The Colonel's wife tittered behind her hand. It was forced and brittle.

"Oh, my lady! You are from the highest levels of society. You mix in circles where a husband's infidelity is a fact of life the wife must endure. I live in the depths of the country now and am a country mouse. Or perhaps I am more hedgehog than mouse, for there is nothing petite about me! I grew up in a Westminster townhouse. My father was a physician and my mother the daughter of an earl. Such an unequal match, but Adolphus and I, we did see our noble grandparents, and right up until their deaths. So I think that you do indeed understand what I mean when I say they are *known* to one another."

Selina stopped and faced her.

"Are you telling me your husband and my housekeeper are-are
—*lovers*?"

"Were. I do not think they are now, although…"

"But just then—"

"Yes. Perhaps…" Mrs. Bailey thought a moment, a crease between
her fair brows. Finally she nodded, as if reaching a conclusion. "Yes.
Yes, I think you are right, my lady. After what we just witnessed
between them, they must indeed still be lovers—or lovers again. Or
perhaps they always have been and the Colonel lied to me…"

"You have always known about their—about their affair?"

"Why, yes. I accepted it as a necessity. And then, later, when I
thought he would no longer need her, I minded. Now, at my age, I
am in two-minds if I care enough, or not. I shall have to give it more
thought."

Selina was unsure of what to say to such a cool response. Had it
been Alec in the Colonel's boots, she would have been devastated,
heartbroken, furious, and every other emotion in between. She most
certainly would not have been calm.

"That is magnanimous of you, Mrs. Bailey."

Mrs. Bailey shrugged. "When it comes to matters of the flesh,
men cannot help themselves. She is to blame. Certain females, particularly those of the lower orders, have a way of ensnaring men—"

"But it is obvious she is not happy with the arrangement!" Selina
blurted out before she could stop herself.

Far from being surprised or shocked or upset, Mrs. Bailey
straightened her spine. Gone was the breathless obsequiousness.

"My lady, if you are implying my husband would force himself on
your housekeeper, I respectfully must tell you that you could not be
more wrong. Their *arrangement* has been ongoing for many years. She
has permitted him to take liberties with her body, no doubt for remu-
neration known only to themselves. Perhaps he—her husband—
knows what compensation she is receiving. In fact he must, or this
arrangement could not proceed as it has. So how then can she be
unhappy as you seem to think? That my husband allowed himself to
show his concern for her in public when seeing her in distress tells me
he cares for her more deeply than makes me comfortable. But I shall
seek solace in my faith, and Adolphus will help me pray for my

husband's soul. And rest assured these unseemly public displays won't happen again." She bobbed a curtsey. "I see that His Lordship and the other gentlemen have returned to the tea trolley. Lord Halsey will be anxious to assure himself that you have suffered no ill effects from this afternoon's dramatics, so let me return you to him. Oh, and please, let us say no more about this regrettable incident. I ask that what I just told you about the dear Colonel and your housekeeper remain between us."

"Y-yes, of course," Selina replied without thinking. But as soon as she was alone with Alec later that night she did not hesitate to break her promise.

TWELVE

A~~LEC~~ WAS JUST AS EAGER TO DISCUSS THE DAY'S DRAMATIC
events with Selina. Though he would not divulge to her the grisly
details of Hugh Turner's murder, or the fact the gamekeeper had
discovered two right hands, meaning that one of the other boys with
Hugh had most likely been murdered, too. But who would want to
kill two boys out poaching? Scare them off, yes. Possibly give them a
beating, if they had encroached on another poacher's patch, but
murder? No. There was something more than poaching at play here,
his intuition told him so. But what?

Shaking his thoughts free of poor Hugh and the fate of his friends
as he came into his wife's dressing room, he found Evans braiding her
mistress's hair ready for bed. So he went and waited by the undraped
window to admire the clear night sky, hands deep in the pockets of
his silk banyan. Selina slipped on a pair of soft kid mules with Evan's
assistance, then joined her husband at the window, a hand to the
middle of her aching back.

"Shall I rub it for you?" he asked, kissing her temple and drawing
her closer.

"Please. But—later."

Evans was still at the dressing table tidying away brushes, pins,
and ribbons. She must have sensed she was being watched, for she
glanced up into the looking glass and caught Alec's reflection. It was
enough to make her fingers all thumbs, and she quickly turned and

scurried to the servant door. But she was not quick enough. She heard Alec wish her a good night. She paused, turned, bobbed a curtsey without lifting her eyes, mumbled *good night* in return, then fled in a rustle of petticoats into the passageway, and so fast that it had Selina smiling.

"You are a fiend!" Selina said without heat. "Poor Evans. You know she can never look at you again, for fear you'll stroll in here naked—"

"Once. It happened once. And it was *she* who strolled in on *me*."

She looked him up and down and pouted. "You're still dressed under that banyan."

"Yes. I'm doing my best to behave."

She was not fooled by his look of contrition.

"I wish you wouldn't!"

Alec gave a bark of laughter.

"Then I won't—but later. First Uncle and I are sharing a tiff of brandy in the Picture Gallery."

"I may be asleep by the time you return."

He nuzzled her hair and drank in the scent of her. "I could wake you…"

"Do. But you won't have to because I lied. I won't be asleep."

She turned in his arms and pressed herself against him, her kiss insistent and needful. When she sighed her frustration that her pregnancy made it impossible for him to take her completely in his arms, he smiled, seemingly able to read her mind.

"You do realize that we are three already. That he or she will now and forever be with us in some way or another…"

"I do. And I am happy we are soon to be a family. But in here, in our rooms, it will only be the two of us. Here I want you all to myself. If that is selfish, I am not sorry. Oh why oh why weren't we allowed to have our first year of marriage without me in this condition! All I want to do is shut out the world and romp with you in our bed."

Alec grinned.

"It was our romping that got you in this condition, and dare I say it, before we were married."

"If we have the Halsey luck, we may only have the one son,

though I won't mind spending the rest of our lives trying for another!"

"Wicked creature. Flippancy aside, surely you don't wish to deny our son brothers and sisters? Besides," he added, walking hand in hand with her into the bedchamber, "you forget I had a brother, too. That surely means whatever ill luck there was in the family has been broken."

"If it is ill luck then it has been visited not only on the Halseys but the other landowning families in this district. You heard what was said at nuncheon. All accepted it as fact that their families produced only one child per generation, and that child a son and heir." She watched Alec grab a couple of the down pillows from the four-poster bed, plump them then arrange them at one end of the chaise longue. "Their reasoning for such impossible odds being that 'it's just the way of things down here', is-is ludicrous. It's not possible. If I did not know these people, or your uncle, or you were not a Halsey, I would say that it has the whiff of being all so—so—"

"*Contrived...?*"

"I was going to say fantastical. But if you like, it could be contrived," Selina answered as she joined him by the chaise. "What other explanation is there? Take your pick, be it by sorcery or design. It's certainly more plausible than saying 'it's just the way of things at Fivetrees', as if it were commonplace for these families to have genera-tion after generation of male-only children. You might as well blame such an outcome on something in the drinking water, or the milk, or the eggs being different in this part of the country to everywhere else! All are perfectly acceptable explanations for such an anomaly if you want to believe the notion that it just is what it is—What?" she added, concerned when he looked up and was no longer smiling. "Am I being too rational? Or have you thought of some other explanation?"

"No. Not at all. I love that you are rational. But you may not like the conclusion I have just drawn from your rationality. You need only take the next logical step and you will see what I mean."

She thought for a moment about what he said, and the sparkle died in her eyes. "Oh, no. Surely not," she said with a shake of her head. "No. That can't be. That is—that is—"

"—a plausible explanation."

"—*diabolical*." She teared up and swallowed hard. "You think these couples, over many generations, deliberately chose to have only one child, by discarding those pregnancies that were unwanted or which were not male? Did you come to this conclusion because this is what I did, rather than give George babies?"

"No. Of course not, darling. What you did was not based on choosing the sex of your child and ridding yourself of those that were not male. What you did, you did to survive. Besides, how could these couples know beforehand whether they were having a male or a female child? They could not. But what they *could* do was choose to abstain from fornicating once their longed-for son arrived." Alec shrugged. "And then there is the possibility—though you will tell me the odds are beyond what is plausible—that perhaps there is a natural tendency for families in Fivetrees to have only male children. Perhaps there is something about the female line that is weak, and daughters do not survive?" He picked up a coverlet that was over the end of the chaise and laid it out, folding back the end closest the pillows. "If you have a better explanation, given you are the mathematical genius in the family, I am very willing and hopeful of hearing it."

Selina shook her head and absently toyed with the white silk ribbon tied about the ends of her long braid of apricot hair. "I don't want to think beyond what you have told me. Not tonight. Tomorrow." She suddenly came out of her abstraction and pointed her braid at the chaise longue. "What are you doing?"

"I thought you might prefer to sleep here—"

"Why would I want to do that when I just told you I can't sleep without you?"

He smiled to himself at her outrage.

"Not without me *all night*. Just until I return. The bed is high. You have trouble getting up the bed steps as it is. And what if you want to get down again?"

"Why? Why would I do that?"

Alec tried not to smile but failed. It was his turn to shake his head. There was no reason to be coy. They were man and wife after all. "My darling, in your present state I help you get up and down those steps at least three times a night."

Selina blushed scarlet at his oblique reference to her weak bladder. And when he went to her side of the bed, opened the top drawer of the bedside table and took out her porcelain bourdaloue, she was speechless. He might as well have brought out the chamber pot stored in the cupboard behind the tapestry dressing screen in the far corner of the room, such was her embarrassment. But when he set the portable urinal on the side table by the chaise longue she'd found her voice again.

"Thank you. You do help me, and without complaint. And I wish this baby weren't pressing on all my organs so that I feel one may burst at any moment!" She cradled her roundness as if holding it up. "I feel as if I'm about to birth a-a hippopotamus! That is nothing to laugh at," she grumbled. "I just want him out of me. I've had enough of being pregnant. There! I've said it! I am the worst female imaginable to have a child. What sort of mother I'll be, I cannot hazard a guess!"

She then burst into tears and covered her face, feeling utterly deflated and foolish. When Alec drew her to him, she collapsed against him as best she could, forehead on his chest.

"You will be a wonderful mother," he murmured soothingly. "Whether it be to a fat jolly boy, or a hippopotamus. It will be ours, and that's all that matters to me."

She gave a watery laugh and felt better for it. Dabbing her eyes with his handkerchief she said with a sniff, "You are the dearest man, and too infuriatingly kind for your own good. I know I've said it before but it's true: I don't deserve you."

He kissed her temple. "Today has been exhausting for you—"

"My exhaustion is as nothing, and neither is my self-centered petulant wish for this pregnancy to be at an end, when I think of the poor Turners and their loss. To lose their boy in a hunting accident—"

"Yes. It is very sad for them," Alec cut in, not wishing to contradict her about it being an accident. "By all accounts Hugh was a caring, lively boy who enjoyed gardening; Lady Ferris told me." He caught up her hand and kissed her fingers. "I'm sorry you had to witness that scene between Colonel Bailey and Mrs. Turner. It must've resurrected painful memories…"

"It did. I cannot deny that. But the sense of panic I sometimes have when I'm reminded of those years with George—the terror that used to overwhelm me anticipating his violence—does not stay with me for very long these days." She smiled up at him. "That's because I have you. I just think of you, and I know I'll never experience that sort of cruelty again—"

"Never. On my life."

"Thank you. I do know that…" She rallied and said, thinking back on the day, "I had the strangest tête-à-tête with Mrs. Bailey right after that shocking display between the Colonel and Mrs. Turner…" She gave him a précis of that conversation, adding, "So if what she told me is all true about her husband and Mrs. Turner being lovers, then perhaps other landowners in Fivetrees took a mistress from the lower orders so they—"

"Mrs. Turner is our housekeeper and wife of the estate steward. That is hardly the lower orders."

"To you, and to me, and to your uncle, perhaps not. But to the landowners of Fivetrees, and to most of the people of my acquaintance in Westminster, if one does not own land, and does not have a pedigree, then everyone is of a lower order! And it is from the lower orders that men like the Colonel and his ilk find women with whom they can fornicate so that they need not be a burden on their wives— with physical intimacy, or with procreation. Mrs. Bailey said so herself, to me."

Alec helped Selina ease down on to the chaise. He then sat beside her to gently rub the small of her back.

"There was something visceral in the way Bailey grabbed Mrs. Turner and would not let her go," he said quietly. "And there was something decidedly odd in the reactions of those around them. No one showed surprise or made comment, not even her husband. Why didn't Turner do something, *anything*, to stop his wife being manhandled? Why didn't he defend her? No matter he's a steward and the Colonel a local squire, in this circumstance he had every right to do him a physical harm. I'd not let anyone so much as lay a finger on you!"

"Thank you, my love. I take comfort in the fierceness of your protection. And I'd want you to put your fist into the Colonel's face. Right between his eyes!"

"Ha! Turner didn't so much as flex his fingers."

"He's known all along about the affair. He must," Selina reasoned.

"It can be the only explanation for not defending his wife's honor, and his own. Either that or he is an odious coward."

"I agree. Either he can do nothing about it, or he doesn't want to. And as no one else moved a muscle, it must be common knowledge as to what's going on between that couple. Even my uncle knows! I was the only one who has no idea—and I should have done something."

"What could you do? You were as stunned as I. And if Sir Tinsley and Lady Ferris know, then you can be assured everyone within twenty miles or more do! Why don't you ask your uncle about it when you share that tiff with him?"

Alec did not answer immediately. He would ask his uncle about the Turners and the Baileys, but he had a far more pressing matter he wished to discuss with him first, and that was about Lady Ferris's confidence at nuncheon that his father and uncle were selfsame twins. Even with everything else that had happened that afternoon he had not forgotten that revelation. And the sooner he had it out with his uncle for hiding it from him, and why he would think he needed to, the sooner they could all move forward. He wanted a clear head for tomorrow's search of the wood where the grisly remains of Hugh Turner had been discovered by his gamekeeper.

Stopping his thoughts from wandering to questions of who would want to murder two boys, and cut off their right hands, and what had happened to the third boy, Alec finally got to his feet. He looked down at his wife, hands shoved in the pockets of his silk banyan, the fingers of one hand about his spectacles case. A black curl fell into his eyes but he hardly noticed, such was his concentration. And though he was looking at her, Selina sensed his thoughts were miles away. She remained silent and waited patiently, and then he said abruptly,

"I think we've been asking the wrong question."

"About the Colonel and Mrs. Turner?"

"No. About the families in this district, and their lack of offspring —sons and daughters."

"Oh? You know why that is? Do tell!"

He shook his head. "That's just it. I don't. But we don't necessarily need the answer to *how* these families managed to limit their offspring to one son and no daughters. What we should be asking is *why* they considered it necessary to do so."

Selina blinked up at him, and her lips parted slowly.

"Oh! You *are* clever," she said, awed. Her brows contracted as she thought more deeply about what he had just said. "And then there is the fact this state of affairs has been ongoing for so long now that it seems to have become some sort of Fivetrees tradition for the landowning families in this district. And as it is now a tradition no one seeks to question it. That is reinforced by the inscription in the market place, isn't it? Who would dare argue with words carved in stone and in Latin! It's as if they were lifted direct from the Scriptures themselves."

"That is an excellent line of reasoning, sweetheart. Though I wonder why my uncle has not sought to question it. He questions everything else!"

"He may have and gotten nowhere. Just as no one blinked when the Colonel manhandled Mrs. Turner. It is accepted. It is wrong, but it is still accepted..." She shuddered. "Life in the country has me flummoxed at times."

Alec did not point out that the Colonel's rough treatment of Mrs. Turner had little to do with a country mindset, and everything to do with a society that permitted females to be the chattels of their male relatives, be it fathers, brothers, uncles, and husbands, and to do with as they pleased. But he did not want to further upset her by reviving painful memories of her own appalling mistreatment at the hands of a violent misogynist. He wanted to take her mind as far from such traumatic experience as possible, and he knew what he was about to tell her would not please her at all, but it would suitably divert her.

He leaned in and kissed her forehead, and when he straightened pulled a letter from his pocket and held it out.

"I hate to be the bearer of ill tidings, but this cannot wait until tomorrow. It's from your brother—"

"Talgarth?"

"Cobham."

The light of expectation died in her dark eyes. "Cobham?" Frowning, she reluctantly took the letter. It was addressed to Lord Halsey, and the script in her elder brother's usual stilted fist. The seal was broken. "What does he want?"

"I don't know—yet."

"But you've read it..."

"I have. But he doesn't say what he wants. Just that he has invited himself to stay—"

Selina half rose up off the cushion, agitated. "Oh no, Alec! You know I can't bear him at the best of times. I positively won't receive him like this! You must write tonight and tell him to stay away."

"I wish I could refuse him. I'm sure he's well aware of the reception he'll receive, and does not care. No doubt he got an earful from Olivia, too. But that would be to no avail. He's traveling down with her and Sybilla—"

"With Aunt Olivia? Why didn't she refuse him a seat in her carriage!? He listens to her."

"As a dutiful nephew must. But she could not refuse him upon this occasion. He merely had to put on his Head of the Foreign Department hat and tell her his visit is of national importance—"

"*National importance*!?" She crushed the letter in her fist without realizing it. "He's such a self-important intermeddler! What could possibly be of significance to the nation down here?"

"Perhaps I am…?" he quipped.

"You?" She pouted, too annoyed to hear his levity. "Surely whatever it is can wait until after our happy event—which is far more important to *us* than whatever it is my ninny of a brother has to say to *you*."

Alec swept her a bow with a grin, then chucked her under the chin.

"I couldn't agree more, my darling. But this time he has managed to outwit the three of us—you, me, and Olivia. God knows how he achieved it, but he has."

"If he's managed that, then it was someone else's idea or nudging that won the day," Selina grumbled. "Cobham has never had an original thought in his life."

"Yes. I think you're right. But he is not as insensible to your feelings or mine, as you may think. Which is why he sent that letter by courier, and after Olivia's carriage, with him aboard, had left Buckinghamshire. They are already on their way, and should be here sometime late tomorrow."

※

ALEC WAS STILL SMILING TO HIMSELF AT THE STRING OF ABUSE his dear wife was able to pour forth when describing her elder brother, when he sauntered into the Picture Gallery. He was also thinking about his godmother Olivia St. Neots and how she was possibly giving her nephew an earful whilst shut up with him in her carriage. The only person he truly felt for was Olivia's daughter Lady Sybilla. The poor woman would be beside herself with anxiousness, and no doubt would spend much of the journey with her gloved hands to her ears in the hopes of blocking out her mother's eloquent swearing.

He was halfway along the long room before he noticed the entire length of the gallery, with its red velvet upholstered furniture under the row of family portraits, was bathed in candlelight. In heavy frames, the portraits provided a timeline of the Halsey family's rise to greatness. Painted in their finery, ancestors peered out from stark white faces with severe expressions. All were adorned in the height of fashion of the time, from gentlemen in their copotains festooned with feathers and ladies in fillet and braids caught up in hair nets studded with jewels, to noblewomen in silken farthingales, and couples with natural hair—hers curled either side of rouged cheeks, and his, also natural and long, with well-groomed and waxed mustaches.

And there was his uncle, sipping brandy and peering up at one enormous canvas in particular. It was the family portrait of Alec's grandparents, the Earl and Countess of Delvin, with their two sons. One of the boys was a young Plantagenet, the other his brother Roderick, the father who had rejected Alec before he was even born. All were dressed in black velvet and white silk, the earl in an impressive full-bottomed wig, and his Countess with an elaborate coiffure framed by white silk fontanges to her frelange headpiece.

Alec had time to peer up at the portrait before Plantagenet Halsey came to life beside him. When the old man turned a shoulder, squeezing tight the bridge of his bony nose and drinking down his brandy, Alec wondered if he had been too wrapped up in his thoughts to be aware of his presence. But when his uncle finally turned to greet him with a wan smile, the reason for his hesitation was obvious. The old man's eyes were rimmed with tears.

THIRTEEN

"Are you all right?"

Alec asked the question instinctively, the words out before he realized his uncle was not physically unwell; the tears were brought on by something else entirely. Perhaps it was peering at the portrait and reflecting on his youth, or the loss of his parents, or his brother, or all three. Alec had no idea, and tried to recall the last time he had seen his uncle brought to tears. It only took him a moment—the day of his mother's funeral.

He gave his uncle time to collect himself by digging in a pocket of his silk banyan for his eyeglasses. He then stepped up to the large canvas, gold-rimmed spectacles perched on the ridge of his bony nose, and took a closer look at the noble family. Wearing his glasses, and at such close quarters the brushstrokes came into focus. He had never stopped to truly study this portrait before. And his aunt was right. The two boys did have different hair coloring. Yet, in every other respect they could have been the same boy. It was as if the artist had been too lazy to be bothered to paint them as individuals. This was unsurprising. Artists of bygone eras were known to paint children as identical beings, as if they were not worthy of being singled out as individuals with separate personalities until they had reached adulthood. There was nothing new in this treatment of offspring. Many died in infancy and some well before reaching adulthood, so that they were not painted at all. Often the names of brothers or sisters who had died were used again, Alec suspected, in the hopes that this offspring would survive, and the name of a past relative live on too.

Regarding the brothers dispassionately, Alec's first thought was not to think here were selfsame twins. All he saw were two boys near in age. Had his aunt not told him the reason for the differing hair color, he would have been none the wiser, and not thought anymore about it. But now that he knew the reason for differentiating the brothers, he was inclined to wonder if there was something more to it than the obvious, some hidden meaning perhaps known only to the parents, or the boys themselves. Why bother to highlight difference when painting sameness in siblings was more often the norm? No, he did not think the artist was lazy, or the parents indifferent, upon this occasion. His grandparents had chosen to highlight difference in their sons, and this made the portrait all the more intriguing. He was about to comment on this family grouping in the hopes of having his uncle open up about his boyhood, when the old man spoke first.

"How's our girl?"

Alec stepped back from the canvas and removed his eyeglasses. "Emotionally exhausted after today's events. But I left her with the news Cobham is on his way here. She's furious, and thus suitably distracted."

"Ha! Good for you! She needs distraction. What she don't need is that plaguey brother of hers makin' a fuss. Though I'd have thought such a cold fish as Clive Vesey, Earl of Cobham, would prefer to visit the Outer Hebrides in winter as come within a mile of a headstrong virago of a sister who's about to give birth!"

"Believe me, we'd all prefer it if he were on his way to a remote island. But he's not coming here to give us the pleasure of his company, but to see me."

"Couldn't it have waited until after the happy event?"

"That was Selina's outraged response. Obviously not. I have some idea of what he wants because he mentioned Midanich. He counseled that it was a matter of national importance, and vital I keep this to myself. So I am keeping it to myself by telling you."

"Bravo! Damned bloody presumptuous of him to show his face after he sent you into the middle of a civil war goin' on in that very country! I'm itchin' to plant him a facer for puttin' all our lives at risk."

"As he is sharing Olivia's carriage, I've no doubts Her Grace is giving him a rather sizeable slice of her mind about Midanich, me, and anything else that upset her while we were abroad."

"He's foisted his company on his aunt?" The old man chuckled. "Good God! What an imbecile! He must be desperate indeed to see you. She'll be strippin' the layers off him every mile they travel, be assured of that. It was thoughts of what she was goin' to do to her nincompoop of a nephew when we got back on English terra firma that kept her spirits up the entire return journey through rough seas. Here," he added, handing Alec a glass of brandy. He held his up. "A toast to redoubtable females," he said with a soft smile. "May they always be in our lives."

Alec joined in the toast. He took a second sip of the amber liquid, then looked up at the portrait. Without his spectacles the brush-strokes were a blur, as were the stern expressions of the adults. "Was my grandmother a redoubtable female?"

"Good Lord was she! Olivia and our flame-haired girl are vira-goes, that's certain, but neither of them can hold a candle to my mother. Rod and I were more than a little afraid of her." The old man turned to regard the portrait as well. "She had this way of lookin' at you when she was displeased. No need to speak. And if she did, no need to raise her voice. All it took was that look. Terrified us! Not that she was cruel or mean or heartless. Far from it. She just didn't suffer fools or fiends. And she was not one to coo, cluck, or cuddle an infant or small child. Rod and I had to look elsewhere for that sort of affection. She didn't have much time for children, generally. Still. She did her duty by us."

"And my grandfather—your father? What was he like?"

"Ah, now here comes the cant phrase—but it was true—chalk and cheese! That was my parents. He was light to her dark. He was a gentle giant of a man. Kind. Honorable. A good master. Believed in justice. Hated bigots. Never talked down to us because we were chil-dren. Led by example—"

"You take after him."

"Do I? Yes, I-I suppose I must," the old man muttered self-consciously, gaze on the portrait. "At least in temperament, if not in action..." he added cryptically.

"Did they marry for love, or was it an arranged union?"

"Arranged. But they grew to love one another. M'mother was a faithful wife; m'father had several affairs, and one long-term mistress —daughter of a sugar planter by one of his slaves. She lived in Canterbury with her father's family until my father set her up. He— m'father—sired several mulatto brats with her. My valet Joseph Cale he—he was one of 'em. When his mistress died in childbed, m'father brought their children into this house, and m'mother raised them. Until then she'd ignored that side of my father's life; out of sight was out of mind, as far as she was concerned."

Alec kept his eyes on the portrait. "Your mother must indeed have been a formidable woman to accept her husband's natural offspring by his mistress and raise them here—"

"That reminds me!" Plantagenet Halsey interrupted with a huff of laughter, and turning the subject, "I only ever saw my mother laugh when in my father's company. I can't recall what he said or did in particular to make her do so, but only he could do it." He smiled at Alec and raised his glass again. "Thank you for making me remember that about her…"

"You're very welcome. Thank you for telling me. I know so very little about them, so I'm grateful for anything you'd care to share. Tell me more about your boyhood… I'd like to know about you and my father as brothers."

There followed several seconds of complete silence, underscoring that the entire house was eerily quiet. Renovations had stopped for the night. Any servant not retired to the servant areas of the house was quietly padding about their tasks, candlestick in hand, doing their best not to disturb their masters. It was so quiet, in fact, that had Alec a pin he could have let it drop and heard it hit the floor-boards. But what the deafening silence highlighted most was his uncle's extreme reluctance to be more forthcoming about his brother. And yet he had been accommodating about his father's infidelities. Alec was about to explain his reasoning when the old man finally spoke, and in a voice that was colder than a January wind.

"Is that why you asked to see me here in particular?"

"Not specifically. But yes, one of the reasons."

"How many reasons—or should that be questions?—have you got?"

"That depends on what you are prepared to answer—"

"Damme, Alec! Stop with the silver-tongued démarche! I'm no fool! I'm not Cobham."

"No one but Cobham could be Cobham," Alec quipped, trying to lift the mood because the arctic coldness in his uncle's normally warm friendly voice was a surprise.

But Plantagenet Halsey did not want to banter, nor did he wish to be appeased. He threw back the last drops of brandy and crossed to the window where he'd left the bottle. He snatched this up and glared at Alec. "She put you up to this, didn't she. Well? Did she?"

"No. Not to seek you out in this way. But Selina has been urging me since before we were married to find out more about my family. With the baby due any day, she's anxious, as am I, to supply our infant with a name. But I suspect she wishes to satisfy a burning curiosity. She tells me it is perfectly natural to want to know about one's grandparents and great-grandparents, aunts and uncles. She says I am the odd one out, not only because I know so little about my familial connections, but also because I've never felt it necessary to my existence to know." He smiled lovingly at the old man. "You are all the family I've ever wanted or needed."

Alec's smile and his sincerity cooled the old man's enmity in an instant. He brought the bottle across and splashed a generous drop into both their glasses. "Forgive me, my boy," he said, much subdued. "It was wrong of me to direct my anger at you. It's natural for her to want to know about your family. In her condition family is all she must think about. But your—our—family is-is—different, more so than you can ever imagine, or need to know."

"So it would seem, given your valet was your half-brother!" Alec quipped.

"So you picked up on that detail, did you?" When Alec lifted an eyebrow, as if to say how could he not, he let out a breath and shrugged and diverted the conversation by adding, "I guess today's events—particularly that young lad's grisly death—have affected me more than I realised."

"How are the Turners?"

"Not well, either of them. She's fallen all to pieces, which is understandable. And Turner doesn't know what to do about it to fix it. Not that he can fix it, can he? The lad's dead. And the boy's brother has taken himself off somewhere to grieve in whatever way he needs

to. The Turner boys weren't close, but they were brothers." Plantagenet Halsey shook his head. "Got me mystified why anyone would
kill Hugh. He was just a boy. They both are, because Adams is
convinced there is a second body out there. But cuttin' off their
hands, well that's a warning to other poachers, aint' it?"

"It is?" When the old man nodded, Alec added, "Could it have
been travelers passing through? Perhaps the boys discovered them
killing deer and they were killed to silence them?"

"There ain't any need to silence a couple of lads from around here.
Everyone knows there ain't any poachin' in the wood—"

"Even when there is?"

The old man raised his glass. "Aye. Even when there is," he admitted. "It's a fine line we all tread, but it's there, and if you play by the
rules, for the common good, then no one gets prosecuted, not even
travelers passin' through, and we all go on livin' our lives."

"And how does His Lordship walk this fine line if he's unaware of
these rules, or does he not need to bec—"

"Oh, I walk the line! Everyone walks the line," Plantagenet Halsey
insisted, adding in a rush, realizing too late Alec had been referring to
himself, "But I didn't want you to be bothered with the quirks of
livin' in this part of Kent, not yet... You've a far more important
matter to spend your time worrin' about, than worrin' about walkin'
lines, real or imaginary! And so I told Adams and the others. So we
agreed to leave botherin' you until Selina and the babe had come
through the ordeal and you were less clouded with worry."

Alec decided it was best to ignore his uncle's slip of the tongue—
for now. If nothing else the old man's retort, which bordered on the
boastful, confirmed to Alec what he suspected from the beginning of
his tenure at Deer Park—that the servants, the tenants, and his neighbors all deferred to his uncle first and foremost. He had not been
imagining it. Something—many things—had been going on behind
his back since he'd inherited the estate. And while he believed that his
uncle had his best interests at heart, and that it was a desire not to
bother him while he waited the arrival of his infant, he could not
shake the suspicion there was more to it than that. He was missing
something fundamental, and he had been kept in deliberate ignorance. How did he discover what that was? As Lady Ferris had
reasoned, he could not ask if you did not know what to ask about.

But he did not want to discuss that particular quandary tonight, or the murder of Hugh Turner. Intuition told him the death of those two boys was somehow linked to the understanding everyone in the district had about poaching and poachers, and that Hugh and his friend had been murdered because they had transgressed these unwritten rules. What rule, and who had murdered them—well that too could wait until tomorrow, when he was fully cognizant.

Tonight he had come to the Picture Gallery seeking answers about his uncle and father. And knowing Selina would be sleeping fitfully, if at all, until his return, he decided to come straight to the point and tell his uncle about the conversation he'd had with Lady Ferris. Plantagenet Halsey beat him to it.

"When I said she put you up to this, the *she* I was referrin' to wasn't Selina. I was referrin' to Lady Ferris."

"You think she was being intentionally mischievous?" Alec asked evenly. "She was certainly surprised by my ignorance of the family history but not, it seems, that you chose to keep me ignorant of it."

"Chose to keep you ignorant?" Plantagenet Halsey repeated softly. He shrugged a shoulder. "Aye, that's true. But there's nothin' sinister in my intent. I thought it for the best—for your peace of mind—given the circumstances. I stand by that decision. She had no right to disturb you. No right at all!"

"What circumstances would disturb my peace mind?"

Again the old man shrugged but this time he stuck out his lower lip, dismissing the question as if it was facetious. He eyed Alec speculatively. "So she didn't say anythin' specific about that inscription in the market square?"

"She mentioned it, just as the others at nuncheon did. In fact she was indifferent, saying the inscription—which she referred to as a sort of blessing—was possibly the least odd thing about Fivetrees."

"Ha!"

"I'd rather hear it from you than any other. What does it mean, that inscription? To be blessed with one son and no daughters is rather specific, and, yes, odd."

The old man threw up a hand. "We don't have time for this now. I'm tired. You are too."

Alec put up an eyebrow. He wasn't going anywhere.

"You may have gotten away with dismissing me like that when I was a child, even when I was a youth, but you seem to have forgotten, I'm thirty-six. You can't dismiss this—or me—so arbitrarily."

"I know how old you are! It's not likely I'll ever forget unless I go senile. But your age don't matter a whit, whether you be fifteen or fifty. I won't allow the life to be sucked out of you as it was me, m'brother, m'father, and—" He made a wide arc with his arm to encompass the room. "—every male in our family, and as far back as the Conqueror. And I ain't exaggeratin'! It's a burden too much for anyone to bear."

Alec tried to contain his astonishment. He knew his uncle was prone to the melodramatic, but this pronouncement was even more sensational than usual.

"You don't think—knowing me as you do, as an adult, and all that I've been through—I have the shoulders to carry this burden? You have. And if every other Halsey male in our family has, then why not me? What about my brother? Was Edward called upon?"

Plantagenet Halsey shook his head. "No. Fortunately for him, he died before he married."

"If the requirement for taking on this family obligation is marriage, then I am eminently suited. The question is: Why did you shoulder this burden when you've never been married?"

The old man's eyes narrowed, yet he was all admiration for Alec's reasoning. "Clever…" He took both empty glasses and put them on the side table under the portrait of his parents, which gave him time to construct a considered reply.

"But I was unique, and it put m'father in an awkward position. He felt obligated to inform me, to inform us—my brother and me— both, and he did so at the same time. But it was m'mother who counseled him that he could not keep me in ignorance."

"Whereas you feel you can keep the truth from me?"

"Alec, I—"

"Lady Ferris said the discovery would be unpleasant—for me," Alec continued as if his uncle had not spoken. "But she said I deserved to be told the truth—the truth about my-my *birth*, and everything that came before it. Now that's the part that intrigues me —the *everything that came before it*. I can only assume that what she meant by that was the events leading up to my birth are the reason I am here at all. So I have to wonder what she meant and, more importantly, how my birth and this family burden are linked. And why you think me undeserving of the truth."

"Undeservin'? *Undeservin'* of the-the—*truth*?" repeated the old man. He smiled crookedly, yet he regarded Alec with sadness. "Now there's somethin' that's easy for me to answer. You are not *un*deservin'. You are exceedin'ly deservin'. Of all the Halsey men, I'd say you're the most deservin' of the lot of us! But what you deserve is a good life, one with a contented lovin' marriage, and a happy family. That's all I've ever wanted for you, you do know that, don't you, m'boy—a happy life?"

Alec smiled and nodded. "Of course. And with you I've had a happy life. Life with Selina is but an extension of that, and you are part of this life, with us."

"It's more than I deserve. But I'll take it because it's what I want. And what I also want is for you to abandon this need to know, just this once, for me. There are some family secrets not worth diggin' up. You have to trust me that this is one of 'em. Knowin' it will change everythin' between us—" He clicked his fingers. "—just like that. In an instant—"

"Nothing could ever change how I feel about you."

"Alec! Alec!" Plantagenet Halsey grabbed him by the shoulders and looked him squarely in the eye. "Do I need to shake sense into you, my boy? It *will* change everythin' between us, as it changed everythin' between m'brother and me. You have to take my word on it." He let his hands drop but did not move away, and took a deep breath. "Listen. There were men in our family who weren't resilient. They should never have been burdened in the first place, but it was their duty, a duty passed down through the ages, and one they were obligated to fulfill. But the burden weighed them down. It pressed too heavily on their hearts. Y'know what they did? It's not spoken of because it doesn't do to have feeble-brained men in any family, it's considered shameful. But I don't blame 'em. I only feel sadness for their plight. But I do think it cowardly, to leave behind a grieving widow with a small son, and no one the wiser as to why a seemingly contented husband and father would take his own life. Some managed to make it through until their son was old enough to take on the burden themselves. Others were driven to madness. One of your ancestors walked into the duck pond and kept walkin' until he drowned himself. Another was found hangin' by his cravat in the cellar. A third refused food and water until he was too weak to partake of either."

"You think if this family obligation were revealed to me there is a possibility I, too, won't be able to bear it, and I'll go mad, and-and —*kill* myself?" Alec asked quietly, face drained of color. "Good Lord! I can't begin to imagine what would drive a man to suicide. But I could not do such a selfish thing to you, to Selina, to an infant not yet born. Whatever madness there is in the family, surely by now it is obvious I didn't inherit it!"

"Of course you're not mad!" blustered the old man. "But I don't think those men in our family who killed themselves were mad either. They were driven to it. Sent mad by the weight of family obligation, and a murky ancestral history."

Alec's gaze swept the family portraits bathed in candlelight. Every ancestor stared out of a canvas with a confident air and natural superiority of their place in the world. He recalled the first time he and Selina had strolled its length, sun streaming through the windows that overlooked Stone Court. She had remarked on the old furniture and carpets, that with a good dusting, beating, and airing, some polish, and a lick of paint, and perhaps different arrangement, this would be a lovely room for the family to gather on a rainy day. She had even remarked that it would be good for their children to spend time with their ancestors peering down on them, to know from whom they were descended. To which he had rolled his eyes and quipped that someone in the family needed to know, because he certainly couldn't distinguish one stern, humorless face from another. They had laughed and walked on, and he had never given the gallery or its silent watchful occupants much thought afterwards. How blissful was ignorance!

He returned his gaze to his uncle, who was regarding him with a concerned frown.

"And those men who could not shoulder this burden, they are here in this gallery now?"

"Yes. All of 'em, and no one the wiser as to how they died." The old man smiled thinly. "You're not selfish, but I am. I've spent my life makin' certain you've never been troubled by the family history. And by God, I'll not let all those years of parentin' go to waste now, not with you at the precipice of fatherhood."

Alec knew he would not get more out of his uncle tonight, and that he would possibly have to employ other means to uncover this secret about his ancestors that his uncle was unwilling to share with him. So he diverted the conversation to his original purpose for asking the old man to meet him here in the Picture Gallery.

"Then tell me about your brother."

Plantagenet Halsey's sigh of relief was audible.

FOURTEEN

"Why isn't your brother's portrait here amongst the Halsey forebears?" Alec asked. When Plantagenet Halsey's gaze shot to the family portrait, Alec lifted his eyes and shook his head. "Don't point to that picture. I said a portrait. He was a proud man. Surely there's one of him in his ermine, as there is of his countess in hers, just down there by the fireplace. And if every other family has a portrait, then why not this Earl and Countess of Delvin and their son and heir?"

"You've never shown the slightest interest or cared a drop for—"

"Whether I care for him is unimportant. I am curious as to why this gallery has no pictures of him beyond the age of eight. Is it because, as Lady Ferris thinks, you wished to keep from me that you and your brother were selfsame twins?"

"Dear Lady Ferris just had to slip that little morsel into the nuncheon conversation as if it were the most natural thing in the world, didn't she," grumbled the old man. "So Rod and I were self-same twins. What of it?"

Alec huffed incredulous laughter. "Aside from the fact you were one of twins who were identical in every respect? You cannot be so dismissive. It's extraordinary. But what is more so, is to think you and your brother were, for all intents and purposes, one and the same person yet no two men could be more dissimilar! I was forsaken by him; you loved me. He was a self-serving nobleman who cared for nobody but his own interests. You champion the plight of the poor and dispossessed. He is night to your day."

"I suppose it must look to you as if that's the case, given your ordeal in Midanich, with the Margrave and his mad sister being twins—"

"Would you have told me you were a selfsame twin had Ernst and Johanna turned out not to be mad?"

Plantagenet Halsey shook his head. "No. I'd have kept it from you for as long as possible, regardless of all else. Forever, if I'd been able. That business in Midanich just gave me more of an excuse not to tell you. But not because Roderick was mad, or evil, or night to my day. We weren't two sides of the same coin, with him the bad and me the good. For the longest time, for all of our youth in fact, we were that same coin, and inseparable. He was me, and I him, and we were the best of friends."

"When did it change between you?"

"Not long after our father died—that was the start of the estrangement between us. Your birth was the final nail in the coffin of our closeness as brothers." He smiled sadly. "And yes, as your aunt said, what came before it."

"You must've been dreading the day I met Lady Ferris."

Plantagenet Halsey's blue eyes flickered up to meet Alec's. "Oh, I've been dreadin' dear Lady Ferris for a lot longer than that… But that's a story for another day. You asked about why there are no pictures of m'brother here in the gallery. There was once. But only two. And you're right. One in his ermine and coronet, a twin to the portrait of your mother in hers. And one of the two of 'em with Edward on your mother's knee."

"What happened to them? And where are they?"

"Your mother had them taken down almost straight after Rod died. As to where they are…my guess is they're stored in the attic rooms, or in the cellar. Either way, they'd need a fair bit of restoration if you intend to put him back up—"

"Why did she have them removed?"

"Do you want to put them back up?"

"I've not thought that far ahead. Regardless of my lack of feeling for him, he was the Earl of Delvin, and so he has a right to be here in the gallery. Whether he's earned it… But if my mother had both portraits removed, effectively banishing him from his place amongst his illustrious relatives, it gives me pause. Why did she do that?"

"She said those pictures were a constant reminder of *her* failin's."

"What gave her the right to keep her portrait in ermine and coronet upon the wall and not his? Why should she be permitted to show off her trappings of title and wealth when her failings—"

The bitter flippancy in Alec's tone hit a nerve and the old man rallied.

"Your mother was the sweetest, most gentle and lovin' creature to walk God's earth, and you barely knew her, so don't you dare take it upon y'self to cast aspersions on her character or talk of her failin's!"

"You're right. I barely knew her. But that was through no fault of mine. And just like the portraits of the Earl, she cast me out of her life—out of sight, out of mind—no doubt so she could rest her head easy at night. Are they the actions of a sweet and loving creature? Methinks your feelings cloud your judgment."

"You think she had a choice? You think she wanted to give you up? Have I ever said that she did?"

"No. But—"

"No! Not once in all your years have I ever blamed your mother for what happened."

"Because you loved her and are a good man, and you did not want me to think ill of her because she was, after all, my mother."

"Rubbish! I loved her, yes. And she loved me. But I don't know why she continued to do so after what I did! But as I said she was a sweet, gentle creature…and you're wrong. It's got nothin' to do with you not thinkin' ill of her, but you not thinkin' ill of *me*. I told you— I'm selfish."

"Yet, she gave me up. She did not fight to keep me because she could not, could she? And why would she when I was not my father's son but the product of her affair with your valet, who I found out tonight just happened to also be your half-brother—"

"That's utter porridge!"

"But I have her letter. The one where she calls herself an adulteress. Where she blames herself for what happened to me—"

"Oh, for God's sake! Alec! Stop with the sanctimonious blamin'! Listen to yourself! I tell you it was not her fault but mine and yet you refuse to believe me—worse! You continue to believe ill of her. No mother *chooses* to give up a newborn. It was forced upon her by circumstances beyond her control. Beyond anyone's control to alter. So don't you dare—don't you *dare*—malign her."

"If you say so."

"I do."

"Then if you want me to believe you, tell me the truth about my birth."

The old man ran a hand over his face and up over his grizzled hair, jaw tight and eyes closed, as if steeling himself for what he was about to say and its aftermath.

"You're not goin' to let this rest until you've drained every last drop of truth from me, are you?"

Alec pulled a face and shrugged his resignation. "I cannot. I need to know. I didn't think I did. But the closer Selina is to giving birth, the greater this need in me to know about my own."

Plantagenet Halsey nodded. "Olivia said it would come to this…"

"Olivia?" Alec blinked his surprise. "You've spoken to my godmother about-about—*my birth*?"

"That surprises you? You're often uppermost in her thoughts."

"Yes. But not about this, surely?"

"Why not? It's not only about you, y'know!"

"But…you confided in her the truth?"

"I did. But as part of a deeper confessional," the old man stated bashfully. "She needed to know all the sordid details of my past."

For some reason Alec was offended, and bemused. "Why would you tell her, and yet keep it from me?"

Plantagenet Halsey became sheepish. "Your godmother is a good girl. Always has been. She wasn't goin' to take me on without a full and frank confession of all my past sins."

Alec blinked, none the wiser. "Take you on…?"

"And because we're not gettin' any younger, and she means the world to me, I told her everythin'—every last drop." When Alec continued to stare at him, nonplussed, he felt his face warm. "Oh, for pity's sake!" he added, exasperated. "Don't tell me you didn't have an inklin' of how matters stand between us?"

"Stand between…you—you and-and *Olivia*? Good—Lord!"

"What? Did you think we were too old to romp between the sheets?"

"I knew you were fond of each other but—but not—but not *this*... I wonder if Selina has any idea?"

"More idea than you, I'll wager!" Plantagenet Halsey retorted. "So now you know. But you'll keep it to yourself because she wants to be the one to tell you. And she will, tomorrow when she gets here."

"What precisely is my godmother going to announce?" Alec asked with a chuckle. "That she, a noblewoman of the highest moral fiber, and a rabble-rousing MP with republican sentiments, are lovers?" He put a fist to his mouth to hide his grin. "I-I—can't wait!"

His amusement offended Plantagenet Halsey. And because the old man had said more than he intended about his intimate relationship with the Duchess of Romney-St. Neots, and because he was tired, and because he wanted to get this confessional over with, his next words were blunt and uncompromising. With little regard for the consequences it would have on its recipient, thirty-six years spent carefully constructing and nurturing the past was set to the torch, went up in flames and turned to ash.

"You asked for the truth about your birth, so let me give it to you straight so we can both get to our beds. We have an early start in the mornin' if we're goin' with Adams to find out what happened to the Turners' poor boy." When Alec lost his smile and waited silently, he swallowed hard and continued. "The first truth is I lied to you. I've been lyin' to you about your birth your whole life. And for the longest time I let myself believe the lie, too. Because it was far easier than tellin' you the truth.

"The lies are goin' to stop now, here, from this day forward. It must, for my sake as well as yours. The truth—and I told Olivia this, too, so you can verify it with her—is that I took you from your mother barely an hour after her exertions of bringin' you into this world. Her attendants had cut the cord, wiped you over, and swaddled you. And then I took you away... I took you to the sounds of her sobbin' her heart out. It was the most appallin' thing I've ever done in m'life, and I've never forgotten the sound of her utter misery at havin' to give you up.

"But she knew the terms of the agreement between m'brother and me, and she knew if you were to live, then I had to take you there and then, and get you away from here as fast and as faraway as possible. I took you north, to one of our tenant families. The woman had a litter of children and it was she who nursed you and cared for you for the first two years of your life. And in that time, Edward came along, and she consoled herself, but she never, *ever* forgot you, her firstborn.

"And she knew that if I'd not taken you away, you'd not now be standin' here about to become a father yourself. I don't regret what I did. She didn't regret it either. We never did. That's the raw and unde-niable and shockin' truth. But I do regret havin' to keep up the lie all these years. I didn't think about that at the time. All we thought about was keepin' you alive. And I did what I did because I loved your mother, and we did what we had to do because we love you. Love is inexplicable and strange, and often people do the wrong thing but for the right reason. I'm too tired to tell you more, so I'm for bed. And there's more, a lot more, but that'll have to wait for another day. Good night, m'boy."

𝓨𝓬

ALEC CRAWLED INTO BED AND SNUGGLED INTO SELINA'S warmth, without any memory of having left the Picture Gallery. Lady Ferris's revelation at nuncheon had left him dazed but his uncle's raw confessional drained him and left him emotionally numb. Perhaps that's how his mother had coped with losing him almost at birth, by thinking him dead. It was only near the end of her life that she had finally made contact. But even then he had always felt a stranger, a distant relative at best. Not once did she mention he had been taken from her, not because she wanted to give him up, but because she had been forced. Not once had she cast blame in direction of the Halsey brothers. Perhaps she had preferred to put the harrowing episode behind her by severing all emotional connection. And she had had another son, and no doubt gave him all her love and attention, thoughts of her firstborn becoming more distant with every passing month. But the overriding question for Alec, for which his uncle had not provided an explanation, was why the brothers had needed an agreement in the first place which stipulated Alec must be removed from his mother at birth. And if he was not the product of his moth-er's affair with the mulatto servant Joseph Cale, as his uncle now strenuously denied was the case, then who was his father?

Into these mental musings he felt Selina stir. Half-awake she searched out for his hand under the covers. Fingers entwined, she mumbled something he did not catch, but it was enough to bring him out of his preoccupation and into the present to concentrate on her. She was on her back, propped on pillows. It had been impossible for her to sleep on her side for many weeks now. The candlelight fell across the covers and the silhouette of her round belly—a hump in the bed clothes. He was suddenly overcome with the need to protect her and their unborn child. And he knew she slept soundly beside him confident he would do so at any cost. And as he drifted off into an unsettled sleep, a burning resentment began to fester within him for the man whom he loved like a father and now knew had been a willing participant in robbing his mother of her infant, and him of his mother's love.

⚘

HE WAS AWAKENED WHAT SEEMED TO BE FIVE MINUTES AFTER HE fell asleep. In fact it was several hours later but the sun was not yet up, and Selina remained asleep beside him.

The sound of water being poured into a porcelain basin at his dressing stand reinforced the need to rise and dress at once, if he were to be in time to join Adams and the men assembled, ready to head out into the woods. He was grateful for his valet's silence while he dressed, but the two attendants who assisted Hadrian were padding about the closet and dressing rooms as if the slightest sound would unbalance their master's delicate constitution. And this made him wonder if he presented as if he'd spent the night in excessive drinking, for while he was awake, it was much too early for him to function properly. But when Hadrian shooed his assistants out of the room, and they scampered away as if they feared for their lives, Alec was not so dull that he knew something was up. He didn't have long to wait to find out.

Dressed in thigh-tight, knitted riding breeches, long feet encased in jockey boots, it only remained for him to be shrugged into his linen riding frock over his waistcoat to be ready to go downstairs to join the search party. He had eaten a roll and had a cup of coffee while dressing, to save time, and now stood before the long looking glass to take one last look at his reflection before departing. But when his valet left the frock coat on its hook and requested that His Lordship return to sit on his dressing stool, Alec turned back into the room with a frown between his black brows.

"Is something the matter?"

Hadrian swallowed and nodded and indicated the dressing stool. "Please sit, sir. It would be better said if you were seated."

Alec didn't move. "Can't this wait until after I—"

"No, sir. I need to talk to you now, before you go off. We have about an hour until the men gather at the stables."

"We do?"

"Yes, sir. I got you up early so we could have this talk."

Alec took a step forward. "You *what*?"

"Please sit, sir."

"No wonder Phillips and Putnam dashed out of here."

"Yes, sir."

Alec sat on the padded dressing stool and waited. And then his valet further surprised him.

Instead of telling him whatever was on his mind that could not wait, Hadrian crossed to the door which led to the servant stairs and passageway into which the two attendants had vanished. Out of the darkness emerged the last person Alec expected to see. Tam came into the room. He and Hadrian spoke in hushed tones by the closed servant door, and then they both came to stand before Alec.

If a feather had been to hand and he'd been prodded with it, Alec was certain he'd have fallen off the stool. Seeing these two together, and at such close quarters, and being amicable, was almost too much for his dull brain to comprehend at this time of the morning. But his overwhelming feeling was one of relief that the two young men were no longer at loggerheads. And it put him in a charitable mood to listen to whatever it was they wanted to speak to him about, even if it meant he'd been tricked out of an hour of much needed sleep. But first he had to ask the question,

"How are the Turners?"

"Not bearing up at all, sir," Tam responded, pushing the red curls out of his eyes and pulling on the points of his dark blue linen waistcoat. He looked to have dressed in a hurry, as if he had only remembered at the last moment that he needed to be somewhere before dawn. That he shifted from foot to foot was indication of his nervousness. "I gave Mrs. Turner a draught of laudanum. And I gave her enough that I'm hoping she'll sleep most of the day away. She'll wake thinking yesterday was a bad dream. But it wasn't, and I've no doubt she'll feel worse, and curse me for interfering with her grief."

"And Mr. Turner?"

Tam shook his head. "He says he doesn't need anything. And as he wants to be the one to retrieve poor Hugh from the wood, it's best he keeps a clear head. Though I see his suffering is no less than hers."

"And Hugh's brother—forgive me, what's his name—"

"Roger, sir. Roger's not been seen since before dinner. And as the Turners are in no fit state to be asked, and no one wants to upset them further by telling them their other son is now missing, too, we're hoping he'll return in his own good time. Truth told he's probably hiding out at the laundry. That's where he spends his time—he's keen on one of the laundry maids—But that's for another day…"

"Perhaps a servant should be sent to the laundry to check on him—"

"I did that before I came here, sir."

"Thank you. The boy should be with his parents at this time… And we can only hope that a search of the wood yields them some answers. Though I'm afraid nothing is going to heal their grief."

"Yes, sir. And it won't. My cousin Hugh was a bit of a rascal but he had a huge heart, and he was his mother's favorite. He believed in what Mr. Halsey calls *causes*. He didn't like the hunt, and he wanted it outlawed. And he cared what happened to the itinerantes who scavenged in the wood."

"Do you have any idea who would want to harm him?"

"No, sir. Everyone liked Hugh. He was likeable. Now if it'd been my cousin Roger…" Tam shrugged. "But no, I've no idea who'd want to do Hugh a harm, least of all kill him!—or his friends from the village, for that matter. There's plenty of belowstairs gossip hoping it's all been a misunderstanding and Hugh'll be found alive, but that's wishful thinking—"

"Yes, I'm afraid it is. I've no reason to doubt Adams has identified the body as Hugh's, have you?"

"No, sir. None. Everyone from around here knows—I mean *knew* —Hugh."

When Tam glanced at Hadrian, and Alec remained mute waiting

for either of the two young men to speak, Tam added apologetically, "But we're not here to talk to you about Hugh or Roger, sir, or the Turners' grief for that matter."

"Aren't you? Then what is it I can do for you—do for you both?"

"It's not what you can do for us, sir," Tam replied, a glance at the valet. "But what we can do for you."

FIFTEEN

"Do for *ME*?"

"Yes, sir."

Hadrian and Tam looked at one another, and with a nod the valet let Tam explain further.

"Sir, Mr. Jeffries needs to tell you what he's found out about Stone Court. He came to me for advice, and I told him to tell you—everything. And I'm here now because I need you to know that I believe every word of what he told me. Neither of us wants to believe it true, but it is, whether you at first think it can't be. So please, sir, hear him out before you dismiss it as fantastical nonsense. Like me, Mr. Jeffries has only your best interests at heart. I truly believe that."

"Thank you, Mr. Fisher," Hadrian murmured, face flushed with the embarrassment at such overt praise, particularly coming from one who had until recently been an adversary.

"You're welcome, Mr. Jeffries. But what I say and why I'm saying it, is to help out His Lordship. I'd not be here otherwise."

"I know that, Mr. Fisher. But still I thank you for believing me."

Both young men then looked to Alec, who had sat back with arms crossed and was smiling at them. When they remained mute, he realized he was being called upon to affirm their sincerity, which he did.

"Mr. Fisher. Mr. Jeffries. I shall do as requested and listen with an open mind. So what's this about Stone Court?"

"May I just add, sir, before Mr. Jeffries tells you what he knows, that we also believe Mr. Halsey has only your best interests at heart, too. It may not seem so when you hear what Mr. Jeffries has to tell you, but there can be no other explanation for why he did what he did. If that makes sense?"

"It doesn't—yet," Alec replied, not understanding at all. "But I will be sure to do as you say, and keep it in mind while listening to Jeffries, if you think it will help?"

Tam grinned and nodded, satisfied. "Yes, sir."

"So, Mr. Jeffries, what do you have to tell me about Stone Court?"

The valet glanced at Tam, swallowed, and then stated bluntly, "You need to know that under Stone Court, where the paving has collapsed and left a hole, there's a secret vault, and Mr. Halsey doesn't want you to know about it."

"Well that is blunt and to the point," Alec replied evenly. But the look on his face told both young men that His Lordship had no idea about a vault under Stone Court, and that Plantagenet Halsey had been successful in keeping this a secret. "How do you know this?"

In a few short sentences Hadrian told him about crawling under the desk in the library and overhearing the conversation between Plantagenet Halsey and the estate steward.

"And you learned about this secret vault from eavesdropping on their conversation?"

Hadrian did not hesitate. "Yes, sir."

"And you're not mistaken because you committed the conversation to memory. Is that right?"

"Yes, sir. I did. For you, because I thought it important to do so."

Alec let out a breath and nodded. "Very well. Go on."

"You can truly do that? Commit a conversation to memory?" Tam interrupted in wonderment staring at Hadrian. When the valet nodded, he retorted, "And that applies to lists of things, too? You never once had a piece of paper concealed on your person when asked to repeat a list?"

"No. It is an easy thing for me to commit a list to memory—"

"How do you do that?"

Hadrian was bashful. "It's not only lists… But conversations, if I need to. And I can paint a picture in my mind of a scene, and then recreate that scene—"

"Which is why my dressing table is always orderly," Alec added.

"That's right, sir," Hadrian replied. "Everything has its proper place, and in this way order can be maintained."

"But why would you—"

"Later, Tam," Alec interrupted quietly. "We don't have all morning…" He turned his attention to Hadrian. "Why does Mr. Halsey want to keep this vault a secret from me? And, please, I don't need the reply to be word for word of what you overheard. Tell me in your own words."

"Yes, sir. But when necessary, I will use the words I overheard, because then you'll know I'm telling the truth—"

Alec held his valet's gaze. "I know you would never lie to me, Hadrian."

Hadrian swallowed and nodded, awed. It was only when Tam gave him a friendly nudge that he found his voice, coughing into his fist first, and then saying quietly,

"Mr. Halsey did not say outright why the vault had to remain a secret from you, sir, only that he had spent his entire life trying to forget its existence, and he was going to make certain it was kept secret and sealed from you, too."

"Was there any mention of the vault's purpose? Why it's there? Who put it there? Any talk of that nature?"

"Only that the vault has been there for a long time. Mention was made of the Conqueror. And that heads of the Halsey family had used the vault for generations. Why it's there has something to do with what Mr. Halsey called *to honor the ancient family practice of interment*—"

"Interment?"

"Yes, sir."

"Did Mr. Halsey use the vault?"

"Why would he, sir? Mr. Jeffries never mentioned Mr. Halsey having anything to do with it. Did you, Mr. Jeffries?" Tam stuck in, and then quickly closed his mouth when Alec frowned at him.

When Alec repeated the question, Hadrian said calmly, "No, sir. It—the vault—has been closed up for a long time. Mr. Halsey said that it was his father who had it bricked up. And it was Mr. Halsey's brother who had it reopened so he could, as Mr. Halsey put it, *revive the ancient family practice of*—"

"—interment. I see…" Alec shifted on the stool and said as casually as he could, "And Mr. Turner…? What is his involvement?"

"Mr. Turner told Mr. Halsey that he only found out about the vault when he took over as steward upon his father's death. There's a document in his safe—"

"In the steward's safe?"

"Yes, sir."

"That concern the vault and its purpose?"

"That's right, sir."

"And what did Mr. Turner discover about the vault when he became steward?"

The valet paused, sighed, and then replied without hesitation, "He said it was not his nor Mr. Halsey's right to judge Mr. Halsey's ancestors for practicing interment. Mr. Turner said it was the family's only recourse if they hoped to flout the law, a law put in place before the Conqueror—"

"Flout the law?" Alec interrupted. "Is that what they said was the purpose of the vault, to allow my ancestors to defy the law?"

"Not only your ancestors, sir, but other Kentish landowning families in the district flout this law, too."

"Did they say what this law was?"

"No, sir. But mention was made that this vault helped them flout this law, and flouting this law meant they could preserve their estates intact."

There was a long pause, and then Alec said, addressing them both, "You do realize that none of this conversation between Mr. Halsey and Mr. Turner will make complete sense to me until I speak to them about it—"

"No! You can't, sir!" Tam burst out, adding quickly when Alec grimaced at being so forthrightly addressed, "Of course you can speak to them, we can't stop you, nor would we, but I don't think it would be in your best interests to do so, that's all."

"Why not…?"

Tam let Hadrian explain.

"Mr. Halsey doesn't want you to know about the vault, or what's in there, or what it's been used for. He said—Mr. Halsey said—that nothing justifies murder, and that's what his family has been engaging in for centuries—"

"He said that? He used that word? He used the word *murder*?"

The valet did not blink at Alec's incredulity. "Yes, sir. He used that word. He said that your family—his family—has been engaging in murder for centuries, and so have other landowning families. And that Mr. Turner did not need to guess what was interred in the vault."

"I see…" Alec muttered, though he did not want to see at all, or speculate as to the murderous contents of the vault under Stone Court. Tam said it for him.

"But he wasn't the one who committed murder and disposed of bodies in that vault, was he?" Tam argued.

"You think that's what's in that vault?" Alec stated without heat. "The bodies of men murdered by my forebears?"

"I-I don't rightly know what to think, sir," Tam said quietly. "But Mr. Halsey did use the word murder…"

Alec stood, and so quickly the padded stool under him rocked on its legs. The two young men took an involuntary step back, breath held, and watched as Alec paced the space between his dressing table and the long looking glass, flexing his fingers. A change had come over his features, too. Gone was the friendly light in his eyes. He stopped and looked at Hadrian and Tam.

"He may not have done the deed, but the very fact he knows murder has been committed and he is prepared to keep it a secret makes him almost as guilty as those who did."

"Sir! You can't think Mr. Halsey would—"

"Tam, I don't know why he wants to keep this appalling family secret from me, but now that it is no longer a secret, it needs to be investigated, and the truth discovered, and, if at all possible, the perpetrators brought to justice."

"Respectfully, sir, how do you intend to bring your ancestors to justice?" Hadrian asked calmly.

Alec threw up an arm, exasperated. He was annoyed with himself. "Obviously, that's impossible. But what I can do is ensure it never happens again."

"In Mr. Halsey's defense," Hadrian said into the protracted silence, "he did mention he wanted the vault and its contents kept secret particularly at this time because Her Ladyship is so close to her lying in... So mayhap he intended to tell you after the happy event?"

"Perhaps..." Alec muttered, believing the former but not the latter. He came out of his abstraction and asked, "How did my steward and my uncle intend to keep this vault and its contents a secret from me? Particularly as there is now a gaping hole in its roof, and half my workforce is itching to throw in ropes and climb down into the blackness."

"To tell you a truth, sir, this plan seems more wishful thinking than any rational thought—"

"Wishful thinking?" Alec couldn't help a flicker of a smile. "You mean they convinced each other they could keep me in ignorance without any real plan for doing so?"

Hadrian found himself smiling, too. "Something like that, sir. Yes. Though they hoped to rely heavily on the fact it is no easy thing to enter the vault from its original entrance, hole in its roof aside. And as the ceiling is now unstable, you would not send men into such a perilous predicament for fear of risking their lives. So it was more a matter of waiting and hoping for the best..."

"Meaning?"

"Mr. Halsey's reasoning was that with the birth of your infant you would be sufficiently distracted to forget about the hole. And by the time you came out of your—um—abstraction, it would be patched up, and the vault would remain unexplored."

Alec's brows lifted slightly. "That, Mr. Jeffries, is wishful thinking at its finest."

"It is indeed, sir."

"So how does one enter this secret vault, if not via the gaping hole in its unstable ceiling?"

Hadrian told him about the bricked-up entrance in the cellars, concealed by an old musty carpet hung on the wall. He described the vestibule to be discovered behind this concealed bricked up entrance, and once in the vestibule, that there was an oak door, bolted and padlocked. And then he told him who held the keys.

Alec huffed his surprise. "The keys are at the chambers of Yarrborough and Yarrborough?"

"Yes, sir. That name was mentioned twice.

"Sir—!" Tam said abruptly, a glance at Hadrian, "As it was your ancestors, and not Mr. Halsey or you who had anything to do with this vault, surely you can leave it be? Just have the roof patched up and the inside left untouched. That way Her Ladyship and everyone else are none the wiser as to what's in there, and you can forget about it being there, too."

Alec smiled at him in understanding. "But it's not that simple, is it? And it was you and Hadrian who told me about the existence of this vault. You came to me, wanting to tell me what Hadrian had overheard in the library, and offering to help me."

"I did, and we did," said Tam. "But—but I don't want you and Mr. Halsey to have a falling out over what must've happened decades, or even centuries ago, and has nothing to do with either of you!"

"Do you think it possible for us to go on living our lives knowing that under our feet there is a vault with—who knows how many bodies, and how those bodies came to be there—just below us?"

Tam shrugged and looked glum. "That's what's been happening for centuries, right up until now, hasn't it? I mean, your ancestors just got on with their lives knowing full well there was a vault under Stone Court, didn't they? And by all accounts they remained unaffected by it, and mayhap that was because they did what they felt was in the best interests of the family and the families here in the district?"

"And that justifies their behavior—that justifies murder? Because it was in their best interests?"

"No! No! Nothing justifies murder!" Tam stated vehemently. "I didn't mean it like that. I don't know what I mean. What I do know is that Mr. Halsey is no murderer. Nor are you, and so it is unfathomable to me that any of your ancestors could be either."

Alec immediately thought of his brother Edward and how easily he had killed his best friend in a duel, and done so without remorse. And then he recalled what his uncle had said to him in the Picture Gallery the previous evening: That some family secrets weren't worth digging up, and certain ancestors had killed themselves, either because they could not bring themselves to continue on a family tradition they had found abhorrent, or they had been struck with remorse for having done so, and gone mad in the process.

"You're right, Tam. Nothing justifies murder. But the only reasons that vault remains a secret are either because my ancestors were too ashamed to admit to the murderous activities of their forebears, or they were murderers themselves and did everything in their power to ensure their unspeakable behavior never saw the light of day. I cannot live with such a secret under my feet, nor can Her Ladyship. Nor will I allow my children to be saddled with an appalling history that was not of their making. They—we all—must be able to live in this house, on this estate, unfettered in mind and body. And, sadly, I think some of my ancestors were not as unaffected by the actions of their forebears as perhaps history would have us believe. Not all walked these halls and courtyards with an easy mind once they knew the family secret and the purpose of that vault."

"Do you think Hugh found out about the vault and that was why he was killed?"

Alec was startled. "Hugh? I have no idea, Tam. But it's a great leap to take to attach Hugh's death in the wood while poaching deer with his friends, with a family vault and who or what may be buried within its walls."

"Unless Hugh discovered something about the vault and was silenced," suggested Hadrian, more to offer support to Tam than he believed there was a connection. "After all he is the son of the steward… Perhaps he overheard a conversation, too—"

"That logic would then suggest either my uncle or his own father killed him to shut him up," Alec replied more harshly than he intended. "They are the only two who know of the vault's existence, according to your own eavesdropping, and so it stands to reason that—"

"Mr. Turner and Mr. Halsey would never commit such a heinous crime!" Tam stated, an angry sidelong glare at Hadrian. "And not against Hugh!"

"You cannot blame Hadrian for extrapolating on an idea that you voiced in the first place," Alec counseled. "And thinking of poor Hugh, I will be late to the stables if I don't finish dressing. But first, I must deal with the vault. And you both can help me—"

"Willingly, sir!" Hadrian and Tam interjected in unison, and then grinned at one another for voicing the same thought.

"Thank you. And for coming to me with this. It took great courage and I will treat what you have told me with the utmost confidence. And I would appreciate you both also keeping this to yourselves. No one is to know what we know. And now I need you both to do something while I'm away from the house this morning. Tam, I want you to deliver a letter to Yarrborough and Yarrborough, and have one of the attorneys accompany you here, and with the keys that unlock the vault door, and any family documents being held at their chambers. Take my town carriage from St. James's Place. It will allow you and the attorney a more comfortable journey upon your return."

"Yes, sir. Happy to oblige. What if Mr. Halsey or anyone else asks why I'm off to London?"

"Surely you have business to conduct with your assistant at your premises in St. James's street? Supplies to procure for the apothecary shelves here perhaps. Plants from the Chelsea physic garden you need to run your eye over before taking them into your possession. I'll leave it to your imagination."

Tam grinned. "No need to use it, sir. As it so happens I have all of those tasks awaiting me."

"If there is nothing specific you wish me to do this morning, sir, I'll get on with assisting Her Ladyship in the library," Hadrian said, helping to shrug Alec into his riding frock coat.

"Ever been down to the laundry?"

Hadrian's back stiffened and his nostrils quivered. Alec saw these signs of affront in the reflection of the looking glass as his valet adjusted the sleeves of his riding frock. And by his grin, Tam saw them too, but he quickly turned his back lest Hadrian did too.

"Well?" Alec asked, meeting his valet's eye in the looking glass. "Have you?"

"No, sir. Phillips and Putnam go to the laundry. I do not."

"You will today—Tam? What's the name of the laundress Roger has his eye on?"

"Sally, sir."

"Hadrian, you will visit the laundry and make Sally's acquaintance. When I return from the wood, you can give me an appraisal of her, and what she knows about Roger, and his whereabouts."

"As you wish, sir."

With his valet momentarily gone from the room, Alec opened the top drawer of his dressing table. He took out his spectacles case and slipped it into a pocket. He then searched deeper in the drawer and removed a small velvet-covered box the size and type which held a ring, and with it, a letter affixed with his seal. He handed both to Tam.

"I was wondering how I would get these to London. Your visit provides the perfect cover. Keep them out of sight until town. Deliver them to the person and direction on the letter, and before your visit to Yarrborough's chambers. And you must place the box and letter into the lady's hands yourself. Insist upon it. No one else is to do it."

Tam nodded, intrigued as to the identity of the lady and what could be in the letter. Never mind the little box. He itched to read the letter's direction, but curbed the instinct to glance down, and quickly put both items in a frock coat pocket. "Yes, sir. You can count on me."

"It is a relief to know I can. You're the only one I do trust with this, Tam."

"Of course, sir. Should I wait for a written reply?"

"No need. As soon as she opens the box you'll know her mind, and she will tell you. Of that I am assured. And, Tam… No one else —and I do mean *no one*—within this house must know of this particular visit."

Tam held Alec's gaze and nodded again. He knew at once to whom he was referring. His Lordship had no wish for his wife to discover that her husband had sent a ring to a mysterious lady in London. Intrigued, Tam could hardly wait to make her acquaintance. And on his ride into Westminster, he was filled with thoughts of her and what would be her reaction to the little box from the Marquess Halsey. As to Alec's connection with this lady, he did not wish to hazard a guess, though he let his mind wander to possibilities, for he was well aware of His Lordship's roguish past and his affairs with a string of beautiful women, here in England and on the Continent. That was all behind him now as a devoted husband and soon-to-be father. Still, speculating on the lady's identity and relationship to His Lordship was a more pleasant way to channel his thoughts and while away the time on horseback than let his mind wander to what unspeakable horrors awaited to be uncovered in the secret vault, or to wonder at the state of his poor cousin Hugh's remains, which were at that very moment being exhumed from a shallow grave of leaves deep in the wood of the Deer Park estate.

SIXTEEN

The boy's body was where the gamekeeper had left it undisturbed the day before, in a shallow depression of leaf litter between a hollow tree log and a rack hacked from a mighty stag. Several hessian sacks secured with stakes covered the body, put there by Adams and his men to ensure the remains were not interfered with or carried off in the night by scavengers.

It was just after dawn. Muted light filtered through tree tops which rustled in a cool morning breeze, and a low mist hung close to well-worn tracks through ancient forest. Birdsong heralded a new summer's day, which would be warm and bright and cloudless. But not for Hugh Turner another summer's day. Three nights had come and gone since he had last tilted his face to warm in the sunshine. Now that young face was discoloring with every hour that passed, and his once thin frame was bloated and starting to decay.

The gentlemen on horseback had dismounted, but they hung back at a respectful distance while Adams, with Paul Turner and Plantagenet Halsey, crossed to the site.

Several of the gamekeeper's men were already in position by the log, ready to do what must be done to remove the body and place it on a canvas litter to return it to the house. But they, too, hung back. All had removed their hats, and kept their heads bowed and their eyes lowered until commanded to do otherwise.

The steward stood tall, eyes front, and walked with a firm tread, as if he were about to inspect a mantrap, not the remains of his dead son. But it took only a glimpse of the well-worn sole of his son's boot, peeking out from beneath the hessian, for Paul Turner to crumple and slump sideways against Plantagenet Halsey. If not for the old man's quick reflexes, the steward would've buckled up and fallen into the leaf litter. Plantagenet Halsey put his arm about him, whispered in his ear, and propped together, they advanced as one to stand beside the gamekeeper. Several seconds passed. There was not a sound but that of birdsong and the barking of the dog pack, and the shouts of men searching the woods for Hugh's missing companions. And then Paul Turner could no longer contain his grief. He threw himself on the sacks and howled like a wounded animal, his agonizing cries piercing the stillness and the hearts of the men gathered around him.

It was almost too much to bear. Yet, bear it they did, with fortitude, for the steward of Deer Park whom they had known all their lives, and for his son who would now be forever young. They possibly would have remained silent and motionless for a lot longer had their solemn reverie not been broken by the approaching search party.

The contingent of laborers and a small band of Alec's outdoor servants were led by a pack of hounds and their handlers, and had fanned out, trudging through the leaves and bracken, kicking up the undergrowth, alert and on the look out for anything unusual. They were still some distance away, yet their movements and noise were close enough to wake into action the men standing about the grieving steward.

It was left to Plantagenet Halsey to coax Paul Turner away from his son so Adams and his men could get on with carefully removing the body for transportation back to the big house. But when the steward was reluctant to allow the men to get on with their tasks, it was Colonel Bailey, not Alec, who stepped forward. He suggested to Alec that they offer their assistance to Plantagenet Halsey.

"We should help your uncle," the Colonel murmured at Alec's ear.

"Yes, we should," Alec replied tersely, gaze on his uncle who was stooped over the distraught steward, a hand to his back. Yet he did not move, and when he did not, the Colonel hesitated.

"My lord, mayhap it would be better for you to approach Turner alone. Turner and I don't see eye-to-eye, and he might not appreciate—"

"Why?" Alec asked, turning his back on the distressing scene and staring hard at the Colonel. "Why doesn't my steward have time for you?"

"Eh? I-I think—*I know*—why. But-but I'd rather not say—not here, not *now* because-because—"

"—he would see your offer of assistance as insincere because you're sleeping with his wife?"

"*What?*" The Colonel could not have been more dazed had Alec punched him between the eyes. "Sleeping with—You think—You think Eliza and I—You think we're—*lovers?*"

"Well? Are you?"

"Oh my God!"

The Colonel covered his face with his hands and turned away. He took a few heavy steps, as if he were wading through the course of a fast flowing river, and staggered away. Alec followed him. Through the branches he caught sight of a cottage. A thin trail of smoke was lazily winding its way out of the single chimney. Reasoning this must be Old Bill's cottage, Alec stepped back over to the magistrate, told Sir Tinsley he and the Colonel were going to call on the cottage's occupant to see what they could find out. Before the magistrate could reply, Alec was gone to rejoin the Colonel, who was still walking towards the cottage. But his hands were no longer covering his face, they were by his side, and they were balled into fists.

"Bailey! Colonel! Wait up!"

The Colonel stopped, but did not turn about.

Alec glanced over his shoulder. Everyone else was occupied, and he and Bailey sufficiently distant so as not to be overheard if they kept their voices lowered. He stepped in front of the Colonel and waited for the man to raise his gaze to his.

"You deny you and Mrs. Turner are lovers?"

The Colonel's jaw set hard, hands still clenched.

"Of course I bloody well deny it!" he hissed through his teeth.

"But—yesterday, at nuncheon—Your behavior, and hers. I'd not have said a word but that display—"

"Bloody fool!"

Alec flinched. "I beg your pardon."

"Not you, my lord. Me. I'm the bloody fool." The Colonel sighed heavily and relaxed his jaw. Something amused him, because he smiled crookedly. He shrugged. "Gave the game away, didn't I? But I couldn't help myself, seeing my poor girl in such distress. Felt it keenly. Too keenly…" He peered at Alec. "Does Mrs. Bailey think Eliza and I are-are—"

"—lovers? Yes. She confided this in Lady Halsey. In fact, it seems she has thought it for some time."

The Colonel nodded unsurprised. "If I'm not mistaken in my memory, I'd say my dear wife could put her finger on the exact date, were a diary presented to her, of when she suspected Eliza and I became—er—lovers. It was her fourteenth birthday—"

"*Fourteen?*" Alec blurted out. He took a step closer and lowered his voice. "You've been visiting Mrs. Turner—"

"—Fisher. She was a Fisher back then. They all were. Yes. Her fourteenth birthday… It was the day my son Daniel was born. They —Eliza and Daniel—share that momentous day." He met Alec's troubled expression with glazed eyes. In his mind's eye he had returned to that day. "It should have been the happiest day of my life—the birth of a son! I should have been with my wife. But I abandoned her and the infant almost at once. All I could think about was Eliza, and what I'd done to her."

Alec did not want to ask, but he did. "What happened to Mrs.— to Eliza?"

"Do you believe me when I say I did not violate that poor girl *in that way?*"

"Yes. Yes, I do," Alec said without hesitation, and because he did believe it.

The Colonel nodded and walked on towards the cottage beside Alec.

"You're a decent man and a gentleman, Halsey. There's not many men in this world who are. But you—your uncle is right in his estimation of your character… Not that I agree with some of your notions—putting a stop to the hunt for one—but that's by the by. Just as I don't see eye-to-eye with much of what Plantagenet rails about, but you're both gentlemen. And as you are, I'm going to tell you what I've never told a living soul because I know you'll keep it to yourself. I don't want Eliza to be caused any grief. She—Eliza—she knows the truth. She's known since her fourteenth birthday. That's when she asked me outright. I could not lie to her. Though I've lied to everyone else. I dare say I'll burn in hell for what I did." Suddenly his shoulders shuddered with silent laughter, and he shook his head. "I'll have plenty of company. The Fivetrees Five'll be joining me!"

They had almost reached the front door to the cottage when Alec stopped and turned, anxious for the Colonel to confide in him before they were interrupted. He regarded the man with a steady expression he hoped masked his apprehension.

"Do you have any idea what I'm blathering about?" the Colonel asked when Alec remained silent.

"I would not be so discourteous as to surmise what it is you wish to confide."

The Colonel nodded and took a deep breath. After all, he did not know what would be the Marquess's reaction to his confession. Though he reasoned the nobleman could think no worse of him, having believed he and Eliza Turner were lovers.

"Every day of her young life I wrestled with my conscience, wondering if I had made the right decision, not by Eliza, but by my forebears, who had sacrificed so much. Was I a coward for allowing her to live when I should have left her out on the hillside to perish as had been done to the generations before her? As had happened to countless daughters and unwanted sons born to the Fivetrees Five. But one look at this tiny creature—flesh and blood of my making— and I knew I had to find another way, a better way. And while I wrestled with my conscience, my prayers were answered. The Fishers came calling."

The Colonel's eyes opened wide. Alec dare not ask who the Fishers were. He knew the man was itching to confess all.

"To this day I do not know how Mrs. Fisher knew my wife had just given birth to a daughter, but she did. Thinking back on it, I suspect the physician who attended my wife's lying-in told her. But I cannot know for certain, and as he has gone to meet his maker, I never will. But the day after my wife gave birth, Mrs. Fisher with three of her five children in tow, arrived at my door seeking shelter. Their cart had broken an axle and the weather was closing in. They were from Delvin—your Deer Park, but there was no chance of making it through the wood to their cottage on such a night. I let them stay in the stables. When they left in the morning Mrs. Fisher took Eliza with her, no one the wiser that there was an extra mouth to feed who had not been with them upon their arrival."

"You gave up your newborn daughter to this Mrs. Fisher?" Alec could hardly believe his own question. He tried to suppress the horror from his tone. "And your wife—what did-what did she think happened to her infant?"

"My wife was told the infant died. Infants die all the time. And so I did what I had to do. The alternative was even more horrifying. Other men, with stronger stomachs and iron wills—my own father— have done what I could not do. I salute them their courage. But I could not. And I do not regret that she lives. I regret that I lied to my dear wife, and that I could not give Eliza the life she deserved as my daughter. But upon my death she will have what is rightfully hers. I am determined it will be so, and so I have assured Paul Turner, though he does not believe me."

"Paul Turner knows you are his wife's father?"

"She told him, and he has kept our secret on her wishes. Though I know he privately has a disgust of me… I do not think she has had an unhappy life, particularly once married to Turner, who, despite his animosity towards me, is a decent man. But this tragedy… The death of Hugh…"

"You said Eliza has known since her fourteenth birthday that you were her father… Who told her? The Fishers?"

"No. No one told her. She's a clever girl. You see, Halsey, there's never been a Mr. Fisher, and yet Mrs. Fisher added regularly to her offspring—offspring that bore no likeness to her or her sister, and who were often too close in age to be born of either woman." He smiled weakly. "And there is the indisputable fact Eliza does have the look of a Bailey."

"Pardon my ignorance, but why did you have to abandon your daughter?"

Surprised, the Colonel stared at Alec as if the answer was self-evident. "The inscription—*Et benedicta tu quae uno filio tantum, non et filiabus nomen tuum.* May you be blessed with one son only, and have no daughters to your name—It's the Fivetrees Blessing. Since the conquest. One son. No daughters. Only then can our estates remain undivided and be passed to an only son."

"By ridding oneself of offspring that are superfluous to require-ments?" Alec stated tongue-in-cheek.

"That's right. You do understand."

But Alec did not understand, and he never would. He could no more abandon a newborn as plunge a dagger into his true love's heart. As for taking away her infant, and letting her believe that infant had died, and allowing her to grieve for all eternity at such an insur-mountable loss? Surely, only a monster was capable of such a wicked and reprehensible act. But regarding the man who stood before him, Alec did not think the Colonel a monster, nor did he think him intentionally evil. He truly did not know what to think, such was his shock. Yet, now the Colonel had unburdened himself, and used the inscription in the market square to justify his actions all those years ago, Alec had a foreboding that there was something, something fundamental and much worse and thoroughly evil, that was being kept from him. He wanted the Colonel to tell him more about the inscription and its links to his abandonment of his daughter, yet knew this was not the time or place for that. But he did ask one ques-tion that was niggling him, one he hoped had a much simpler answer.

"What did you mean when you said Eliza was *a Fisher back then. They all were?*"

"All the infants brought to Mrs. Fisher were given the surname Fisher. Stands to reason, doesn't it?"

"Does it?" Alec asked with a frown. And then his eyes brightened with new knowledge. He glanced at the Colonel. "The inscription— *...and have no daughters to your name...*"

"Eliza could never have my name and be a Bailey. To live she became a Fisher."

"Any unwanted sons and daughters—the ones that were not left to perish on a hill—they were taken in by the Fishers," Alec stated more to himself than to have the Colonel confirm his suspicions. He had a sudden thought. "Tam—Thomas Fisher—the apothecary—"

"He's one of Mrs. Fisher's brats."

"Do you know who are his parents?"

"No one asks, and so no one knows. Only Mrs. Fisher knew. And sometimes she didn't. Just as when infants are abandoned by nameless parents on the parish doorstep. They're taken in, looked after, and most never know where they'd come from, least of all who their father could be."

"How many Fisher children are we talking about?"

The Colonel shrugged. "That's a question none of us can answer. Eliza lived with Mrs. Fisher up until her marriage when she was seventeen. But that's not to say she kept count. And now's not the time to ask her."

"No. It's not," Alec muttered. He asked, though he had already figured the answer, "How did Mrs. Fisher feed and clothe all these children?"

The Colonel smiled crookedly. "The Fivetrees Five made regular donations to the church. There's a special parish fund. Donations were passed on to the Fishers. A salve to the collective conscience!"

"The parish priest was in on this—this—*scheme*?"

"Not my brother-in-law. Purefoy is an odd fish. Vehement in his sermons and zealous about saving his flock from evil, but that's all talk from the pulpit. There's no harm in him. But the vicars before him? They must have known, or how else did all those Fisher children get fed and watered?"

Alec ruminated on this for a moment. "I'm surmising, given the ages of my neighbours and that their offspring are yet to marry, there hasn't been a Fisher born for quite some time?"

"You'd be correct, m'lord." The Colonel permitted himself to smile thinly. "But you're mistaken to think it's only the unwanted offspring of those of us who are married which were taken in by the Fishers. Rumor has it your brother fathered at least two Fishers in his youth—"

"*Edward*? Edward, Earl of Delvin?"

"He is the only brother you have? But as to the number and the names of his brats, your uncle may know."

"I shall add it to my list," Alec quipped; that list was growing by the hour. He had one last question. "What did Mrs. Turner mean yesterday when she shouted at you that 'You're all to blame. Every *damned* one of you.'? I had assumed she was referring to the death of her son—"

"Eliza is right. We are damned. We're damned for what we and our ancestors did to our offspring, and to our wives, and we shall all meet again in he—" said the Colonel, the final word cut off when he was distracted by the cottage door creaking open.

A girl appeared out of the gloom and blinked up at them.

"Ah! Good morning. Be good enough to tell Old Bill—" Alec began. "No! No you don't!"

Alec would've had the door slammed and bolted in his face had he not stuck out a boot and wedged it in the gap between the door and the jam. He then put a shoulder to the wood paneling. The girl didn't have the strength to offer any resistance. She stepped away, and the door swung wide on its rusty hinges and banged against the wall.

A growl came from deep within the cottage.

"Old Bill ain't receivin' visitors!"

SEVENTEEN

THE COLONEL DID NOT FOLLOW ALEC INTO THE COTTAGE. AND when Alec turned to see why he gestured over his shoulder.

"They may need my help…"

"Of course," Alec replied, stooped under the lintel. "I'll rejoin you as soon as I discover what Old Bill knows, or does not. And it goes without saying, but I'll say it anyway: What you confided in me will go no further."

"Thank you, my lord. That would be for the best. Most particularly for Mrs. Bailey. Her mind would surely unravel if she ever found out what I'd—Thank you," he repeated in a mutter, the sadness in Alec's eyes enough to make him swallow hard.

As the Colonel trudged back down the path, Alec entered the cottage. He was pleasantly surprised at how snug it was. And as he adjusted to the low light, a small wooden table by an undraped window came into focus. It was set for a meal, with utensils fashioned from deer antler and a couple of tin plates and mugs. In the center of this arrangement was a crusty loaf of bread partially wrapped in a linen cloth.

"Fresh bread? And stew. Venison?" he asked rhetorically, a glance at the simmering contents of an iron pot suspended over a crackling fire.

"That it is," replied a thin-shouldered young man sitting crossed-legged at the far end of the table. "The best venison to be had from His Lordship's prize herd."

"Then I shall certainly have to taste—"

"Sorry, friend, but there's not enough to go round."

Alec came further into the space and regarded the young man who had not looked up from twirling a small knife with a polished wooden handle, the point of the curved blade anchored in a gnarl in the table top. He was well dressed in a frock coat without darns, and clean knee breeches. And for all the dirt on his boots, they had recently seen polish. He had clean hands that were unused to manual labor, nails short and smooth. So he was not one of Alec's farmhands or an imported worker up at the house. In fact he did not present as a servant at all, and his cadence suggested he'd been educated far from Kent.

"I presume the bread also belongs to His Lordship and is branded with the Halsey cipher?" Alec asked lightly.

"You can't be from around here if you have to ask," the young man replied with a sigh of boredom. His gaze remained fixed on twirling the knife. "But it don't need a cipher to be considered as belonging to His Lordship. That jug by the loaf, it's full of elderflower wine. The elderflowers were picked from hedgerows belonging to His Lordship, and distilled in his distillery. That means it belongs to him, too." He glanced up with a sneer, the knife balanced on its point with one finger. "So in the spirit of full disclosure, all of this was procured without His Lordship's permission. That's generally known as stealing. So if you eat or drink with us, you're stealing too." He went back to spinning the knife.

"Thank you for your honesty, but I'll take my chances—"

"You didn't hear me, friend. I told you: There's not enough to go round."

"There's more than enough in that pot."

The youth slammed the knife on the table, and keeping his hand over it half rose from his chair. "Look, friend—!"

"That's just it. *You* need to look. And I am not your friend—yet."

At that the young man put his buttocks back on the chair with a heavy sigh, and slowly lifted his gaze. As it appeared to be an effort for him to do even this small movement, Alec resisted the urge to smile and roll his eyes at such adolescent behavior. Instead he dropped a disapproving gaze to the dirt floor beneath the lad's feet. To which the young man again sighed and made a fuss of pushing out his stool and reluctantly stretching his legs to stand tall. If he did take a good look at Alec and realize who or what he was, he hid it well with a sneering untroubled half-smile.

But Alec's silent rebuke was about manners and showing respect for an elder, and not, as he suspected the young man supposed, a need for an acknowledgment of his superior societal position. If indeed the lad realised he was in the presence of a nobleman, and not any nobleman, but the lord and master of all he surveyed in any given direction. Alec suspected not, because he kept his hands clasped in front of him, still holding the knife, and did not respectfully lower his gaze, but met Alec's blue eyes squarely, if not as an equal, then as one defying the status quo.

"Just so you aware of His Lordship's views on stealing," Alec said evenly, and ignored the overt insolence when the young man let his mandible drop and his eyes roll back. "If the food taken from his larder, or his distillery, or an animal killed on his estate, is used to feed those under his care who are hungry, that is not stealing. But if that food is stolen to be sold on for profit, or his deer is illegally slaughtered for the mere sport of killing, then yes, that is stealing, and he will prosecute the offenders to the full extent of the law."

Far from being reassured, the young man crossed his arms, glancing across the room before regarding Alec with skepticism. "You'll have to pardon me if I swallow my own tongue in disbelief."

Alec saw the glance and wondered if the young man's bravado was being fuelled by his audience, a girl and a boy huddled together on a cot opposite the table. The girl had opened the door to Alec, and once he stepped inside she had scrambled back to join the boy. Neither had dared make a sound or look up at him, or at the youth with the knife. Alec now wondered if her fear was not because he had come calling, or because of the sounds of activity just beyond the cottage, of the shouts of men and the barking of dogs scouring the woods for two missing village boys, but because this young man was possibly holding them against their will. This gave Alec added incentive to make the youth see reason, and to disarm him of the knife he was jealously guarding.

"What part do you disbelieve?" Alec asked, ignoring the girl and boy for now. "Lord Halsey's views, or that I would know his views?"

"Both. You might be his best friend. I don't know. You're certainly dressed like a lord's best friend. And he might've told you what you just told me, but that would make His Lordship, and me and my ma, the only three on this estate who think that way!"

"*Me and my ma*? I confess to being a little dull at such an early hour. So if you would care to elaborate…"

The young man closed his eyes and swallowed, as if it was the most difficult thing in the world for him to explain himself. Yet a few seconds later he opened his eyes and complied. "Me and my *mother* aren't involved in profiteering at the expense of this estate. No! I stand corrected. Ma's cousin isn't a thief neither, even if he is Lord Halsey's footlicking apothecary."

"I'm pleased to hear it." Alec put up his brows. "What about Lord Halsey? If you're skeptical of his word, then perhaps you think he is caught up in this profiteering venture too?"

The young man blew out his lips, incredulous. "Now I know you're funning with me! Are you sure you're his friend?" he added, staring hard at Alec. "Because if my cuz is to be believed His Lordship is the most self-righteous gent this side of the Atlantic! Besides, what has he to gain from poaching his own deer and selling it on? It don't make sense."

"He could be saying one thing and doing another?" Alec suggested lightly.

"What d'you mean?"

"He could be turning a blind eye—"

"Like the old man?"

"Old man?"

"His uncle."

There was a slight pause before Alec asked for confirmation.

"Plantagenet Halsey is turning a blind eye to poaching on the estate?"

Without hesitating the young man nodded.

"So my ma says. She says His Majesty made Lord Halsey a lord, but around here it's the old man who is lord of all he surveys."

"If, as your mother says, Plantagenet Halsey is lord of this estate in everything but name, why would he turn a blind eye to poaching?"

The young man shrugged and pulled a face. "Perhaps he ain't blind. Perhaps like your Lord Halsey he don't consider killing to feed oneself poaching. That's what my br—that's what's said in the village.

"But your mother still doesn't approve of Plantagenet Halsey?"

"She's none too happy that the old man has my pa in his pocket. She says if His Lordship ever gets a sniff of what's going on under his fine nose, it will be Pa for the gallows, not Mr. Plantagenet Halsey esquire."

"To be clear, you're saying His Lordship's uncle and most of the inhabitants of Fivetrees are neck-deep in illegal pursuits?"

"*Illegal pursuits*? If that's a fancy way of saying poaching and thievery, then yes." The young man leaned in and said confidentially, jabbing his finger on the table to punctuate his point. "And if His Lordship has a mind to put a stop to it then he'd not only have to round up the entire village, but those self-seekers who pretend to be law-abiding citizens. I tell you, that lot are the worst offenders, and *they* should be the ones who need prosecuting, not the villagers who do their bidding. As if the poor can stand up to the likes of them? As if any of us can!" He scoffed. "Pretending to be upright members of society when they're the ones running the *illegal pursuits*, and so making the greatest profits—"

"Besides Plantagenet Halsey, do you know which upright members?"

The youth blinked, suddenly wary.

"Why? Who wants to know?"

Alec kept his features neutral and forced himself not to smile, because the young man's earnestness reminded him of his uncle. It was refreshing to see such moral outrage in one who was barely out of his teens. He met the lad's frown with a look of enquiry and said equably,

"I want to know. And I agree with you. If, as you say, these upright members of society are engaged in profiteering at His Lordship's expense, then they are not upright at all, are they? They're not only setting a bad example for those who look up to them for guidance, but they are stealing and should be brought to justice."

The young man was not to be so easily convinced. While he was elated to be taken seriously and made to feel his opinion had worth, and by someone who dressed and sounded like a lord, he was wise to the ways of the world. Men who called themselves gentlemen, who were born of a certain class, who were related by birth and wealth and land ownership, they stuck together. Any accusations of wrongdoing were taken care of within their own ranks, if taken care of at all. And if those accusations came from outside their ranks, they were not given due consideration or were dismissed without those wanting justice receiving satisfaction. So it was pointless to seek justice in the first place. He might rail against what was going on at Fivetrees and be bitter about it and wish something could be done, but he wasn't prepared to stick his neck out. Because speaking up meant speaking out against the local magistrate, and Sir Tinsley would sooner have him strung up as be uncovered as a self-serving mountebank.

And so he had told his brother. He had warned Hugh time and again that no amount of protest would see a change for the better for the poorest inhabitants of Fivetrees because the local magistrate, the old man, and Adams, not to mention their own pa, were the ringleaders. They would never be hauled up before the Assizes for any wrongdoing. If Hugh made a fuss, the only ones who would be punished were those he sought to champion. Not that he cared tuppence for the vagrants and travelers who eked out an existence in this wood. But Hugh had cared, not only about poaching and thievery and the mistreatment of the poorest wretches, but the hypocrisy of their so-called betters. And where had his protests got him? Dead at thirteen and his mother's heart broken.

He didn't want to think of Hugh, or his mother's heartache, or the murderous fiend who had slit his little brother's throat and left him to drown in his own blood, alone and terrified. But he wanted vengeance and Hugh's killer brought to justice, and Sally's brother Nic was going to tell all he knew, because he'd been with Hugh, so he knew something. But if Nic kept his mouth shut, then he could go hungry and they'd all stay here in this cottage until they starved and rotted away.

And suddenly he wasn't thinking of Hugh at all when a hand gently pressed his shoulder and told him to sit. And so he sat. A fine white linen handkerchief was pressed into his hand and he was told to wipe his face. And so he wiped his face not realizing it was damp. And within a few quiet moments, while he calmed listening to the spit and crackle of the fire, a bowl of stew and a fist of bread was put before him. No one had to tell him to eat.

He was starving, and spooning up the meaty stew before he realized his tirade had not remained in his head, but had been said aloud, and to the gentleman who now sat opposite him sipping elderflower wine from a mug.

"I must compliment my cook," Alec said, finding the wine surprisingly delicate and refreshing. "This is excellent."

He glanced over at the cot. The girl and boy were eating hungrily, enjoying the thick meaty broth and fluffy white bread. But considering what was going on just beyond the cottage door, Alec had no appetite, and had declined an offer of a bowl of stew. He accepted the wine as a courtesy, and over the mug he addressed the girl.

"Were you the one who brought the stew and wine from the big house?" When she swallowed quickly and nodded without hesitation, he added with a smile, "And are you the Sally who works in my laundry?"

EIGHTEEN

THE GIRL'S BROWN EYES WIDENED, AND SHE SHOT A LOOK AT the young man at the table before again nodding mutely. Never in all her days would she have dreamed of being spoken to by their lord and master, and here in Old Bill's cottage of all places! And she could have been knocked over by a puff of smoke to think His Lordship knew her name.

Of course she knew who *he* was. What she couldn't fathom was that Roger Turner, the smartest boy of her acquaintance, who had attended university and would one day be steward of this estate, had not the faintest notion that the stranger who had come calling was in truth Lord Halsey. She recognised him on sight, because she had once had to present herself to His Lordship's valet, who had specific instructions about the care of His Lordship's linens. None of the other laundry maids had been brave enough to go, but Sally was inquisitive. She had not even minded being berated by Mr. Jeffries, not when it gave her the opportunity of a lifetime to be in such magnificent surroundings. And then His Lordship had strolled into the closet dressed as he was now. She had stared. She could not help herself. But what surprised her most was that he apologized for intruding and left without a word spoken to Mr. Jeffries. She couldn't even recall how the interview ended, for she was downstairs sitting at the kitchen table with a lemon cordial relating to the cook all that had happened, before she came to her senses, wondering if it was a dream.

But she wasn't dreaming now, and she couldn't afford to be. She had to protect her brother. Nic's life depended on it.

"And your companion—this is your brother?" Alec asked. He smiled when the girl instinctively leaned into the boy. "You share the same nose and coloring. He could of course, be your cousin—"

"Brother!" Sally blurted out, then added in a less strained tone, "Nic's m'brother, m'lord. He's nine. He's too afeared to speak. He ain't said a word since it happened. So you'll have to pardon his manners."

"Nic had best start remembering his manners," the young man threatened. "And that he's got a tongue! Or I might have to make him remember!"

He went to snatch up the knife to flourish it about, but it was no longer on the table. He frowned, wondering where it had got to. Perhaps he had dropped it. But one swift glance across the table and he saw that Alec now held the knife. He blushed scarlet. Disarmed in more ways than one, he hated to admit it, but he was glad he no longer had it. He wasn't about to hurt Nic, and he didn't want to scare or disappoint Sally. But someone had to do something to get Nic to talk. He sat back and crossed his arms and pretended offence; it wouldn't do to show further weakness in Sally's eyes. He'd already blubbered like a baby as it was, and how did a man ever recover from that?

"Has Nic been at Old Bill's cottage since *it* happened?" Alec asked the girl, surmising that the 'it' was the death of Hugh, and after the young man's tearful confession knew that Sally's brother was the third boy of the trio who had gone missing. When Sally nodded, he asked, "And aside from losing his manners and his voice, has he suffered any physical injury?" When Sally shook her head, he smiled, a glance at her brother. "I'm pleased to know that."

Alec then made a show of shifting on his chair to look about the small room before turning his attention to the young man whom he now knew, and had assumed almost from the moment he had stepped into the cottage, was his steward's son, and Hugh Turner's elder brother, Roger. "As this is Old Bill's cottage, are you Old Bill?"

"*Me*? Old Bill?" The young man snorted. "You must need spectacles if you think—"

"As it so happens, I do wear spectacles. For reading, and any close work. But I see you clearly enough, Roger Turner." Adding with a crooked smile when the young man gave a start, was about to protest, but then closed his mouth tight. "But it was you, was it not, who growled out pretending to be Old Bill?"

"Aye, it was," Roger said with a sheepish grin. "To warn you off."

"Why?"

"Why what?"

"Nic isn't the only one to have lost his manners," Alec murmured, adding firmly, "Why what—*sir*."

"But you're Lord Halsey, and I should address you as m'lord at the very least."

"So now we've established who we are, if I feel so inclined, I am perfectly within my rights to tell you to address me as 'sir', as your cousin Tam does. But if you want to be exactingly formal—"

"No. No. I'll do as you request—sir," Roger said, as if it was being forced upon him. The fact that he sat up taller and could not keep the smile off his face to think he was being give the same privilege as his cousin told a different story.

"Why warn me off?" Alec repeated.

Rather than answer the question, Roger said, "I gather from your enquiry, sir, that you've no notion there is no such personage as Old Bill?"

"That's correct. I did not," Alec replied truthfully. "More to the point, if I did know no such personage existed, why would I be warned off by you pretending to be Old Bill? Surely that would only intrigue me further to find out who was impersonating a phantom?"

That made the young man shake his head in recognition of Alec's logic. He confessed.

"There was an Old Bill. Pa said there's been an Old Bill at this cottage for over two hundred years or more. A'course not the same man, obviously. But men calling themselves Old Bill came and went. The last Old Bill died twenty-odd years ago."

"Do you know why the last Old Bill wasn't replaced?"

"Can't rightly say—"

"A bright lad like you, and a university graduate? I'm sure you could give me at least an educated guess."

"If you want my expert opinion, sir, that opinion is I don't rightly know why the last Old Bill wasn't replaced. But after traipsing behind Adams and his sluggards for a month or more, I got a fair idea of what was goin' on here at the cottage. And all I needed to do to confirm my suspicions was to go rummaging through the implements stored out in a hut out in the backway—"

"The *backway?*"

"There's a yard behind the cottage," Roger explained. "That's called a backway down here in Kent. Anyway, as I was saying… There's a hut in the backway and it's kept padlocked. One day it wasn't, so I sneaked a look. There's a chain and hook and a draining pit—"

"A makeshift game larder, like the one at the far end of the kitchen gardens?"

"Yes, that's exactly what it is. But this one's not brick with a fancy roof and a tiled floor, like the one up at your house. You'd not know what it was but a tumbledown hut from the outside, but inside it has everything you need to cut up a carcass."

"We don't need to think too hard where our poachers got their hands on the equipment… So when a deer is brought down without permission, it comes here to be cut up and moved on for sale?"

"That's my reckoning of it. And I reckon Old Bill was the butcher in the operation."

"That's what I think too," mused Alec, suddenly and over-whelming mentally tired.

His day had begun before sunup with Tam and Hadrian telling him about his murderous ancestors, and the possibility of there being bodies in a sealed vault beneath Stone Court, and that his uncle was doing his best to keep this from him. Then the Colonel made the astonishing confession that Mrs. Turner was in truth his daughter, whom he had disowned as an infant and placed in the care of a Mrs. Fisher, a woman who made a habit of taking in unwanted infants and bringing them up as her own. And then there was the horrific death of Hugh Turner. What type of monster slit a boy's throat and cut off his hand, and the hand of his friend? Rampant poaching and stealing seemed the least of his worries.

But his most immediate concern was keeping these children safe. They could not remain here at Old Bill's cottage, yet he did not know whom he could trust. If Roger was to be believed, then he certainly could not trust the men presently in the wood. He wondered if the Colonel had told the others Old Bill's cottage was occupied. The plume of smoke from the chimney was indication enough, but not precisely who was in residence. And it was only a matter of time before those involved in the cutting up and distribution of illegal venison returned with a fresh carcass.

Alec was about to ask Roger how often poachers came to the cottage when a persistent thumping on the door had the children holding their breath. And then Roger and Sally entreated Alec not to let whoever it was inside, and most definitely not to alert them that Sally's brother had been found, she pleading,

"Please, m'lord, please don't let 'em in. I beg o' you! Nic's afeared. His brain's addled. But he'll come right. But the men out there—

"—are looking for Nic, like they're looking for Will," Roger Turner interrupted.

Alec reassured them no harm would come to Nic, or to any of them. They were under his protection. He was lord and master at Deer Park. No one else. Everyone answered to him. This calmed them sufficiently that they nodded their understanding. They expected him to send whoever it was banging on the door on their way. And Alec was about to do just that when he had an idea...

He asked Roger to open the door. The youth hesitated, frowning, and stood his ground. But at Alec's smile of encouragement he finally trudged across and yanked it open. Without looking up, he stood back and let the visitors enter.

Alec's gaze was on Nic. The boy did not disappoint.

ℋ

COLONEL BAILEY, PAUL TURNER, AND ADAMS THE GAMEKEEPER entered the cottage on a stride, then stopped as one. Turner instantly saw his son and would have gone to him, but a lifetime of deference held him back. He removed his cap and waited for Alec. The steward looked to have aged ten years; his face was drawn, gray eyes vacant, and he was hunched as if in pain. It was too much for Roger, who pushed past the Colonel and threw his arms around his father to be gathered up in a loving embrace.

"We've located the other bod—" the Colonel started to tell Alec, then stopped. He had been about to say body, but with the Turners within earshot he thought better of it, and came over to Alec and continued in an under-voice. "He was found by a fallen log. Piece of branch straight through his eyesocket—"

"Jesu…" Alec muttered, wiping a gloved hand over his mouth and briefly closing his eyes. "That's what killed him?"

"Aye. Looks as if he tripped and fell."

"Possibly while he was fleeing… And his hand?"

"Missing."

Alec was taken aback. "Removed after he was impaled?"

"Looks that way. Both bod—boys are being taken to the Turner house. Sir Tinsley and Dr. Riley have been sent for. I offered to go with them, but Turner is in the right. Mrs. Turner doesn't need a houseful. I'll be returning to Mrs. Bailey. She'll be wanting news… I trust Your Lordship will let me know if and when there are any developments."

Alec nodded, keeping Nic and Sally in his peripheral vision. Neither had moved. More importantly, Nic had not reacted to the presence of Adams, Turner, or the Colonel. The boy remained listless beside his sister. If he did anything, it was to snuggle closer. His lack of response was a relief. Had he reacted to their presence in any other way but as he had just now, had he shown fear, or been terrified, Alec may have been closer to knowing the killer's identity. But he was not, and so he must look elsewhere. He hoped also that with Nic and his sister back at the house and feeling safe, the boy's tongue would loosen and he'd be able to tell him what he had seen while out in the wood with his companions.

Alec hated himself for thinking the worst of these men, that one of them might be a killer. But after today's revelations he wasn't even sure he knew his own uncle—the man had raised him and he loved him as a father. They had spent almost every day of the first twenty years of his life together, and yet it was as if the Plantagenet Halsey he knew in London was a different Plantagenet Halsey to the one everyone on the estate and the Fivetrees community looked to for direction. That Plantagenet Halsey was a stranger to Alec. And that singular thought made him miserable.

It must have shown on his face, or in his eyes, because when his uncle hailed him from the doorway with an expectant smile and he did not react, the old man's smile dropped, and so did his gaze.

He joined him by the cot and smiled at the boy and girl, saying in a friendly tone, "I trust Master and Miss Fisher have been behavin' themselves in His Lordship's company?"

"Fisher? Why does that not now surprise me?" Alec muttered. "We became acquainted over a bowl of venison stew," he added audibly. "So well acquainted in fact that Sally and her brother Nic are returning to the big house as my guests. If you wouldn't mind taking Sally up with you, Uncle, I'll take Nic. That's if you're not wanted by the Turners?"

"No. I'll ride back with you. But you'll be needed over at the steward's later on, or you can always send for Dr. Riley and Ferris—"

"Yes," Alec replied more tersely than he intended. He glanced at Nic and then back at his uncle. "And now all three boys have been located, the search can be called off."

The old man knew at once to what Alec alluded—that Nic was the third boy who had been out with Hugh and Will that fateful morning—and he opened wide his eyes in understanding. When his name was called, he glanced over his shoulder. It was the steward. But he hesitated, a sheepish glance at Alec.

"Please. Go to him," Alec said with sympathetic smile. "He needs you. He's a father who's just lost his son, and in the most appalling of circumstances."

Plantagenet Halsey nodded but he did not move. He held Alec's gaze . "Aye. There's nothin' on this earth more agonizin' than the loss of a child."

"You missed a word between *the* and *loss—unintentional.*"

The old man's eyes went dull, and his tone lost its warmth. "I told you how it would be. I told you knowin' would change everythin' between us, and it has." He threw up a hand in dismissal. "It ain't your fault, it's mine. So be it." He dropped his chin. "Excuse me, my lord."

With a sudden dryness in his throat, Alec watched Plantagenet Halsey return to Paul Turner's side, and with Roger between them, they left the cottage. He had no idea how dazed he was by his uncle's comment until a tug on his sleeve had him looking down. It was Sally, and she was smiling shyly up at him.

"Did you mean what you said, m'lord, about Nic and me bein' your guests?" When he nodded, she said naively, "I'm only sorry we're not in our Sunday best for you and Her Ladyship."

For some unknown reason—he wasn't sure if it was the girl's trusting smile or her disappointment in failing him, or a delayed reaction to his uncle's coldness—but his chest tightened and he felt an overwhelming responsibility, not only for this girl and her brother, but for making things right with the world on his estate, most importantly for his family, and between him and his uncle. And with this feeling came the need to return to Selina, to reassure himself she was well, and so, too, their unborn child. More than anything, he wanted an hour's respite with her alone, knowing the planets of that small domestic world were in alignment, even if everything else around them was in chaos.

NINETEEN

It was certainly chaos, but a well-ordered chaos, upon their return to the stables. Stable boys ran every which way, riders dismounted, horses were taken to their stalls, and the pack rounded up by their handlers to be returned to the kennels to be watered and fed. In amongst all this frenzied activity, and to one side of the wide expanse of stableyard, was the mud-spattered and dusty traveling coach of the Duchess of Romney-St. Neots; grooms unhitching weary horses, their hooves inspected by the estate farrier before being led away. And doing his best not to be in the way of handlers and animals was Hadrian Jeffries.

He came across to where Alec and his uncle with the two children had dismounted, and gave his master the cryptic news that the men were assembled and awaiting his presence. Alec knew what he meant by this. Before heading off for the wood, he had left Hadrian with several tasks, one of which was having Stephens the foreman select five of his strongest laborers and the tools necessary to demolish a brick wall. After breakfast they were to go down to the cellar. These men were there now. The dank carpet covering the particular part of the brick wall to be assessed had been taken down. If His Lordship would care to join them at his earliest convenience…

Alec did. And he wanted to make sure the men got on with that job before he welcomed his newly-arrived guests. But first he had to make sure Sally and her brother were cared for, and he wouldn't leave them with just any servant, not with the boy still mute with fear.

"If you're needed elsewhere, I'll see them safely to the servant hall," Plantagenet Halsey offered, ignoring the fact he had interrupted a conversation between master and servant that, by Alec's frown, was not meant for his ears. Masking his sadness with a smile, he said to the boy and girl, who stood so close to Alec's back he wouldn't have been surprised to find them clutching at the skirts of his frock coat, "Guests of His Lordship need to be clean, which means it's a scrub in a tub of soapy water for the two of you, and no argument." He looked to Alec. "Mrs. Dawson can find clean linens for them too." He jerked his head in direction of the traveling coach. "Best if they remain belowstairs for the time being; and you never know what I might get out of 'em on the way up to the house…"

"If anyone can extract chatter out of a child, it's you," Alec said with a smile. "You have a knack for making children comfortable."

The old man wanted to quip that he wished he hadn't lost that knack with *him*, but he just smiled and nodded and silently watched Alec stride off across the courtyard with Hadrian Jeffries at his side and his greyhounds loping at his heels. He must have stood there a good few minutes, because master, servant, and dogs reappeared making their way across the sloping lawn up to the house. They did not head towards the archway that housed an external stairwell giving access to the apartments Alec shared with his wife, but to the archway under the Nursery Gallery that went through to Stone Court. Which made him wonder if more of the flagging had collapsed into the vault below.

His first thought was to send word to Turner to make sure the men remained vigilant, that Alec continue to believe it was too dangerous to investigate the hole. And then he remembered the steward was mourning the loss of his youngest son, a boy of thirteen who'd had his throat cut. That tragic circumstance suddenly brought everything into perspective. The anxiousness drained from him, leaving him curiously numb. And just as poor Hugh Turner had been unable to fend off his attacker, Plantagenet Halsey realized he could not fend off fate. Nor could he control it where Alec was concerned —not any longer. Ironically, the tables had turned. His fate, the fate of Deer Park, the future of the Halseys, now rested not with him, but with his nephew—*his nephew*! He shook his head. He had been lying to himself and everyone else for so many years now that he had convinced them and him the lie was true. That, too, was now out of his control.

He took the brother and sister by the hand and left the stables to enter the house where every Halsey heir had been born since Henry Tudor's time. Only this time he gave himself permission to enter it without a care in the world. The woman he loved was waiting for him, and, he thought with a chuckle, waiting to berate him—let the verbal sparring begin!

THE CELLAR WAS DARK, DANK, AND COLD ENOUGH TO KEEP ICE blocks from melting. But in the farthest corner, beyond the barrels, boxes, and rows of wine bottles, there were enough flambeaux burning to light up the area like a summer's day. Stephens was still in his coat, but his men had stripped to their shirtsleeves with various implements at their feet. They stepped aside, removing their caps, when Alec approached with Hadrian Jeffries.

The foreman gave Alec an assessment of the brick wall, now the carpet had been removed. It was his opinion there were two courses of bricks for most of its length, except for the section covered by the carpet, the small size of the bricks and the type of mortar attested to this. What was immediately apparent to Alec, with no need for Stephens to point it out although he did, was that the carpet only managed to partially cover the bricked-up archway. As to when the archway had become a wall, Stephens would hazard a guess this occurred no earlier than the turn of this century, and possibly as late as last Tuesday. The latter was a lame attempt at humor, that had his men chuckling out of politeness, and Alec nodding, such was his abstraction. Stephens coughed and dropped the levity,

"Though it is beyond me to speculate why the carpet was nailed here at all, my lord, because, as we can all see, the archway and the brickwork extend above and below it."

"Perhaps it wasn't meant to conceal but to indicate the entrance to the room beyond?" Alec opined, smoothing a gloved hand lightly over a section of wall where old brick met new. "One flambeau doesn't cast much light, but it would quickly show up the difference between brickwork and a tapestry…"

"Aye, it would that. And be more inviting than, say, a black hole some men might be afraid to enter," Stephens agreed. "The carpet could've served as a curtain of sorts."

Alec looked about him, spied the carpet discarded over by a wooden door, and went over to it, one of the laborers following behind with a flambeau. He nudged the tapestry pile with the toe of his boot. "I want this rolled up carefully and taken to the laundry. The women maybe able to do something to rid it of mould."

The rest of the men came forward, and two pulled the carpet flat on the flagging in preparation to roll it up and take it away. They hesitated when Hadrian Jeffries, who had come across to stand by Alec, went on his haunches by the carpet. He indicated for one of the men to bring a flambeau closer so he could better see. There was mould in places, and it was filthy, but there was enough of the color and metal to the threads to shine through the filth for Hadrian to instantly recognize the pattern. He felt the cloth between his fingers, then stood, satisfied.

"Sir, I've seen this before. Not this particularly, but a gouache painting of it in a folder about your family's history. Her Ladyship was perusing the folder the other day and remarked upon it. This isn't a carpet but a baldachin—a canopy cloth."

He returned to his haunches beside Alec, who was inspecting the cloth through his eyeglasses, one of the laborers close with a flambeau. Something glittered in the weave, and Hadrian continued.

"I remember it particularly because Lady Halsey read out the inscription. It said the canopy was specially made for the royal visit of Queen Elizabeth to this house. And that it was used again when Queen Anne paid a visit the year after she ascended the throne."

"And you called it a-a baldachin?"

"That's right, sir. Lady Halsey told me a baldachin is a special canopy that is suspended over a throne, and that this one was used with the Delvin Settee, which can be found in the Great Hall."

"So the house has its own throne… Dear me, Mr. Halsey won't like that at all!" Alec waved the laborer away and stood, and his valet did likewise. "But I dare say he wouldn't mind that it ended up here, in the cellars. Though what Her Ladyship intends to do with it now it's found, is anyone's guess."

"Perhaps for the next royal visit?"

"God forbid, Hadrian! Still, we had best save it, as it is part of the house's history. You go with the men to the laundry and explain its significance, so they take special care with it."

"Yes, sir. I know where the laundry is now—"

"Good. But Sally wasn't there, was she? Though she has since been found. And no need for you to return here. I'm sure you've got enough to do, now there is a houseful of guests. And I had best be getting back upstairs," he added, turning to address Stephens. "I'm assuming you're confident you can remove the bricks from the archway without disturbing the rest of the wall or the roof?"

"Aye, my lord. There'll be no problem with it. And it won't take much effort. The mortar is very poor. I'd say the archway was bricked up in a hurry. But we'll take our time as we don't know what's behind it, if that is agreeable to Your Lordship."

"Yes. Do. And I'm reliably informed there is a vestibule on the other side of that archway, and beyond that a heavy oak door with a padlock that opens into the room whose roof has collapsed above in Stone Court."

"When we make it through to the door, do you want us to break the padlock?"

"No need. I'll have the keys in the next day or two. And until then, I want this demolition kept between us, here. Post two men at the entrance to the cellars at all times. No one is to come in here. And I do mean no one—my family included."

"Very good, my lord. There were two lads guarding the cellar's entrance when we came down here but they soon scampered away when we showed them our—um—muscle."

"On whose orders?"

"Mr. Turner had them guard the entrance, my lord."

"My steward and his men won't bother you further. And Turner has other concerns occupying his time at the moment."

"We heard about his wee son, my lord, and are all very sorry for his loss. I trust I might take the time out of my day to pay our respects at the funeral…?"

"Yes. Yes, of course. That is a touching gesture, Stephens. Thank you. Oh, and Stephens, should you find anything other than an empty vestibule and a padlocked wooden door behind that wall, however trivial you may think the find, send for me at once."

With that, Alec called his greyhounds to heel and returned to ground level. He thought about taking the stairs up to his private apartments to change out of his riding habit. But he had sent Hadrian off to the laundry, and he did not want to keep his guests waiting. More importantly he could not leave Selina in the company of her brother, not even for an hour. If anything or anyone could bring on an early labor, it was Clive, Lord Cobham.

But he was pleasantly surprised to find the members of his extended family enjoying a convivial morning of tea and cakes in the Great Hall.

Selina had her stockinged feet resting on a velvet-upholstered footstool, the habitual hand smoothing her round belly. Their newly-arrived guests had been divested of traveling cloaks and hats and were lounging about on the sofas and chairs arranged around the giant hearth that did not have a fire in its grate for the first time this wet hot summer. They were drinking tea and nibbling on strawberry tarts. His godmother, the Duchess of Romney-St. Neots, her daughter the Lady Sybilla, and his brother-in-law and head of the Foreign Department, Lord Cobham, his mouth stuffed with tart, were all waiting to greet him.

TWENTY

"OH, MY BOY, YOU'RE HERE AT LAST!" OLIVIA ST. NEOTS
announced, up off her chair. She swept up to Alec in a rustle of
painted cotton petticoats, matching mules clacking on the stone flagging as she left the oriental rug, and met him halfway across the
cavernous space. And there she forestalled him, a hand to the front of
his buff linen waistcoat. "I've done all I can to steer the conversation
away from the reason for Cobham's visit," she told him in an undervoice, up on tiptoe to receive his kiss. "But Selina is too bright for her
own good. And Cobham is as thick as an old oak, so he's going to
blurt out the lot if I don't keep his mouth stuffed with those most
excellent strawberry delights."

"I applaud your ingenuity, my dear Olivia," Alec replied with a
grin. "But the outcome was inevitable the moment you allowed him
into your carriage. It's done, and I will deal with the consequences as
best I can."

"Of course you will. You always know what to do, but—" She
eyed him speculatively. "You think it wise for your very pregnant wife
to know just who is anxiously awaiting you in London?"

Alec patted her bejeweled hand. "Wise? I had no idea that word
was still in your lexicon, what with you now openly entertaining an
avowed republican—"

"Entertaining?" She snorted, dots of color in her cheeks, and
grumbled, "It's nothing of the sort! It's—it's—"

"—none of my business. And you are within your rights to tell me so." He drew her hand up to kiss it. "Thank you for making the journey. We'd both be lost without you—without you and Sybilla. Selina will be less fretful now you're here."

The Duchess smiled bravely.

"You must not fret either. Every female's first birth is the most traumatic because there are so many unknowns. What I do know is that she and the babe will pull through this; I am determined."

"I believe you, Olivia. But it does not make me any less fretful. For Selina's sake I do my best to appear confident. And to be entirely truthful, I've been keeping my mind off her confinement with an entirely selfish worry. I should put it out of my mind until after the birth. Nothing should cloud our happiness, but I've been thinking back on my mother's confinement, and I have this foreboding…"

"Foreboding?" asked the Duchess, trying to appear as if she had no idea to what he was alluding.

But she could not fool Alec. The corner of his mouth twitched at her play-acting.

"Your republican beau confessed to snatching me away from my mother, but he has refused to tell me why. But you know why, don't you?"

The Duchess did her best to remain impassive. Plantagenet had confided in her about his sad history and Alec's birth, and she had sobbed in his arms, long and hard until her lungs ached. He did not spare her even one morsel of detail, such was his need for a confessional. They had been aboard ship, on the return journey to England from Denmark. She had not cried like that in many decades, and she hoped she never would again.

"Yes," she confessed, and when Alec nodded added, "But I made a vow to your—to Plantagenet, and I cannot break it, not even for you."

"Nor should you. But he can't be a coward all his life. He should tell me to my face rather than leave it to me to put the pieces of the puzzle together."

"I agree, and so I told him—Not that he was a coward, because he is not. He is the bravest man I know—you both are. But he is also infuriatingly idealistic and stubborn! Damn him!"

She bustled away, head bowed, leaving him stranded in the

middle of the oriental rug. He was not alone for long. Lady Sybilla came across and presented her upturned flushed cheek. And Lord Cobham swallowed down the last of a tart, and brushed his sticky fingers on his breeches to offer him his outstretched hand.

Alec joined his wife by the fireplace and stooped to kiss her forehead, saying near her ear, "Forgive me for coming straight from the stables and not changing before joining you."

"You're here. That's all that matters," she murmured. "Besides," she added with a cheeky smile, "you are most desirable when disheveled—"

"Selina!" he hissed, embarrassed. The color in his cheeks glowing when she giggled behind her fan. "Behave, madam wife!"

"Or what, my lord? You'll have your way with me? I wish! *That* is a distant memory."

He flicked out the skirts of his riding frock to sit on the footstool, and put her stockinged feet on his lap. "Hardly distant, my love," he contradicted with a knowing smile, and lightly squeezed her toes.

Selina was about to make a further quip and thought better of it, her smile dropping into a frown of concern at the tiredness in his eyes.

"Are you all right? I should have asked at once, and I wasn't being insensible but doing my best to take your mind away from this morning's awful events. And it was awful, wasn't it? Did you—did you find what you were looking for?"

"We did. And I will be fine directly."

She did not ask him to elaborate, wondering if he was withholding details because of her pregnancy. At any other time she would have insisted he tell her, but she was mindful and so did not ask.

"Of course… But where's your uncle?" she asked, changing the subject, and loud enough for the others to hear.

"He'll be here as soon as he's settled our other guests—two children from the village. They need a bath and fresh clothing."

"Village brats?" Cobham gawped, bushy red eyebrows shooting skywards. "What? No parents?"

"Not that I am aware."

Lord Cobham was skeptical. "Umph! Likely story! Beggars! Take my advice, Halsey. Charity begins at home, your home, with your family. Not with some nameless beggar's brats wheedlin' their way into your good graces. They'll start in the kitchen, eat you out of produce and preserves, and next thing you know they've found their way upstairs and are ransacking the good linen and making off with the silverware. Start this sort of thing, Halsey, and they'll be no stoppin' the hoards. Word will go out you're simple."

"*Simple?*"

The word was uttered in horror by all three ladies present, which considerably lightened Alec's mood. He took no offence at his brother-in-law's unwanted homily, and to divert him from providing more thoroughly pointless advice, he asked him about the journey from London. It was the last thing he wanted to hear, Cobham being a thoroughly dull conversationalist. But with his brother-in-law droning on about every mile traveled, Alec hoped to have some respite from thinking at all. He was quite adept at knowing when to nod and look as if he were taking an interest. It was a skill he had perfected while a junior minister in the Foreign Department and been forced to listen to the pontificating monologues of elder statesmen who did not want advice, just a sycophantic audience.

Alec also knew his wife. Selina was putting on a brave performance of sisterly rectitude, but it could not last. Being heavily pregnant no doubt accounted for her uncharacteristic charitable complacency. But when she had flinched at his suggestion, he knew that five minutes into Cobham's travel monologue and she would be scratching the thread from the upholstery. Ten minutes and she'd bring it to an abrupt end by using her pregnancy as an excuse to escape, taking her aunt and cousin with her to her sitting room, to talk all things infant and birth related. He would be abandoned to entertain Cobham on his own, a justifiable punishment in her eyes for giving her brother free rein to blather on.

It was the outcome Alec was counting on because he could then whisk Cobham away to the privacy of the library. There they would have the conversation Cobham, as Head of the Foreign Department, had come all the way from London into Kent to have with him at His Majesty's behest.

But Alec's best-laid plans were upset by the Lady Sybilla. When Lord Cobham had to stop mid-sentence to take a breath or faint from lack of air, she saw it as her opportunity to contribute to the monologue.

"Lina, you'll never guess whom we encountered on the outskirts of Fivetrees," she said breathlessly, a glance at Alec.

"I won't try, so tell me," Selina replied, fingers hard gripping the chair arm. But when Alec winked at her, she pulled a face at him and did her best to ease the tension her brother always managed to induce in her.

"The boy apothecary who was once Lord Halsey's valet. Terrence Fisher, or is it Theodore?"

"Thomas Fisher. But we call him Tam," Selina corrected, adding with a quizzical frown when Alec remained silent, "Are you certain it was Tam because he is staying here with us—"

"Oh, yes, very sure, Lina. I recognized him upon first glance, despite the hat pulled down practically over his eyes. He has a red queue, and so the same coloring as you and Lord Cobham," Lady Sybilla prattled on. "Though his coloring is more carrot, like Lord Cobham, whereas your hair is a lovely soft apricot—"

"Damned rude to pretend he didn't see us, hat or no hat," Cobham interrupted, an eye on the remaining strawberry tart. That he felt compelled to show some manners in another man's house and leave it on the plate made him even more irritable than usual. "The fellow made Her Grace wave her fan from the window in a most undignified manner, all to get his attention. What with a flock of sheep between us, and she leaning out so far her fan was practically ticklin' his snout, he could do nothing but finally acknowledge her efforts! Imagine! A duchess having to make herself known to a peddler of potions!"

"Tam is a fully qualified apothecary, Cobham," Selina replied irritably. "And a very good one at that."

"I admit to being overly anxious," Olivia St. Neots confessed under Alec's raised quizzical eyebrow. He knew her methods of extracting information firsthand, having walked in on her interrogating Tam when he was his valet. "I naturally assumed that with the boy on his way to town, Selina must've already delivered, for why else would he abandon her? And I wanted news—"

"And did you get news?" Selina asked, a suspicious sidelong look at Alec. "I hope he hasn't been called away on some urgent matter?"

"That's what I said to Mama," Lady Sybilla interrupted. "I said if Mr. Fisher is off to town, then it must be urgent, because he wouldn't leave Selina so close to her confinement, not without good reason. We all know how in demand he has become as an *accoucheur* since attending on the Duchess of Cleveley. All the young pregnant ladies of Westminster must have him call on them. It's the fashionable thing to do—"

"*Fashionable?*" Lord Cobham pulled a face of disgust. "It's-it's —*degenerate*, that's what it is!"

"Don't be ridiculous, Clive!" the Duchess said stridently. "As Selina pointed out to you, Thomas Fisher is a qualified apothecary. And as Sybilla says, he is also a much-in-demand *accoucheur*. And if the Cleveleys have put their confidence in him as their *accoucheur*, then it stands to reason everyone else will too! The boy obviously knows what he's about."

"Knows what he's about?" Lord Cobham blew out his cheeks. "If you ask me a woman's—a woman's—*parts* is no place for a man to be about, however qualified he may be!"

Selina burst into a fit of the giggles and clapped a hand to her mouth, and Alec grinned. It was a moment of levity that broke the tension in the room, but it did not divert Selina from asking her husband sweetly, when she had calmed herself, "What errand has caused Tam to abandon me and go galloping off to town?"

"He has not abandoned you, my darling. And he'll be away two nights at most," Alec replied.

"That does not answer my question, sweetheart," Selina enunciated with a tight smile.

Alec grinned. "It doesn't, does it…"

Selina opened her mouth, but the Duchess interrupted, dabbing at her moist eyes, her own laughter finally under control.

"Good Gracious! No small wonder why you and Caro have yet to breed, Clive! No! I don't want to hear another word about that or Thomas Fisher, or why he has gone gallivanting off. And why, pray tell, does Selina require the services of a fashionable *accoucheur*, when she has me? Have you all forgotten I had *a dozen* lying-ins. There isn't a man or woman alive who knows more than I do about a woman's *parts and* childbirth."

"Please, I beg you, Aunt, say no more," Lord Cobham uttered, feeling bilious. He mopped his damp brow with his handkerchief.

"There are some—*matters*—for which men are best left in ignorance. Childbirth being one of them."

"Oh, I quite agree, Lord Cobham," Lady Sybilla replied earnestly. "Men who are not *accoucheurs* have no place in—"

"I most certainly do *not* agree!" Selina answered stridently. "Men who want to be fathers, who want heirs, should know precisely what their wives must endure to bring their offspring into the world. I'm told that all that blood, sweat, and toil, not to mention screaming, as the baby is pushed out of—Cobham? Cobham? Oh dear," she said without sympathy, a knowing mischievous smile at her aunt and cousin. "What did I say to make him run off like that?"

TWENTY-ONE

"DEAR GOD, HALSEY, I WAS NEVER MORE GRATEFUL TO YOU FOR following me out of there!" Lord Cobham announced on a heavy sigh of relief, as the double doors to the library were thrown wide by two liveried footmen. Alec let him go before him. "Not that I'm a coward by any means. Not about *manly* matters. But this childbirth business..." He shuddered and briefly closed his eyes. "Who'd be a female, eh?"

"I doubt I possess the bravery to endure childbirth—"

"Well! Well! What a lot of fusty old books you have," Cobham burst out to change the subject, receding chin skywards to take in the floor-to-ceiling book shelves of yet another expansive room. "Are all your reception rooms equally as large and well appointed?"

"I'm afraid so," Alec apologized, smiling to himself at Cobham's unconcealed envy. "We're replacing most of the furniture because it's uncomfortable. But what you see in here I had brought down from the townhouse. As to the silverware..." he added, watching his brother-in-law crane his neck in all directions to try and take in the entire expanse of the ornate plastered ceiling, "I've not counted it, but there is quite a stockpile, and it's locked away in the butler's room, along with the gold plate."

Cobham's chin came down. "Silverware?" he repeated, bemused. He'd forgotten he had all but accused Alec's belowstairs guests of being thieves. "No good asking for my advice. I know nothing about such domestic arrangements."

He followed Alec to an assortment of sofas and chairs grouped about a low table and sat heavily at one end of a sofa, only to lift a buttock in an effort to extract a plump tapestry cushion from under his backside. This he dropped over the upholstered arm to the floor before resettling himself.

"Lady Cobham has one too many of these fringed articles lyin' about. Damned annoying." He rolled his eyes and made a face, as if to say Alec as a fellow male would empathize with him. "Never will understand all the fiddle-faddle females insist is needed in a house. Since getting leg-shackled the number of cushions on settees has multiplied. And at the London abode, I keep finding small porcelain pots with open wire lids scattered about the rooms. They're filled with dried flowers and spices Lady Cobham tells me is some Frenchie bloody nonsense called *potpourri*. She says this French muck gives off a pleasant odor about the place. Have you heard the like? Of course you haven't! Not bloody likely. What man has?

"But if this potpourri has the wife spendin' her days in town directing servants to fill up these useless pots with dried leaves and whatnot, keeping her busy with domestic trivialities, I can get on with what's important, with no interference from her, then who am I to argue? Of course I don't have to worry about this potpourri nonsense when we're in the shires. Plenty for her to occupy her time on the farm. She was born and bred on the adjoining property y'know."

"So Selina mentioned—" Alec began and was cut off, with Cobham barely pausing to take a breath.

Alec bit down on his tongue and patiently kept silent, hoping there was a point to this wandering monologue. Recalling his time in the Foreign Department, when he was compelled to listen to Cobham's long and rambling speeches, it had quickly become apparent that the Head of the Foreign Department measured his intellectual mastery of a topic not by the content, but by the number of sentences he uttered and repeated. And those around Alec knew this too. They too were compelled to hold their tongues, and at the end of the monologue exchanged furtive eye rolls. They then went about their business in spite of their superior's pontificating. More than once, in the Commons, Plantagenet Halsey had used Lord Cobham's sinecure as the prime example of the idiocy of such a system, why it should be abolished and a structure based on merit instituted within governmental departments. And while Alec agreed with his uncle on sinecures, he was not completely dismissive of Cobham, if only because in amongst his verbal detritus, and unbeknownst to the man himself, there was often a pearl of intelligence worth extracting.

Alec applied past practice now, as his brother-in-law continued his monologue about Lady Cobham, and landowning in general.

"Means to an end, owning land, as far as I'm concerned. Which is why I married Lady Cobham in the first place. Not that she isn't a fetching female. But if she hadn't come with acreage, what would've been the bloody point of installing her in my drawing room? Thought long and hard before I committed, I can tell you, Halsey. Marriage is a bloody difficult undertaking, but I'd have been a complete noodle not to take her on. She's an only child, and there were no male relatives to pull the land out from under her. So she inherited the lot and no argument. Of course, if she'd had brothers, aside from a dowry, then the only parcel of land she'd have been entitled to would be the estate down here in Kent. But it's a worthless piece of dirt. It's been divided amongst siblings over so many generations I'd be surprised if the wife's portion amounts to more than clod of earth sufficient to grow a bean! Bloody shocking state of affairs. Shocking waste of good estates, but there's nothing that can be done about it."

He suddenly looked hard at Alec as if seeing him for the first time. He waggled a fat finger at him and his lips undulated as if he had a lot to say, but his mouth wouldn't cooperate and let the words out. Finally he burst out,

"Good—Lord! Your estate's in Kent! *This* estate is in Kent!"

"Yes, Cobham," Alec confirmed, suppressing a grin. "We are in Kent—"

"How many acres have you got, Halsey? Here. Here in Kent. Not anywhere else. Here. This estate."

Alec shrugged. "Twelve, perhaps fifteen thousand acres—"

"Fifteen *thousand* acres. Bloody hell! But how did—how did you —your forebears—manage to keep it all?"

"I imagine in the usual way. Eldest sons inheriting from fathers, land gifted at the time of a marriage contract—"

Lord Cobham shook his head vigorously, so vigorously his wig slid to the left. He hardly noticed.

"No! No! No! That can't be it. This is Kent, man. It don't work that way down here. You can't keep an estate together even if you wanted to. Trust me. I've tried. It's a bloody travesty, but eldest sons have no more rights than do their younger brothers and—you'll be as horrified as the rest of us to learn—their *sisters*. That's right. *Females* have *rights* to *land* in Kent. *All* siblings have *equal* inheritance to an estate under an archaic and frankly bloody stupid law called gavelkind. Surely you've heard of it? You must have! *Gavelkind*," he enunciated, as if to a small child. "Scheme of land tenure peculiar to Kent. Surely you were advised about tenure inheritance when you came into this pile. Didn't your attorneys, your steward, your uncle, give you the bad news?"

"Is it such a bad notion for children to inherit equally?" Alec asked mildly, instantly thinking of Selina who was as deserving, and certainly more capable, than either of her brothers.

Yet his mind was racing, trying to recall if he had ever heard mention of the word *gavelkind*, least of all had such a law explained to him, at any stage since inheriting the estate. Perhaps when he'd first come down here after Edward's death, when he had been accused of his brother's murder and been a recluse, shunning all invitations. Attorneys came and went, informed him of certain particulars and legalities, and he had nodded his understanding without listening. His uncle had been there. So had the steward. They had told him not to concern himself. And he had done just that—not concerned himself. All he had thought at the time was what a huge, unwanted responsibility he'd been given. How insurmountable the repairs to the house, and what a major expense it was going to be to get the house livable and the estate up and running again. He'd thought it a millstone around his neck. The last thing on his mind was marriage, children, and, far into the future, their inheritance. And now, in two short years, his outlook and life had dramatically changed for the better. He and Selina would raise their family here...

"Such a bad thing?" Cobham repeated in a reed-thin voice. He coughed loudly into his fist, forcing Alec out of his abstraction, and said sternly, but in a tone one uses on a puppy who has hidden a stocking and won't tell you where it is, "Look here, Halsey. You're no longer a junior member of the Foreign Department. You can't be. Not now His Majesty has seen fit to elevate you into our ranks. You're a peer of the realm. You do understand what that means, don't you? And you're a landowner, quite a substantial landowner. Most important to me is you're married to my sister. Selina and I may never have seen eye to eye on anything—between you and me, she scares me breechless sometimes—but she's blood and that's that. And as you're married to her, we are now forever connected for better or worse. So what I thought of you and what I said about you in the past, and what you are—"

"A half-caste savage of indeterminate lineage?"

Cobham waved this away. "No longer relevant! Forgot all about it. The thing is you're my brother-in-law and that—"

"—negates my poor heritage?"

Cobham touched his nose and smiled. "Precisely! Knew you'd understand. Good man! And as my brother-in-law you have certain privileges, but it also means I and the rest of your peers have expectations of you. There are unwritten rules you must abide. And as we are now connected by blood, and I am Head of the Foreign Department and have His Majesty's ear and his confidence, and you're a peer of the realm, you can't talk treasonous drivel."

"And expressing the desire for all my future children to share equally in an inheritance is treasonous drivel?"

"Of the lunatic kind, Halsey," Cobham replied darkly, and with such a grave expression that Alec wanted to burst out laughing. He did not, and so his brother-in-law continued in the same solemn tone. "You utter anything of the sort in the clubs or in the Lords and you'll find yourself on a cart headed for a straw bed in Bedlam. What's worse, eyes will turn in my direction. Questions will be asked why I bloody well didn't have a word to stop you making a fool of yourself." He leaned forward on the sofa as much as his paunch would allow and tapped his temple. "Think, Halsey. It's one thing for that old windbags of an uncle of yours to spout the treasonous ravings of a bloody lunatic in the Commons. He can do that because he ain't a peer. He's as free as a bird to say and do as he pleases, however ludicrous. But you're not, and no longer ever will be. You can't turn your back on your title and pretend it never existed. Who in their right bloody mind would? Only a lunatic. You have to keep in mind that your peerage goes on after you. Your son will inherit it, and then his son, and so on and so forth. That's how the system works and will forever work. That's how we keep order. And how the filthy masses expect us to keep order. You have a responsibility to your eldest son to make certain he inherits this great pile. But as to how you do that when you have this mucky gavelkind business to contend with, I bloody well don't know." He gave a snort of laughter, having just had an idea he thought ludicrous in the extreme. "If the luck's with you perhaps Selina will give you only one son and you won't have any female children to muddy the land inheritance waters; that'd do the trick!"

"*May you be blessed with one son only, and have no daughters to your name,*" Alec repeated, immediately recalling the Latin inscription in the Fivetrees village square.

"Exactly! If I were you, I'd add that line to your nightly prayers."

But Alec wasn't thinking about his future children, but those born here in the past, and about his uncle in the here-and-now, and he voiced his thoughts aloud.

"By your reckoning, if this estate comes under the law of gavelkind and sons and daughters inherit land equally, then my uncle, being one of twin brothers, inherited a stake in this estate from his father. And when his brother died, and my brother Edward inherited, then I must have inherited along with him as his brother. Edward's dead, but my uncle is very much alive. Which means he still has part ownership of this estate with me. And that means I am not the sole owner, and am not at liberty to pass the estate on in its entirety to an eldest son, even if I wanted to and could, by some legal miracle, remove this law of gavelkind."

"Look here, Halsey. I have no idea what you're talking about, but it sounds a messy business, and one you'd best sort out with your uncle sooner rather than later. I don't know the ins and outs of the legalities, but Aunt Olivia is adamant that this estate is yours, and yours alone."

Cobham had all Alec's attention. "Olivia? What does she know about—"

"No! Not at liberty to say. Made a promise I must keep or Her

Grace will have my ballocks for breakfast—er, her words, not mine. Not that she told me much. She can be as closed as a bloody mantrap when she wants to be. But as you and I are now bound by blood, and we fellows must stick together against a conspiracy of females, I will tell you that arrangements were made—"

"By whom?"

"Keep up! Keep up! Arrangements made by your uncle about the inheritance of this estate," Cobham enunciated and rolled his eyes. When Alec went to speak, he shook his head and waved a hand, mentally exhausted. "No! I can't tell you anything else. Told you. Aunt Olivia will have my ballocks. Talk to your uncle. That's if you can get a sane bloody word out of him. But I'm done. Didn't come down here to sort out your business. Because, frankly, it's none of my bloody business. It's yours. And to be blunt, my business is far more important. It concerns the nation, and His Majesty's honor, and is of some urgency."

"Then we had best fortify ourselves," Alec said as he crossed to the side table.

He returned with a brandy decanter and glasses, and slowly went about pouring out into two tumblers. Watching the amber fluid spill into the glass gave him a moment to mentally put to one side all the questions that filled his head about what Cobham had just revealed to him. He knew he would not get anything more out of his brother-in-law while he was now wearing his Head of Department wig, even if it remained crookedly over an ear. His questions would have to wait until he could confront his uncle, and if he was not forthcoming, then there was always the attorney from Yarrborough and Yarrborough whom Tam had gone to London to fetch. Either way, he would have his questions answered within the next few days. Returning his thoughts to the here and now, he handed Cobham a glass and raised his. His brother-in-law did likewise.

"Normally wouldn't imbibe until after dinner," Cobham confessed, and greedily downed the contents in one. He stuck out his glass to have it refilled, and Alec obliged. "But what I have to tell you calls for it."

"So why is it the Head of the Foreign Department needs my help?" Alec asked smoothly.

"Why? I'll bloody well tell you why!"

Lord Cobham almost screeched the words. The brandy had revived him. He sat up, straightened his wig and waggled the glass at Alec as if it were his sword. All his assurances that Alec was no longer a junior member of his department disappeared into dust. He addressed him as he did all those in the Foreign Department whom he considered beneath his notice, which was everyone except himself.

"Halsey, you got this country in this mess, so you're bloody well going to get us out of it!"

TWENTY-TWO

"Mess?"

Alec put aside his empty glass and crossed his arms. He was not at all rattled by Cobham's heated outburst, and waited for him to elaborate as if he had all the time in the world.

"Y'know, a-a difficulty," Lord Cobham finally mumbled, considerably chastened under Alec's fixed stare.

"I understand the terminology. Was it His Majesty who suggested I was responsible for the country being in some difficulty or did someone suggest it to His Majesty that I was the cause?"

Lord Cobham waved a hand in dismissal. "Not His Majesty. To His Majesty." He snorted his superior incredulity. "How would the King have any idea what was going on unless I told him, eh?"

"So it was you who told him I was to blame."

"Listen, Halsey. Who said what to whom don't matter now. The problem is there and you're the only one who can fix it. Which is why I came all this way to see that you do."

Alec pretended not to understand. He cocked his head in thought. "There seems to be two opposing contentions here. One is that I caused the country to be in some difficulty; the other is that the problem, whatever it is, can only be fixed by me, who, you say caused it in the first place? Which is it?"

Lord Cobham pulled a face, having no idea what Alec was talking about. But to cover his ignorance, and because he had an overinflated opinion of his negotiating skills, as no one in his department had dared to tell him otherwise, he said with a sniff and a crooked smile of superiority, "You know what these foreign courts and their rulers are like. They envy us. They will say and do anything to be our friend, whilst stabbing us in the back with the help of our enemies."

"Hedging their bets as it were."

"Precisely!"

"As your government was hedging its bets with the outcome of the civil war in Midanich?"

"Exactly! I knew you'd under—No! No! That's not what our government was doing at all!"

"Oh? Then you personally didn't describe the Margrave of Midanich as a-er—*bloody nobody ruler*, or call Midanich *an insignificant principality in the middle of God-knows-where in Europe*?"

Lord Cobham's buttocks lifted off the sofa while his feet remained firmly rooted to the carpet. He swayed. "Who told—Why would I—"

"That it didn't matter to you who won the civil war, Prince Ernst or Prince Viktor, as long as His Majesty's government was seen to have supported the winning side from the very beginning?"

"Where did you hear—?"

"A letter to me describing you and your opinions of Midanich and its Margrave. I don't believe I misquoted the letter, or you."

"But how did—"

"Surely you are aware that as Head of the Foreign Department you're not immune to being spied upon. I would go further and say you are possibly the most spied-upon man in the government."

"But these foreigners don't understand the English tongue, least of all understand what I—"

"Who said anything about foreign spies?"

Lord Cobham was up on his feet. "That's bloody treason, and heads will roll!"

"Sit, Cobham. This isn't Tudor England. Our monarch is not about to behead his own spies for reporting what the Head of his Foreign Department says and does in the name of the Crown. And what you said about the Margrave of Midanich and his principality has displeased the King because the Margrave is displeased. Is that not the case?"

Alec did not need the question answered because he already knew. He'd received letters from a number of correspondents over the course of the last six weeks, most from Midanich. And one had come from the Earl of Salt Hendon, whom the King had requested head up a welcoming party for the London visit later in the year of the newly-installed Margrave, the first visit by that country's ruler to England. Lord Salt's letter explained that arrangements for the Margrave's visit had stalled and the situation wasn't being helped by the Head of the Foreign Department.

So Alec was well aware a diplomatic crisis was brewing between England and Midanich. And while he did not know the mind of his king, he did have the confidence of the Earl of Salt Hendon, and of Midanich's Margrave. Both wanted a resolution, and quickly. And the Margrave wanted Alec to resolve it, no one else. He was putting his trust in his Baron Aurich of Midanich, which is why he had sent an emissary, in secret, to London. But Alec was also the Marquess Halsey of England, and his fealty was to King George. And so the Earl of Salt Hendon had reminded him.

He was about to walk a diplomatic tightrope—that is, *if* he was prepared to step out onto that rope and act as diplomatic go-between. As if he didn't have enough going on in his life on the estate! But Cobham was now his brother-in-law, the Earl of Salt Hendon was a trusted friend, and so, too, was the Margrave. And then there was the private visit to London of the Countess Rosine, and to whom he had sent a letter via Tam. How could he refuse?

First he had to end Cobham's misplaced confidence in his own paltry abilities. For he also knew His Majesty was furious with his Head of the Foreign Department and had threatened to strip him not only of his sinecures but also of all his positions of high office.

Alec splashed brandy into Cobham's empty glass and told him to drink up. And then he took control of the situation.

"Let's be clear. The fix, as you call it, our government is in with a foreign power was not of *my* making, but of yours—"

"Now listen here, Halsey, I—"

"Of *your* making," Alec enunciated with an unblinking stare.

He pointed to the sofa, for Cobham to put his buttocks firmly back on the cushion. And when he did just that, Alec continued.

"Your ill-informed, and dare I say inflammatory, opinions of

Midanich and its ruler have left His Majesty in an embarrassing predicament. The Margrave, who had already accepted His Majesty's invitation to visit England, then discovers that his country and his person have been maligned by none other than England's Head of the Foreign Department. What is he to do?"

"Forget all about it! Forget I said a word. That's what he should do if he wants us to—"

"I don't require you to answer the question, Cobham. Your remarks were inked for all to read. This is not mere rumor the Margrave can brush aside, it is fact."

"No one can say it was in my handwriting, least of all that German upstart!"

"We all know you said it, Cobham. The Margrave, his courtiers, ours, Lord Salt, the Spymaster General, and His Majesty. And because we all do, the Margrave is within his rights to cancel his visit to our shores, and His Majesty cannot take offence, or there'll be a diplomatic incident. But there is a diplomatic impasse, and it is of *your* making."

"Why would the man do such a bloody-stupid thing as not come to England, eh?" Cobham questioned belligerently. "Being invited here is a high honor, indeed. And it's the first time Hanover's neighbor has been invited, so a double honor for him."

"That may yet save you and your department, and also save face for the Margrave."

"Eh? How's that?"

"Because His Majesty will invite the Margrave, not as his Britannic Majesty of Great Britain and Ireland, but as Duke of Brunswick and Elector of Hanover. Which means he will entertain the Margrave as his German cousin and friend."

"Sounds reasonable. The Margrave can't object to that, surely?"

"It means His Majesty will be free from the usual parliamentary and ministerial constraints to which monarchs of Great Britain are generally subject. And it also means those involved in the visit from our side will be the King's German advisors, and not their English counterparts." When Lord Cobham made no comment, Alec spelled it out for him. "There will be no place for England's Head of the Foreign Department, or the department itself, in the visit, or in the negotiations for—"

"What?! That's outrageous! This is bloody England! I am Head of the Foreign bloody Department. I won't—

"—be Head of the Foreign Department much longer if you continue with this belligerent approach. That is fact, Cobham. If you do not step aside for this visit by Midanich's ruler, take some time to visit your estates and play concerned landowner, you may find yourself relegated to a life of filling little porcelain bowls with potpourri for the rest of your days. I'm sure that's not what you want?"

Lord Cobham shook his head, bottom lip stuck out, empty glass held between his knees, and double chin pulled back in his stock. He was the model of contrition. The only indication of his inner turmoil was the movement of his small dark eyes, flitting from side to side. And then his next words dashed Alec's hopes that his brother-in-law was at last taking responsibility for his actions. But what did not surprise Alec was that Cobham lived up to his reputation as the least-qualified man to run a department devoted to diplomacy.

"The fellow's got to have the thinnest hide this side of a bloody starved horse, if he took m'remarks to heart! Besides, we all know he can't afford to be insulted. Not with his country in a shambles after that civil war with his mad brother, and needing the ready to rebuild. He wants to find himself a stronger jawbone and pull it up and forget he was ever insulted, because if he don't, who says we'll take his bloody troops, eh?"

"Cobham, I think you fail to understand what is at stake here. It is not for the Margrave to come cap-in-hand to us. He can easily find another foreign power only too willing to hire such well-trained and respected fighting men as Midanich produces. The country has the best fighters in Europe. He may need the income to rebuild his country, but he can get that from anywhere. We—England and His Majesty—cannot find such troops just anywhere. To put it bluntly: England needs Midanich more than Midanich needs us."

Lord Cobham nodded, but he did not look convinced. "Frankly, all that matters is getting the Margrave's signature on those documents, giving us his troops for hire. If that means I've got to go down to the country and wallow in pig manure, than so be it. But I won't, y'know—"

"Won't what?"

"I'm not going anywhere. I'll be in London where I'm needed."

Alec drew in a great breath and gritted his teeth before saying calmly but firmly, "Why have you come here if you're not prepared to listen to me?"

"Told you: Need your help. Margrave won't talk to any of us, not even His Majesty. Will only talk to you. Says he ain't coming to London in November unless you're there alongside His Majesty to greet him."

Alec wanted to throw up his hands and bellow *Hallelujah!* The Head of the Foreign Department had finally asked for his help with a problem he knew only Alec could solve.

"I will help you, Cobham—"

"Good! About time you agreed to come to the aid of King and country—"

"—but I will only help you upon two conditions."

Lord Cobham put the empty glass on the cushion beside him and got to his feet. He threw up a hand, as if such details were petty in the extreme.

"Name these conditions, and they're yours. And now, if you don't mind, I'd like to change out of this traveling raiment for something more presentable for dinner. Got to keep up appearances, particularly for our females, even if we are in the country. I hope you do, too. I will say that for m'sister. Always looks fetching wherever she is... Well? Keep up! Keep up! Don't just stand there, tell me your conditions! My man will be waiting for me."

"You will stay well out of negotiations with the Margrave. And you and your subordinates, and the Spymaster General and his minions, will follow my lead."

Alec stuck out his hand.

Lord Cobham pulled a face, bushy red eyebrows waggling, and shrugged a shoulder. He then tugged at the lace at his wrists, and stretched his thick neck in its linen stock, making Alec wonder if he intended to refuse to shake hands. But he finally did so, adding sulkily,

"Very well. Not that I wasn't about to suggest we all follow your lead. After all, you speak the *lingua franca* better than I. Never was that good at French at Eton... And you also speak German, which grates on the ear; sounds like a lot of meaningless God-awful gutteral utterances."

Alec bit down on his tongue and nodded to the footmen to open the double doors. They did so, and in strode Plantagenet Halsey and Sir Tinsley Ferris in heated argument. Both were brought up short by the Head of the Foreign Department, who blocked their entrance further into the library.

"Sir Tinsley, this here is Lord Cobham, Lady Halsey's brother," Plantagenet Halsey stated with a heavy sigh, as if it were a struggle to make such introductions. The two strangers politely bowed to one another in greeting. "Cobham, this is Sir Tinsley Ferris, the local magistrate and neighbor. That's all the time we have, so you can go on your way. And as you reek of a horse and cart, you'd better get in a tub and scrub, or you'll offend the ladies—Now, my lord," he said to Alec, stepping past a speechless Lord Cobham, "Sir Tinsley and I need a word."

"No, there is no *we* about it," Sir Tinsley stated with a sniff of annoyance.

It barely registered with the magistrate that the man standing before him, with the head shaped like a cod and a paunch that declared the glutton, was an exalted member of the Privy Council and Head of the Foreign Department. Such was his self-importance in his role as local law enforcer that he considered himself the most important man in the room, and next on that list was his host, Lord Halsey. So he followed Plantagenet Halsey deeper into the room without a second glance at Lord Cobham, whose mouth was at half-cock at being so summarily dismissed by one man, and ignored by the other.

"I and I alone in my capacity as magistrate must speak with Lord Halsey, and without your interference in this murder investigation!"

"Interference!?" blustered Plantagenet Halsey, a step behind Alec, who had returned to the group of chairs he had just vacated with Lord Cobham. "You should've heeded m'advice, and perhaps the boy would've been more willin' to talk."

Both the magistrate and the old man were so caught up in arguing with each other they were deaf to the berating Lord Cobham gave the two hapless footmen standing to attention by the open double doors. Alec was not. He watched Cobham storm out of the library, and nodded for the doors to be closed. It was going to be a long day…

TWENTY-THREE

"I told him the lad won't talk," Plantagenet Halsey said to Alec in a much more subdued tone than when he had first entered the library with Sir Tinsley. "If he ain't openin' up to his sister, then he ain't goin' to say boo to a magistrate, now is he?"

"Your advice was noted, Halsey, but as magistrate, I have certain duties to perform. The Turner boy was murdered, and while the death of the blacksmith's son may have been accidental his body was interfered with, his hand cut off by person or persons unknown. And the only witness to both crimes is Nicholas Fisher. So he must and *will* talk. And if not to me, then he will be handed over to a higher authority to be interrogated. The fact that he refuses to speak at all can lead one to surmise that he is implicated in the murd—"

"That's complete pig's swill, and you know it!" Plantagenet Halsey spat out, a roll of his eyes at Alec. "That boy ain't much more than a saplin'. Hugh Turner was a strappin' lad, and three years older than Nic Fisher, whose arms are no more than the width of a broom handle. You tell me how a boy like that could overpower and slice the throat of one friend, and then when his other friend fled the scene, catch up to him, find him impaled, and then casually as you please cut his hand off. It just ain't possible. Besides, why would he do that to his two best friends, and in such a gruesome and tellin' way? No. He had nothin' to do with it. And the reason he ain't talkin' is he's scared witless and in a state of great agitation. And he'll stay that way if you keep pesterin' him. He'll talk in his own good time."

"I agree it is improbable the boy had anything to do with this horrifying state of affairs," Sir Tinsley replied in an about-face. "My hypothesis was a conclusion others might draw by his continued silence. But if he doesn't open his mouth, I'll be forced to hand him over to others who do not know him. And they'll be keen to place the murder at someone's feet to satisfy the grieving parents, and to appease a village that is also frightened out of its wits that there's a murderer loose in the woods who is preying on innocents. As Nicholas Fisher was there at the time the boys were attacked, he is the only one who can tell us anything; he may even know the identity of the killer or killers. So no, we don't have time to wait until the boy decides to talk. Which is why I am here, my lord, to request that you allow me to take Nicholas Fisher into custody and—"

"Sir Tinsley, unless you have reason to believe Nicholas Fisher committed these crimes, then I'm afraid I cannot grant your request," Alec said without apology. "The boy and his sister will remain here, under my care and protection."

Sir Tinsley bowed his head. "Very well, my lord. However, you leave me no choice but to send to London to Bow Street, and allow others to take over this matter."

"Why are you so quick to jump off the prosecution wagon, eh?" Plantagenet Halsey asked. "Normally you're eager to point the finger yourself, but not now. Why?"

"Uncle, were Nic and Sally given a bath and put into clean clothing?" When the old man nodded, he asked, "And their discarded clothes were kept aside as I ordered?" Again the old man nodded. "And when you examined their clothing, what did you find?"

"Rags. The garments were threadbare, darned beyond repair, and the boy's were louse-ridden. I dare say the girl's petticoats were cleaner and vermin free because she has employment, and spends most of her days knee-deep in laundry liquids!"

"What has this to do with anything, my lord?" Sir Tinsley asked in exasperation.

"If, as you postulate, Nic Fisher was involved in a gruesome murder, it is expected that his clothing would be covered in the tell-tale signs of his criminal activity."

"Meaning?" asked the magistrate with a deep frown.

"*Blood*, Ferris!" the old man interrupted. "There was no blood, not even a speck, on any of the clothing worn by those children. You can examine the rags for yourself. They've not been touched or altered or cleaned. It stands to reason that if you cut the throat of an animal there's lots of blood *everywhere*. And bein' farmers we all know how that goes, don't we?"

"The boy was missing for days—he could've changed out of his rags," Sir Tinsley argued lamely, thinking over what the old man had said about the lack of blood stains on Nicholas Fisher's clothing, and feeling foolish for failing to enquire about it.

"Changed out of them into what?" Plantagenet Halsey scoffed. "He's a Fisher! I'd wager he's wearing hand-me-down rags as it is."

"He spent those days hiding out in Old Bill's cottage," Alec said to Sir Tinsley. "And as far as I could see there were no blood stains—"

"Your Lordship has been to Old Bill's?" the magistrate asked warily.

"What surprised me most, aside from the fact there is no such person as Old Bill presently residing there, is that for a woodsman's cottage, it is remarkably well kept—too well kept." Alec looked at both men when he added with a wry smile, "And I assume that is because keeping it maintained is part of the agreement amongst you all, but it is the padlocked hut in the back—*backway*? Yes, out in the backway, that is the more important building. But I digress, and what I want to know now, Sir Tinsley, is how Nic reacted to your presence?"

"My lord? He did not react in anyway other than I expected," the magistrate repeated slowly, because he was still digesting the news that Lord Halsey had not only visited Old Bill's cottage, but knew the purpose of the hut. "Why do you ask?"

"Perhaps, as you were too caught up in doing your duty to notice it would be better if my uncle, who was an observer, tells me."

"The boy has lost his tongue," Plantagenet Halsey replied. "He kept close to his sister. And even when she tried to coax him to talk, he wouldn't. But why would he open his mouth with Ferris here bent over him breathin' in his face, and threatenin' the gallows if he did not cooperate."

"So he wasn't startled, but scared?"

"Startled? No. Not out of the ordinary. Nic and his sister know Ferris is the local magistrate, so naturally they're afraid of him; what villager isn't? They expected to be questioned. The sister willin'ly spoke up, while her brother remained mute."

"So if he wasn't startled, was he terrified?" Alec persisted, looking from his uncle to the magistrate and back again.

"Not terrified either," Plantagenet Halsey affirmed. "To be honest, he wasn't anythin'. Meanin' he showed no emotion. Ferris here could've been questionin' a brick wall and received the same response, which was nothin'."

"That tells me vastly more than you can presently know."

Both the old man and the magistrate looked at one another and then at Alec, mystified by the line of questioning, and by Alec's response. He enlightened them.

"I ask because if Nic had been startled or terrified to be in Sir Tinsley's presence, it would lead me to think that the boy recognized him as being there in the wood when Hugh and Will were set upon. And if that were the case and he had seen Sir Tinsley take a knife to Hugh's throat, then Sir Tinsley would know that too, and hope to silence him."

"But-but that's-that's—outrageous! Outrageous!" Sir Tinsely stuttered. "To what purpose would I kill two boys in the wood? My God, my lord, but I am offended by your supposition and ask that you retract it at once or—"

"—or what? His Lordship is only puttin' two and two together, and comin' up with more than you have! What's to say you *weren't* in the wood stalkin' deer? Come to think on it, Bailey could've been with you, and the two of you set upon those three boys because you didn't want them knowin' you were huntin' His Lordship's prize stag."

"Don't be ridiculous, Halsey!" Sir Tinsley said dismissively. "Everyone in Fivetrees, from the blacksmith, to the vicar, to Adams the gamekeeper, and the itinerates and gypsies who pass through, know we hunt His Lordship's deer; that includes those boys. And that includes you, too. You've drunk too much brandy!"

"Everyone knows, it seems, but me," Alec said quietly, and smiled weakly when both men suddenly looked at him as if they had just divulged the biggest secret ever told to them. Alec would have laughed at the guilt writ large in their expressions, but the occasion was a solemn one. Thinking of Hugh and Will he said bluntly, "You're correct, Sir Tinsley. As hunting and poaching my deer is common knowledge, it is not a reason for anyone to kill. But thank you for confirming what I had already worked out for myself—"

"Alec, I—" began the old man, and was cut off. Alec did not look at him.

"As you've just said, Sir Tinsley, everyone knows about you hunting on my lands. Thus I presume that everyone from the village fool to the vicar, my own gamekeeper, and my landowning neighbors, and my uncle, are all involved in some way in the poaching of my deer and the illegal selling and distribution of venison—"

"Alec, it's not what you think! I—"

"Halsey is correct, my lord. It's not what—"

"The time for explanation and excuse have passed. You've both had ample opportunity to explain yourselves." Alec finally looked directly at his uncle. "And you have had more time than anyone, and more reason to tell me. No! Allow me to finish, and then I may give you the opportunity to speak. To be honest, organized poaching on my estate is the least of my concerns. My steward's son has been murdered, and his friend is dead, both children—" He stopped on a thought and frowned. "Uncle, may I presume that Turner knew about the poaching? Of course! He must have been heavily involved for the scheme to work at all…"

Plantagenet Halsey opened his mouth to reply, then closed it and pressed his lips together when Alec's frown deepened.

"Do you… Do you think, my lord, that Turner's involvement in such a venture is somehow connected to the murder of his son?" the magistrate asked timidly.

Alec shook his head. "No. That is, I am reasonably confident that is not the case."

"After all, those boys were poaching deer for themselves, and had brought down one of your prized stags," Sir Tinsley continued silkily, emboldened by Alec's continuing frown of thought, and Plantagenet Halsey's uncharacteristic silence. "That is no mean feat. The beast was fourteen points or more. That they were not following the usual process would cause discontent amongst the Fivetrees populace who felt they were, in their own minds at least, being robbed of revenue… Perhaps Adams, or some of the villagers, or Turner himself, were furious those three had dared to defy the Fivetrees way. And you said yourself, my lord, Nicholas Fisher was at Old Bill's hut, which is off limits to all but a select few—"

"Oh no you don't, Ferris," Plantagenet Halsey burst out. "Don't you foist the blame on those who will never be given the right to defend themselves against the likes of you! How convenient if all this could be made to go away by pinnin' the murder on an indiscriminate villager, or Adams, or even the steward! Adams and Turner won't talk because they are loyal, and wouldn't want to implicate others. And who will listen to the ravin's of a poor villager against the word of the respected local magistrate? I know your story. If you're forced to take this to Bow Street, you're worried that it would come out that you not only turn a blind eye to poachin' and what goes on at Old Bill's, but that you take your pound of flesh—or should I say venison—to keep that eye blind. You're just as caught up in all this, and as common a thief and a poacher as anyone in Fivetrees. You've got a nerve! I'd show both your eyes my knuckles here and now but I don't want to sink any lower in His Lordship's good opinion. So I'll leave it to him to verbally strip you bare and pummel—"

"Dear me, Halsey, I will never understand you," Sir Tinsley interrupted on a tich-tich and sad shake of his head. He glanced at Alec, as if he would be in sympathy with him. "We all tolerate you because of your blood line, and me because we are related through your kinship with my dear wife. She's always maintained that the wrong brother was elevated to the earldom, which I never could fathom because as far as the rest of your neighbors are concerned, your brother was a fine Earl of Delvin who understood *noblesse oblige* and the dignity of upholding tradition and position. You, on the other hand, are an aberration."

The magistrate glanced at Alec and emboldened by the fact he had not interrupted him but was looking steadily at the old man, he continued with a note of superiority.

"What you have always failed to understand, no matter how many times it is told to you, is that Colonel Bailey, myself, and the Halseys are not poachers, but sportsmen. Poachers kill to eat or to sell. We, on the other hand, hunt deer for the sport of it, for the thrill of the chase and the pleasure of the kill, not for any mercantile purpose. That there is venison on our table from our kill is an end product of the sport, not a means in itself."

"Allow me, uncle," Alec demanded quietly, watching the old man flexing his fingers and clamp his jaw shut.

Alec's blue eyes flickered over the magistrate and fixed on the condescending smile that came when talking about those beneath him with those he considered his equal. Alec quickly disabused him, and had the hollow satisfaction of watching Sir Tinsley's smile drop and the color drain from his face only in the next instant to glow red in a mixture of outrage, embarrassment and guilt.

"Poacher or sportsman, both kill for their own gain or gratification. And yet those who kill because they are starving are the ones who are punished? Where is the morality in that? I understand the farmer who culls the herd to ensure its survival or because he must to protect his crops and those of his neighbor, those means justify the ends. Yours do not, and never will. You also knew my wishes that hunting cease on my estate, and was only to be permitted during the cull, and yet you defied my edict. By what right do you think yourself above the law? No! Let me finish!

"You knew poaching was being committed on my lands, and yet you, as magistrate, did nothing. As an upholder of the law, that is unforgiveable. As magistrate it is your duty to enforce the game laws and the Black Act, whatever your personal views on the matter. That you did not is a blessing in disguise for me, who, like my uncle, finds the Black Act abhorrent. Many in this country do. You think because I lived most of my life in the metropolis I do not know what goes on in the counties? The newssheets are filled with argument and counter argument about the Black Act, and for years I have heard my uncle discuss its inequities and brutalities. Why should landowners have the right to hunt game when ninety-nine percent of the populace are forbidden from even owning a gun or keeping a lurcher? I also know that there is widespread evasion of the Game Act and that this is tolerated. How else does pheasant, partridge, and venison end up on the tables of those who can afford to buy it by underhand means, but do not own wildgame, least of all have access to hunting such creatures?

"If I thought you were turning a blind eye to poaching to address this inequity or to allow the poor to put food in their mouths, I would be the first to be your champion. But as a landowner and a sportsman, you saw it as your prerogative to kill my deer, and to prosecute poachers when it suited you?"

"My lord, I respectfully disagree. Your summation is incorrect on a number of points. And I protest in the strongest language possible and must disabuse you of a falsehood that—"

"Don't you think you've said enough to incriminate yourself in His Lordship's eyes, Ferris?" Plantagenet Halsey interjected with a meaningful stare at the magistrate.

But Sir Tinsley's affront and his need to rehabilitate his character with the Marquess Halsey meant he ignored the old man's warning. And in the rush to repair his good name and standing he dug a far deeper and wider metaphorical hole, not only for himself, but for the old man.

"Please, Sir Tinsley," Alec stated, ignoring his uncle. "I welcome you to persuade me otherwise."

"I wish to do so, my lord," the magistrate replied stiffly, a sidelong glance at Plantagenet Halsey. "Putting aside your—er—*peculiar* opinion of the Game Act and of those of us who hunt, I cannot allow you to continue under the misguided belief that your neighbours would hunt the deer on these lands without the landowner's knowledge and cooperation. We are gentlemen after all, and as gentlemen, we would never hunt without permission. That would indeed make us as common as any poacher! But we were given permission to hunt. Not by Your Lordship but by—"

"—my uncle."

"That is correct, my lord. We—Colonel Bailey, the Reverend Purefoy, and I, desired to come forward and lay our case before you, but Halsey assured us he would take up the matter with you. He persuaded us to continue on as we have always done."

"Alec, I—"

"Then I owe you an apology, Sir Tinsley," Alec stated, cutting off the old man before he could say more. "That you were given permission, and told to ignore my wishes, I appreciate why you continued as if nothing had changed on this estate. Your indignation at my homily is understandable. My uncle's vocal stance in the Commons on the Black Act, and his views on hunting, are widely reported in the newssheets, and I agree with those views. Yet, here in Kent, on this estate, he allowed his neighbors to hunt with impunity? You must indeed think him a hypocrite, and me a dupe for believing his word."

"Alec! My boy! I can explain my—"

"*Don't*. I am not *your boy*," Alec hissed through his teeth as he passed Plantagenet Halsey to return the used glasses to the sideboard. He stood there a moment to collect his thoughts and to cool his anger, head bowed and palms flat to the polished surface. When he turned and rejoined the two men he could not bring himself to look at his uncle for fear he would be overcome with emotion and not be able to speak at all; what that emotion was—fury, confusion, disappointment, overwhelming sadness—he was uncertain. All he knew was that he had a hundred words on the tip of his tongue, words he bit back and would not say until he was alone with him. First he had to get rid of the magistrate.

"I suggest we limit ourselves to your investigation into the deaths of Hugh Turner and Will Bolen," he said quietly. "Catching their killer, finding justice for those poor boys and peace of mind for the Turner and Bolen families in their time of grief are to be our main concerns. Hunting on the estate and everything associated with it can wait to be discussed at a later date."

The magistrate nodded, but he was not insensible to the tension between Alec and Plantagenet Halsey. He stepped up to Alec and said with a hint of contrition, "I will do as you suggest, my lord, but I must make a final comment, lest you think me utterly corrupt, which I am not. You need to know that I have always done my utmost to ensure that every man, woman, or child from Fivetrees brought before me were not prosecuted for poaching or any of the multitude of offences as stipulated in the Black Act, if just cause could be found for their actions. If, as you say, they had taken one bird, not a brace, or received a parcel of venison from a neighbor to feed their family. And that is due to the agreement made with your uncle. Mr. Halsey holds by his principles, and has never wavered, however—*odd*—we his neighbors find them. In exchange for permitting us to course across this estate, I gave my word to be charitable and ignore the Black Act where possible. I have kept my word. Is that not so, Halsey?"

"Aye. That's the way of it, Ferris. Kept your word and been benevolent to the villagers of Fivetrees."

"I appreciate you explaining matters to me, Sir Tinsley," Alec replied, dry in the throat and not a look at the old man. "As to whether this arrangement continues, that can wait for another day. You have more pressing matters to attend to with this murder investigation, and anything I can do to assist, I am at your disposal."

"Thank you, my lord."

"I hope you will allow both families to bury their boys as soon as possible?"

"Yes, my lord. With the summer heat unrelenting, the sooner the better."

"That will be a small comfort to the parents. Oh, and Sir Tinsley, I intend to pay for both funerals, the burials, and associated costs. It is the least I can do to lessen the burden on their families."

"That is very generous of you, my lord. It will be particularly welcome by the Bolens, who have a large family and thus little to spare in any given week." The magistrate glanced at Plantagenet Halsey before asking diffidently, "I presume the invitation that was graciously extended to my dear wife and me for tomorrow evening is still open? Of course, we would understand if Your Lordship decided to postpone, given the circumstances today, which must be most upsetting for Lady Halsey, particularly in her present delicate condition."

"No, Sir Tinsley. Lady Halsey and I look forward to your company, as does Her Grace of Romney-St. Neots. It will be a subdued affair, given the Turners' bereavement, but it will be a full table, what with a handful of house guests staying with us until after the happy event. The Colonel and Mrs. Bailey and the Reverend Purefoy have accepted their invitations."

"Lady Ferris and I will be honored. And look forward to making the acquaintance of Her Grace. Lady Ferris is particularly desirous of meeting her—"

"I'll wager she is!" Plantagenet Halsey interrupted with a harsh laugh. "The feelin' is mutual." And with that cryptic comment and a curt nod to the magistrate, he strolled away.

Sir Tinsley did not know what to make of the old man's aside, and hesitated until Alec gave him leave to depart, which he did in silence.

It was only with the footmen closing over the double doors that

Alec turned into the room. He found his uncle standing at the long table at the back of the sofa Hadrian Jeffries sat at while assisting Selina with her research into the Halsey ancestry.

Plantagenet Halsey held several sheets of paper he'd picked up off the table to give himself preoccupation while the magistrate took his leave, and time to collect his thoughts. After what Sir Tinsley had just divulged about their hunting arrangement, he knew Alec had every right to his fury at such subterfuge and the hypocrisy of his actions. He had some explaining to do, and he had best do it sooner rather than later.

And then something about what was inked on the papers in his hand caught his attention. It was a family tree. Beside the branches of the tree was the pencil sketch of a flower and two smiling faces, crudely drawn by a child, though the family tree and writing were in the script of an adult. He stared at the branches, looked at the names, and knew precisely what it meant. His hands began to shake. Without a second thought, he hastily folded the sheet into quarters and slipped it into an inner pocket of his riding frock. He then needlessly pulled the hem of the skirts, as if adjusting the folds.

Two sheets of paper remained. Taking a deep breath he cast his gaze over the top one. It was folded in two, and he opened it out. This was what he had been searching the shelves for when he was up the ladder and Selina had asked to speak with him. He wondered who had found it, and surmised it must have been Hadrian Jeffries because it was atop his diary. The burning question was, had Her Ladyship seen it?

It was a drawing of a square like that made by a draughtsman under an architect's direction. Three lines were drawn top to bottom and three lines left to right so that the grid pattern formed sixteen smaller squares. Each of the squares contained two crosses. The crosses were not in a particular pattern with some being in the corners, and others in the middle, so that it looked as if these had been added at a later date and merely to indicate that each square contained two of something.

Along one side of this square was a length of hatching and the word 'wall' written in precise handwriting. And off to one side of the square was another smaller square marked with the word 'entrance'.

Plantagenet Halsey itched to do with this as he had the first sheet, to put it in his pocket. But he knew Alec was watching him. As casually as he could manage it, he folded it again, and shuffled it behind the third and final piece of paper.

It was a list of male Christian names, and the script in a feminine hand he recognized—Helen, Countess of Delvin. The first entry was for 1215, the year of the Magna Carta, with the name Linus, and the final name Ralph was inked beside the date 1689, a year after the Glorious Revolution.

He had little idea what this list meant, but then as he continued to frown down at it, he had a flash of clarity so blinding he swayed. Hastily, he opened out the plan of the draughtman's square with its grid lines and crosses. He then looked again at the list. There were thirty-eight names. A quick tally of the crosses and he counted thirty-eight.

He could hardly believe his eyes. But here it screamed at him in ink. The large square surely represented the Halsey vault. Each cross represented a life, a life extinguished soon after taking a first breath. It was confirmation of what he had been told but never wanted to believe was actually the truth: He was a descendant of a long line of ancestors who practiced filicide.

TWENTY-FOUR

PLANTAGENET HALSEY THOUGHT HE MIGHT THROW UP THERE and then. He thrust out a hand to grab the edge of the table to stop himself pitching forward.

Why, he wondered, should those crosses and a list of names affect him in this way when he had known, since his twenty-first birthday, that he had been born into a family of murderers. His father had not called it murder, and nor, he supposed, had their ancestors. But to him, and those of his kin who had not been able to cope with the knowledge and had taken their own lives rather than take another, it was murder, plain and simple. The Greeks had practiced it, exposing unwanted newborns on dung heaps and rubbish piles. And had not Euripides written about Medea who killed her two sons in an act of revenge when she was abandoned by their father? The Romans had written infanticide into law: A father had the right, and was protected under law of *patria potestas*, to kill his own children. These were civilizations that had achieved greatness, and yet they had condoned the murder of innocents.

But they were also barbaric and heathen, and this was a Christian nation with Christian values. Murder was not sanctioned for any reason, and the murder of innocents was particularly condemned. And so he had said to his father. His father agreed and assured him that his parents had never participated in the family tradition. His father had also made him and his twin swear on the family Bible never to do so either, and never to open the family vault. It was to remain bricked up and in time it would be forgotten to history. Plantagenet and Roderick had willingly agreed. Neither wanted to explore the family's murderous history. And then his parents had died, and everything changed.

Why, he wondered, had Helen seen fit to make a list of names, and and why was this list with a plan of the vault? The infants would've been nameless, like those exposed on dung hills, and all boys, as his father had told him, to ensure that only one son inherited an estate that remained intact and was not divided up amongst siblings. What happened to daughters remained a mystery. According to his father, there had been no officially recorded births of a female in the family in over fifteen generations. Didn't his father find this strange? He did. But he had not offered any further explanations or answers for this anomaly. It was only later, much later, that he learned the truth behind the inscription in the village square, and the fate of females born to Fivetrees landowners.

The old man could only think that Helen had not wanted these abandoned infants forgotten to history, so had given a name to each of the thirty-eight crosses. And were the crosses on the map representational or actual crosses? Were the infants buried in the vault and a cross placed over them, or did the crosses indicate where an infant had been left, forsaken? And who would draw up such a map, and why? But his overriding thoughts were with Helen, and how traumatic it must have been for her to come across such a map. And to think her firstborn could have been the nameless thirty-ninth cross, destined to join these nameless newborns who had died unloved and alone in the freezing darkness underground, was for him unbearable. He fell all to pieces. His arthritic knees buckled, his hands slid from the table, and he crumpled to the floor. His world went black.

ℋ

ALEC HAD BEEN WATCHING HIS UNCLE SHUFFLE PAPERS AND peer at them at close quarters, wondering how best to deal with his recalcitrance. Sir Tinsley confirmed his suspicions that his uncle was involved in systematic widespread poaching on the estate. Indeed, he was the one in charge of operations, turning a blind eye on the local magistrate and his neighbors when they hunted deer with impunity. Alec had believed his uncle to be sincere in his denunciation of hunting as barbaric, the Black Act as abhorrent barbarism not worthy of a civilized country, and the Game Laws as a blight on the poor man's right to hunt and gather to feed his family. That was not poaching, that was subsistence, plain and simple. Most MPs considered his uncle a thorn in their side and dismissed his condemnations of his own class and his championing of the poor as the ravings of a madman. Cobham had branded him a lunatic.

Alec could not recall a time when his uncle wasn't pilloried in the Commons and in the newssheets, often caricatured for his beliefs and his causes. Yet he stood by his convictions and counseled Alec to do the same. Alec was all admiration for his steadfastness. He remembered well the men who put their knees under their dining table. As a youngster he had listened in wide-eyed interest as gentlemen argued and declaimed and made what were considered by polite society treasonous and often blasphemous utterances, while passing around the beef and potatoes, and pouring wine to overflowing as if it were from their cellar. And there were always one or two men who said nothing, who ate greedily, and were dressed in clothing that had seen better days. Alec had wondered if these men were beggars his uncle often picked up off the footpath and invited in to warm themselves by the fire and enjoy a decent meal. And sometimes this was so. More often than not, these men in their ill-fitting clothes were like-minded scholars without independent means; unable to find regular employment, they lived on the charity of their friends.

And as an eight-year-old Alec had asked why such men did not have family to whom they could turn. His uncle had told him they were not wanted by their family, because they were considered an embarrassment for not conforming. And Alec had responded that these men then were like them, because his uncle was a nonconformist, and they had no family either. "Are we an embarrassment to our family, Uncle?" he had asked, swinging his thin little legs from the cushions stacked on the chair so he was at a comfortable height at a table of loud, opinionated men. To which his uncle had said that in their case, it was their family who was the embarrassment; they were better off without them. He had winked and smiled and said Alec was all the family he needed, and Alec had hunched his shoulders with delight and replied his uncle was all the family he needed, too. They had then clinked glasses and his uncle had rejoined the conversation while he went back to eating the slices of beef on his plate, black curls falling into his eyes, and with ears wide open.

For the longest time it had been just the two of them as a family, and neither had needed or wanted anyone to join them. And now, even though he was married and he and Selina were about to welcome their first child, he could not imagine his family complete without his uncle.

Plantagenet Halsey MP may have defied Alec's wishes and allowed Sir Tinsley and the Colonel, and neighbouring landowners to hunt, but Alec knew his uncle was no hypocrite. He was very sure he had given his permission in exchange for the magistrate's leniency on the local poor. Sir Tinsley had said as much. And he could only think that whatever monies were collected from the illegal sale of venison, his uncle would have used for charitable purposes. It was not in his uncle's nature to profit from another's misfortune. He wouldn't have been at all surprised to learn that this arrangement had been ongoing for decades, and so entrenched in the local population that it was a way of life; no wonder Fivetrees had the lowest criminal rates in the country!

He was not angry at his uncle for making these arrangements with Sir Tinsley and his hunting ilk, but because he had not informed him of how matters stood on the estate. His gamekeeper, his steward, and any number of other servants all knew what was going on, so why had he not been told, too? Surely his uncle knew he approved of turning a blind eye to the Black Act, to allowing the poorest of the poor to continue to eke out an existence in the woods. As for Sir Tinsley coursing on Halsey lands, that was another matter, but something could have been arranged.

That his uncle had seen fit to keep him in ignorance, and to go behind his back, and to act as if he were the master of this estate made him recall what Cobham had told him about the law of gavelkind. That made him suspect that his uncle had inherited half of the estate upon the death of his father, and thus he had every right to be considered its master, too. This did not bother Alec in the slightest. In fact, he welcomed it. It was not as if he needed the income from the estate to survive. His mother had left him a considerable fortune, which meant he was independently wealthy. What he could not fathom was why his uncle was keen to see Alec sole master of Deer Park, and why he had colluded with the estate's employees and servants to keep up this pretense. Why did his uncle feel the need for such secrecy? Which made him wonder, what else was he keeping from him?

And as he ruminated about this, watching his uncle from across the room, he saw the old man's knees buckle, the papers in his hand flutter up into the air, and he fall heavily to the ground. Plantagenet Halsey's head hit the carpet with a thud before Alec could reach him. And all Alec could think about as he dashed to his side was that his uncle must not die, not now, not when they were on the cusp of a future as an extended family. How could he go on without him?

A FEW QUICK STRIDES AND ALEC WAS ON HIS KNEES BESIDE AN unconscious Plantagenet Halsey. He barked at the footmen standing by the door, who had already rushed halfway across the room, to send for the physician. He demanded a basin, a jug of ice water, and towels, and to fetch the brandy decanter and glass. He then gave the old man his undivided attention. By his ashen pallor he appeared to have taken gravely ill. Alec wondered if he had suffered a severe palpitation of the heart—if indeed his heart was still beating. He checked and was relieved that he had a pulse; it was fast but not irregular, and he was still breathing. His uncle may have knocked himself out, but there were no cuts, and he appeared not to have fractured any bones, though it was likely there was a nasty bump to the back of his head.

He made him more comfortable on the carpet, and then gently smoothed the old man's disorderly hair back from his temples. Speaking in hushed tones, and placing a cool hand on his forehead, Alec told him he'd taken a fall and urged him to wake up. He said that his arthritic knees had finally got the better of him, and lovingly chastised him, accusing him of not assiduously applying the drops as Tam had instructed him to do. At that his uncle's eyelids fluttered and he slowly opened his eyes. When he saw Alec, he smiled, but a thudding in his head made him wince and put a hand to where he felt most pain.

"Damme! That'll be a nice egg tomorrow…"

"Not surprising. You fell like a stone. Can you move?"

When he nodded, Alec helped him to sit up. Once settled and he was confident his uncle wasn't about to sway and fall, Alec poured him a brandy, and urged him to take small sips.

"Are you in pain?" he asked, a frown of concern flickering over the old man to assure himself he wasn't trying to be stronger than he really felt. "You gave me a hell of a fright."

"You and me both, my boy—er—apologies you don't want me to ca—"

"I'm an ass. I was angry. But I should never have lashed out at you in that way. I-I—"

"You had every right," the old man cut in when Alec faltered. He leaned against the table leg, careful not to touch his throbbing head to the carved wood, and briefly closed his eyes, saying with a sigh of resignation, "I'm the ass. And a bloody fool. I've been treatin' you like a child. We all have. I thought I was protectin' you, when what I was doin' was not wantin' to face the truth m'self. I'm a damned selfish coward, and I wouldn't blame you if you never found it in your heart to forgive me—"

"Dear me, you did take a nasty knock if that's what you think!" Alec quipped, trying to rally him out of his melancholy. When the old man stared into his glass, Alec lost his smile and gave his arm an affectionate squeeze. "You know I can forgive you anything because you always act with good purpose. You are a good man. In all my years I have never known you to be vindictive, frivolous, or insincere."

"But I am a liar and a coward, and I took you from your mother."

"Yes, you did. But after the initial shock subsided of your confession the other night, I must assume you were compelled to do so for my own good."

"I had to get you away from here as fast as possible before—before m'brother changed his mind. But years later, after his death, when your mother was still livin' and wished to see you, I kept you away." Plantagenet Halsey met Alec's gaze squarely. "That was selfish, and it was cruel." He smiled crookedly. "I told you the other night that the lies were goin' to stop, and they have. Ask me anythin'; I'll do my best to answer you."

"Why did you keep me away?"

"Ah! And here was I thinkin' that the first question you'd want answerin' was why I took you from your mother as a newborn."

"I do want to know that, too. But tell me first why you did not want me to visit my mother in her widowhood."

"I didn't think you were ready for the truth. But she—your mother—she wouldn't have told you. In that we were in accord. But if I'd brought you down here when you were younger, there was every chance you'd meet your mother's sister, and I couldn't have her whisperin' in your ear—"

"Lady Ferris? Why?"

"Because she would've delighted in tellin' you about your parents. I couldn't take that risk. It's not her right to tell you. If anyone is goin' to, it's me." He stuck out his glass and Alec splashed brandy into it. He savored the heady liquid as it slid down the back of his throat, and he collected his thoughts. "I never expected to be tellin' you all this sittin' on a carpet in the library of this house! But somehow it's fittin' we're here at floor level. I can't sink any lower."

"Why was Lady Ferris keen for me to know about my parents?"

"To hurt your mother. To hurt me."

"That presumes she felt you had both hurt her..."

"The only hurt was in her mind. She never understood why I preferred Helen when she was prettier, and, so she thought, smarter. But just because your mother was a sweet creature with a heart of gold did not mean she was unintelligent. She just wasn't one for puttin' herself forward in the way her sister did. And even when Helen's sister was told the truth about our—about our—*relationship* —and that it was impossible for your mother and me to be together, she—Lady Ferris was determined to replace Helen in my affections. Which was ludicrous. *She* was ludicrous."

Alec frowned, not entirely sure he understood what this relationship was between the sisters and his uncle, but he was very sure of what was driving Lady Ferris's actions.

"I told you love is inexplicable and strange," Plantagenet Halsey said, interrupting Alec's frowning silence. "There was no rhyme or reason to why your mother and I fell in love. It just was. We made each other happy. It's just a pity we—that she—that it could not last..."

"You say you made each other happy and that you were in love, and yet she became Countess of Delvin?"

"Yes."

Alec kept his gaze on his uncle. "May I provide an explanation? I've given a lot of thought to what you told me in the Picture Gallery."

Plantagenet Halsey smiled. "I don't doubt it. Explain away!"

"Did she marry your brother because she expected to be Countess of Delvin? That when you eschewed the earldom for your principles and your brother became Lord Delvin, she married him. You say she was sweet with a heart of gold, but that does not mean she understood your principles. She possibly thought them a lot of intangible nonsense that wasn't worth giving up your position and title for. Perhaps she thought that as your brother was your selfsame twin, he would not be so different to you, and mayhap he was not. After all, it seems that you both made the switch without any consequent drama. I must suppose the upper servants, the steward, and anyone intimately connected with you both would have been in on the swap. No doubt my aunt was, too. And you didn't want her telling me? Perhaps it didn't matter to these upper servants which one of you became earl, as long as one of you did." Alec gave a wry smile. "How did I do?"

"I'm astounded! When did you make the leap that I'd given up my birthright?"

"Don't be too impressed. I have Cobham to thank for providing me with the pearl."

Plantagenet Halsey's lean cheeks diffused with color. He was too stunned to speak. Alec's smile widened, and he was relieved to see the color back in his uncle's face. He enlightened him.

"Occasionally, if one listens attentively, there is a pearl of wisdom amongst our Head of the Foreign Department's long-winded diatribes—"

"As only you could find, my boy! I'm all admiration for your patience. The man's a dullard. Not surprisin' you say pearl, because an oyster is more captivatin'! Don't it amaze you—it does me—that he and our golden girl emerged from the same womb?"

Alec grinned. "I am very sure that crosses Selina's mind upon every occasion she is forced into her brother's company."

"How did the oyster give you this pearl?"

"He offered me his advice—"

"My astonishment increases by the minute!"

"—that as His Majesty has bestowed upon me a marquessate I can no longer do or say as I please. I must conform and be as one with my brethren lords. That I cannot, even if I wished to, turn my back on my title and pretend it never existed. And anyone who had such thoughts wasn't in their right mind. Only a lunatic would dare act in this way. And that got me thinking about you—"

"—being a lunatic? Ha!"

"In a way, yes. Because to Cobham and his ilk your beliefs are Bedlam utterances. But what he did say was that you can spout treasonous drivel because you are not a peer and thus you are as free as a bird to say and do as you please. And so I thought if I were you and I had a selfsame twin, and he had a burning desire to be the earl, and I had a burning desire to champion causes in the Commons, then it would be an easy thing to swap birth order. He would have the title, and I would have my freedom to say and do as I pleased, and we would both of us be satisfied."

"I'm all admiration for Cobham's acuity, though I suspect he's oblivious, which is just as well because he'd make a mess of usin' it, and be more obnoxious than he already is." Plantagenet Halsey glanced at Alec and set down his glass on the carpet between them and chose his next words carefully. "Your assessment is not too wide of the mark, but let me set you straight. And perhaps I may even surprise you, which is no small thing because I don't think I've managed to surprise you since you were in your teens. And yet, I am constantly surprised by you! You do know how proud I am of you, m'boy—"

"As I am of you. To stand by your convictions and give up your birthright, an earldom at that! That takes courage."

The old man grimaced. It had nothing to do with the thudding pain to the back of his head. "The thing is… I married Helen."

"You and my mother were-were—*married*?" Alec blurted out, incredulous.

"Ha! So I finally have surprised you! Of course I married her. I loved her. We were in love. Shame on you for thinkin' the worst of us!" he added teasingly. "I told you once your mother and I were not lovers, and we were not. At least I didn't lie about *that*!"

"Uncle—I—Leave it and go! *Go!*" Alec demanded harshly, annoyed at the interruption when two footmen set down a porcelain bowl, towels and jug of ice water on the carpet beside them. "And close the door! And don't let anyone enter—no one!"

"That's the harshest tone I've ever heard you use with a servant," Plantagenet Halsey commented with a sad shake of his head. But the twinkle in his blue eyes belied his criticism. "And here was I thinkin' I'd taught you better. After all, you know they can't answer back."

"I do know that, but—damn it! This—this is far more important," Alec argued, face ablaze with mortification.

He went to pick up the jug to pour ice water into the basin, but the old man waved it aside, and he set it down again. He was surprised to find his hand was shaking. It had nothing to do with his uncharacteristic bad manners towards his servants, and everything to do with the answer to a burning question that had plagued him all his life, and yet he had never asked it for fear of it not being true. He still could not bring himself to be direct.

"If you were married to my mother, how is it that she remained here with your brother when he became earl in name if not in law, and did not go with you to London?"

"I married Helen while our parents were still livin'. They were against the union; always had been. Never could give us an adequate explanation for their opposition. Helen was an heiress and a cousin, and so by all accounts it was an excellent match. But we didn't let their opposition stop us. We married in secret. I found an Anglican clergyman in the next parish and paid him off. It was before Hardwicke's Act, so it was all legal. The only person who knew was my brother. Not even Helen's sister was told... Pass me that cloth, m'boy. I think I do need it now."

Alec scrambled to pour ice water into the porcelain bowl, head full of unanswered questions. He soaked a cloth, wrung it, folded it, and made a pad which he passed to his uncle, who gingerly pressed it to the back of his head where it was most painful.

"Did she refuse to go with you because you had given up your earldom for your principles? How then can you say she loved you?"

The old man shook his head and relaxed a little, the cold cloth numbing the pain. Yet he was gripped by a sense of urgency, that he had to get through this confessional, to tell Alec everything, before someone else did, before they were interrupted. And he still hadn't explained about the vault and what he would find there.

"I need to tell you somethin', somethin' fundamental. Somethin' I think now you will be able to accept and understand, which you would not have at a younger age. It won't make much sense until I tell you all of it, so let me finish. Besides, I'd say we don't have much time before our relatives are poundin' on that door wonderin' where we are." When Alec nodded he continued. "I told you, your mother and I were married in a church ceremony. But we kept our union a secret because my father had not returned from London, and we wanted both parents to hear our news at the same time. Truth is, we were a little afraid of their response, particularly m'mother, who I told you was formidable. She never took to Helen and her sister when they came to live with us. M'father did his best to be a parent to them, but m'mother kept her distance. Helen said she always felt m'mother thought she and her sister were interlopers.

"Several months went by and then Helen's sister discovered our secret. She went straight to m'mother, and m'father returned from the city *subito*. They were furious and appalled, tellin' us there was, what they deemed, an *insurmountable impediment* to us bein' married. But when they wouldn't tell us what it was, I refused to believe them. It was just m'mother's prejudice against Helen. And as we had been up before parson there was nothin' they could do about it. Helen and I were married, and that was that."

When he took the cloth from the swelling because it was warm and went to soak it again, Alec did this for him. The cloth wrung out and cold again, Plantagenet Halsey gingerly put it to his head, held it there and continued, Alec silent and grave and not daring to interrupt.

"M'father returned from the city ill, and soon m'mother was ill too, both with the influenza. News of our marriage made 'em worse. So did our determination to remain married. M'mother never rose from her bed again. M'father demanded that I disavow the union; Helen and I were to act as if it had never happened. If we did this, then we would be forgiven and we'd all go back to how it was before, no one outside immediate family the wiser. He had me and Roderick to his bedside and demanded the parish records be destroyed. He made us promise to keep the entire episode a secret. O'course I was havin' nothin' to do with his edicts. We were husband and wife under the eyes of God. I was confident there was nothin' that could tear us apart.

"But m'brother, bein' the good and obedient son, gave our father his secret solemn promise to do his bidding. He hoped this promise would improve our father's health. What Rod didn't tell me was that our father, in his relief, or perhaps it was in the delerium of his fever, then confided in Rod that our mother had been right—he should've left the girls where they were, to be cared for by others, and not brought them into this house. He then confided in Rod the-the *insurmountable impediment.*

"M'brother waited his opportunity. It came mere weeks later when our father passed away. I made good on my promise to Rod and he became the earl of Delvin in my stead. His first act as Lord Delvin was to carry out our father's wishes. He had the parish records destroyed. He paid off the vicar who had married Helen and me, and sent him to a remote parish in northern Wales. But most devestatin' of all—and somethin' for which I never forgave him—he told Helen the reason why our parents had opposed our marriage… And then he told me. That was the end—of everythin'—m'marriage, our hopes and dreams for the future, and Helen's peace of mind… And it was the end of any brotherly love between Rod and me."

The old man's gaze flickered up to meet Alec's unblinking stare. Emotion choked his words, making his voice hoarse.

"Rod took from me everythin' that I loved in this world. And I thought he would take you, too. I fought hard to keep you, Helen and I both did. It was only after much persuadin' and promises made by us both that he finally agreed to release you to me."

"What promises?"

"That I never allow your mother to see you. That I agree to the fiction that Helen and Roderick were married—"

"But if your parents were against you marrying Helen, and so too was your brother, and there was this insurmountable impediment, how then could he maintain a fiction of being married to her? I presume, as your marriage to her was still legal, despite the steps taken to void it, that they pretended to be man and wife? Was he in love with my mother too?"

"Their marriage was a fiction, and it remained so for the rest of their lives," Plantagenet Halsey revealed bluntly. "They were man and wife in name only. In every respect they lived separate lives, yet maintained the pretense of being married when called upon for public occasions. As it turned out, the arrangement, such as it was, suited them both, and it suited me. He was Earl of Delvin, she was Countess of Delvin, and I agreed to keep my distance."

"If it was a fiction, then where did my brother Edward come from? Perhaps, if their marriage was in name only, she had committed adultery. In her letter she said she was forced to give me up in penance for her adultery, and—"

"Nonsense! All of it! The adultery was part of the larger fiction that she and my brother were married, and the reason why you were livin' with me and not with them... Believe me, your mother considered being branded an adulteress a small price to pay for your life. As to Edward's paternity..." He took a deep breath and shrugged. "I never asked and they never told me. And frankly, given all other considerations, I was beyond carin' one way or t'other. He was entitled to a son and heir, and as I'd ruined enough lives what did it matter how he came by him. And I ruined Joseph Cale's life—"

"Did Cale agreed to the fiction of being my mother's lover because he was your half-brother, and you asked it of him?"

"Somethin' like that... No one knew his intimate connection to us. M'father kept that close to his chest. And as Joseph looked more the son of a slave than he did a Halsey, m'father never owned to him. Though Joseph knew, and he told me much later, after he had become my valet, about our father's visits to the house he shared with his mistress, and the years they had as a family until Joseph's mother died giving birth to her third child, a girl."

The old man sighed, overcome with sadness.

"Joseph was a good man. He reminds me of our father in many ways. And not once did he cast blame, or show his anger at what had happened between Helen and me. And he allowed my brother—our brother—to publically humiliate him and accuse him of bein' the father of Helen's infant."

"I hope he was suitably compensated for his sacrifice!" Alec quipped bitterly.

"I paid him off so he could have a better life across the border in Edinburgh."

"Were there any other promises made, other lives ruined, all to get your brother to hand me over to you?"

The old man heard the hurt and sarcasm, but continued to ignore it. He made a concerted effort to keep his gaze on Alec and his voice steady.

"I gave Rod my word to never tell you the truth about your parentage in his lifetime or in the lifetime of his son and heir. Had Edward not been murdered, had he lived to a ripe old age—at least outlived me!—it would've meant that you may never have found out the truth about your birth, and we would never have had this conversation."

"Because you would have kept your word," Alec stated flatly. "Through thick and thin, through every accusation and rumor leveled at my head. Despite a lifetime of doubt, of not knowing the truth about my birth, or as Lady Ferris told me *what came before it*—which now I gather means what led to my conception—you would not have told me?"

"Alec, once given, I could not break my word. Not when it was given to save your life. You understand that, surely?"

"I wish I could say I did. But I don't."

Plantagenet Halsey's shoulders slumped and his breathing became shallow. The unhealthy pallor returned. Alec should have stopped interrogating him there and then, but he could not rest until he knew it all. The question he asked was not the one the old man was expecting.

"How did Lady Ferris discover you had married her sister?"

TWENTY-FIVE

Alec waited for Plantagenet Halsey's answer, gaze steady but heart beating hard. He was waiting for him to tell him what he had always wanted to hear and what he always believed in his heart to be the truth, but which no one had dared voice, and which his uncle had lied about on numerous occasions. And, so it seemed, had a lot of other people; none of them even hinting at the truth in all his thirty-six years.

"Lady Ferris discover that Helen and I were married?" Plantagenet Halsey repeated, as if he'd misunderstood the question. But the heat in his face told a different story, and he mentally criticized himself for his newfound prudishness. He blamed Olivia. Or perhaps, as the thudding pain in the back of his head reminded him, he'd had some sense knocked into him when he blacked out and hit the carpet. He smiled bashfully. Ye Gods! He *was* growin' prudish in his old age! "When two people are in love there are consequences, and we could not hide Helen's pregnancy forever—"

"*Finally*. There it is! And *still* you can't come out and say it!" Alec demanded explosively. "Haven't I given you enough opportunities to tell me of your own free will without the need to extract it from you like a good tooth in a young head?"

He scrambled to his feet and stared down at the old man as if he were a ghost, before covering his face with his shaking hands to try and control his overwhelming emotion. Long fingers splayed through his disorderly curls while he squeezed tight his eyes and took a deep breath. And then he let his arms drop heavily to his sides, not knowing whether to laugh or cry. He thought he was in control, but he could barely get the words out.

"All these years. All those nights as a boy, praying that what I wanted most in this world would, by some miracle, turn out to be true. I dreamed of you coming to me with the most astonishing news, of making the announcement at breakfast, that there had been a misunderstanding or a mistake or some such thing, and you would tell me just like that, as if it were the most ordinary circumstance in my day—that I was not your nephew and you were not my uncle. I didn't care a three-penny bit about how it all came about. All that I ever cared about was us, you and me. All I ever wanted you to tell me was the truth, the truth as I believe it in here, in my heart. And yet you cannot tell me, now, to my face, even after all these years… What's farcical is that I'm incapable of saying it out loud until you say it first. I have this irrational fear that if I do, it will turn out to be false and that dream will die inside me, and that part of my heart will die also. You must say it. Unless you do, it can never be—"

"Alec, how can I tell you—"

"It's a simple enough sentence to say, isn't it?"

"In our case nothin' is simple."

"For pity's sake! Are you going to continue to make excuses? To make me believe the web of lies you, your brother, my mother, and your half-brother spun to keep the truth from others, and from *me*?" When the old man hung his head, Alec frowned. Bitter disbelief sounded in his voice. "If you can't say it to me here, now, then at least tell me you have no intention of ever saying it, because then I will know that you don't want to say it!"

Plantagenet Halsey prevaricated, and it was too much for Alec. He threw a hand in the air as if to say he had had enough, and walked off. He didn't know what he was going to do or say or even if he could continue this conversation. But as he strode down the length of the library, into his mind's eye came the rememberance of being a small boy sitting at a very long table, alone with his uncle—*his uncle, ha!*—and being shown how to crack the shell of a boiled egg with the back of a spoon. That made him smile, and all the anger drained from him. He sank into the closest wingchair, exhausted, put his head in his hands and gave himself up to an overwhelming sadness.

ℋ

Plantagenet Halsey slowly struggled to his feet and was about to follow Alec when he saw the papers he'd had in his hand before he'd taken his fall and blacked out. They were at the edge of the carpet. He scooped them up and put them back on top of Hadrian Jeffries' open diary, knowing he still had the piece of paper with the family tree tucked away in his pocket. He had only taken a few steps when the double doors were flung wide, and this despite Alec giving orders they were to remain closed.

The Duchess of Romney-St. Neots sailed over the threshold, fan fluttering furiously, deaf to the entreaties of the two red-faced footmen hopping about at her back. She went straight up to the old man and tapped the closed sticks of her fan on the front of his waistcoat

"Why has a physician been summoned?" she demanded, peering up at him. In her periphery she caught sight of the jug, bowl, and discarded cloths, and she swiveled about to take a closer look at these articles in the middle of the carpet. "What's happened? Are you ill? Where's Alec?"

"Took a fall. But nothin' to—"

"Who took a fall?" She turned back to face him with a swish of her petticoats. "You? *You* did? Show me!"

Before he could protest, she grabbed his coat cuff and pulled him to a sofa, where she pushed him onto a cushion. When he gingerly put a hand to the back of his neck, she pulled him forward by his lapel so she could look over his shoulder to inspect his head. Seeing nothing, she gently ran the tips of her fingers through his grizzled hair until she came upon a lump.

"What made you fall—Good grief! That's quite a lump! You must have hit the floor hard. No skin broken and so no blood. Thank God! A cold compress will help take the swelling down." She stood straight and gently pushed him to sit up. "What you need is a dose of James's Powders and a lie-down before the physician gets here. What a pity Thomas isn't here to—"

"Your Grace. Olivia," he interrupted quietly, and when he had her full attention said in a voice he used only with her, "Livvy. Livvy, it's not m'head that's bruised. I couldn't—I didn't—tell him, but he knows…"

Olivia St. Neots's eyes went wide, and when he pulled her onto his lap, she did not resist but sat in a crumple of petticoats, steadying herself by putting her arm about his shoulders. "About us? You told him?"

He shook his head with a smile, and then contradicted himself. "Not that. I did tell him somethin' about us but you made me promise to wait, and I have. No. About him and me. About Helen—"

Her back went ramrod straight. She was aghast. "He knows about you and-and Helen? How? Did your meddlesome sister finally manage to tell—"

"Livvy, no. Not her. Me. I can't—I can't do it. I didn't do it. I'm—I'm a coward," he whispered in anguish. "He thinks I don't want to own him. How wrong can he be? But if I can't tell him the truth after all these years of lyin' to him, what can he think me but a miserable cur who—"

"Nonsense! You are nothing of the sort!" She smiled resignedly. "Did I not advise you to tell him as soon as you came down here to stay. You know you must tell him, so what are you waiting for?"

"But if I tell him part of it, I have to tell him all of it. And I-I don't think I can because as you now know the truth is far worse than had he been the product of an adulterous affair—"

"Rot, you silly man!" she castigated him lovingly. She whispered near his ear, "Tell him the part he *needs* to hear. That's all he has *ever* wanted from you. The rest can wait."

He pulled back and regarded her with such anguish that she held her breath on a sob. Neither were aware there was anyone else in the room, least of all that Alec had walked back up to join them and in time to hear what Plantagenet Halsey said next.

"Perhaps—perhaps you're right. That can wait—"

"I've waited this long, why not," Alec stated flatly, without apology.

The couple jumped and looked about and there was Alec standing before them, one of Stephens' workers, cap in hand, shuffling into the room when Alec motioned for him to do so.

"Please—Don't move for my sake," he added flatly. He made his godmother a bow. "I hear congratulations are in order?'"

The Duchess looked mulish and sheepish at one and the same time, if that were possible. She pouted. "We were hoping to tell you and Selina and the rest of the family when we are all gathered at dinner."

"Then I will hold my exuberance," Alec replied, still not a glance at the old man. "Dinner with the family will make your announcement that much more entertaining. Particularly with Cobham present. Now you must excuse me."

"Where are you off to?" the Duchess demanded. And when Alec cocked an eyebrow as if to say it was none of her business but was too polite to say so, she sat up taller on Plantagenet Halsey's lap and tried to appear imperious. "Your wife is about to give birth any day now, so it is imperative I—*we all*—know your movements, so we can find you at a moment's notice."

At that Alec did glance at Plantagenet Halsey before saying cryptically, "If I am needed, you can send word to the cellars." He motioned for the worker to come closer. "What has Mr. Stephens to tell me?"

The man bowed nervously, not a look at the couple on the sofa.

"Master says to let y'Lordship know archway's been breached. There's somethin' untoward and so Master is waitin' your instructions. Apologies, m'lord, and he did add to ask y'Lordship to be quick about it."

"Tell Mr. Stephens I will be there directly." He swiveled on a boot heel and addressed the old man. "Well, *uncle*, I don't know about you, but I for one want to know what our forebears were up to. Care to join me?"

"Down in the cellars?" The Duchess was shocked. She scrambled to her feet and shook out her petticoats. Any embarrassment she felt at being discovered sitting on Plantagenet Halsey's lap vanished, and such was her concern for his welfare that she was brusque with Alec. "He's had a nasty fall, and there's a lump the size of a hen's egg to the back of his head, and you want him to go with you into a musty old cellar? No! He—

"Olivia—"

"No I say!" she responded angrily to the old man's interruption, and again addressed Alec, "He will wait here with me for the physician and—"

"Livvy," Plantagenet Halsey began again, "I'm all right. And this is far more important than a hit to my clodpoll." When he grabbed at her hand she would not let him take her fingers and shooed him off. "Your Grace—"

"Don't *Your Grace* me in this way! Who's to say you won't black out again. What if that happens in a dark cellar where the floor is uneven? You would fare far worse than collapsing on a soft carpet! How are they to carry your long carcass out of there? It's foolhardy and just like you to—Don't! Don't you dare try to hold me! Not here. Not before-before—Damn you!"

Plantagenet Halsey held her against him for a long moment, until he felt her go still, and then he whispered he would be careful, kissed the top of her head and stepped away. The Duchess fussed with the sit of her bodice, fiddled with her fan, and kept her chin down, not a look at either man. Plantagenet Halsey regarded her with frowning concern, but Alec smiled, finding the scene touching. It dissolved the harshness from his tone.

"I only wish you to come with me if you feel up to it," he said gently to Plantagenet Halsey.

"I do and I am."

Alec put an arm about the Duchess's shoulders and leaned down to kiss her cheek. "I'll take good care of him and he'll be returned in time for the physician's visit. I promise."

Olivia St. Neots nodded, but still could not lift her chin. By the time she did, the double doors were closing on the backs of the two men who meant most in the world to her.

TWENTY-SIX

NEITHER SAID A WORD UNTIL THEY HAD REACHED THE TOP OF the cellar steps, and then Plantagenet Halsey waylaid Alec with a hand to his arm. Alec instantly thought him unwell but the old man shook his head, though he did lean his shoulders against the stonework to steady himself. One of two of Stephens' men who were guarding the entrance below started up the stairs with a flambeau, but Alec waved him back down, sensing Plantagenet Halsey wished to speak privately with him.

"I tried mighty hard for you not to find out what's down in that cellar," the old man confessed apologetically. "I thought it best for your peace of mind…"

"But until we do know, not knowing will hang over us like a black cloud," Alec replied steadily. "I don't want that for either of us, or for my family. I'm not angry with you for trying to shelter me. I realize it is just another of your efforts to protect me from our dreaded and, dare I say, despicable ancestors. But you don't know what's in that vault any more than I do, do you?"

"If you mean have I ever explored the ghastly place, no! I got the family history from my father, who got it from his, and so forth. That was enough for me."

"Then, other than being told that there is a vault in the cellar that was used to—what was the phrase…? Ah yes! *Honor the ancient family practice of interment*—you don't know for certain—"

"Alec! I didn't need to go in there to know what m'ancestors got up to. That phrase about honor and ancient family practice is a lot of elegant pap to justify the fact they were engaged in—" He leaned in close and whispered the word *murder*, before putting his shoulders back up against the stonework. "And there are supportin' documents and maps. The steward has some ancient papers locked away in his safe. And today I found a map of the vault in the library. It has thirty-eight crosses marked on it. They aren't there for the hell of it! They are *crosses*, for God's sake! I think they give a fair indication of what we can expect to find, don't you?"

"Thirty-eight?" When Plantagenet Halsey nodded grimly but remained silent, Alec took a deep breath, adding evenly, though he was anything but calm, "If there are thirty-eight bodies, then deal with it we must. And as your father didn't use the vault, and it seems, neither did my great-grandfather, then there hasn't been a body interred there for a hundred years—"

"Not since 1689," the old man muttered.

Alec's eyebrows shot up. "How precise."

"Don't ask me how I know that *now*, but I'll show you when we return to the library. There's a list."

"Then your brother, though he threatened to, and had the brick-work removed from the archway entrance, didn't use the vault either."

"Small comfort. But I'll take it."

"Then it's been seventy-five years, that's three generations, since our ancestors shouldered that burden you said was too much for some of them to bear. A euphemism for justifying murder—"

"There's more to it than them bein' a pack of murderers," Plantagenet Halsey burst out, and then lowered his voice. "Our ancestors committed a particular kind of murder, a kind so appallin' I can barely comprehend it. And I wish you didn't have to know about it!"

"Every murder is appalling. Think of the poor Turners. Hugh was just thirteen. So too his friend Will. Murder is murder, and those boys are forever taken from their families, and it happened just a matter of days ago! The Turners and the Bolens will have to bear it as best they can, and for the rest of their lives. Our ancestors committed murder for decades under the guise of respectability and being gentlemen and using words such as honor and burden. As you rightly said, that's a lot of elegant pap. But we are able to distance ourselves from our ancestors' crimes, and the fate of those poor wretches, because time is a great healer. We have seventy-five years between us and murder. Not so the Turners and the Bolens.

"And we are nothing like our ancestors, and our family never will be again. You took me away from here at birth. You turned your back on your murderous ancestry and you have spent your whole life trying to alleviate suffering and inequity. You and I must hold to the fact we are good men and we will continue to do good. So too will my children because they will learn by the example I set and which I learned from you—"

"Ah! My boy! I don't deserve your praise, not after what I've put you through. And this—" He made a gesture towards the steps. "Any way you cut it, havin' to deal with this is a burden, regardless there is a span of years that allows us a certain detachment. With you about to become a father you must feel it even more keenly. But you don't have to shoulder this alone. I'll be right here beside you."

"Thank you. It's because I am almost a father that I have the impetus to close this chapter of our family history once and for all," Alec told him gently. "I should warn you… If that vault does contain the ancestral remains of thirty-eight of our kin, then I intend to have them removed and given a proper burial—"

"Alec, Alec, have you not worked out what-what kin they are? You can't speak of them as *remains*, they're not remains. Those thirty-eight crosses belong to-to—*infants*. Each cross represents a-a *baby boy*—a-a *newborn*. They were sacrificed—*sacrificed*—on the high altar to inheritance by our ancestors, all to make certain an only son inherited this estate. Any male siblin's were disposed of—*murdered*— to keep land from bein' subdivided amongst them. It's so unspeakable, I can barely fathom the ancients carryin' out such barbarity, least of all our ancestors practicin' it to keep a few clods of earth together. Is it any wonder men killed themselves rather than carry out such a horrific deed? What manner of-of—family *monster* turns it into a macabre tradition perpetuated down the ages? It's got a name, this type of murder—filicide. And it's got to be one of the most horrifyin' words in the English language."

"Yes. Yes it is," Alec agreed croakily and quickly cleared his throat of a phantom obstruction. "I cannot answer for our ancestors, or even begin to understand what drove them, how they convinced themselves to commit murder, to justify in their own minds that it was perfectly acceptable to kill an infant. A newborn is a precious life, a defenceless life, a gift from God. It is a life a father must love and cherish and protect with every fiber of his being. As I will protect my child, and as you protected me—"

"Oh! Ah! My dear, dear boy," Plantagenet Halsey cried out in anguish. "And a fine protector I turned out to be—lyin' to you, allowin' you to grow up not knowin' your mother or your father. Allowin' others to think you were cast out and undeservin' of this place, your birthright, and the title. Truth is, that part of you which came from your dear mother—her blood and her ancestry—is far nobler and honest than anythin' the male line could provide. Never forget that. I don't deserve you—"

"Nonsense!" Alec cut in and tried to rally him. But while he managed to keep his voice strong, the flush to his lean cheeks and the tears in his eyes revealed the depth of his emotional turmoil. "You are too hard on yourself, as always." With a gentle smile he stated simply, "You are and always will be my exemplar."

The old man fell all to pieces, and through a mist of tears, he pulled Alec into his arms and hugged him as if his life depended on keeping him in his arms and not letting him go. Finally he released him. Gaze locked on his, he said in a voice filled with emotion, "You are the finest son a man could wish for. I've dreamed of this day for so many years now that I thought it would always remain a dream—of finally bein' able to call you my son. For that is who you are—*my son* —and always have been. And I love you with all my heart."

"Father!"

They embraced again, this time so overcome in the moment that time was lost. They would have stayed locked that way far longer if not for the interruption from the base of the steps, when Stephens called up to them. He then sent one of his men with a flambeau to the top of the steps.

Stephens apologized for the urgency. The sunlight was weakening and soon would be gone altogether behind black clouds that were rumbling in from the south. A thunderstorm was brewing, Stephens explained when Alec and Plantagenet Halsey came down the steps to meet him. And as rain was likely at any minute, the tarpaulin would have to be put back and secured over the hole in Stone Court as soon as possible. So if His Lordship wished to see inside the vault without flambeau, it was possible now while it was being lit from above.

"*Inside?*" Alec was surprised. When the foreman nodded, he glanced at his father, asking Stephens, "How is it possible you saw this light? Isn't there a door, and a padlocked one at that, between the vestibule and the inside of the vault?"

"There is a door. But it is best I show Your Lordship. Then you'll understand what I mean."

When Alec nodded, the foreman turned and waved for the worker with the flambeau to walk before them. Alec took Plantagenet Halsey's arm, lest he was unsteady on his feet, and arm in arm they silently followed Stephens deep into the cellars. When they arrived at the archway, the bricks that had been removed were piled either side of this entrance way, some stacked neatly but others more haphazard. The foreman explaining that once it became apparent sunlight was streaming down from above, which indicated the space was open to the elements, and that news from up top told them there had been a change in the weather, there came a greater sense of urgency to get the job done before the heavens opened. Hence the messiness.

"The strong gusts were playing havoc with the tarpaulin," the foreman explained. "My men found it had come loose from one of its moorings, and with none of Mr. Turner's men keeping an eye on things—"

"The tarpaulin?" Alec cut in, anxious.

"Once we'd breached the archway and could see in, we were taken by surprise by a shaft of light, at times intense and at other moments it disappeared altogether," explained Stephens. "That's when I realized the tarpaulin must be flapping about above. And now it's been removed altogether, you should have enough light to explore that room without the need for a flambeau. But we'll take one with us just in case the thunder clouds roll over the sun. I predict it's going to be quite a storm—"

"Then let's get on with it!" Plantagenet Halsey interrupted gruffly. "Can't be standin' about wonderin' when they'll be a thunderstorm. It'll happen regardless, and sooner rather than later if you keep gabbin' on!"

"Yes, sir," Stephens said evenly, taking the old man's grumpiness in his stride. "If you'll both follow me."

The foreman went under the archway, and Alec and Plantagenet Halsey followed. Neither said a word or exchanged a look, sensing the apprehension in the other.

The vestibule was unremarkable and was like any other cellar room, with rough-hewn plastered and whitewashed walls, a low ceiling, and a brick-paved floor that was covered in a fine layer of dust, kicked up and disrupted for the first time in many decades by the boots of Stephens and his men. And it was dark. If not for the flambeau, it would have been pitch black.

But it was at the farthest wall straight ahead, opposite the archway, that Alec stared. No wonder Stephens had set his men to quickly dismantle the bricks. A shaft of light beamed down through the gaping hole in the courtyard and into a room beyond the vestibule, sunshine illuminating a pile of rubble in the middle of the floor. And then the light disappeared, as if a candle had been snuffed. Just as quickly the beam reappeared, and brighter than before. It all became clear to Alec why it was possible to see sun shining into the vault. Plantagenet Halsey voiced his thoughts first.

"I don't think this bump to m'head has affected m'sight... That door is wide open!"

TWENTY-SEVEN

THE HEAVY OAK DOOR TO THE VAULT WAS AJAR, THE PADLOCK and chain nowhere to be seen. Alec quelled an angry outburst, thinking his orders had been defied, to say with restrained curtness, "Mr. Stephens, I made myself plain that we would wait the arrival of my attorney with the key."

"You did, my lord. And we didn't touch a thing," Stephens explained. "This is how we found the door when we broke through the archway. It was open and there was no padlock or chain as you described. Take a closer look, my lord. You'll see there are no boot-prints across the threshold. I told my men to hold back. And we did. We fetched you straight away."

Alec and Plantagenet Halsey looked at one another, and had the same thoughts: Who had a key to the vault, and why had they unlocked the door and left it ajar?

"Would Your Lordship care to take a look? The weather won't hold much longer…"

At the entrance to the vault, Alec turned to his father and said in an undervoice, "Whatever we find in there, know this: We are not our forebears."

He then held out his hand and they walked into the room hand in hand, father behind son.

※

THERE WERE SMALL NICHES CUT DEEP INTO THE STONEWORK, one row above the other and running the length of two of the white-washed walls. To anyone who did not know to what purpose this room had been put, it looked to be an extension of the wine cellar. Perhaps that is what it had been long ago, thought Alec, because the niches were bricked compartments able to hold more than a dozen bottles of wine and were no different in shape or size to those on the other side of the wall. What was different about this room was that there were no sconces to allow for tapers, and it had none of the para-phernalia that comes with wine storage. In fact, the room was eerily empty with a heavy mustiness clinging to the bricks and in the air, indicating years of being sealed, the oak door padlocked against trespass.

The only sign of life came from the sunlight which streamed in through the collapsed ceiling, straight from the heavens, illuminating the space with an ethereal otherworldliness. The sunshine beamed down on a pile of rubble, formed when the brick roof collapsed, and the stone flaggings and bricks crashed and splintered upon hitting the stone floor. Alec presumed this was the most activity this room had seen in decades, for the bricked niches not only remained untouched —they were empty.

For Alec this was a huge relief. Plantagenet Halsey had an alto-gether different response.

The old man stomped up and down the line of niches and looked in every one. He did this with a thoroughness that suggested to the foreman and workers that he was searching for something specific. He went so far as to stick his head in some, to stretch a hand down the length of others, and finally to squat to look up under the top of a few, as if he would find whatever it was he was looking for hiding there.

Alec wasn't surprised to find men crowded around the doorway eager to know what was in the room for which they had toiled to remove a wall of bricks in record time. And when the beam of light disappeared again and one of the men came forward with a taper, he was reminded a heavy downpour was predicted at any moment. So he went up to Plantagenet Halsey, who was repeating his search of the empty niches, and gently touched his arm.

"I need to let Stephens and his men secure the tarpaulin before the heavens open up—"

"What? Yes!" Plantagenet Halsey replied, giving a start. He was so deep in thought, he had no idea what Alec had said. He was preoccupied, and he was livid. "It's all been a damned lie! There never were any bodies! It's a myth. Has to be! Of all the tricks to serve—"

"You want there to be bodies?"

"What? A'course I don't want there to be bodies," the old man hissed, pulling Alec aside so the foreman couldn't hear them. "What I want is the truth. There were thirty-eight crosses on that plan, and for centuries Halsey men have followed that God-awful edict etched in the market square, and our family not the only ones! More fool us, and my father for believing what he was told by his father!"

"Our ancestors who commited suicide did so for good reason," Alec argued. "And there is a reason that saying was chiseled into the square. You forget. The numbers do not lie."

"The thirty-eight—"

"Not the thirty-eight. What I should have said is the *lack* of numbers. You heard Selina at nuncheon. It's all but impossible for a family to have only one son and no daughters for generation after generation. That is a *contrivance*." Alec looked over his shoulder at his patient and silent foreman, and then back at his father. "We haven't even touched on what happened to the daughters born into our family, though I have a theory about that."

"You do? So do I."

"Good. We'll exchange theories later. But for now, you can forget that there is a myth or you've been duped. Just because we haven't found what we were expecting here, doesn't mean what we think happened didn't. Remember the door was unlocked..."

The old man's bushy brows shot up. "You think they were removed?"

"Is there another plausible explanation?"

"Not that I can think of at this precise moment," Plantagenet Halsey said in a much more subdued tone. He smiled weakly. "To tell you a truth, I ain't feelin' quite the thing. This damned bump to m'head is threatenin' to turn into a megrim, so if it's all the same to you, it would be best if we reconvened after I've had a lie-down—"

"—and had a visit from the physician. Olivia insists. And so do I."

Leaving his father to grumble good-naturedly under his breath about interferin' relatives, Alec went over to his foreman.

"If it's acceptable to Your Lordship, we'll get this rubble cleared away. Once the tarpaulin is secure, we'll make a start on getting the scaffolding up. I have men prepared to work all night to repair the ceiling. But it will depend on the severity of the downpour as to how much we get done."

"Thank you, Stephens. And thank your men for getting the job done as quickly as possible. They can all have a double ration of cider for their efforts, and an extra loaf of bread."

"Much appreciated, my lord. I had word from the steward's lodge that the Turner boy's funeral is tomorrow..."

"I'll be giving the senior members of my household leave to attend the funeral, so if you wish to take the wagon with them to the parish church, you are welcome."

"Here's hoping the storm passes tonight and the sun is shining for the lad tomorrow."

※

SELINA HOPED SO TOO, WHEN SHE CAME INTO ALEC'S DRESSING room an hour later, a hand to the middle of her aching back, the other holding a sheaf of papers. She found her husband soaking in his bath, up to his neck in suds, with an arm dangling over the side, and dozing. She wondered how he could sleep through the pelting rain, gusting winds, and thunder claps. She jumped every time there was a flash of light, waiting for the inevitable boom of thunder, and praying it was far off and not, as her brother insisted, directly overhead.

There went another loud clap, and not only Selina but Alec's valet and two assistants gave a little jump. They then made themselves scarce, leaving the couple alone. She came straight up to the bath, picked up one of the hand towels, and lightly trailed it along Alec's arm, so as to wake him gently. When he opened an eye, she said,

"Clive thinks our house will be burned to the ground in this lightning storm."

"What? In a deluge? Are you worried?"

She shook her head with a smile. "No. But he is! And so I agreed with him. And I never agree with him, so now he is truly worried. Fool."

Alec grinned and sat up, careful not to splash water over the edge of the bath, and smoothed the wet ringlets out of his eyes. He took the hand towel from her and wiped his face dry.

"Thank you. And for waking me. I suspect your brother is wanting his dinner and I am keeping him waiting."

"He can wait. Besides, when I left Aunt Olivia, she was still in the dressing stage. She wouldn't let Dr. Riley leave until she was truly satisfied your uncle had suffered nothing more than a bruise and a bump. And now Riley can't leave because of the storm. So he'll be staying the night. Are they lovers do you think?

"Who? Riley and your aunt?"

"Silly! You know perfectly well I'm talking about my aunt and your uncle! They certainly act like an old married couple."

"I thought them acting like a newly-married couple."

"But we don't fuss at each other like they do."

"Oh? Is that what old married couples do, fuss?"

"Yes. A lot. Well, those that still care for each other do. Are they lovers?"

"Would it bother you if they were?"

Selina shrugged. "If they are, I envy them. At their age, they can enjoy the carnal delights of the bedchamber without the conse-quences."

Alec chuckled. "And Olivia hasn't earned that, what with ten adult children married off and too many grandchildren to count? Besides," he added, grabbing her hand and kissing the back of it before looking up at her, "You don't think, at their age, it might be more about companionship than bed-hopping?"

"You may be right, but I do hope it is a bit of both, for their sakes. They deserve to be happy... And I'm being inordinately petu-lant because I am thoroughly consumed with wanting our baby in my arms and not still in me! And that is one of the reasons I'm here. Aunt Olivia says I must walk, *a lot*. Apparently it will help bring on the contractions. And if it doesn't, this dreadful storm just might!" She studied her husband a moment, and asked, surprised and suspicious, "Why the self-satisfied smile? You look the cat given cream. And please do not say it is because you are eagerly awaiting fatherhood. *That* smile is different from *this* smile."

Alec's smile widened and he shook his head. Despite mental exhaustion causing him to fall asleep in his bath, and in the middle of a storm no less, he was exultant. Emotional revelations concerning his ancestors aside, nothing could take away his happiness in finally realizing a boyhood dream of knowing his father. A lifetime of uncertainty that had been a void within him was now filled to the brim with contentment. He wanted to share this with Selina, and the wider world. But something made him hesitate to confide in her. He wasn't sure why but a gut feeling warned him to wait, that there was more he had to learn, about his birth, about his mother, and about his parents' relationship, before he could make such an announcement. And he felt he owed it to his father to seek his permission before disclosing any details to anyone, and that included his wife. And while he was uncomfortable withholding anything from Selina, he justified this, as he did keeping from her the horrifying details of Hugh Turner's death, and of his ancestors' murderous behavior, by not wanting to upset her in anyway while pregnant, particularly when it was Olivia's opinion the baby was due any day. Such news could wait, everything could wait, until after the baby's arrival.

So instead of answering her, he did what he had made a habit of doing over the course of Selina's pregnancy, he deflected unpleasantness by asking a question of his own.

"Is that the other reason you've invaded the male inner sanctum?" he asked, indicating the papers she held.

She was not fooled by his deflection but it did remind her why she had interrupted his bath. She held them up.

"I found these in the library. They were atop Jeffries' diary. One is a list and the other a map. I haven't had a chance to ask him, and would never do so here—"

"List? Map?" Alec interrupted, trying to keep his voice steady. He recognized the handwriting on the paper his wife held up as that belonging to his mother; he also remembered his father mentioning a list of names while they were in the cellar, and that he, too, had found this in the library. "A list of what, pray tell?"

"Names. But the list is not in your valet's handwriting and there are dates, too. And they are all male Christian names—"

"How many names?"

"Thirty-eight. Why? Is the number more odd to you than the fact all the names are male?"

"Not necessarily. You said the names were male. The next logical question was the number of names…" Alec replied evenly. "Which makes me then ask if the number thirty-eight is of more significance to you because of your peculiar affinity for numbers?"

Selina smiled. "His Lordship knows me well. Yes! It is the number which interests me, because on this second piece of paper is drawn a map, and it has upon it thirty-eight crosses. And that corresponds to the number of names—"

"Coincidence?"

"That is a possibility. But given these papers were together, with one being a list of names and the other a map, and the numbers correspond, I think it obvious."

"It is?"

"Yes. Look at the layout of the map. See," She unfolded the paper and held it up, but then just as quickly let her arm drop, a flush to her cheeks. "Forgive me. I forgot. You need your glasses…"

"I do. No matter. You tell me while I submerge all but my head in this tepid water. But I will have to get out soon."

"Of course. I am keeping you from dressing," she muttered, suddenly awkward at her self absorption. "You must be cold."

"I am, but what is more important is that you have forgotten all about the storm raging overhead. There have been three loud thunderclaps in the last little while and you did not jump once. What is the significance of the number thirty-eight?" he prompted.

"It's not the number, but that the two pieces of paper correspond, names and crosses. I think this map is a drawing of a cemetery—"

"Because there are names and crosses?"

"The way the map is drawn up and the placement of the crosses makes me think so. The fact all the names on the list are male, leads me to wonder if what is buried in this cemetery are favored dogs, or horses, or perhaps both, or pets in general. And it is an ancient cemetery, because the first entry is for a Linus in 1215. Linus sounds like the name one gives a trusty steed, doesn't it? What?" she asked when Alec's mouth turned down. She took this as a sign of disbelief and baulked. "You think I'm being fanciful!"

"Not at all. Your theory is as good as any I've heard—"

"So you've known about this list and the map all along?"

"—for why the two marry up so well," Alec continued smoothly, ignoring her accusation. "And I do not see why the family would not want to bury favored animals in their own plot—

"That at least is something you have in common with your family —a love of animals," Selina argued. She gave a jerk of her head towards Cromwell and Marziran who were curled up beside the bath, as close as they could get to their master without jumping into the water with him. "Your four-legged children are going to feel somewhat unloved when this little one arrives."

"They don't like storms any more than you do, my darling. And you wrong them. They will be protective older brothers, you'll see."

"So it's not fanciful to think this is a pet cemetery, is it?" Selina persisted with a smile of triumph.

"No. It is not. And I would love to give your list and map further consideration when I am dressed."

"There is one last odd circumstance about the number thirty-eight. And I should dismiss it as mere coincidence... My logical mind tells me to. But that same mind also tells me there are few instances which are coincidence when one sees a pattern, so perhaps there is something to it."

"Trust your instincts. I do."

"Good. Then I shall. Thirty-eight names. Thirty-eight crosses. Thirty-eight white roses."

"Roses?"

"The number of white roses Lady Ferris had cut from a garden she told us is in the far corner of the walled meadow on the other side of the house. It was planted by your mother, and it seems it has been somewhat neglected since her passing. Lady Ferris had one of our gardeners bring me a bunch for the table at nuncheon the other day, don't you remember?"

"I do. And you counted them—?"

"I was bored. It was while the young Mr. Ferris was rabbiting on about his good fortune... I did my best to appear interested, and counting the number of roses in the bunch helped with that—You're frowning again."

"I was remembering something my aunt said when I thanked her for the roses. She said the garden was in a spot that was not the best place for roses to thrive, and yet these roses were thriving. She said there must be something particular in the soil—"

"She said that? She used those words '*something particular in the soil*'?" When Alec nodded, Selina's eyes shone with triumph. "That's it then! It must be a cemetery! Those dear animals have fertilized the soil for the roses to bloom. Lady Ferris must know what's buried there, but she didn't want to say so at nuncheon for fear of upsetting us. Or possibly she did not wish to upset me." She made a face at Alec that was half glare, half smile. Whatever it was, Alec knew she was not angry with him when she said imperiously, "It seems you aren't the only one trying to shield me from any unpleasantness. It must be a universal inclination to want to keep pregnant women in ignorance for fear of upsetting them!"

"Perhaps she was merely being polite?" Alec suggested lightly, not refuting her assertions.

Selina thought about it a moment then nodded. "I suppose here in the cultural wastelands of the country, people are far more concerned with what is and what isn't polite conversation at the nuncheon table, than the content of the discussion. Whereas we town dwellers don't seem to mind in the slightest what is discussed, as long as it is interesting; politeness be damned."

"Remind me never to mention pet cemeteries at our dinner table here at Deer Park ever again."

Selina giggled. "Silly!" She leaned down as far as she was physically able, to kiss Alec, and this was achieved when he half rose out of the bath to meet her. "When the weather breaks and the sun is shining again, I'd like to be taken to see this family pet cemetery."

"Any particular reason other than to satisfy your curiosity and to confirm that you are in the right about this list and the map?" Alec asked in what he hoped was a light tone. What worried him was not taking her to visit a cemetery, but if that cemetery—if indeed that was what the rose garden turned out to be—was not the last resting place of favored pets, but something far more sinister and heartbreaking. So he added, hoping to put her off, "Could it not wait until our infant arrives? After all, it is quite a walk to the farthest corner of the walled meadow, and I would not want you to go into labor so far from the house; nor would Olivia."

"There is that, but I am keen to see it sooner rather than later, because after I will be preoccupied for quite some time. Perhaps I could be taken in the sedan chair?"

"We have a sedan chair? Here at this house?"

"We do. It's presently in the Countess's room. That's what I call the guest bedchamber closest the stairs. It was your mother's room, and the sedan chair hers. Your uncle told me it was his idea, so she could get about the place and not have to walk."

"Because of her arthritis?" When Selina nodded, Alec had a sudden tightness in his chest to think he had not known, or that his mother's arthritis had been so debilitating. What sort of son must she have thought him? He and Edward both had not treated her well... He shook himself out of his self-castigation and tried to dissuade Selina. A thunder clap just then was apposite. "Even were you to use the sedan chair, I doubt the ground would be dry enough tomorrow to allow for the chairmen to convey you without mishap across a soggy lawn, do you?"

"There is that... Do pet cemeteries have headstones?"

"I have no idea. Why? Do you want headstones?"

"No! I'd rather there weren't any. Just the rose bushes."

"Because?"

"I thought that obvious. I don't want our son finding out his parents chose his name from a pet cemetery!"

"Have we chosen a name...?"

"Linus."

Alec returned her triumphant smile. He hoped his looked genuine because he did not like the name at all. But he wasn't going to tell her, or why he thought it no coincidence the first name on that list was Linus.

Ever since he'd been told about the list, the name Linus had been bothering him. Not because of his dislike, but why the name Linus was chosen, and that it must mean something. It came to him while drifting off to sleep in his bath to the sound of rumbling thunder. He recalled his classics education, and Homer in particular, and the reason given why a mournful song was known as a *linus*. It was said that a princess named Psamathe, from the city of Argos, bore the god of manly beauty, Apollo, a son—Linus. She then exposed that son on a mountainside where it was devoured by dogs, and in retribution

Apollo plagued Argos until he was satisfied its people had made reparation for the death of his infant son.

Alec had then woken with a start, shivering, not from cold or because a flash of bright light from a strike of lightning lit up the mullioned windows and penetrated his eyelids. Selina's artist brother Talgarth called him Apollo, and so did Selina when she was at her most teasing. Thus the last name he would ever choose for his son was Linus.

Perhaps he'd tell Selina about the story of Apollo and Psamathe and their son Linus. That should be enough to convince her to find a more suitable name they could both agree upon.

Tomorrow he would confide all this in Plantagenet Halsey and if the weather cleared take the trek across the parkland to the far reaches of the walled garden, and without Selina.

TWENTY-EIGHT

WHY, ALEC WONDERED, WITH A HOUSE THAT COVERED approximately seven acres, was it in his private apartment, specifically his dressing room closet, that he had the most interruptions to his day? Was it because his servants and his family unconsciously considered him cornered, and thus he could not easily escape them? Not that he wanted to hide, but he did crave some respite at the end of a long day. And this day had particularly dragged, beginning with being woken an hour before he needed to be, and ending with heated words exchanged between Selina and Cobham after dinner in the drawing room, Lady Sybilla doing her best to play peacemaker.

He wasn't sure what was more stormy, the weather outside, or the thunder and lightning argument between the siblings. It made him glad to have been brought up an only child, and pray that his own children were not as chalk and cheese as were Selina and her brother.

Sitting on his dressing stool in his banyan, he tried to recall who or what had started their argument. And then his valet came soft-footed into the closet and interrupted his train of thought. He had already said good night to Hadrian Jeffries, and here he was again, standing in the doorway holding what looked to be folded bedlinen.

"Sorry to disturb, sir. This came for you while you were at dinner. I took the liberty of thinking it important enough for you to see it now, rather than wait until morning. And I did not want to leave it lying about in case Her Ladyship ventured in here and asked about it.

So I wrapped it up in a couple of pillowcases. It's delicate. May I put it on the dressing table?"

That Hadrian Jeffries did not want Selina to see it intrigued Alec enough for him to wave his valet closer.

"Shall I move your handiwork, or do you want to do that?" he quipped, glancing across the exacting placement of his personal grooming implements on the dressing table.

"If you would put the hairbrushes across to the left, sir, that should provide enough space."

Alec did as requested and held his questions until Hadrian Jeffries had slowly and carefully placed the wrapped item on the table. He then watched his valet unfold the cloth. He wasn't sure what he was looking at when it was revealed to him other than whatever it had been it was now in pieces and looked to have been dropped from a great height or flattened under a great weight. Either way, it was irreparable.

"I'm afraid the men who found it were slipshod in collecting it all up," Hadrian apologized. "And again, I took a liberty, and did my best to reconstruct it. But as you can see, pieces are missing, and as they were possibly pulverized to dust, there is little chance of it being repaired."

Alec put on his spectacles. "If anyone can reconstruct a puzzle from shards," he mused, peering closely at the pieces, "it's you, Hadrian."

"Thank you, sir."

"Whatever it once was," Alec said, carefully lifting a splinter of wood between thumb a forefinger, "where was it found?"

"Sorry, sir. I should've said. Mr. Stephens' men found it in the cellar—"

"Where in the cellar?"

"Mr. Stephens said it was under the rubble in the vault. He thinks it was flattened when the roof caved in."

"That would certainly do it. Do you think it was at one time, before the Stone Court flagging gave way, a small wooden box with brass hinges and a lock?"

"Yes, sir. That's exactly what I do think. So does Mr. Stephens. He brought the pieces to me personally, saying you would not want anyone else knowing about it, on account of where it was found."

Alec took off his gold rims and looked at his valet. "This is all very intriguing, but it can't be the reason Stephens came to you, or why you came to me at this hour." When Hadrian Jeffries could not stifle a thin smile and bowed his head in acknowledgement, Alec asked as calmly as he could manage, "What was in the box?"

"It's there, sir, sandwiched between the top and bottom layer of splinters. I put it where I thought it would've been before the box was smashed."

"How exacting of you." Alec put his spectacles back on and carefully removed the top layer of wooden splinters, putting the pieces to one side on the cloth. "A letter!"

"Yes, sir. And unopened. The wax seal is still intact."

Alec extracted the folded piece of paper with its seal and lightly blew across the surface to remove dust and debris. And then he just sat there staring at the words inked across the face of the parchment. The letters were shakily formed, as if whoever wrote them had an unsteady hand due to age or an infirmity. But he knew it to be the latter, because he recognized the writing as belonging to his mother. But what he found remarkable were the three words written in her fist —*For my son.*

"I'll say good night again, sir…"

"Yes. Yes. Do that…"

Alec had no idea what his valet had said and in some sort of trance he opened a dressing table draw and put away his glasses. And with them he left the letter, to be opened when he was wide awake, and with his father present. Tomorrow…

⚭

HE CARRIED AROUND HIS MOTHER'S LETTER IN HIS FROCK COAT pocket for most of the next day. In that pocket was also the map and list Selina had brandished about while he was having his bath. And it wasn't until early afternoon that father and son were finally able to meet up.

Alec managed to slip away from the drawing room, and a subdued family gathering, the argument between the siblings still bubbling just under the surface. He used the excuse the greyhounds needed a run with the weather clearing, and it was now or never because their guests were arriving for dinner later that afternoon and he would need to dress. It was all true, and Selina sent him off with a kiss and a smile.

Her smile hid the fact her intuition told her she knew where he was headed. Intuition and the fact she had spent a good ten minutes that morning looking for the map and the list to show her aunt and cousin, and neither she nor Evans could find it. And now she suspected her husband had them all along, and was off to see this pet cemetery for himself, and without her. She should have been annoyed he was excluding her, but she was too tired to feel anything at all. She and Alec and their personal servants had spent a sleepless night, everyone thinking this was the night, in the rain, the hail, and the lightning, when the baby had decided to arrive. Then the pains subsided and she finally drifted off to sleep before dawn. She suspected from the darkness under his lovely eyes and the fact he was unshaven, Alec had not slept at all.

Thinking his wife none the wiser as to his destination, Alec strode out across the open expanse of sodden meadow within the walled garden with his four-legged companions bounding ahead of him, tails wagging to be out in the fresh air. And behind him, each carrying a wicker basket of gardening implements, were two of the gardeners, extracted from the teams working to clean up after the previous night's storm. Evidence of the storm's destructive force was every-where, from snapped branches and felled trees to flattened crops and garden fencing. And even here, within the protection of a high brick wall, a substantial rose garden, overgrown and trailing the wall, had not been left unscathed, a gale whipping through the bushes and shaking free a thousand white rose petals.

$$\mathcal{H}$$

PLANTAGENET HALSEY RETURNED FROM THE STEWARD'S HOUSE to find Alec's valet waiting for him with the cryptic message: His Lordship could be found in the most northerly corner of the walled meadow, gathering white roses for Her Ladyship's dinner table. The old man had no idea what it all meant, but he was all for slipping away before he could be pounced on by the females of the household waiting for his précis of Hugh Turner's funeral.

He'd had a restless night's sleep too. Only because he had refused to take the laudanum prescribed by Dr. Riley. Thus he spent the evening with a splitting headache, pretending he did not have one, because Olivia was anxious and angry with him for being as stubborn as an old mule. It was the word old that bothered him most. And when she stomped off to her own rooms, satisfied he was not in any danger because anyone that stubborn could not be that ill, he spent the rest of the night tossing and turning, head thudding, and feeling sorry for himself.

That was the last he saw of the Duchess, because he had not gone down to dinner, too ill to do so, and he had breakfasted in his rooms. All this would further inflame her, because she had worked herself up into a mental frenzy about making their announcement to the family, and his absence would be a further black mark against him. He did not blame her. It was his fault. Yet the thought of enduring it all with that cod-faced Clive Cobham at the table gaping at him, and he with a thudding headache, was all too much.

And now he was avoiding her altogether. Alec's cryptic message couldn't have come at a better time. He changed into a pair of old riding breeches, worn frock coat, his second-best riding boots, gingerly pushed a hat down over his grizzled hair, and was out of his rooms and heading across the sodden meadow in record time.

When he arrived at his destination, he was out of breath and staring at what he supposed had been, before the storm, a delightful, if overgrown, and well-ordered garden. The rose bushes were planted in neat rows, but even he could see that they had been left to go wild, with the more robust bushes now climbing and clinging to the bricks. And all would have been heavy with blooms before yesterday. Now rose petals were strewn across the ground, watered in by the torrential rains. There were so many that from a distance it appeared as if snow lay undisturbed under the boughs. Petals stuck to the boot treads of two gardeners going about the business of bringing order to chaos, and to the long snouts of Alec's greyhounds, snuffling about on the gardeners' heels.

Alec came over to join him. Both smiled at one another, words unnecessary to convey that after yesterday's emotional revelations, their relationship had gone from strength to strength. The old man would never again lie to his son, and his son wanted to include him in everything. But before Alec could explain why he had brought him out here, the old man needed to get something off his chest.

"Apologies for not makin' it to dinner last night. Our announcement put off yet again by my absence!" He rolled his eyes and smiled sheepishly, then frowned, saying, "But that's not what's troublin' me, why I couldn't sleep. Nothin' to do with the lump to m'head either, which is fine, by the by. It's those two children, Nicolas and Sally Fisher. I looked in on 'em before I went off to Hugh Turner's funeral. The housekeeper says the girl is as bonny as can be, but the boy still clings to her as if at any moment he expects a ghost to come out of the woodwork and make a grab for him! Poor saplin'!"

"He's had an exceptionally traumatic experience, one that will haunt him for a long time to come. But I am hopeful that once the killer is brought to justice, he'll no longer feel he's in danger, and he'll begin to talk. Living here under my protection should also help him feel safe." Alec smiled thinly. "But it's not their safety that's worrying you most, is it?"

"You're right. It ain't. I know they're safe here with us. It's somethin' else. Somethin' about them... I can't put m'finger on it."

"They remind you of someone."

"That's it!" Plantagenet Halsey said with a snap of his fingers. "I thought it was the bump to m'head givin' me such thoughts. But I didn't have a bump yesterday at Old Bill's cottage—" The old man peered at Alec. "They remind you of someone too, don't they."

"Can you guess?"

Plantagenet Halsey waved a hand. "Wracked the brain and came up with nothin'. You tell me."

"Sir Tinsley—"

"What? *Ferris*? You think those two children are his?"

"No. Not directly."

"What d'you mean—*not directly*?"

"That they are related to our magistrate, but perhaps in the second degree..."

"Not his children, but the children of his children or something like that?"

"Yes. Exactly like that."

The old man scratched his shaven cheek and pursed his mouth in thought. "He and Lady Ferris had two children, but both died young, so I don't see how Ferris can be related to Nic and Sally Fisher..."

"Come now! This is Fivetrees!" Alec was thinking of the Colonel's confession about giving up his newborn daughter, but he would not betray that confidence if he did not need to. "It was not uncommon in Fivetrees for the infant daughters of our forebears, and those of our land-owning neighbors, to be given to the Fishers, was it? So why not illegitimate offspring also?"

"I suspected..."

Alec was incredulous. "You didn't know female infants were given away? You didn't wonder at the meaning of that part of the saying chiseled in stone in the market square: *...and have no daughters to your name?*"

"I said, I suspected," Plantagenet Halsey confessed, annoyed, a guilty blush to his cheeks. "But I never asked. No one ever did. Cowardly, I know. But I was afraid of what the answer might be."

"Your father never mentioned anything about Halsey daughters when he confided in you what happened to those sons born after their eldest brother?"

The old man shook his head but conceded, "That don't mean to say he didn't know, and about his neighbors too. He sired only two sons with m'mother, and from what I can gather that was the end of their marital relations. Because dealin' with selfsame twin sons was enough of a dilemma for them, without havin' to worry about other legitimate sons and daughters—"

"—because under the law of gavelkind, all siblings, male and female, born of a legitimate marriage have equal rights to an estate?"

"Aye. That is the way of things down here in Kent," huffed the old man, guilty blush deepening further.

"Before you ask, Cobham explained gavelkind to me." Alec grinned when his father pulled a face of disbelief. "I told you my brother-in-law provides the odd pearl, if one listens... You can correct me, but if I extrapolate what he told me, then you inherited an equal share in this estate with your brother upon your father's death. Which means that when Edward inherited from your brother, he inherited half of a half, because I inherited the other half of a half. Which meant Edward only had a quarter of the income from this estate, so no wonder he was heavily in debt and could not turn a profit from this place!"

"It's more complicated than that, but in essence, aye," Plantagenet Halsey confessed. "My father left the estate to his two sons equally, but as part of the agreement I had with Rod, I gave up my claim in my lifetime, in exchange for you—"

"Oh, Father! No," Alec interrupted on an intake of breath, shocked. "I had no idea…"

The old man shrugged. "Why would you? I've no regrets. And in a way it made life much simpler, for Rod and for me, not to have a finger in what was his pie once he became Earl of Delvin. You weren't meant to know any of this until my passin'. I'm tellin' you now because I promised we'd have no more secrets. And I should also tell you then that I ran an illegal poachin' operation from this estate for over thirty years, so we—you and I—could live in London, and the poor of this parish had food and necessaries on the table. Turner, father and son, Adams and his father, and the Old Bills that came and went in that cottage in the wood, were all in on the scheme. So were Ferris and Bailey, who turned a blind eye on it all, in exchange for huntin' privileges and venison for their table. I'm confident Rod knew somethin' was goin' on, but as long as it didn't interfere with his life, he let me get on with it. A'course all that will stop now, and I've told the others, too, now you're in charge. And I should've stopped it long ago, but there are people out there who rely on the income and—"

"I understand," Alec replied with a gentle smile. "I had long ago guessed you were the vital cog that made the poaching wheels turn! And I appreciate why you felt the necessity to flout the law in the past. Which has made me think long and hard about what we can do —together, and within the law, such as it is. But it will take time, the involvement of our attorneys, and the cooperation of Sir Tinsley."

"Don't see our magistrate bein' a problem, do you? He's so puffed up with self-consequence to be the closest neighbor and uncle by marriage to a marquess that he'd lick y'boots if you asked him! As for the estate and y'inheritance, best to have the Yarrborough brothers down here to explain the legalities to you, and this time more fully than they were allowed previously."

"They can advise us both. A representative of Yarrborough and Yarrborough will be here tonight or tomorrow."

"You have been busy behind this old man's back, haven't you, Son," Plantagenet Halsey quipped dryly.

Alec's eyebrows shot up. "No more busy then you, Father."

They both grinned and laughed, and then the old man lost his smile and mused with a frown, "I'm still flummoxed how Nic and Sally Fisher are connected, however remotely, to Ferris."

"I fear that the connection which I think the right one, you may think fanciful."

"I still want to know, if you're willin' to share…"

"I am, with you. But I have only my intuition and the fact all three have an uncanny resemblance to Ferris—"

"Three? But there's only two of 'em."

"Their father is the third. I believe Nic and Sally Fisher's father is Edward—"

"Edward?" Plantagenet Halsey was astonished. "Your brother Edward?"

"Why not? You told me my mother's marriage to your brother was in name only, and that Edward was not their son. Yet how do you explain his resemblance to the Halseys? And if you carefully study Sir Tinsley—which I've had the time to do since coming to live here—you'll see that Edward and Nic and Sally Fisher resemble him, too. How is that possible unless our magistrate and my mother produced Edward—"

"No! Never!" Plantagenet Halsey was emphatic. "Your mother would never betray her sister by committin' adultery with her brother-in-law. Now, on the other hand, if it was Lady Ferris's morality we were questionin'… But that don't work, because Rod and I would never cross that line, ever. Upon my honor and his."

"Very well then. There has to be some other connection…which is eluding me at the moment. You do concede there is a resemblance to the magistrate?"

The old man nodded. "Aye. Now that you've pointed it out, I can't *not* see it! But don't ask me how that came about." He shook his head. "And to think Edward fathered two brats on some poor lass and didn't give a farthin'…"

"He must have cared more than a farthing, because whomever she was, she gave him not one but two children," Alec quipped. "And who knows, she may still be here amongst us. But until I can find the direct connection between our magistrate, Edward, and Nic and Sally Fisher, best we keep this between us. And they are not the reason I asked you down here…"

"I'm intrigued. This side of the house don't get much attention, other than a place for sheep to graze and ducks to gather at the decoy," Plantagenet Halsey admitted. "Rod and I would swim in the decoy's pond in the summer."

Alec took out the map, list, and letter from his pocket and told him where the letter was discovered. He then turned over the letter and showed him the three words written on the front. If his father's jaw could have dropped to the muddy ground, it would have, such was his astonishment. And while he was mute Alec added further to his incredulity by telling him Selina's theory about what the map and the list signified.

When he had finished, he looked out on the rose bushes with their damaged stems, decimated blooms, and litter of petals, and was certain that if he counted them they would number thirty-eight. Not seeing either of the gardeners, or his two hounds, he said with a sad smile, "I don't think this is the last resting place of favored family animals. And by your mute disbelief, neither do you. Which means you agree with my theory: That this garden is the last resting place of those infants abandoned in the vault."

"Aye, my boy. But on my life, your mother told me nothing of this. Why would she keep it from me?"

"Perhaps this letter will tell us. But I presume, now that I know more about you both and your shared painful past, she didn't wish to upset you further with what she had discovered about the vault." He put the map and list back in his pocket and took out his spectacles. "Let's go over there under the shade of the wall and read this together…"

To my son Alec

I address this letter to you because it gives me comfort to do so.
Not because I have expectations that it will be you who finds it.
Edward has succeeded to the title, and thus a drop of my blood
but not of my body is now Earl of Delvin, and thus the strategem

*concocted by His Lordship and my sister has come to pass. I
cannot be bitter, for it is a convenient outcome for everyone. And
what else were we to do? If blame is to be apportioned then it goes
to our father. Yet, I do not blame him either. He could not have
foreseen the consequences the Fivetrees legacy would have on his
offspring.*

*Whoever is reading this, I pray you do not possess the faintest
notion of what I speak, which is also a comfort. It is my dearest
wish that you are living far into the future where my brothers,
sister, and I are nothing more than old fusty paintings upon a
wall.*

*Though you will have to indulge an old lady because I have
fanciful thoughts about a future where my son is in possession of
the truth about his parents' marriage—that they loved deeply and
for all their lives—but that he never discovered the tragedy of
their shared history as to why they were forbidden from
remaining together.*

*But this letter is not about my son or his parents. It was left here
to give the Halsey descendants who found it peace of mind.*

*The only truth you need know is that I had this evil place
emptied of its unblemished souls, and set them free. Do not weep
for them. Do not allow your present or your future to be over-
shadowed by our ignorant ancestors. They knew no better. Somehow, along the way to the accumulation of wealth, lands, and
titles, they lost their humanity and committed unspeakable
crimes. It horrifies me to this day that I cannot ink it here, or
anywhere.*

*It is ironic, is it not, that history is littered with horrors perpe-
trated by men who justify their abhorrent behavior as necessary to
prop up their name in the annals of history. But nothing justifies
what they perpetrated all for power and prestige. And no name
can claim to be illustrious, built as it is on death and the destruc-
tion of innocence.*

Despair not that all your ancestors were tainted with the same murderous brush, because my father refused to carry on the family's barbaric tradition so this estate could remain intact and inherited by an only son. As he had twin sons and knew not which to choose, and so did not, he made them swear to follow his example. And with the birth of his grandsons, Alec and Edward, the practise finally passed into legend. The stain on the family history, God willing, will fade with time and never resurface.

As you are here, now, with this letter, you must have a hundred questions but I will answer only one. To answer more will surely open a wound that has finally healed.

You wonder how it is that I, a female, know of this place, when it was a great secret kept down the ages amongst the Halsey men and favored family vassals. Ah! If only those men had not thought themselves exceptionally cunning and perpetuated the horrors of their ancestors, this unspeakable practice would have stopped long ago. Thus, it was left to the females in the family to take matters in hand and work counter to the practice carried out by their sons and husbands.

It was my son's grandmother, his father's mother, who confided in me of the vault's existence. It was an expediency. She was breathing her last and duty-bound to pass her secret knowledge to the next most senior female member of the family. To her credit, Lady Delvin did so regardless of my tenuous blood connection to the family name, something she never acknowledged, nor would she allow our father to do either. It is a circumstance she bitterly regretted in her dying hours, for it was the cause of so much heartache between my beloved and me.

The secret she confided, which was given to her by her mother-in-law, and one I promised to carry out should the need arise (though, thankfully it never did) was that for the many hundreds of years while the Halsey men ensured there was only one son and no daughters to inherit the estate after them, their wives and mothers were spiriting unwanted infants away to live out anonymous lives elsewhere. In much the same manner, legitimate female infants were taken in and raised by the Fishers.

I will not be the one to cast the first stone at our ancestors and condemn them. That does not mean I understand how they could do what they did, and indeed some men were unable to cope with what was expected of them and either ended their lives or remained bachelors so that they need not be required to make such a decision.

Sadly, over the centuries, there were infants who did not make it out of this vault. I like to think that these little ones died a natural death, as often happens with newborns. It is these infants that are now resting forevermore in ground consecrated by my priest. They are finally at rest in the most peaceful corner of the walled garden. Thirty-eight little lost souls with a rose bush planted over them in remembrance.

A list of names and a map were deposited with our family attorney, copies of which exist in the library, though I don't seem to be able to locate its secret hiding place. I could not allow these infants to be buried without naming them. Several were found in the vault with a date inscribed in ink on their swaddling. A truly heartbreaking sight that almost undid me, but did not cripple my resolve. I have only marked on the list the first and last dates, so you will know an approximate period of history when these infants were interred. The most recent date is the most important, for it shows that for almost two generations now, no infant has found its way into this ghastly place.

All I ask is that this list be put away with the family documents so that these infants do appear in the family record in some capacity, and are not lost to history.

My other request is that this rose garden be tended and the blooms cut once a year to fill the house with their beauty and

*their scent—a tribute, not only to the infants who lie here deep in
the soil, but also for those children and their descendants living
out their lives in every quarter of this county and beyond, who
will never know their true family history.*

*If I have one regret in my life, it is that my infirmity cut short my
time before I had the privilege of truly knowing my son. Perhaps
if it is Alec who finds this letter, he will do me the honor of
cutting a single rose in remembrance of his mother who
loved him.*

*Helen Cale Halsey
Countess of Delvin*

TWENTY-NINE

THE VOICE SEEMED SO FARAWAY. BUT IN FACT ONE OF THE gardeners was standing before him, cap in hand and waiting patiently for a response. Alec lifted his gaze over the rim of his spectacles at the intrusion, unaware tears were streaming down his cheeks. He did not hear the gardener's question. He was still coming to terms with his mother's letter. He realized his father was no longer beside him. He had walked a little way off, amongst the rose bushes, back turned, no doubt to be alone with his thoughts and feelings.

Mentally shaking himself free of the past, he quickly removed his glasses and dried his face with his white linen handkerchief, grateful the gardener had lowered his gaze to the petals underfoot. He asked him to repeat his question, which he did, keeping his eyes lowered.

"How many roses does His Lordship want brought back up to the house?"

"Thirty-eight—no! Make it thirty-nine. If you can find that many worth saving."

"Right you are, m'lord. We'll get right on it!"

"Wait!" Alec commanded when the gardener turned on a heel without ever looking up, and put his cap back on. He dug into another of his pockets and pulled out the small knife with the curved blade and polished wooden handle he'd confiscated from Roger Turner in Old Bill's hut. "You can cut the stems with this. It is a rose knife, is it not?"

"Aye, m'lord it is. Thank you, but I have m'own rose knife. All us gardeners do."

"It is a rather particular implement. I dare say you would know your own knife amongst others, yes?"

"Aye, m'lord. Never let it out of our sight. Hard to come by, and we all have our own particular quirks—"

"Such as…?"

"The way the handle is shaped. What type of wood. That sort of thing. Once you have a good knife, you hold on to it forever. If you don't mind me askin'—Did His Lordship find this one amongst the petals?"

"I found it, yes," Alec replied, without having to lie to the man. He held out the rose knife. "Would you know who owns this one?"

The gardener inspected it, turning it over in his sturdy hands. "I've not seen it before, but I reckon it belongs to a woman, and so I might know who does…" When Alec remained silent and Plantagenet Halsey joined him, the gardener addressed them both. "Her Ladyship—Lady Ferris—she was lookin' for her knife the other day when she came down here to have roses fetched up for Your Lordship's good lady wife. I gave her mine to use."

"Does Lady Ferris come here, to this rose garden, often?" Alec asked.

The gardener screwed up his face in thought and then shook his head. "About once a year regular like. Around this time. She were lucky to have fetched up those roses just days ago because after this storm it—"

"You think that knife belongs to Lady Ferris?" Plantagenet Halsey interrupted tersely, stabbing a finger in direction of the knife.

"I can't rightly say for certain, sir. I only know she told me she lost hers, so she used mine. But see here. There are initials inlaid in the wood: TCF." The gardener pulled a knife from the wicker basket at his feet and held it up with a grin. It had the same shape blade, but the wooden handle was thicker and more worn. "This is mine. Initials: BRF. Though Her Ladyship's F is for Ferris, and mine's for Fisher."

"I know who you are, Brun Fisher!" the old man said gruffly, and stuck out his hand for Lady Ferris's rose knife. Something about it bothered him more than it should. "If His Lordship don't have any more questions for you, you'd best get to work on those roses for Lady Halsey. We can't wait all day, and guests are arrivin' at any hour —What?" he hissed at Alec when the gardener bowed and went on his way with his wicker basket, and Alec stared at him with raised eyebrows. "Just 'cause there are lot of Fishers in Fivetrees don't make 'em all blood relations, y'know! They breed on their own, too, just like all the Smiths and Browns around the place." He held up the knife. "I thought she was worried about a lost pair of scissors, and it turns out it was her rose knife she misplaced."

"Do you think she lost it in the wood while out hunting, because that's where it was found…"

"Why would she need her rose knife in the wood?"

When Plantagenet Halsey gave him the knife Alec slipped it back into his frock coat pocket before saying levelly, "There's no blood on it now, but I am very sure this knife was used to kill Hugh."

"Jesus! No! The boy was slit with a *rose* knife? But who—no!" He said with a shake of his head when Alec continued to stare at him impassively, "Never! She wouldn't. I can't believe Tabitha would—no!"

"Tabitha? Is that my aunt's Christian name? You've never said it before."

"I don't say it—The shock… You think she killed Hugh?"

"I have yet to make up my mind. That her knife was used certainly makes me wonder—Why don't you say her name?"

"It annoys her. And anythin' I can do to annoy her makes me feel better. It's petty retribution, but I refuse to use her Christian name. And haven't since she betrayed your mother and me to our parents. If she'd left well enough alone, we could've continued our lives in blissful ignorance, no one hurt and no one the wiser. Tabitha's tale-bearing ruined m'life. So she don't deserve my familiarity, only my civility."

"She must've been not much more than a child."

"She and Tinsley had been married for almost a year. So she bloody well knew what she was doin', all right!" the old man spat out. "She came into my room one night and tried to seduce me. *Me*. A married man, and married to her sister, and we were expectin' our first child. Ye Gods! She said the truth about what came before our marriages didn't matter; it was all in the past. Well the past bloody well mattered to me, and to the rest of us! And so did my marriage vows. Even if she took hers with a pinch of salt! I was never more revolted in my life!"

Alec regarded his father steadily, trying his best to digest his impassioned outburst and make sense of it. Yet an inner voice warned him not to venture down this particular path of inquiry. It was the same inner voice that had niggled at him after reading his mother's letter. He took his own advice, for now, saying instead, "And yet, for all your loathing of her behavior, and that you can never forgive her, you refuse to entertain the idea she may have killed Hugh Turner?"

"That was different. This is different. It don't make any sense why she would do such an appallin' thing."

"Our ancestors justified filicide, and Hugh Turner isn't even a blood relation!"

"Don't be flippant, Alec!" Plantagenet Halsey growled.

Alec held his tongue on a retort and looked out over the rose garden. He said quietly, "I've sent the stonemason into the village to chisel into oblivion that Latin inscription. It no longer has relevance for the Deer Park I inherited, or in the future I wish for my children, and the children of my tenants, villagers, and neighbors."

"Bravo. That should've been done a long time ago."

"And I am determined to catch Hugh Turner's killer, and today. I will need your help—"

"Anythin'!"

"Keep an eye on Nic and Sally Fisher. I intend to bring them before our guests and announce they are now my wards. It's at Nic I wish you to direct your energies, and should he—no! that will be *when* he breaks down, will you please take him in hand, hold him tight and tell him he will never be in harm's way again. I hate to do this to him, but…"

"He's goin' to spot our killer!"

"I'm sure of it. And when he does, he will be very afraid. I have no way of knowing what this will do to him. And I will be distracted, ready to ensure our killer does not do him or themselves a harm before we have a confession."

"Does our girl know what you're up to?"

Alec shook his head and smiled at his father's affectionate moniker for Selina. He liked it. "I've kept her in the dark about most things the closer she gets to her confinement. I don't like doing so, but I worry all this would have a deleterious effect on her and the baby."

"She won't thank you, y'know. Nor do I think she's as unacquainted with what's goin' on around her as you think. But I don't blame you. She has enough worrin' her about the birth, and I don't blame her for that! God-awful nerve wrackin' business—Forgive me," he added, patting Alec's arm when he winced and swallowed hard. "Y'know she and the babe are going to pull through this. She comes from sturdy breeding stock. Look at her mother and her aunt! Those sisters have enough births between 'em to start their own squadron!"

Despite not being able to shake a gut-wrenching apprehension every time he thought of his beloved enduring the pain and hazard of childbirth, Alec smiled and nodded, and said quietly, "If we have a son, Selina wants to call him Linus..." He recounted the story of Apollo and the princess of Argos and grinned when his father swore. "That was my immediate reaction too. Best hope we have a daughter."

He stepped forward and whistled to his greyhounds. When they came to heel, he and his father set off across the meadow towards the house. Cromwell and Marziran took off through the long grasses and summer flowers, leaving far behind the gardeners clipping the rose bushes back into shape and filling their baskets with the last of the summer blooms.

♓

AT THE BASE OF THE ORNATE CARVED STAIRWELL THAT LED UP to the family's individual apartments, Alec stopped, sending the hounds on up ahead of him, which would alert his personal servants that he was not far behind.

"I've invited our neighbors to dine, not only to hopefully catch a killer, but also because with Her Grace and our Head of the Foreign Department present they'll be subdued and attentive," he explained. "Sir Tinsley and Colonel Bailey are more likely to bend to my will with such illustrious company present. And before I have Nic and Sally Fisher brought in, I intend to make an announcement on how we will all go forward from this day—you and me, my family, and this estate. I'll call in as many of the servants as can fit into the Great

Hall, too, so they hear my proclamation. I'm having Jeffries write it up—" He had a sudden thought. "I ought to employ Hadrian as my secretary."

"You should," Plantagenet Halsey agreed. "That young man's talents are wasted as a valet. He's a walkin' repository of information. And he's fluent in almost as many tongues as you. Was staggered when I heard him break into Dutch when we were in Emden! Besides, you'll need an ally when you return to the Foreign Department to sort out this Midanich mess." At Alec's surprise he explained awkwardly, "Olivia told me what Cobham had inadvertently confided in her. Y'know she has a talent for gettin' anythin' out of anyone!"

"Pillow talk? No! Don't answer that. It was gauche of me—Where was I?"

The old man leaned against the ornately-carved newel and crossed his arms. "Your Lordship was tellin' me about a proclamation…"

"Ah yes! I'm having Jeffries write it up and intend for our neighbors to sign it, so that we are all in accord as to how we will conduct ourselves in this little corner of Kent."

"I gather then there will be no more huntin' and poachin' here or around Fivetrees?"

"Not the illicit kind. I'm not adverse to my neighbors hunting when Adams deems we need to cull the herd. But I'm afraid I'll be shutting down your illegal trade in venison."

"It's a relief to be honest. But knowin' you as I do, I expect you have a solution to how the poor of our parish are to feed themselves, and not be prosecuted for merely subsistin' when they take the odd rabbit or bundle of kindlin' from your wood."

"I do. And Sir Tinsley will aid me in this endeavour if he wishes to remain magistrate and on good terms with his illustrious neighbor —that's me, by the way."

The old man grinned and made a show of bowing his head. "Aye, I knew that, my lord."

"I'm also making Roger Turner steward—and before you say it, his father has been an excellent steward but I need someone who is on my side."

Plantagenet Halsey tried to keep the skepticism out of his tone. "And that's Roger?"

"I realize he has a lot of growing up to do and presents as surly, but for all that he has a strong sense of justice and he won't be easily swayed. Given responsibility, I have high hopes he'll step up. And he'll have two years to prove he can take on the position permanently. I'm not putting his father out to pasture just yet."

"Glad to hear it. Paul is a good man and loyal to a fault." The old man sighed. "Loyal to me, that is. So I understand y'motives. And no one would be prouder than he to see his son take his place. I don't doubt he'd like to spend more time improvin' his own patch of land, particularly now he only has Roger…"

"I did not ask you about the funeral."

Plantagenet Halsey threw up a hand in resignation. "What is there to say? But it's as well women don't attend such heartbreakin' occasions, because we fellows would never get through it otherwise. I passed on your condolences, and did as you wished. Paul will come up to the house when you send word."

"And you, Father, will you accept what is rightfully yours of this estate?"

"That's unnecessary, my boy. I don't need—"

"Accept it or I'm afraid I will take measures to make sure you do. And my measures include my godmother."

"Don't bring her into this!" the old man complained, wiping a hand down his face. "She's already pesterin' me to talk to you about settin' matters to rights, but this estate is yours and I won't have it split up!"

"It doesn't have to be. But you will accept an income from it, or I will call upon Olivia to convince you to do so."

"I've no defence against her, y'know," Plantagenet Halsey confessed, unable to stop a blush washing over his face. "It was the same with y' mother. But I never expected two females to affect me in the same way! And me, actin' like a greenhorn. Ha! But for God sake's don't tell Livvy—"

"Don't tell Livvy—what?" asked the Duchess of Romney-St. Neots, peering over the banister rail on the first landing.

Both men swung around, square chins in the air, looking like naughty schoolboys caught out of class. They watched her come down the half dozen steps to join them. It was Alec who found his voice first.

"He does not want to let on to you how nervous he is that you're

finally making your announcement at dinner. He's faint with antic-
ipation."

"You'll keep," the old man muttered under his breath.

Alec winked at his father, and smiled angelically at his godmother.
"Now if you'll both excuse me, I need to change for our guests."

Plantagenet Halsey could have kicked him up the stairs, but all he
did was grin stupidly and nod. The Duchess saw through his nonsensical façade in an instant, and burst into giggles.

THIRTY

THE ONLY TOPIC OF CONVERSATION AT DINNER WAS THE weather, more precisely the fierce lightning and hail storm of the previous day. There was flooding and fires, with widespread damage to property and crops. Livestock were killed, and so, too, a couple on the outskirts of the village when a large oak was felled by lighting and collapsed on their cottage. A coachman who brought his passengers in after midnight to the Fivetrees Inn reported that the storm was sweeping toward London. Closer to home, the Bailey and Ferris farms were fortunate in that they only suffered minor stock loss and crop damage. Less fortunate was the Reverend Purefoy's pigeon loft, which was struck by lightning, with a loss of half his precious flock. A most distressing occurrence, but he assured the dinner guests that when weighed against the immeasurable loss the Turners had suffered in burying their youngest son earlier in the day, a few pigeons dead was as nothing.

Following a general murmur of consensus came a heavy silence, only broken by Selina, who as hostess, did her best to lift the mood by reporting that here at Deer Park they were fortunate that none of the buildings were struck, and the only flooding had occurred at the lowest point within the walled gardens, which was down in the village, at the laundry and bakery. But thankfully there were no fires and the scaffolding covering much of the façades of the buildings looking into Stone Court suffering only minor collapse. What everyone wanted to know was if the hole in Stone Court had caused flooding and damage to the cellars below. Alec chimed in to report that his London foreman and team of men had worked in shifts through the night to repair the collapsed ceiling and make the cellars water tight. The tarpaulin was still in place to protect the brickwork, and when sufficiently dry, the flagging would be relaid. To which news everyone heaved a sigh of relief and applauded.

The Colonel then recommended the installation of Franklin rods, in particular, to affix a Franklin rod to the Deer Park clock tower, which would help prevent a lightning strike. The American Benjamin Franklin's invention, the rods were said to have saved numerous properties and churches in the Colonies. Lord Cobham was the first to scoff at the very idea of putting rods atop buildings, because they would merely attract a bolt of lightning to it with catastrophic results. To which Selina replied—with more patience than she usually showed her brother, but they had guests—that attracting lighting to the rod was the object of the exercise. She then explained to her rapt audience that the Franklin rod was affixed to the highest point of a building, and attached to it was a length of wire that ran down to a second rod which was buried in the earth. Thus when a lightning bolt struck, it traveled down the rod, and down the wire to the rod in the earth, where the energy from the strike dissipated.

Plantagenet Halsey applauded her explanation and the ingenuity of Mr. Franklin. But because he never agreed with anything the Republican rabble-rousing MP said on principle, Lord Cobham's sneering disbelief became fixed and no amount of common sense was going to make him budge from his position that a Franklin rod was a dangerous device. The only person to agree with him was Mrs. Bailey. But her support did little to stop the ensuing vigorous and rather heated argument between the siblings. Two camps of thought formed on the merits and hazards of such rods, and whether they caused rather than prevented lightning strikes. Secretly, as far as the old man was concerned, the argument could go on all night, as long as it continued to divert the Duchess from making her announcement.

With his guests suitably preoccupied in heated debate, Alec took the opportunity to turn to his aunt, who was seated on his right, and who had been remarkably quiet throughout the meal.

"I trust the storm did not unsettle you, Aunt? You do not seem yourself."

"I am not unwell. It was not that wretched storm which upset me... It's those roses... You know, don't you?"

Alec looked down the length of the table at the crystal bowl full of white roses set before his wife. But a single rose he had kept aside and placed in a tall tumbler of water before him.

"I do—now."

"Was the garden much damaged?"

"Thankfully, no. And with the proper care and attention it will receive from now on, I am hopeful there will be even more blooms next year."

Lady Ferris set down her silver knife and fork, and lifted her gaze from her plate. There was little emotion in her features, but Alec sensed here was an altogether different creature from the one who had shared confidences with him at nuncheon. Gone was the playfulness and smug self-assurance. He knew she was referring to more than just the rose garden and what had been buried in the soil; she was talking specifically about him and his history. And it was the single rose in front of him, and what it represented, that had garnered her ire.

He decided to have his suspicions confirmed so asked in his customary tranquil manner (after all, they were seated at a dinner table and he did not wish to upset her, or his guests), "On your previous visit you confided in me about the Fivetrees Blessing in the village square, the Halsey brothers being selfsame twins, and your disappointment in my woeful lack of knowledge of the family history—"

"Someone needed to give you a push in the right direction! Imagine being head of the family and a marquess no less, and unaware of the sacrifices made by your ancestors to keep this estate secure. Without it, I doubt this magnificent collection of buildings would exist, and you certainly wouldn't have a deer park."

"Yet... I don't think the push you wanted to give me was in the direction of the *family* history but to make certain I discovered my *personal* history."

She shifted on her chair. "You cannot know one without the other, surely?"

"True. But it is not the thirty-eight blooms that bother you, but this single rose and what it represents, which is—"

"I wish the storm had decimated that garden!" she grumbled.

"—the unconditional love a mother has for her son."

Lady Ferris rolled her eyes. "Helen was such a sentimentalist."

Alec heard her derision and slowly set down his wine glass. "Why is that trait something of which to be ashamed?"

"There is no place for sentimentality in great and noble families. Marriages are contractual obligations made by parents who know what is best for their children."

"Which is why you accepted the match with Sir Tinsley?"

"It was eminently suitable for both of us. And I came with a dowry of five thousand pounds."

"But you only accepted him after your hopes were dashed; you wanted to be a countess. You were told marrying either of the Halsey brothers was an impossibility and to resign yourself to being the wife of the local magistrate. It was more than your sister could hope for—or so you thought. And then your world unraveled when Helen married Plantagenet in secret. You could not bear the idea of her being Countess of Delvin so you informed on them to Lord and Lady Delvin. Sadly for everyone concerned, your betrayal started a chain of events that opened up the family's sordid history, and in ways not even you could have foreseen."

In the silence which followed Alec selected strawberries from the bowl placed before him. He put several on his plate and looked across at his aunt with a smile of enquiry. "Discovering one's personal history means I get to know yours as well."

"I never did find my sewing scissors, y'know," Lady Ferris began, with a vague frowning glance about her. "I am very sure I had them when—"

"Come now, Tabitha," Alec drawled. "Your performance of vaguery at nuncheon had me almost convinced. But not today. Oh, I believe that you do have episodes of memory loss. Perhaps they are becoming more frequent, and that frightens you and makes you irritable. But not here, and not at nuncheon the other day, and not today."

Lady Ferris did not try to deny it. She chuckled and her eyes sparkled for the first time since sitting to dine. "I do love the way my name rolls off your tongue!" She glanced down the table at Selina. "I wonder for how long she will hold your interest before some sultry little thing rubs herself up against your silken thigh."

"I am my father's son. Once the heart is captured, all else is too," Alec replied stonily, affronted by her tasteless comment. "Let me be frank: You hoped that by setting me on the path of discovery that led to the vault, and the diabolical meaning behind the Fivetrees Blessing, I would also discover the truth about my birth. I did, and I have also found my father, and for that I thank you."

"*Thank me*? Good grief, my boy! You should be cursing my name from the clock tower! Perhaps now you know the truth, you wish you'd remained the bastard son of a mulatto footman and a countess."

"Let's drop the pretense, shall we? You and I know little requires changing in that statement to turn tawdry gossip into fact. My father was not a footman, nor was he the mulatto. But my mother was certainly a countess." When Lady Ferris made an off-hand gesture at the use of the definite article, he knew she understood he was referring to her and his mother being of mixed race. After eating one of the strawberries, he added conversationally, "What puzzles me—and I know you can enlighten me—is why my mother was not permitted to keep me. No one would've be the wiser as to which twin was the father; they were identical…"

"Do you truly not know the answer and are wanting me to tell you?" she asked, surprised, leaning in so he could hear her clearly, because a remark made by the Duchess of Romney-St. Neots had everyone laughing.

"Would you like to hear my theory?" he asked, and when she nodded, taking one of the strawberries from his plate, said, "Roderick Halsey rejected his brother's son as a suitable heir because you had assured him of an alternative."

"My dear boy, how wide of the mark you are! Your father's brother rejected you because you are a preternatural being. You should not exist in nature. You certainly have no place amongst good society. No one knew what to expect, not least of all your mother, who was justifiably terrified as to what type of ungodly creature she would birth. You want the truth—"

"Please."

"—we—the family—all hoped her infant would be stillborn, or

so hideously malformed that it would not live outside the womb. Ah! I stand corrected," she added with a tight smile and raised her glass as if in a toast. "Plantagenet was ghoulishly optimistic in the face of the facts. But he always was one for championing the downtrodden, the shunned, and the socially misfit of our society. He refused to give up on you. And see how you have repaid him! He is so proud—and laughing on the other side of his face at the rest of us—that his-his —*creation* is an Adonis amongst men, and managed to take the family name further than any of his ancestors, to the dizzying heights of a marquessate!"

"I can do little to alter who or what I am, but I can offer you my sympathies," Alec replied evenly, though he was shaken by her vitriol. "You wish it were your son Edward sitting in my chair, presiding over this table as Lord Delvin. You had every right to expect that. He succeeded to the earldom as Roderick and Helen's son. Tragically, he did not live long enough for his favorite aunt to fully enjoy her victory over her sister, and over Plantagenet Halsey. And now, here I sit, the creature who should never have been. But here I am, and here I intend to stay."

She leaned her chin on her fist and smiled at him, dark eyes glittering, furious with him and heartbroken for the loss of her son.

"What a wonder you are!" she sneered. "I can see why Edward loathed you, why he called you Second with such derision."

"Because his favorite aunt planted a garden of hatred and loathing in his head."

"How florid! But I am interested in how you worked it all out. Go on! Tell me the rest. We have time. This lot are too wrapped up in thunder and lightning and the inventions of Mr. Franklin to bother us. I believe they have moved on to discussing his kite and key experiments. Besides, the longer you give me your singular attention the more it is getting under the skin of your godmother. And what woman wouldn't want to outshine a duchess!"

Alec decided to play along with her infantile jealousy, if only to see if it sparked anyone else at the table to also show their true nature. He had noticed that more than one of the guests had withdrawn from the banter and were straining to overhear the conversation between their host and his aunt.

"Please let me know if I wander from the family path," he said, as if they were discussing the latest play at Drury Lane. "I do not know for certain, but I assume that Roderick, while keen to be Earl of Delvin, was less than enthusiastic in producing an heir to carry on after him. And not because he had no wish to follow in the family tradition set out in the Fivetrees Blessing, but because he was uninterested in female—um—companionship. Hence, his willingness to enter into a sham marriage with Helen, and why it was successful. She could not be with the brother she loved, but she could still lead a life of privilege and remain in the family home. And then you made the couple an offer they could not refuse. You were pregnant with your second child. Better he live and be raised as the heir to an earldom, than left out to die, or locked up in the family vault, or taken away to be placed and raised by strangers. You knew your sister would never refuse your child, a child that had a drop of her blood but was not of her body—"

"He had a drop of Roderick's blood too."

"He did. But Helen never betrayed you, or him—or any of you."

Lady Ferris smiled. It was not pleasant. She lifted her wine glass in a toast. "To Helen, the sentimental favorite of the family. And to loyalty in all its forms."

Alec wasn't sure what she meant by the latter, but he followed her lead and lifted his glass. "And to Edward—"

"Despite what you must think, I am not my sister," Lady Ferris mused. "Once he was hers, I never gave him another thought... Well, not until he was much older... Babies do not interest me, whereas Helen was born to coo and ahh over infants. She raised my son, but she never got over the loss of you."

"You may not have given him a motherly thought, but I do not doubt you derived an immense satisfaction watching your sister bringing up your second son. That he was heir to an earldom appealed to your sense of twisted justice, so did my mother living an earthly purgatory, having been forced apart from the man she loved, and to give up her infant, all because of the circumstance of their birth."

"*Circumstance*? Oh no, that won't do at all," Lady Ferris purred with a sad shake of her head. "You are far too polite. Say it as it truly is."

"That my parents, ignorant of the truth, fell in love?"

"Not that pap!" Lady Ferris hissed, angry impatience getting the better of her. "Admit you are an aberration. Go on. *Say it.*"

"My dear Lady Ferris! Are you perfectly well?"

It was Mrs. Bailey. For how long she had been standing at Alec's back, he had no idea. But she had finally come forward to pacify her friend as Lady Ferris leaned across the table and snarled in Alec's face. She put her arm about her, coaxing her to return to her seat, addressing Alec with breathless apology.

"I do not know what has come over her, my lord. She is some-times inexplicably gripped by some fright or other—Oh! Sir Tinsley! Look, my dear. Here is your husband come to help you…"

Sir Tinsley replaced Mrs. Bailey at his wife's side. Yet Lady Ferris was oblivious to everything and everyone but Alec, and she demanded he confess to her the truth about his parentage. And no one and nothing was going to stop her getting him to speak, not her husband, not her friend Mrs. Bailey, and not Dr. Riley when he joined them.

Alec remained frozen in his seat, doing his utmost to remain impassive. It took all his concentration to bring the wine glass to his mouth with a steady hand. He was aware that Lady Ferris continued to stare at him, while demanding of those around her to leave her be. But Alec was beyond words. And when Sir Tinsley insisted that Dr. Riley attend to his wife, and said so in a strident voice, Lady Ferris suddenly became aware of her surroundings, and that the entire company had fallen silent.

Conversations were cut off mid-sentence, and dissected fruit paused on the way to mouths. Lord Cobham's was wide open and half a peach suspended between his parted lips. It was a moment of absurdity Alec needed to ease the tension, and he wanted to laugh out loud. But he returned his focus to his aunt, all admiration for her acting skills when she looked about her as if unaware of her surround-ings. She put a hand to her cheek and then to the front of her husband's waistcoat, and blinked up at him.

"Tinsley? Oh, Tinsley, there you are! Mrs. Bailey? Whatever are you doing at this end of the table? Oh? Did you find my rose knife? Did that boy take it like we presumed?"

"Your rose knife?" Mrs. Bailey was perplexed and she gave a little titter of nervousness. "Whatever can you mean? What boy? And it was your sewing scissors you misplaced. Do you not remember? I am sure of it—"

"Unfortunately we have yet to find your knife, my dear," apologized her husband. "Mrs. Bailey, it would be best if you resume your seat. Dr. Riley and I can deal with dear Lady Ferris now."

"Of course! Of course!" Mrs. Bailey agreed, saying to Alec as she stepped back. "I had no idea Lady Ferris had lost her rose knife. Her scissors, yes. Do you know what she means, my lord?"

"Come away, my dear," ordered the Colonel, stepping up to herd his wife back to her seat, and muttering an apology to Alec as he did so.

"You've had one of your little episodes," Sir Tinsley was explaining loudly to his wife. "Dr. Riley is here to help you—"

"Dr. Riley?" Lady Ferris looked nonplussed. "What are you doing here? Is the baby on its way? Is someone ill? Not my nephew—?"

"No, my dear. Everyone is perfectly well."

Sir Tinsley looked pleadingly at Alec, who was still immobile and mute, and so it was left to Selina to move time on, and make the announcement. She had been watching the interaction between her husband and his aunt with increasing alarm, and the woman's snarling attack left her mentally reeling. Yet she managed to mask her feelings and put in a performance herself, and remain serene.

"Coffee, cake, and sweetmeats in the Great Hall," she announced. "Others will be joining us there, but not straight away. Cobham, if you would lead the way with Aunt Olivia…"

There followed a great deal of commotion as everyone proceeded to follow Lord Cobham and the Duchess of Romney-St. Neots towards the archway that would take them through to the Great Hall. It was at the opposite end of the room to where Alec still sat motionless. So none of the guests passed him or were impolite enough to stare over their shoulders to discover why their host remained seated. It was left to Plantagenet Halsey to walk against the tide. But first he whispered a few words in Selina's ear, and only after she went off leaning on the arm of her cousin Lady Sybilla, did he make his way to Alec. He sat in the chair vacated by Lady Ferris and hard-gripped Alec's forearm through his linen sleeve to get his attention.

"Alec, m'boy. Y'don't have to tell me what she said, but tell me you're all right."

Alec nodded, and reached out to him, and when his father took his hand in both of his, he returned his smile.

"Do you remember I was told that what came before my birth would disturb my peace of mind?"

Plantagenet Halsey bit down on his tongue to stop himself making an injudicious remark about Lady Ferris. He knew why Alec was asking the question, and he knew this day would come. Yet, no matter how prepared he thought himself it did not make it any easier. He nodded, and as he always had with Alec since he was a small boy, he gave a matter-of-fact response.

"I do, and I see that they have. But what came before your birth was not somethin' contrived or depraved. Your mother and I never discovered the tragedy of our close connection until after we'd married, and you were on the way. Don't you ever let anyone convince you it was otherwise!" When Alec nodded and smiled bashfully, he returned his smile, adding, "Anythin' else?"

"How is it you believed I would be born whole, and not an aberrant being unfit for purpose? Why did you not give up on me?"

His father's response was simple. "Love, my boy. I loved your mother, she loved me, and we loved you. That was all that mattered. And it is all that should matter to you."

THIRTY-ONE

"I'M SORRY, OLIVIA," ALEC APOLOGIZED, STROLLING INTO THE Great Hall five minutes later feeling more himself, the Duchess sweeping up with a frown between her brows. "This has postponed your announcement yet again—"

"Never mind that!" she responded, a glance over at Lady Ferris who was being attended to by Dr. Riley, and fussed over by her husband. She tapped the front of Alec's cream silk waistcoat with the closed sticks of her fan. "She upset you! And don't say she did not! If you ask me," she whispered loudly, "she did it—she killed that poor boy! Evil hellcat of a woman!"

"Naturally, this accusation is based on fact, and not on your emotional involvement with my father?"

"Oh! Oh! Dearest boy!" It was the first time she had heard Alec refer to Plantagenet Halsey as was his due, and she was so overcome she burst into tears and covered her face.

"Good God! What did you say to upset her?" the old man demanded, having followed Alec into the Great Hall in time to witness, if not hear their exchange.

Alec lifted his hands as if to say he had no idea, and it was left to Selina's brother to steal the moment and revive his aunt.

"I warned you, Halsey," Lord Cobham stated darkly, addressing Plantagenet Halsey, and walking up to them needling his teeth with a toothpick. "First it was Lady Ferris, and now it's Her Grace. All this talk of electricity and Franklin rods ain't suitable chatter for the female mind. Gets 'em overwrought."

"Do shut up, Clive!" the Duchess snapped, and with an outward flick of her fan, bustled off in direction of the tea trolley, leaving the Head of the Foreign Department red-faced and feeling every inch a schoolboy.

ᚼ

THE DINNER PARTY GUESTS CONGREGATED ON SOFAS ARRANGED before the enormous hearth in the Great Hall. There was a fire roaring in the deep grate but it did little more than provide a focal point and something to stare into if one didn't want to join in the conversation. Colonel Bailey was doing just that, and leaving her husband to brood in silence, Mrs. Bailey took the opportunity to mingle amongst the guests. She spoke with Lord Cobham, exchanged a word with the Duchess, and enquired of Sir Tinsley if dear Lady Ferris was feeling any better. And this with his wife sitting beside him, but with her eyes closed and appearing for all the world to have fallen asleep from the headache powder given her by Dr. Riley. She would have spoken with Her Ladyship, but Selina had decided to stroll the room on Lady Sybilla's arm, her pregnancy now greatly discomforting her. It was also making her anxious. It was the Duchess's opinion from an earlier observation she had made of her that afternoon in the privacy of her dressing room that she could go into labor at any moment.

"I will not have this baby until Alec has made his speech to the household, and Aunt Olivia has made her announcement, and all these people return to their own homes," Selina stated irritably. She had a sudden thought. "Do you know what it is about?" she asked her cousin.

"Did Alec not tell you—"

"Not that, Silla. Your mother's announcement. Do you know?"

Lady Sybilla shook her head. "She hasn't said a word to me. Which is just as well because you know I couldn't keep a secret from you! Oh! Why have we turned about—?"

"Hush. We are taking another turn because I cannot bear to hear what Mrs. Bailey has to say about Lady Ferris's fit. As it is, I dare not even approach my own husband to ask how he is, which is far more important to me, for fear it will only start our guests hypothesizing again as to what caused his aunt's fit in the first place! Come!"

With the two ladies turning away to stroll in the opposite direction, Mrs. Bailey halted her progress and returned to the assortment of sofas in front of the enormous hearth. She was pleased to see that her husband was no longer alone but deep in discussion with Lord Cobham and her brother the vicar, while the Duchess of Romney-St. Neots and Plantagenet Halsey had retreated to the farthest sofa to drink their tea. Not wanting to intrude on either conversation, she went to the tea trolley to busy herself. Here two liveried footmen stood to attention either side of a large silver urn full of hot water, and where she was surprised to find the Marquess Halsey, seemingly alone with his thoughts, stirring sugar into his coffee. He was in fact waiting for her.

"Tea or coffee, Mrs. Bailey?"

"Please do not trouble yourself on my account, my lord," she replied, equal parts flustered and delighted.

"It is no trouble." Alec held up a clean porcelain cup on its saucer with a smile. "Milk?

She nodded, but with her cup of tea made Alec did not hand it over but suggested they sit together for a moment. He carried her cup to a high-backed red velvet settee positioned under one of the long mullioned windows. It was far enough away that whatever he had to say would not be overheard. And being up against the wall, the settee looked into the room, giving him an excellent vantage point to watch the other guests. That it was unoccupied and nearby hovered a stony-faced footman was no coincidence.

Alec indicated Mrs. Bailey sit on his right, which had her facing away from everyone else and partly obscured by the unusually high sides to the settee. Unaware of the contrivance, and as giddy as any nursery room miss on her first admittance to the heady adult world of drawing rooms, Mrs. Bailey propped herself on the edge of a fringed velvet cushion and accepted the cup of tea His Lordship had personally made for her. And when Alec chose to sit facing her, she felt her throat warm at having the singular attention of this handsome nobleman who was practically a duke.

"I do apologise this sofa is not as comfortable as the others. It's also too ornate for my taste, but I'm told it is a special piece of furniture. So special, that it has a history. According to family lore, it was once used as a throne, having a matching red tapestry canopy, and put upon a dais. Imagine! And it is so famous that it has a name—the Delvin Settee, and travelers come from far and wide to view it, as much as they do the rest of this house."

"I do not doubt it, my lord. One feels quite special seated here."

He sipped his coffee before asking, as if it were a natural progression in their conversation, and hoping it would not remain one-sided, "Did Dr. Riley manage to find a medicinal to settle my aunt...?"

"I do believe he did," she replied. And when Alec smiled encouragingly over the lip of his cup, her shyness disappeared and there was no stopping her confidences. "He has quite a plethora of medicinals in his traveling chest. I was surprised he knew what to find and where! But every little bottle and container is labeled and in a particular order, so that he has everything at his fingertips. I suspect this is most necessary when the situation calls for it and he needs to act quickly." She leaned in a little closer and confided, "I do believe Dr. Riley gave Lady Ferris a headache draught containing a drop of laudanum, to help settle her nerves. He told me he keeps that in a sealed compartment, along with other poisons." She sighed and shook her head and sipped at her tea before adding, "Poor Lady Ferris, I have never seen her so distressed."

"Distressing for you, too, to see your friend have such lapses of memory. Particularly when you have known each other for many years—since you were brides in fact?"

Mrs. Bailey smiled and nodded at a memory, and then frowned thinking of her friend's deterioration of the mind. She rested her cup on its saucer, head to one side. "I do feel for her. It must be a frightening experience to forget one's memories... She and I have shared so much... Her friendship has seen me through many difficult times. When I lost my mother, when the Colonel was away in London, leaving me alone for months at a time... She was there, always."

"And she was there to offer you support at the birth of your children—I beg your pardon. I did not mean to resurrect painful memories for you, but was merely pointing out how important Lady Ferris has been in your life."

He looked out across the hall, and Mrs. Bailey followed his gaze, to where Selina and her cousin had come into view, strolling arm in arm, heads close together. Selina paused and would have come over to him, but she was quick to catch his slight shake of the head and significant sidelong glance at his tea-drinking companion. Instead she lifted her dark brows, turned on a heel and walked on with Lady Sybilla, Mrs. Bailey none the wiser to the silent exchange between husband and wife.

"Dear Lady Halsey is exceedingly fortunate to have the Lady Sybilla and Her Grace with her at this momentous time," Mrs. Bailey commented, watching the Marchioness and her cousin stroll out of her line of sight, she too polite to turn her head away from Alec. "And Your Lordship must not worry. I pray every night, and I know Adolphus does too, that Her Ladyship has a safe delivery, and she and the infant survive the ordeal in excellent health."

"Thank you. At this stage, prayer is all I am capable of." Confiding with a shy smile, "I confess, apprehension has fogged my ability to make decisions for I cannot settle on a suitable name for our infant. I am the most indecisive of expectant fathers!"

"Oh no, my lord, you must not think so!" Mrs. Bailey said with breathless sincerity. Feeling privileged by His Lordship's confidence her nervousness evaporated. And because he had done her the honor of sharing with her, she returned the favor. "Every husband feels as you do at this time. But once you hold your infant in your arms, you will know the name you wish to bestow upon him. I knew as soon as I held Daniel. Sadly, Terence died before he had time to grow into his name—"

"And your daughter?

"My-my—daughter?"

"Surely you had thought of a name for her?"

"Y-yes. I-I called her Tabitha."

"After my aunt?"

"To honor our friendship, and it is quite the loveliest name."

"It is. I do not know why I thought this... Perhaps my aunt told me," Alec continued smoothly, attention seemingly on the contents of his cup, and frowning "but I had it in my head your daughter's name is Eliza?"

"Eliza? Why would you think—why would Lady Ferris—she knows I called her Tabitha." Mrs. Bailey blinked up at Alec, and for the first time since the start of their tête-à-tête, the breathlessness was gone from her voice. "Why would she confide such a thing in you?"

"Perhaps she told me when she was having one of her episodes of memory loss?" Alec responded placidly, his tone at odds with the light in his eyes. He took a sip of coffee, watching her closely. When he saw her relax, and thus accepting of his explanation, he added with a feigned pondering air, "Although—and I am hoping you can help me understand this, Mrs. Bailey—why would she talk of your daughter as if she were alive, if you maintain she died soon after birth?"

He paused, giving her the opportunity to confess the truth or continue to hide behind the dogma of the Fivetrees Blessing. And when she met his gaze, he knew, without her uttering a word, she was going to lie to him. Yet, she could not stop her cup from rattling on its saucer.

"Allow me to have that taken away…"

He gave their cups on their saucers to a liveried footman, who came forward at his nod. He then glanced past the servant to the tea trolley, and was relieved more cups of tea and coffee and plates of cakes and sweetmeats were being handed around; he needed a few more minutes with Mrs. Bailey.

"Upon reflection, you are quite right, my lord," she stated when Alec returned his attention to her, the breathlessness returned. "With her memory fading, Lady Ferris must've become confused and lost all notion of time. She conjured my daughter back into existence, wishfully thinking her alive when in fact she died the day of her birth."

"Mrs. Bailey, I am very sure you have convinced yourself that is the truth. But you know, as does my aunt, and so does your husband, that Tabitha did not die but was taken away and was given a new name—"

"Tabitha *did* die. Eliza is *not* my daughter! She is Mrs. Fisher's daughter!"

"Tabitha *became* Mrs. Fisher's daughter Eliza," Alec corrected, adding with a wan smile, "And you were the first to mention Mrs. Fisher, not I."

Mrs. Bailey blinked, and realizing she had betrayed herself, stumbled and stuttered her way to provide an explanation. "How did you —Why would I—The only Eliza I know is Eliza Fisher who is now Mrs. Turner. So I naturally assumed she—"

"The loss of a child is heartbreaking, whether through illness or accident or because of circumstances beyond the control of the parent," Alec stated calmly, placing his clean white linen handkerchief into her hand because her cheeks had fired red and her eyes become glassy. "As far as you were concerned, you were following an age-old Fivetrees tradition, one countless ancestors had done before you, by placing your daughter in the care of the Fisher women. This tradition has been upheld for so many centuries that it has Fivetrees landowners and their wives in its grip, so much so that it is etched in stone in the village square, for all to see and abide by, and not be forgotten: *May you be blessed with one son only, and have no daughters to your name.*"

"I did what was expected of me as a good and obedient wife," Mrs. Bailey assured him, unconsciously scrunching Alec's handkerchief between her fingers. But despite the few tears that had slid down her hot cheeks, she had had time while Alec spoke to regain her self-control. Gone was the fawning breathless creature, and in her place was a remarkably composed woman, convinced in the rightness of her actions, however heinous. Alec could not but be enthralled by such self-possessed delusion.

"You are quite right, my lord. The local landowning families adhere to the Fivetrees Blessing, just as their ancestors did before them, they who sacrificed so much to keep their estates intact." She sniffed and held out the damp handkerchief for Alec to take back with a smile. "I do not doubt that Lady Halsey knows that what is at stake is far more important than her personal wishes. The future of your estate depends upon it. And Lady Ferris and I are here to ensure she is persuaded and consoled to do what is right and proper. Naturally, we are all praying she delivers you a son and heir."

Alec could not have been more appalled had she offered to take his newborn straight to the Fishers to save him the time and effort. So when she shook out her petticoats and bobbed a curtsey, thinking their tête-à-tête at an end, it took him several seconds to react. And when he did come out of his trance, it was to stop her taking her leave. He was not finished with her yet. He had a cold-blooded killer to bring to justice.

THIRTY-TWO

ALEC SHOT TO HIS FEET AND COMMANDED MRS. BAILEY RESUME her seat. Startled by his acerbic tone, she dropped back onto the settee without a word.

Watching this play out were his family and guests. The Duchess of Romney-St. Neots and Plantagenet Halsey were by the tea trolley, awaiting the opportunity to interrupt. Selina, too, with Lady Sybilla, had strolled past the Delvin Settee for a third time, and now joined the couple. Sir Tinsley and Lady Ferris had not moved from the sofa where Dr. Riley had attended on Her Ladyship, and where the physician had returned to check Lady Ferris's pulse now she had settled enough to take a cup of tea. But all three were also keeping an interested eye in direction of the Delvin Settee. Lord Cobham, Colonel Bailey, and the Reverend Purefoy were the only ones seemingly oblivious to the unfolding drama. They had found kindred spirits and were deep in discussion on the merits of the Sugar Act as a necessary revenue-raising method to defray the costs of defending and protecting the American Colonies.

When the Duchess quietly approached the settee to better hear what was being said, Plantagenet Halsey and the rest of the party followed. Even Lady Ferris demanded of her husband that he take her across to join the group—she was not going to learn secondhand what her nephew and Mrs. Bailey were discussing that the Duchess of Romney-St. Neots found so fascinating.

If he was aware he had an audience, Alec did not show it. He needed to concentrate on Mrs. Bailey, whom he was convinced held the key to solving Hugh Turner's murder. And while it would do no harm to have witnesses, he was unsure if the task of extracting the truth from her was hindered or helped by their presence. He would soon find out.

"Mrs. Bailey, indulge me: You have always believed Eliza Fisher became your husband's mistress when she was just a girl—"

"That is so, my lord. But I do not blame him for—"

"Please, Mrs. Bailey. I am not interested in casting blame, nor do I wish to indulge in the lurid details. All that I wish to know is that if you were aware of this supposed affair, were you also aware that Eliza Fisher was in truth your daughter?"

"I knew of the affair many years before it was told to me that she was the daughter I gave up at birth whom I had named Tabitha."

"How did you discover the truth?"

"Fivetrees is a small community. Nothing remains a secret for long."

"And this same community—and you—believing your husband and Eliza Fisher were conducting an affair, yet upon discovering she was your daughter, you did not seek to put a stop to it?"

"My Lord Halsey, I may hold my tongue, but my eyes and ears have always been wide open. I am from noble stock. My grandfather was an earl and not only did he have a mistress, but the woman lived in the house he shared with my grandmother! I understand husbands —men—must satisfy such carnal appetites. Surely, you, as a peer of the realm, are aware that noblemen frequently fornicate with females who are not their wives—"

"But not with females who are their daughters!"

Mrs. Bailey was embarrassingly amused. And such was her belief that she was in the right that she dared to look past Alec and not only address him, but include those assembled at his back.

"My husband is unaware of their connection. So I cannot blame him. Just as we cannot blame the rest of the poor wretches from this district, all of whom are so closely related through centuries of discarded children being secretly placed into the community that their ancestry is a familial tangle of unholy marriages. Naturally it is a repugnant notion to you and me and any and all who are not from around here; thus it is best left unspoken and unexplored, and I do not dwell. My dear brother Adolphus, as vicar, has devoted his life to praying for their souls, for how else are such abominations to have any chance of entering the gates of heaven?"

"What an utterly heartbreaking situation for all concerned," Alec replied sadly, and acknowledged the presence of the silent audience by turning his shoulder to include them. His next words were full of contempt, not only for Mrs. Bailey but for others with her point of view. "That you lacked the moral fortitude to overcome your prejudices to confront your husband, or at the very least approach your daughter, is unforgivable. She deserved your protection, not your censure."

"But had I spoken up, it would only have made matters worse, for my husband and for Mrs. Turner, for both our families, to learn the truth."

"Had you spoken up, madam, you would've learned the truth!" Alec cut in harshly. "Allow me to extract that weevil from your brain that the Colonel and Mrs. Turner were lovers. They were not, and never were—"

"Wh-what?" Mrs. Bailey half rose off the settee and then sat with a thud. Her gaze searched out the gathering, looking for her husband and her brother, but neither were there, and the only faces that stared at her reflected shock and outrage. She wrung her hands. "I-I do not believe you! I was told—I have it on the highest authority—Adolphus? Where are my brother and my husband? I must speak with—"

"But I am not here to judge you or them on the unfathomable silences between you, but to ask what you know about the death of Hugh Turner."

"Hugh—Turner? I-I do not understand..." she replied, the breathlessness back in her voice, but still wringing her hands. "My silence? What has that boy's death to do with me?"

"I do not know which of you is the better actress, you or my aunt," Alec muttered, adding aloud so everyone could hear, "Let me be blunt, Mrs. Bailey: You believed Hugh the product of your husband's affair with your daughter—"

"I do. I still do. They were having an affair, whatever you say to the contrary, I know it to be true. And that boy is their unnatural spawn—"

There was a collective intake of breath from their audience which Alec ignored, saying with quiet menace, "How extraordinary you refer to Hugh as unnatural."

"He is! He was! He was created from an unholy union. He is an abomination, a creature whose polluted blood is forever corrupted and whose soul is beyond redemption."

"Hugh Turner was a boy. Beloved by his parents, whom he loved in return. He was a boy who reveled in nature, and running wild in the woods with his friends. He was harmless and mischievous and full of life, and he was kind and patient, and spent hours in your garden, no doubt listening politely to your stories, as he did with Lady Ferris, too. It matters not how Hugh came into being. What matters is that he and Will deserved to live to prove themselves as men."

"Hear! Hear!" Plantagenet Halsey applauded. "Well said, my lord!"

The old man's outburst was met with a murmur of agreement, several gazes dropping to the stone flagging when Alec looked their way. He waited while the Colonel, Lord Cobham, and the Reverend Purefoy finally came across to join them, then addressed Mrs. Bailey once more, aware she now had the added attention of her husband and her brother.

"Mrs. Bailey, who referred to Hugh as unnatural spawn whose soul is beyond redemption?"

"Once you know it was obvious: He has a great look of the Colonel."

"What? Prudence!? Who—What is this?" demanded the Colonel, taking a step toward his wife.

"Hush, Bailey!" ordered the Duchess, and stuck out her fan so that he retreated into the group.

"Hugh Turner resembled your husband because the Colonel is his *grand*father," Alec continued. "It is that simple. So I ask again, Mrs. Bailey: Who referred to Hugh as unnatural spawn whose soul is beyond redemption?"

"No one!" she insisted, petulant and unyielding. "*I* said so! It was me."

But Alec saw her glance dart away from him to her right, and he guessed correctly who it was she unconsciously appealed to, without having to turn his head. Before he could ask again, the magistrate decided it was time to make his presence felt.

"Mrs. Bailey, if you do indeed know who killed Hugh Turner and Will Bolen, now is the time to confess—"

"Why would my wife know anything about that gruesome business?" demanded the Colonel, nonplussed. "Retract that accusation, Ferris, or—"

"I am magistrate here, and if your wife, or anyone else present, has any information that could lead to the arrest of a person or persons for the murder of those boys, then I urge that person or persons to come forward and speak up—at once!"

"If you took a breath so they could get a word in, perhaps they would speak up!" quipped the old man, and for his wisecrack got a playful rap on the arm.

"I do not appreciate your tone, Halsey—"

"He's always like that," Lord Cobham stuck in, unaware he had just thrown his support behind his republican nemesis. "Let His Lordship get on with it!"

"If anyone should be getting on with it, my dear Lord Cobham," Sir Tinsley said stiffly, "it is I as magistrate."

"So you said, Ferris," the old man sighed, rolling his eyes.

"Enough! All of you!" commanded the Duchess of Romney-St. Neots. "Allow my godson to finish interrogating this woman! We all want to know the who and why, and if you, Mrs. Bailey, can provide the answers my nephew and the magistrate require, then please do! And be brief. Lady Halsey could give birth at any moment, and that is far more important to me, murderer or no!"

There was a low grumble of assent and everyone went quiet, except Selina, who with one hand cradling her round belly, and the other holding tightly to Lady Sybilla's arm, announced, "You must excuse me... I need to walk... Not a word, Sybilla," she said under her breath as they walked off. When some feet away, and there was no fear of being overheard, she confirmed Lady Sybilla's suspicions, "My birthing pains must not stop Alec catching the fiend who killed those boys! Nor will I give birth before an audience! My rooms. Now."

Alec had permitted the interruption, silently listening to the heated exchange between his guests, not only because it provided a moment of light relief, but because it gave him the opportunity to carefully observe everyone, and two people in particular. And then Selina spoke, and he was distracted and lost his concentration worrying for her welfare. She had smiled his way and tried to appear composed, but Lady Sybilla's frowning concern told him the true state of affairs, and that his wife was more than unusually uncomfortable. It gave him a sense of urgency and the impetus to bring this interrogation—for that was what it was—to an end as soon as possible. So he stepped over to Plantagenet Halsey, asked in a low voice for him to send footmen to have everyone assembled in the Stone Court brought through to the Great Hall.

"Don't you worry. I'll keep Nic Fisher close," the old man assured him, and slipped away.

Alec lost no time in returning his attention to Mrs. Bailey, who remained seated on the Delvin settee, her back a little straighter than before, and no longer wringing her hands. She had regained her composure, and that was no doubt due to her brother. He had joined her, uninvited, and now held her hand, and was speaking to her in hushed tones. Alec interrupted them.

"Do you have any insight you wish to provide, Reverend, as to why Hugh Turner would be branded as unnatural spawn?" Alec asked evenly.

The Reverend Purefoy gently squeezed his sister's hand with a smile, then turned his attention to Alec. "I do, my lord. I fear I must break a confidence to Lady Ferris and tell you that Her Ladyship mentioned the boy by name to me, in a tale she—"

"Nonsense! It wasn't a tale. It was a parable. And it was not about that boy. It was about Tabitha. But I did tell it to Hugh."

"I beg your pardon, my lady," Purefoy replied politely, "but I assure you it most certainly was."

"Why don't you tell us the parable, Aunt," Alec encouraged.

"Very well…" Lady Ferris agreed, enjoying being the focus of attention. "It is about a love that was never meant to be. Tabitha is forbidden from marrying the love of her life when she discovers he is in truth her half-brother. But they cannot imagine being apart. So Tabitha approaches a witch in the wood and asks her to cast a spell to turn the couple into deer of the forest, so they can always be together. The witch agrees, but warns the couple that danger lurks in the wood, danger she has no power to cast aside. The couple cannot foresee what possible danger they could be in, as a stag and his doe are the king and queen of the forest. And so the witch transforms Tabitha into the most beautiful doe, and the love of her life becomes a magnificent buck. But no sooner is their transformation complete than a hunter slays and then cuts the throat of the buck, breaking the spell and turning him back into a boy. Tabitha is left a doe, to roam the wood alone, and dies of a broken heart."

"Good grief! Why would you tell the boy such a ghastly tale?" the Duchess demanded, horrified.

Lady Ferris put up her chin. "He needed to be taught a lesson. The moral being to be content with one's lot in life. He understood, but it didn't change his mischief-making ways—"

"Why call the girl Tabitha?" Mrs. Bailey interrupted, mystified. "You could've given her any name—"

"—such as Eliza?" Lady Ferris pulled a face. "Why would I call her anything but Tabitha, which is by far the prettier name?" She sighed. "That boy was such a good listener." She smiled at the vicar, but it was not pleasant. "You listen, too, don't you, Purefoy. But in a different way. Hugh listened as if he cared. You listen because you are duty-bound to do so. I wondered at the time if you truly had your ears open. So I adapted the tale for you." She looked at Alec. "I told Purefoy the story about a couple who fall in love, and it is only after they are expecting their first child do they discover, to their horror, that they are so closely related by blood that their union would be deemed unholy, their child deemed unnatural spawn—"

"Aha! So it was you! I thought it was you who put a weevil in Mrs. Bailey's brain!" the Duchess of Romney-St. Neots threw at her, unable any longer to contain her feelings, "Conniving, evil, witch of a woman! No one, least of all your vicar, believes your absurd stories—"

"Enough, Olivia," Alec ordered quietly. "No more stories, and no more lies. The story Lady Ferris told Purefoy wasn't about Hugh Turner and his parents, it was about me and mine. And you're right, Olivia, the Reverend didn't believe Lady Ferris. He thought her story the ravings of a confused old lady. But he changed his mind and gave them credence once his sister confided she believed her husband was having an affair with his own daughter, the uncanny resemblance the boy had to the Colonel proof enough in her mind, and then his, that Hugh Turner was unnatural spawn."

"My God, what have you done, Prudence?" the Colonel burst out in anguish and collapsed on the closest wingchair.

"Lionel! Lionel!" Mrs. Bailey cried out, up off the settee. She would have gone to him, but her brother grabbed her wrist and pulled her back down beside him. She instantly shut her mouth and hung her head.

"And because Mrs. Bailey had confided so much in her brother," Alec continued as if not interrupted, "she felt compelled to confess not only to giving up her daughter at birth, but also to the rest of the sad sorry mess. About the Fivetrees Blessing and what that meant for the ancestors of landowners, and for their descendants. What a shocking wake-up for you, Purefoy. To realise you were administering to a flock where it was reasonable to assume a good many of your parishioners were the result of what you considered unholy couplings. So I ask you again, Mrs. Bailey: Who was it who told you Hugh Turner was unnatural spawn?"

"Well, ain't it obvious?" Lord Cobham stuck in, a jerk of his head in direction of the Reverend Purefoy. "He did. The vicar did."

"But she—that mischief making creature—said it first!" the Duchess announced, pointing the closed sticks of her fan at Lady Ferris.

"Unless you are bringing an accusation of some kind against my sister, my lord," the Reverend Purefoy interrupted, up on his feet. "Then I humbly request you desist with this most distressing interrogation!" He looked about at the faces and fixed on the magistrate. "My sister and I have done nothing for which we need answer for here on Earth, Sir Tinsley. Only He can judge us. Truth told, she is the wronged party in all of this, and the Colonel and his whore are the ones who—"

"Dear me, vicar," Alec interrupted with a crooked smile. "You, of all people, are surely aware that of the seven things the Lord hates, lying is one of them. Though, for you, that sin was as nothing to the other six. All of which you were firmly committed to perpetrating once you were set on ridding your congregation of one more abomination, and one closely related to you."

"Wait up, Halsey! It was six things God hated," Lord Cobham rudely asserted. "Lying is one, so is false witness, as is a proud look. Then there's a heart that devises wicked plans, and feet that are swift in running to evil. And something about sowing discord amongst the flock—"

"Sorry, Cobham but there are seven. I wish that weren't true, but it is. The seventh being hands which shed innocent blood... Proverbs six, verses sixteen to nineteen," Alec told him, gaze never leaving the Reverend Purefoy. "Now is the time, Reverend. If you want to save your sister and give her any hope of redemption—"

"It was me! I did it! I killed him! I did. I slit his throat with the rose knife, and I'm not sorry!"

THIRTY-THREE

These damning words were screeched out by Mrs. Bailey, up on her feet beside her brother. Such was the ferocity in her confessional that everyone took a step away from the Delvin Settee on a quick intake of breath. And as they did so, Mrs. Bailey swayed and collapsed at her brother's feet. Shocked into immobility like the rest of those around him, his wife lying unconscious on the floor brought the Colonel to life. Up out of the wingchair and on his feet he was soon down on his knees beside her. And there Dr. Riley joined him. The reverend managed to stay upright, but he was unable to move, face the color of chalk. Alec took a step closer, and then everyone turned at the sound of quiet footfall and low murmuring.

The Great Hall was filling with people. Villagers, laborers, foreign workers, servants, cooks, gardeners, tenants, women and children, old men and young. They came as close as the footmen would allow, silent and watchful, eyes wide and hearts aflutter to be granted permission to congregate as one under His Lordship's roof.

Alec left Mrs. Bailey in the care of her husband and the physician, and went over to where a stepladder had been placed for him to climb so everyone would have a chance of hearing him. But before he did so, he murmured to one of his footmen to have all the exits guarded. No one was to leave the hall without his permission.

Doing his best to put aside Mrs. Bailey's confession and appear calm and unruffled, he took to the ladder and looked down on the sea of upturned, wary faces.

"I brought you all here today to make a speech about the future of our little corner of England, and most particularly our community of Fivetrees," he told them, gaze sweeping out across them all. "But I have decided to spare you the long-winded version, and tell you what is most important. First and foremost—and some of you undoubtedly already know this—is that I had my stonemason chisel away the Fivetrees Blessing that has been a feature of the market square for well over three hundred years. Whether you think you know the history behind the saying, or some version of that history, all you need know is that it will never again hold sway over any of us. Nor will any landowner within this area of Kent follow its odious practise, instituted to honor ancestors who had made choices to preserve their lands for future generations, choices that, frankly, to me are barbaric and incomprehensible, and have no place in this century.

"From this day, all children born in Fivetrees, from the lord of the manor to the dwellers in the wood, will know their parents and be brought up by them. If a parent has the great tragedy of losing a child, it will be from natural causes beyond their control and their best efforts and the efforts of the midwife-physician. Any child who is orphaned and has no family who can take care of them will be brought up by the Fivetrees community at my largesse. And all children from the age of four until their tenth birthday, will attend a village school, under Lady Halsey's gift, to learn their numbers, their letters, and to read.

"And no longer will I countenance a conspiracy of silence throughout our community, with villagers unwilling or unable to speak out for fear of prosecution under the Black Act. Know this. I will not tolerate poaching on my lands for profit. Nor will I allow my neighbors to hunt with impunity and for pleasure, not when most of you are disadvantaged by their behavior and actions. But neither do I support the execution of the Black Act against those of you who are hunting for food and gathering for shelter and warmth. From this day, you may, under direction of my stewards and my gamekeeper, trap in the wood, remove vermin from your lands, and be free from threat of prosecution for the most basic of infringements.

"I hope my words have given you some comfort and direction. In

the coming weeks I will have more to say, and you may, if you require
peace of mind, approach me through my secretary Mr. Jeffries.
Although," he added with a self-deprecating smile, "you will have to
excuse me if I am a little preoccupied with the upcoming birth of my
infant. Thank you. That is all I have to say for now."

There was a widespread chuckle at the mention of his distraction,
and as Alec stepped down from the steps, that low humorous
murmur grew louder, until someone in the crowd shouted "Hip! Hip!
For His Lordship!" causing a deafening universal cheer to go up
amongst them all.

Alec acknowledged this with a wave above his head, face glowing
red under such an effusive reception. And after turning to see if all his
family and guests still remained by the Delvin Settee, he gave the nod
to his footmen to open the doors and herd the crowd back out to the
Stone Court where they would be served refreshment. He was about
to ask about Mrs. Bailey, who had been helped up to the settee and
sat limp against her husband's side while the physician knelt at his
traveling medicine chest preparing her an elixir. But the magistrate
presented himself, demanding to know what was going on, and if
what Mrs. Bailey had shouted was true. If so, he must call in the
beadles and have her carted off.

"One moment, Sir Tinsley…" Alec advised, and was distracted, as
was everyone else, when through the departing crowd Plantagenet
Halsey emerged with an arm around each of the Fisher children.

"He didn't want to come," the old man murmured when Alec
went to meet them. "But she convinced him…"

"I hate to do this to the poor lad, but I'm afraid it is the only
way," Alec replied, and then said audibly, "Come, Nic and Sally. Let
me introduce you both to my godmother. Have you ever met a
duchess?"

Sally's eyes went very wide and she instantly searched out amongst
the small gathering for the woman dressed in the most expensive silks
and jewelry.

"Nic! There she is!" said Sally, rudely pointing a finger at an imperious little lady with upswept powdered hair, dressed all in silks and
dripping in sparkling gems. "See! She's the one wearing diamonds and
rubies, and—what? What is it?"

Olivia St. Neots was about to comment she was not an exhibit at

a fair and that it was rude to point in any situation, but something
made her hesitate and take stock. And when she looked at Alec and
saw his expression, she realized what was going on—these children
were here to help her godson catch a murderer.

Nic Fisher was also searching the group, from the safety within
the circle of the old man's arm. But he forgot all about duchesses,
diamonds, and rubies when his gaze fell on one person in particular.
His fingers convulsed about Plantagenet Halsey's coat sleeve and he
shut his eyes tight before letting out a piercing scream. It was a
scream he could not control, nor could he stop the images of blood
and death which filled his mind's eye.

He was back in the wood, behind a log, where he had run to hide
as soon as Hugh had said the words *hack the head off*, and where he
remained while his friends got down to the grisly business of cutting
up the slain stag. And when he peered over the log, there was Hugh,
on the ground beside the stag, eyes wide open and blood pouring out
of his neck. Kneeling beside him was a woman, and blood dripped
from a blade held in a gloved hand, and blood was splashed across the
front of a wheat-colored riding coat. And then Will ran towards the
log, screaming like Nic was screaming now, and he tripped and hit his
head and went silent. But the blood did not stop and Nic could not
stop screaming.

Plantagenet Halsey scooped up the boy just as he lost
consciousness.

Everyone was shocked into silence. But what shocked them more
than the boy's screaming was when he opened wide his shut tight eyes
and stabbed his finger into the air. He pointed, unblinking, horror
etched across his little blanched face, at a murderer. He was pointing
unwaveringly at Adolphus Purefoy.

ℋ

"ALL THAT SCREAMING HAS SURELY BURST ONE OF MY
eardrums," Lord Cobham complained, setting aside his brandy glass
to wipe his damp forehead with his shirt sleeve. "It's been hours, and I
still can't hear a bloody thing out of m'left ear."

"Another brandy, my lord?" asked a hovering footman.

"Another—*what*? Speak up! Speak up!"

Plantagenet Halsey rolled his eyes and indicated with a gesture for the dazed footman to refill Lord Cobham's glass.

"That's just your paltry excuse for why His Lordship's givin' you a floggin'," the old man almost bellowed. He was comfortably ensconced in a wingchair, legs sprawled out before him and head leaning on his fist. "You don't need y'hearin' to cross swords!"

"We can stop now if you'd prefer, Cobham," Alec suggested, letting his sword arm fall to his side. He scraped back the damp black curls out of his tired eyes and propped himself on the edge of a window seat. Setting aside his foil, he took the brandy the footman offered him. "It's not as if we haven't had a good half hour—"

"No. No. Got to keep you occupied. Got to keep your mind from wandering to the agonies and dangers of childbirth. Aunt Olivia's orders."

"Thank you for not remindin' him why we men have been relegated to the Picture Gallery!" Plantagenet Halsey said with tongue firmly in cheek and another eye roll, this time exchanged with Alec. "I'll wager you use the same deft touch when you're negotiatin' treaties with foreign powers."

"Takes more skill than you can possibly imagine," Cobham stated darkly, with no impairment to his hearing evident. Readjusting his shirtsleeves he said to Alec, "What I still don't understand is why that vicar suddenly cracked and used a rose knife on that boy."

"His Lordship told you," the old man stated. "Purefoy was convinced he saw the devil in Hugh Turner."

Lord Cobham pulled a face. "Well if I saw the devil, the last thing I'd do is attack him with a rose knife—that *is* madness!"

"According to his sister," Alec explained patiently, suppressing a grin at Cobham's look of complete bafflement, "when she and Purefoy came across Hugh Turner in the woods he was elbow deep in the sinew and blood of a decapitated stag. To Purefoy it was as if Lady Ferris's parable had come to life, but with the boy trapped between worlds, earthly and ethereal. Purefoy was convinced he was in the presence of evil incarnate, and the only way to protect himself, his sister, and his flock, was to smite him."

"But with a lady's rose knife?" Lord Cobham asked, unconvinced.

"Yes, with Lady Ferris's rose knife, which Hugh had on him."

Lord Cobham was puzzled. "Did the boy steal the rose knife, or was that Purefoy?"

"Trust you to be stuck on what's important!" Plantagenet Halsey quipped.

"May I remind you, sir, that stealing is a hanging offence, or transportation with hard labor at the very least."

The old man sat up. "But not grounds for havin' y'throat cut by a mad vicar who thinks you're possessed of the devil! And don't get me started on the hundred and one ways this government is usin' the Black Act to murder the innocent!"

"Sir, why didn't Adams the gamekeeper say something to you earlier?" Hadrian Jeffries asked Alec levelly, deliberately cutting off the old man's intended diatribe, and by doing so, hopefully circumventing an argument with the Head of the Foreign Department. "After all, he finally admitted to Sir Tinsley finding the Reverend Purefoy and Mrs. Bailey with a decapitated stag."

"And risk being implicated in a poaching ring? Had Adams come forward he would have created more questions than answers."

"Answers you would have demanded of him, sir," Hadrian responded to Alec.

"With a dead boy, an illegal kill, and a stolen rose knife?" stuck in Lord Cobham. "I would bloody well hope answers would be demanded!"

"Cobham, the boy's body wasn't there when Adams finally turned up at the clearin' or he would've said somethin'," Plantagenet Halsey enunciated. "The vicar had managed to shove poor Hugh's body under some leaves. Adams thought it was a simple case of poachin'. And as that happened around here often enough, he wasn't about to tell His Lordship." He looked at Alec. "Y'know poor Nic Fisher thought the Lord was after him and his friends for killin' that stag. That's what scared him witless. He thought they were all goin' straight to hell, and there was nothin' anyone could do about it because Purefoy was the Lord's instrument here on Earth—"

"What about the sister?" Cobham interrupted, putting aside the empty brandy tumbler and picking up his cork-tipped foil once more. He flexed the blade. "Is she as mad as a March hare, too?"

"Possibly… She insists she had no idea what her brother meant to do," Alec told them quietly. "She supported his wish to set his congregation of unholy unions and abominable offspring on a righteous path. But she claims she was unaware of his more extreme views."

"Such as murderin' innocent children!" stuck in the old man.

"That woman is as guilty as her mad brother, mark my words!" Lord Cobham stated, now hopping up and down on the spot on the balls of his feet and slashing his foil back and forth through the air. "Both deserve to dangle from a rope!" He came to an abrupt halt and pointed the cork-tip of his foil in direction of the old man. "What I can't fathom is how those two mad murderers could possibly be the grandchildren of Lord Moffat. He was an earl, for God's sake!"

"Why does that surprise you?" Plantagenet Halsey asked placidly. "Our ranks are littered with madmen, and more than a few murderers. Wearin' a coronet and sittin' in the Lords don't mean they're as sane as—"

He was about to say *as you or I*, but remembered he was talking with Cobham and quickly swallowed those words back down his throat. A quick glance over at Alec, who was retying the ribbon at the nape of his neck, and saw by his grin that he knew what he was about to say, too, and he returned the grin with a wink.

"So tell me again how you knew it was Mrs. Colonel and her brother the mad vicar who'd sliced up that boy," Lord Cobham asked Alec as he took a few practise lunges with his foil. "From what I've seen of the locals, they're all as slippery as eels, capable of gutting an animal and slitting a throat, and I'm not just talking about the men!"

"Much like yourself then," the old man threw at him. "You've shot, stabbed, cut, and killed any number of defenseless creatures while on the hunt, haven't you?"

Lord Cobham stopped bouncing and dropped his sword arm. He stared at Plantagenet Halsey, jaw swinging. He shook his head. His smile was contemptuous. "Gentlemen hunt for sport and pleasure. Which is another matter entirely."

Plantagenet Halsey threw up his hands and fell back in his chair. "I rest my case!"

"Lord Cobham has a point, sir," Hadrian Jeffries said, genuinely interested, and addressing Alec. "How did you know it was the Reverend Purefoy who had killed Hugh Turner?"

"I do!?" Lord Cobham stuck out his chest. "Er, yes! I do! Appreciate the support, er—er—"

"—Jeffries, my lord. Mr. Hadrian Jeffries."

Lord Cobham swished his blade from Alec to Jeffries and kept it pointed at him. "And what's your connection to Lord Halsey— cousin, colleague, poor relation?"

Hadrian Jeffries couldn't help a smile. "His Lordship's newly-appointed secretary."

"Secretary, aye?" muttered the Head of the Foreign Department. "Trust you know your *linga franca*, Johnson."

"It's Jeffries, my lord. And yes, I speak, write, and read fluently in four languages."

"Four!? That's three too many in my books, but if that's useful to Lord Halsey, then huzza!"

"He is, and they are," Alec replied and smiled at his new secretary. "I am pleased Mr. Jeffries has agreed to take the post."

"Agreed? To be secretary to the Marquess Halsey? Johnson should be bloody *honored*!" Cobham swished his blade about, cutting it through the air as he took up his position to commence another round of fencing practice with his brother-in-law. "Come on then, Halsey! Got to keep your mind off the horrors of the birthing room."

Plantagenet Halsey got up to stretch his legs. "So you're not inter-ested in the answer?"

"Answer? I can't remember the bloody question!"

Everyone chuckled, even the old man, and it put him more in charity with his political nemesis to confess, "I wouldn't have thought I'd ever say this, but I'm glad you're here with us, Cobham. Mind you, ask me how I feel in a couple more hours, and I may give you a different response, particularly if our girl is still in the throes of child-birth. The question Jeffries asked was, how did His Lordship know it was Purefoy who had killed poor Hugh Turner? And let's not forget his friend Will Bolen, whom the vicar claims he didn't kill, did he?"

"According to brother and sister," Alec told them as he walked out into the middle of the Gallery, "when Will Bolen saw Hugh having his throat cut, he fled into the wood. But he did not get far, for Mrs. Bailey gave chase and found the boy dead by a log, having hit his head when he tripped, and a branch piercing his eye. The physician confirmed that not only had the branch penetrated Will's brain, but his skull was fractured, so we must assume she was telling the truth."

"Why cut off the boys' hands, sir?" asked Hadrian Jeffries.

Alec shrugged. "Mrs. Bailey maintains she had her brother remove their hands to make it appear as if poachers had been through the area. And after what Purefoy had just done to Hugh, removing his hand was as nothing."

"I'm with Johnson," Lord Cobham stated. "What was the point of hacking off a hand when he'd already slit the boy's throat? Pointless exercise!"

"Not if you're another poacher," conceded Plantagenet Halsey. "Removin' the hand of a rival is a signal to the poachin' fraternity and a punishment for trespassin' on another's territory."

"I remember!" Lord Cobham announced, and addressed Alec. "How did you know that murdering swine of a vicar was the one who had taken a rose knife to that boy's throat?"

"Once I realised whoever had killed Hugh had to have been seen by Nic Fisher," Alec explained, "it was a matter of watching the boy's reactions when confronted with particular people. He was so frightened that he'd lost the facility of speech, and he stuck to his sister like glue to wallpaper. I was convinced he had not only seen the murderer but also the murder take place. And yet, there was something about his terror… He was ever watchful, as if he was expecting to be found, to receive the same fate as Hugh. In Old Bill's cottage I had ample time to observe this, and then he came face-to-face with Roger Turner, Adams and his men, Paul Turner, the Colonel, and my fa—"

—and me," Plantagenet Halsey quickly cut in when Alec stumbled.

"Forgive me. I should've said. I don't know why I—"

"Not necessary. We'll tell everyone all in good time, but not tonight." The old man smiled and huffed. "You have enough dealin' out this explanation to Cobham, without addin' to his confusion. And I'd rather you told our girl before anyone else."

Alec nodded, took stock and continued.

"Nic did not react in anyway to these men in Old Bill's cottage, nor did he do so with the many villagers out in the wood with the dogs searching for Hugh and Will. In fact he remained indifferent and mute with all of the outside servants, and those within the house too. And I had him mingle amongst the crowd gathered in the Stone Court in the hopes that at least one of their number would somehow fire Nic's fear and get him to speak."

"He fired all right! Damaged my bloody eardrum with his screaming!"

"I must thank you, Cobham, because you gave me an idea of where to direct my enquiries."

"Eh? Me?" Lord Cobham was taken aback, so was Plantagenet Halsey.

"In our meeting about His Majesty's dilemma with Midanich, you mentioned a conspiracy of females," Alec explained. "That had me thinking about the Fivetrees Blessing, and the role of the women of the families in this district. It seemed unbelievable to me that only the men were involved. And for the hundreds of years this blessing was used as justification for filicide? No. Their wives, as mothers, must have known what was going on, and been complicit for the diabolical scheme to work, and become cemented as lore."

"I don't know what any of that means," Cobham confessed, "and I can't recall mentioning any conspiracy…"

"You told me about Lady Cobham's penchant for cushions and her little bowls full of potpourri—"

"The bloody French potpourri! Ye gods! Then I'm not surprised that got you thinking about murder! I want to strangle someone every time I trip over a confounded cushion or Lady Cobham shoves a bowl of that Frenchie stuff under m'nose and tells me to sniff. Once got a piece of dried orange peel lodged up a nostril. Painful bloody business!"

Plantagenet Halsey burst into laughter. He laughed until he had to put a hand out to the wingchair to remain upright.

"Egad, Cobham! That's the best—that's the best story I've heard this year! Forgive me, my boy," the old man added when he could breathe. "Please, carry on!"

Alec lost his grin and said flatly, "The short response is, I could not rule out the murderer being female. And I deliberately brought Nic before my dinner guests to force a reaction from him."

Alec stopped and turned, distracted by the opening of a door at the far end of the Gallery and rapid footfall. Everyone else looked that way. It was a footman. Alec took a step forward, unable to breathe, and hopeful the servant was bringing news of his wife and child.

THIRTY-FOUR

THE FOOTMAN HANDED ALEC A CARD AND SAID WITHOUT A flicker of emotion, "A Mr. Thaddeus Fanshawe, my lord."

Alec did his best not to let his shoulders slump or show disappointment that it was not the news he and everyone was waiting to hear. Seven hours had ticked by since Selina had gone into labor, and it now had to be close to midnight. He stared at the card which proclaimed Mr. Fanshawe as an attorney-at-law with the firm Yarrborough and Yarrborough, then looked past his footman at the individual making his way down the long room towards him, and had a flash of memory. It was of a young man in a disheveled, canary-yellow frock coat who had paid a visit to his St. James's Place townhouse over a year ago.

This was indeed the same young man, and while he was not in canary-yellow, his attire was no less colorful and surprising. His ensemble of frock coat, waistcoat and breeches was a bright grass-green silk with pink edgings and covered buttons, and under his left armpit was tucked a tricorne with pink trim. Something large and shiny dangled from a silk ribbon in his gloved hand. But it was at his head everyone stared. His neat wig *a la pigeon* carried a heavy dusting of pink powder, and as a consequence so did his narrow shoulders.

Thaddeus Fanshawe presented himself to Alec with a smile that displayed prominent buck teeth, and a sweeping bow, that as he straightened enveloped him in a cloud of pink hair powder.

Everyone took a step away, and watched this cloud rise up and then settle about the attorney. Finding his balance, Thaddeus Fanshawe held out a sealed packet, which, with a nod from Alec, Hadrian Jeffries took possession, before offering an explanation to his mute audience.

"From Mr. Fisher, my lord, who sends his most sincere apologies for not accompanying me into Kent. A most fierce storm visited the metropolis the other night and I saw on my way here that these environs were not unscathed. As a result of the said storm, the shop front of Mr. Fisher's apothecary's business suffered minor damage, and looting by person or persons unknown. The letter, however, is from a third party, whose identity Mr. Fisher did not wish to disclose to me. He asked that I pass it on to you, and present myself at your door without delay, and so here I am!"

"You are most welcome, Fanshawe," Alec replied straight-faced. "I hope Mr. Fisher explained that I require your services for a few weeks?"

"Yes, my lord. I have brought with me several changes of raiment suitable for country living."

Alec imagined that these articles of clothing were just as colorful as the ensemble Fanshawe was wearing, for he suddenly remembered that upon their previous meeting, the attorney had disclosed he was color-blind. But if this outfit were any example, he doubted they would be suitable for anything but a city drawing room.

The young attorney sucked in his teeth and bowed again, and again his audience stepped away. When he straightened, he held up a wide silk ribbon from which dangled a large and very ornate and shiny brass key, and presented it to Alec with all the gravity he could muster.

"My lord, may I present the key!"

"Key?" Alec repeated, having a momentary lapse of memory.

Hadrian Jeffries leaned in and whispered, "One presumes to the vault…"

"Ah! Yes! Yes! *That* key!"

Lord Cobham could not contain his incredulity a moment longer. He pointed his foil directly at Thaddeus Fanshawe. "Who—or what —the bloody hell are you!?"

. . .

IT WAS THE EARLY HOURS OF THE MORNING, JUST ON DAWN, with the men sprawled out uncomfortable but asleep on the various pieces of furniture in the Picture Gallery, when word came from Lady Halsey's apartment. Alec was the only one fully awake. How could he not be? He had been up for almost an hour, waiting for the dawn and listening to Lord Cobham's sonorous snoring. He had washed his face, tidied his hair, sent for a fresh shirt and waistcoat, and was standing at the window sipping a cup of coffee. The same door which had opened to usher in the late-night arrival of the young attorney, was now opened by a bleary-eyed footman to admit the Lady Sybilla. She had come herself to fetch Alec rather than send a maid so he would not worry.

Tired and crumpled, but rosy-cheeked and smiling, she came bustling down the full length of the Gallery. Alec had seen her, but after he shifted from the window he found he could not move. Apprehension had taken away the use of his legs. So Sybilla came right up to him and practically fell into his arms. Alec grabbed her about the elbows and looked down, unable to breathe.

"She's—she's well. She's come through it. She was so brave—so very, *very* brave—Oh!"

Alec's knees buckled with relief, but he quickly pulled himself together and swiftly kissed Sybilla's cheek.

"Thank God, and thank you!"

"What's this? What's happened?" Plantagenet Halsey demanded, still half-asleep as he scrambled out of a wingchair and unfolded himself. He ran a hand through his grizzled hair. "How's our girl?"

"When can I see her?" Alec asked. "Is the baby—" He didn't know how to finish the sentence.

Lady Sybilla nodded, blinking away tears. "Yes. Yes. You must come. She's been asking for you—"

"And the-the baby—?"

"Oh! Oh! Yes, of course. The baby! The baby is-is…"

Sybilla hesitated, unsure how to tell him without giving anything away. It was too much for Alec, who swayed, thinking the worst, and was quickly propped up by his father.

"Oh, no! You must not worry," Sybilla assured them. "Selina made me promise not to tell you. She wants to be the one to do so."

Alec grabbed at her hand and held it, searching her eyes. "But they are well? Everything went—well?"

"They are both very well. So well, in fact, that Dr. Riley has left for the day, but he will return this evening."

"And the baby?"

Sybilla smiled. "The baby is—the baby is *beautiful*."

❦

AN EXHAUSTED OLIVIA ST. NEOTS GREETED THEM IN THE sitting room. She went straight up to Alec and Plantagent Halsey and stopped them with a palm to each man's chest.

"If either of you say one word to her about looking tired, I will march you both straight out of there!"

Father and son nodded obediently, and dared not speak. But such was their excitement that they could not contain their smiles, try as they might. It was too much for the Duchess, who fell into the old man's arms and burst into happy tears of relief.

"It's been a long nine months for all of us," Plantagenet Halsey muttered. He jerked his chin in direction of the door. "Go in, my boy. We'll join you presently."

Selina was dozing, sitting up in bed with a silk banyan over a fresh bedgown and her apricot hair neatly braided into one long plait. The room was tidy and quiet. Evans sat in a corner also dozing, and a maid hovered in the doorway that went through to the dressing closet. There was nothing about the scene to suggest his wife had endured a monumental struggle to bring a new life into the world. Except for the tiny wrapped bundle nestled in the crook of her arm.

Alec gingerly approached the foot of the bed. He didn't know what to say or do. But when Selina stirred and put out her free hand across the coverlet, he was there in an instant. He snatched up her hand to kiss her fingers.

"You look tired," she commented. "Have you been very worried about us?"

"Very. But that's all in the past now isn't it? You came through it, my darling, and I am so proud of you—of you both. Today is the start of the rest of our lives!"

"Do you want to see her?" Selina asked, smiling down at the bundle.

"A-a daughter?"

She nodded without looking up. "I'm sorry it's not the boy you—"

"I'm not!"

He was emphatic, which made her glance away from her infant and up at him. His grin and the look in his blue eyes told her he was sincere. She smiled back, glassy-eyed.

"Nor I." She carefully held out the bundle to him. "She is the most beautiful little creature…"

Alec gently took the infant in his arms, still smiling at his wife. And when he had her secure in the crook of his arm, he finally took a peek at his newborn daughter. He drew in a quick breath of surprise and swiftly looked across at Selina with undisguised delight.

"She has my curly hair!"

"Your hair and my temper no doubt! Though your temper and my hair would've been better—no! I take it back. She is perfect as she is."

"Do you have a name?"

"No… Although, I had hoped to call her after my mother—"

"Splendid! Let's do that," Alec replied, unable to take his gaze from his daughter, or the smile off his face.

It was a maid, come in to speak in hushed tones with Evans, that brought Alec out of his trance to realize Selina had maintained her silence. When he looked at her she was smiling in a way that told him he had either done something very right, or very wrong.

"Dear heart, you have no idea as to my mother's name."

Alec pondered this a moment. "True. I only ever knew her as Lady Vesey. But if you wish to call our daughter after your mother, I've no objection. That is, unless her name is utterly awful and unpronounceable…"

Selina chuckled. "It is not unpronounceable, but you won't like it." When Alec put up an eyebrow as if to say 'try me', she told him. "Her name was Helen."

𝓗

"GOOD GRIEF! WHAT IS GOING ON IN HERE THAT HAS CAUSED you both to fall into a fit of the giggles?" the Duchess of Romney-St. Neot's demanded, bustling over to the bed, Plantagenet Halsey on her heels. "Hush! Or you'll wake her."

"We were deciding on names," Selina explained, much subdued but the sparkle still in her dark eyes.

"Please don't tell me you've called that beautiful baby something fashionable or unpronounceable."

"Well, do you think Helen Olivia Jane fashionable or unpronounceable?" Alec began then let the sentence hang and winked at his father. He went over to the old man with his daughter in his arms. "Would you like to hold your granddaughter?" he asked him quietly.

Plantagenet Halsey nodded and cleared his throat. "Very much."

Alec carefully placed his newborn daughter in his father's arms, and stepped away to allow him a moment alone with her. That Plantagenet Halsey could not speak or raise his head but kept his chin on his chest as he cradled his granddaughter spoke volumes about his feelings. There was not a dry eye in the room.

Alec sat back on the edge of the bed and held his wife's hand.

"Olivia, would you care to make your announcement now, before Cobham demands an audience with his niece?"

Plantagenet Halsey looked across at the Duchess and nodded. She sighed and threw up a hand.

"Very well. Although I am certain you know what it is we want to tell you, so what is the point of making an announcement?"

Alec and Selina exchanged a look, and then Alec said, "But my dear Olivia, we might know, but we can't talk about it until you tell us."

"I will make an ambassador of you yet, my boy!" the Duchess quipped, but said nothing further.

"We were married in Copenhagen," Plantagenet Halsey said bluntly. When the Duchess gasped he shrugged. "You were never goin' to say it, Livvy." He smiled down at his granddaughter and then across at her parents. "But we ain't goin' to set up house together. She's happy where she is, and I'm happy with the two of you—if that arrangement still stands—"

"Of course!" Selina interrupted without hesitation and smiled at

Alec when he gently squeezed her fingers in thanks. "We wouldn't have it any other way."

The old man nodded, and overcome again, he went back to gazing at his granddaughter.

Alec and Selina looked at each other and then at the Duchess of Romney-St. Neots. Both had the same thought, and so did Olivia. She straightened her shoulders, put up her chin, and said with all the dignity she could muster,

"If anyone dares to address me as Mrs. Halsey, I may just breathe fire!"

"Yes, Your Grace," Alec, Selina, and Plantagenet Hasley replied obediently in unison, and then laughed so loud they woke the baby.

The End... until Alec, Selina, Plantagenet Halsey, Olivia St. Neots, Hadrian Jeffries, Evans, Tam Fisher, Lord Cobham, and baby Helen return in Deadly Diplomacy.

AUTHOR NOTES

FACT

Gavelkind was a partible inheritance system whereby property was equally apportioned among heirs, chiefly sons. It's said that before the conquest in 1066, all lands in England were subject to gavelkind. It was William the Conqueror who introduced primogeniture (whereby only the legitimate firstborn son inherited an entire estate) throughout the kingdom, except in the county of Kent; where William's Kentish supporters were able to extract the concession of preserving gavelkind.

Such an inheritance system meant that over successive generations larger estates in Kent were divided up. Those with wealth and title acquired estates in other parts of the country to ensure their eldest son inherited an estate that would remain intact. Whatever lands they had remaining in Kent were either sold off or rented out to tenants. Gavelkind remained the chief system of inheritance in Kent until its abolition by the Administration of Estates Act of 1925.

FICTION

So while gavelkind as an inheritance system did indeed exist, how Fivetrees landowners circumvented this system, to ensure their estates were not divided up and passed to an only son, is the work of my imagination.

FACTION

Deer Park, Alec's estate with its deer park and sprawling manor house, is closely based on Knole, Kent's last medieval deer park. Originally built as an archbishop's palace, it became the home to the Sackville family, who still live there today. Knole is situated close to the town of Sevenoaks, which in Deadly Kin is the village of Fivetrees. Knole is also home to the Knole Settee or Sofa (here named the Delvin Settee), possibly the first piece of celebrity furniture, copied down the ages, and replicas can still be purchased from fashionable interior design studios. You can read and explore more about Knole, the Knole Settee, and surrounds, here: www.nationaltrust. org.uk/knole

BEHIND-THE-SCENES

Explore the places, objects, and history in
Deadly Kin on Pinterest.

www. pinterest.com/lucindabrant

CPSIA information can be obtained
at www.ICGtesting.com
Printed in the USA
BVHW070121271219
567842BV00002BA/478/P

9 781925 614510